THE BIG
PICTURE

ALSO BY VANESSA DRUCKER

Winner Takes All

THE BIG PICTURE

VANESSA DRUCKER

CROWN PUBLISHERS, INC.

NEW YORK

Published by Crown Publishers, Inc., 201 East 50th Street, New York,
New York 10022. Member of the Crown Publishing Group.

CROWN is a trademark of Crown Publishers, Inc.

Manufactured in the United States of America

Library of Congress Cataloging-in-Publication Data

Drucker, Vanessa.
   The big picture / Vanessa Drucker. — 1st ed.
   I. Title.
PS3554.R74B54   1992
813′.54—dc20   91-43636
                                                                                   CIP

ISBN 0-517-58490-5

10 9 8 7 6 5 4 3 2 1

First Edition

To I J D

THE BIG
PICTURE

WHO'S WHO

Uptown

Emil Papier—*a Swiss art collector*
Susannah Bishop—*his mistress*
Delphine Papier—*his daughter*
Jacob Karakoff—*his best friend*
Felice Karakoff—*Jacob's wife*
Jim McHenry—*Emil's lawyer*
Nick Jones—*an English yuppie*
Georgia Cavendish—*manager of the auction house order bid room*
Iris and Pansy—*Susannah's maids*
Xavier—*a "beautiful people" hairdresser*

Downtown

Giulietta Giuliani—*an art dealer and friend of Emil*
Peter Dante—*a rival art dealer*
Luke Elliot—*an abstract painter*
Kitty Elliot—*his wife*
Dan Helena—*a heavy-metal sculptor*
Caspar Peacock—*a versatile art maker*
The Wagnerian Hero—*an Expressionist painter*
The Visual Scientist—*his friend; an art theoretician*

Out of Town

Mr. and Mrs. Sanford Vincent Milholland III—*Texan collectors*
Billy Berrymouse—*a Utah collector*
Sandy Pike—*an Australian collector*
Juan Gomez—*a Filipino investor*

Baron von Tislowicz—*an Austrian collector*
The man from Shining Squid—*a Japanese art acquisitions executive*
Rudi—*a Swiss anarchist*
Professor Cecil Rawlings—*a British art historian*
Zachary—*a Tennessee church elder*

DOWN AMONG THE
IMPORTED KNOCKWURSTS

Keep your head down. There's somebody watching us."

"Where?"

"At the top of the stairs."

"Who is it?"

"Dark-skinned guy. Maybe Lebanese, maybe Indian, maybe Puerto Rican. He's wearing a leather jacket and he has a mustache."

"I like it, baby. I like it."

"Shh."

"Is he still watching?"

"Yes."

With the fleshy side of his muscled hand he gagged her mouth, as he felt the little whimpers about to escape. He did not like noisy women. Their cries and gasps distracted more than aroused him. Control was better. Now her teeth sank into the only soft place, at the root of his thumb, as the silent signal of her excitement. Faster and faster.

The man in the leather jacket paused at the top of the subway station entrance at the corner of Delancey and Essex streets, where a long stationary escalator led below street level to a dead-end metal grille. Outside, the glimmer of March twilight fell on the "No Entry" sign at the top of the steps. Next to the sign sat a cross-legged bum, unmoving and unblinking like an ancient toad, waiting for something in the same place he had sat and waited now for many weeks. Unstirred, he watched the man in the leather jacket, who had stopped to watch the couple on the subway stairs.

It was a strange sight, even for New York. The passerby, who worked in a falafel takeout store on Broome Street, did not know much about rich Manhattanites' wardrobes, yet he could tell, even in the half-light, that her high-heeled shoes and pale suede coat came from a place he had never been. She was kneeling on the stinking steps in those movie star clothes, while her tall, lean partner hid most of her body from view as he thrust into her from behind. The witness was granted a glimpse of suede and heels and shaking, shining copper hair, and the two full shopping bags from Dean & DeLuca. He knew it was the most expensive food store downtown; they charged five bucks for a fancy loaf of bread there, maybe a couple of dollars for a banana. And these crazy people had balanced their bags of delicacies on the filthy steps, which smelled so foul even the tramps no longer went down there to take a leak.

For a couple of minutes it was exciting to watch them. He wished the red-haired woman would cry out, or at least make some noise to show she was real. When she did not, it became boring. He turned away and hurried down Essex Street, where the evening light softened the desolation of the Lower East Side. He soon forgot. It takes all kinds of folks.

Down at the foot of the subway steps, the man tightened his grip as he felt his own body shudder and convulse. An instant later he was hitching up her gossamer oyster panties. When he swiveled her body around to face him, they smiled at one another with a flash of gaiety. The bond had been sealed again.

"Time to go uptown," said Susannah Maud Lucile Bishop.

"It's getting late and we've got six scared up for supper. Plus me and Emil." When she pronounced Emil's name you could hear the buried twang of Tennessee, which had become scratched and abraded after years in New York. But not quite lost its southern torpor.

Dan Helena picked up the two bulging Dean & DeLuca grocery bags.

"Emil flew in from Switzerland this morning. He'll be waking up from his nap, and he likes me to be home, in case there's anything needs tending to."

They mounted the last of the escalator steps and turned onto Delancey Street. The Jewish shoe stores and pet stores and opticians were closing for the night. In Orchard Street, people were bringing the racks of garments indoors. Dan switched both bags to one hand and touched her arm with the other. She noticed that the champagne-colored suede coat had picked up some kind of nasty stain down in the subway, a smear with an oily tint. It was at the thigh, where the material had brushed against the ground.

He guided her past the synagogues and Hispanic churches and Korean snack stalls. There were still no taxis; there never were at rush hour in this off-the-beaten-track corner of town. Why should anyone want to be dropped off here amid the racks of garments and small hardware stores?

He plunged an arm in the grocery bag and pulled out a piece of fruit. "What's this?"

"A Japanese apple-pear. I get them for Emil's breakfast."

"Since when?"

"Since his last visit. For the past fourteen years whenever he got to New York he had to have bagels. You couldn't get them in Switzerland. Then, all of a sudden, they start selling bagels all over Europe, and now it's got to be these hybrid pears."

"Why do you bother?"

"You know it's my job to accommodate him. Six times a year, maybe eight, he comes to New York for a week. I see that the food is right. The flowers have to be just so, the way he likes them, lilies and birds of paradise and mimosa. We go out at night with his dealer friends, I spiff myself up and I wear the best jewelry."

"And you fuck?"

She looked away for a minute, toward a vacant lot where the graffiti artists had composed a swirling, blazoning mural. Her sticky crotch was beginning to itch. She wrenched her arm away from him. "It's none of your damn business."

On the corner of Allen and Houston, he thrust at her the cornucopia of delicacies while he ran against the stream of cars for a cab. For a moment, as he held the door, they stood in an island of honking and swearing and yelping brakes.

She heaved the second bag across the seat. "Are you coming uptown with me?"

Dan followed her and slammed the door behind them. He gave the address of the palazzo on East End Avenue. Susannah had just time to notice from the license that the driver was a South American, with an I've-seen-it-all, so-what-else-is-new expression. He stared as if blinkered at the lights ahead. Dan's iron fingers tightened their grip on her arm and he breathed in her ear, "Get down."

"King Jesus! Right here?"

The cars around them were inching slowly. The grocery bags balanced precariously against their knees.

"Do as I tell you."

Before she had time to object, he had already unzipped his fly with deft fingers and clutched a handful of her copper hair. He pulled her face into his lap.

Now she felt only the pitch and toss of the taxi below and smelled the mixture of exhaust fumes and knockwurst and Emmentaler from the grocery bags. He rocked her mouth sternly against his ballooning flesh. She raked it knowingly with her teeth and wondered, Will the cooks have made sure to steep the fruit macédoine in Grand Marnier, and if I wear the de la Renta, will Emil remember that he saw me in it twice when he was here in early February? I'm not hungry at all, and I'm going to have to pretend to eat the overrich slabs of Wiener schnitzel with *rosti* diced potatoes (boiled, then fried, then baked), the heavy, bloating Swiss food that Emil likes best.

"Deeper," Dan ordered. He whispered hoarsely, "All the way in your throat."

She plunged deeper and hoped she would not end up one

day by throwing up, especially on the seat of some cab or movie theater.

She wondered, Would Dan care if I gave him up, would it even superficially wound his masculine pride? Maybe not. That had always been his trick, developed to a fine art: not caring. No one who cared could have lived his whole adult life so solitary, rootless, and almost without possessions. He used to bury himself away in his warehouse on Plymouth Street with hardly a human conversation for weeks on end. There he constructed his twenty-foot sculptures, hammering and welding and battering the final assemblage into place. Unlike most of the artists she knew, he did not listen to music while he worked, and he did not own a television.

Dan's awareness differed from other people's. When he rambled around the city at night, scouting out the netherlife of the dingy bars and side streets, he homed in on details other eyes passed over. When they strolled he pointed out to Susannah a glimpse of a courtyard garden or mysterious patterns of light and angles of architecture. But to his physical comforts he was indifferent. He paid no attention to what he ate, or where he slept, or even the scorching summers and bitter winters of New York City. He had little notion of time, often no idea whether it was Monday or Wednesday or whether he had been working for two or six hours. His life was predicated on avoiding any form of commitment, even an appointment a day ahead.

He took responsibility for no creature except Judd. He had rescued the Great Dane as a puppy, scavenging garbage in Battery Park. Susannah knew that Dan himself occasionally roamed at dawn along the deserted lots of the West Side Highway, looking out for interesting metal coils or pipes or old hubcaps, or helping himself to bits of the bridges, as components for the sculptures. He understood what it was to comb the junk heaps and trash cans. He claimed that was what had made him suddenly adopt the dog, the affinity they shared for vagrancy.

Susannah noticed how he fed and groomed and trained him, with tenderness and exacting discipline. When he grew up, Judd learned to obey his master like a snake charmer. The animal, which accepted no other human being, responded to Dan's minutest voice inflections. Sometimes the pair wandered around the city together. Other days Susannah imagined Judd stretched out majestically in Dan's studio, sleeping and waiting, keeping guard over the warehouse with its works in progress.

She asked him once if he had ever cared about any woman. Instead of answering, he had just stared at her quizzically and asked, "Have you?"

Now he was holding her head, guiding her mouth up and down along the stiff shaft. He's going to come in my mouth, she thought, and she hoped the driver would have the sense not to turn his head.

She knew why she came back to him week after week, month after month. His controlled violence made her feel desirable. It more than compensated for the task of polite glacial sex with Emil, who, after touching her in the obligatory places, would mutter nervously, "Come, please come."

When the shy Swiss millionaire had installed her nineteen years ago as his mistress in the palazzo on East End Avenue, he had made quite clear that he required her to keep up the apartment to the highest standards of elegance and luxury. It suited Emil, who detested hotels, to replicate his Swiss life in New York. Financial business in Switzerland and his other globe-trotting exhausted most of his time, but he told Susannah that she was free to visit him whenever she should choose in the chalet above Lake Leman (and that for those trips he would provide first-class or Concorde tickets). During the early years she had visited, until her strained relationship with Delphine, Emil's adored only child, made the stays unbearable. Moreover, she found Montreux, with its cafes and gardens and casino, was a dull place. She had never quite made friends with the jet set who lived in the surrounding hills.

So she waited instead for Emil's regular visits to East End Avenue, where he would pass a week or two, lunching with investment bankers and nurturing the art collection, his only passion.

He taught her about money and art, about using the bloodsuckers who buzzed around them, and about masochism. For in bed he was the most passive man she had ever known. She often wondered where he found the aggression required to volley into daily battle with the governments and financiers and come out doubling and tripling his great wealth. Perhaps men's natures were neatly cloven. Susannah's job was to stroke and caress and tease and claw him to orgasm; for that he paid her charge accounts, maintenance on the co-op, all telephone and electricity bills, and unlimited accounts at the florist and local liquor stores.

For tonight she had ordered up a case of 1975 Château Margaux, which Emil had remarked on last time they had entertained in February. At nineteen hundred a case, it damned well ought to have body. He would only notice the first couple of glasses, anyhow. By midevening he would be too deep into the bottle to know or care. He had been drinking more recently. When he called her each night from Switzerland at ten (European time), before he went to bed, he rambled and slurred and sometimes made no sense. When she mentioned it Emil made vague excuses. He hated confrontation. He said that he was lonely in the empty chalet at night and overwrought after long days on the telephone with bankers. Besides, he added almost sheepishly, he only drank red wine and never touched whiskey.

She felt the sudden jerk along Dan's body and the spurt in her throat. She closed her eyes tightly and swallowed hard. And again. And once more. Then he was moving away, zipping up his fly, and rummaging for change.

Dan insisted on paying for everything when they were together: taxis, restaurants, the knickknacks they picked up in antique stores, fortune-tellers, street vendors and portraitists, graphologists and clairvoyants. She liked that. He dealt only in cash and carried no credit cards. He never seemed short of money. His sculptures were selling for two hundred thousand these days, and he generally sold two or three a year. He could have been more prolific if he had really cared about the money. As it was, he made more than enough to maintain his barebones life-style: the warehouse studio in Brooklyn, the steel supplies, the Moto Guzzi motorbike, and his sporadic jaunts around the world, when he lived like a gypsy. At the age of forty-one he still traveled on cargo ships.

They passed the flags outside the United Nations. The taxi lurched and came to an abrupt stop at a traffic light. Dan tapped on the driver's glass partition. "Let me out at the next corner."

She sighed. A woman alone, she was stripped of her authority. Now she would be imprisoned all the rest of the way uptown, under the mocking leer of Jose Rolando Ortega, whose black eyes stared at her from beneath hairy brows on his license photograph in front.

Dan kissed her on the lips, almost tenderly.

"Are you going back to SoHo?" she asked. "Will you call me later?"

"Maybe." He thrust thirty dollars in her lap and reached for the rickety door handle.

Before they arrived at her quiet, residential street, she told Jose Ortega to stop off at the dry cleaner. He turned his head to sneak a look at this swanky, crazed nymphomaniac who got off blowing guys in his bouncing backseat. Ortega's glance told her the tip had better be good.

The Greek dry cleaner marked an X with his chalk where she pointed out the stains on her suede coat. Christo, thank God, always beamed guilelessly. She had brought him every relic of her rampages: grass stains and grease, wine and come and lipstick.

The fare came to $14.80. She gave Jose Ortega the thirty dollars. "Keep it."

"Gracias, señora."

Emil was already awake from his nap. She could hear his voice through the half-open door of the study. He was speaking on the telephone, half in German and half in English. She caught the words *neunzig tausend Mark* and *amerikanische Inflation*. To whom would he be talking in Europe so late? In his business dealings, Emil shunted effortlessly among English, French, German, and Italian. Susannah had once signed up for an elementary French course at the Alliance Française, which had hardly enabled her to master the menu and boutique stage of communication.

Straightening her hair, she slid open the study door. Emil was sitting at the Bauhaus desk, the cordless telephone receiver in one hand, a smoldering cigarette in the other. An ashtray brimmed with half-smoked butts. He looked up at her with his frosty smile of welcome. It was their first encounter in six weeks.

He was wearing his brocaded dressing gown and looked surprisingly well rested. After the morning Concorde trip from Paris, he always napped for several hours before resuming business. Although he smoked and drank with an unbridled frenzy, he took care to get plenty of rest. His own father had died of a heart attack at fifty-nine. The dread of a similar end had been hounding Emil since his fifty-sixth birthday last year. Susannah paid lip service to his hypochondria. "Emil's heart is sound as a dollar," she told Dan Helena. "But he'd be mortal affronted if anyone told him so."

He pointed at his empty wineglass beside the delicate Giacometti he so prized. He had snatched the sculpture away at a Sotheby's auction from Baron von Tislowicz, another obsessional collector of surrealist art. He carried on talking, now in English. "Sell dollars short again, Franz. The U.S. economy is hitting a plateau. The Fed will ease on interest rates."

She glided away from the door to fetch his wine. They hardly touched each other these days, except for his peck on the cheek when he arrived fresh off a plane, and he would never interrupt the most insignificant business call for that. She wondered, as she opened the sixteenth-century oak cabinet where they kept the decanters, how long she could go on fulfilling her usefulness as a housekeeper/hostess.

They bickered often; he withdrew and she sulked. Yet they still stopped just short of broaching the subject of a real separation. She had begun to think of it more and more often. She had her unsigned copy of the precious contract, she repeated to herself, which promised her the East End Avenue apartment in the event of any such split not induced by her. The original, signed version of the contract lay in a dusty vault downtown in the offices of Whittaker & Blessing, Emil's New York attorneys. The document had been her idea. The affair with Dan had bolstered her determination; life, for the first time, seemed suddenly precious. Nine years ago she had decided she deserved compensation for the portion of it she gave up to Emil. At that time, when he signed the contract, he had already amassed about fifty million dollars. Her "security" must have seemed a pittance to him. And now he was close to the two hundred million threshold.

Then. Then and now. Whoever was it said that the cruelest memory is that of happiness? Was it some country and western singer, some snatch from Loretta Lynn or Johnny Cash? Just whenever Susannah was beginning to reckon she had outgrown her dependence, some fleeting, treacherous association would recall the Other Emil. He was the wizard, the necromancer who could conjure money out of nothing with his million-RAM brain. She never used to lie to the Other Emil; what was the point in lying to a magician? The Other Emil had been a font of knowledge and instruction. He patiently used to answer all her questions about history and art and politics and philosophy and human motivation. Economics, he taught her, drove every-thing: passions, imagination, sultans, and bootblacks; there was only money and the fear of death. And Emil knew everything about money.

Then and now. Now she was older and had discovered that Emil's topography was so limited. Money, it turned out, was only one aspect. Susannah unearthed other powerful forces. Dan Helena, for example, cared nothing about money.

Need and love and desire plaited inextricably, like a three-way braid. As a teenager, Susannah had believed in the hack-neyed romantic patterns of the country songs. You were in love or you were wounded and battle-scarred; you suffered or you walked on air; you won or lost the war; you checked in and out of Heartbreak Hotel. The day Susannah met Emil, the twenty-two-year-old girl perceived that such sentimentality had no fur-ther use to her. No one had yet written a popular song about the kind of emotion that bridled her to Emil. No Opry ballad identified the faith Emil ignited in her younger self. He had stepped out like a deus ex machina in an atheist's world, offering security. Other people assumed he had roped her with a noose of money. They were wrong. Susannah was absolutely clear about that, after nineteen jumbled years. Of course it was not unpleasant belonging to a millionaire. Particularly as you brushed with forty. The younger Susannah, however, had fol-lowed the man and not the checkbook. She had bowed to the yoke of the Other Emil, whose aura occasionally lingered on a puff of after-shave, or a pair of old ticket stubs, or a scribbled message or a crumpled receipt from 1973 or 1975.

When did love begin to wither? (We'll call it "love," she said to herself. It's the wrong word to describe that plaited rope, but it'll have to suffice. I can't think up a better one.) Whose love waned first, hers or Emil's? Did her affair with Dan Helena precipitate the rot? She gravitated to both men. Besides, Susannah admitted, Dan had not furnished a neat, packaged solution to the soreness of drifting from Emil. On the contrary, lust asked as many questions as it answered.

She poured a glassful of Château Margaux from the decanter and closed the carved oak door. Its exquisitely wrought panels depicted scenes from the Garden of Eden, the tree of knowledge, and the writhing bodies of the eternally damned in hell.

She glanced around the baronial living room, where in a short time they would all soon be sipping and nibbling and talking a mile a minute about the retrospective at the Guggenheim and the latest Whitney biennial and whether Jasper Johns was superior to Rauschenberg.

The grand living room had been designed entirely by Emil, as a home-away-from-home solace to his Swiss soul. Although it was Susannah who must live there, he had not consulted her when he had had the walls all paneled in rosewood from floor to ceiling and replaced the windows with leaded diamond panes. When he was abroad she kept the windows open all evening, to take in the view of the East River and the moon that rose each night larger than life, sometimes pale, sometimes gold, sometimes harvest russet. Right up until June he insisted they burn pine log fires (he was always chilly) and that real candles be replaced every morning in the eighteenth-century Dresden sconces.

It was a stagy room that elicited gasps from the bankers and art dealers Emil invited over to impress. His guests shivered at the double doors as they passed the waist-high statue of the three-headed dog Cerberus, guardian of the Greek underworld. Edging inside, past the menacing animal, they ogled the complete suit of armor, said to be from Saxony or Bucharest, circa 1325.

Susannah rearranged a few leaves of the giant chrysanthemums in the cauldron, as Emil liked them. The florist had sent them up that morning, along with the camellias she had ordered for the adjoining conservatory, where a flagstone path meandered between the moist clumps of exotic foliage. The blue-and-green parrot, Gauguin, lived on a perch over the wicker bench, and learned to imitate the human sounds it overheard.

After Susannah had brought Emil his wine, she stopped by the L-shaped kitchen to supervise the two Jamaican sisters. Iris worked for her full-time, while Pansy came in as auxiliary support whenever Susannah had house guests or people to dinner. Susannah had trained them to cater to Emil's robust Swiss taste: fondues and rabbit with mustard, Sachertortes and pheasant with apple and bacon. Iris was rolling the veal escallops in bread crumbs. Pansy swayed over the stove, stirring sorrel soup.

Susannah opened one of the refrigerators. "Did you remember the Grand Marnier this time?" she asked.

"Yes, ma'am. And the jellied eggs on the bottom shelf."

Susannah tasted the soup to check it was not overseasoned. She took in the rows of *oeufs en gelée,* a European delicacy Emil insisted on. Their American guests had been known to retch and choke on the cold poached eggs in gelatin, but what did Susannah care, as long as her own job was secure? They would all drink their fill of the Château Margaux, that she could guarantee, and if they could not stomach the food, too damn bad.

She climbed the duplex stairs to her dressing room to change. In the corridor outside she ran into Delphine, who had flown in with her father that morning and looked tired and irritable. The two women kissed each other formally on both cheeks. For Emil's sake they kept up civilities on official occasions, when they were forced under the same roof, during the weeks Delphine would visit in New York, at Easter and Christmas, when they gave one another expensive presents, Cartier earrings or antique Derby pillboxes. But they were all gifts bought with Emil's money, and the ritual of exchanging them was enacted to please Emil.

"Good trip?" asked Susannah.

Delphine swept aside a strand of her ruler-straight long brown hair and answered coolly. "Not really. The Concorde was two hours late in Paris. Papa kept saying, all the way across, 'What's the point of taking this stupid plane? We could have flown directly from Geneva.'"

"What an everlasting bore."

"I didn't care. I only came on the dumb Concorde to keep him company. Serves him right, and all those other industrialists."

Delphine, who was a Maoist-Leninist-Marxist, made a big issue of not traveling first class. Property and theft were one and the same, she maintained. Susannah noted that her creed had not deterred her from accepting from her father a three-bedroom co-op across the street on East End Avenue. Because Delphine rarely spent long in New York, and found it more convenient to perch at Susannah's palazzo, the co-op remained quite empty, except for a couple of wing chairs. Emil had picked them up at Christie's on a whim and then dumped them over the road in the empty living room.

"I'd guess I'd maybe better change." Delphine yawned loudly and nodded down at her blue jeans. She spoke a bilingual English, with hardly a trace of a French accent.

"Me too." Susannah ducked into her dressing room.

She was zipping the sea green de la Renta, with its plunging neck and embroidered matador jacket, when Emil came in. He held out two almost identical ties of a somber blue.

"Which one shall I wear tonight?" he implored.

Although she could hardly discern any difference, she pointed at his left hand. Emil liked resolution. "That one," she said firmly.

He stood behind her to knot it in the mirror. She did not turn to help him.

"Good day?" he asked indifferently.

And to think he had not seen her in six weeks. Did he harbor any feelings for her at all, underneath the tepid civilities? She murmured, "I'm sorry I was tardy. I couldn't get a cab downtown."

"What were you doing?"

She fiddled with the clasp on the twenty-two-carat ruby pendant Emil had provided at Christmas. He made no movement to adjust it for her. She avoided his eyes in the mirror while she lied, as she had lied her way through nineteen years.

"I stopped at some galleries. I saw a surrealist photo show you might like. Condoms growing out of bottles."

"What prices?"

"Five thousand, six thousand . . ."

"You buy anything?"

"I wasn't in the mood."

"You have good instincts."

Not in art, she thought wryly. Emil encouraged her to pick up the occasional painting or sculpture that took her fancy. He saw the assembling of a collection as a creative activity in its own right. Susannah secretly considered his theory a lot of hogwash. He collected because he enjoyed writing out the checks and taking things home. So what was the point in spending her own cash on yet more objects to hang on the walls or enshrine in the niches along the staircase? All their houses were already museumfuls, the East End Avenue apartment, the beach house on Martha's Vineyard, the apartments in London and Zurich and Cannes, and even the ski chalet in Val d'Isère.

He leaned over her shoulder to pluck away an escaped copper hair, for he loathed the minutest trace of disorder. Even when he barely touched her she sensed the crisp stiffness of his suit and breathed in the whiff of Monsieur Rochas she always associated with him, squeaky clean and powerful as a tidal wave. "Is everyone coming tonight?" he asked.

She moved over to the ruffled chaise longue to coax her feet into the uncomfortable spike-heeled shoes. Her dressing room was the only place in the thirteen-room duplex (not counting the six bathrooms) where Susannah was allowed a free rein with the decoration. She kept it pretty and puffy and fluffy, with fabrics in fuchsia and shell pink. Emil had bought her the porcelain-topped dressing table, said once to have been owned by Madame de Pompadour.

Susannah had been permitted no hand in the arrangement of their bedroom, *Emil's* bedroom, where they slept. Spacious, it contained no furniture but the bed, with its goosedown duvet, and the side table with four telephones: Susannah's private number, Emil's New York business number, the regular house number, and a special number granted only to Delphine for the nightly call with her father. On the wall above the bed hung three paintings: a dripping Dali watch, a decomposing planetary landscape by Yves Tanguy, and a de Chirico frozen nude. On the side table, when Emil was in town, Susannah filled the Venini glass dish with overripe apples, as he requested. The fruit must be aged a couple of months and emit a faint, musty scent. Whether in New York or Switzerland, Emil always slept in a room redolent with the perfume of apples. He explained to her that the aroma brought back a childhood memory of a certain orchard in Grindelwald.

"Is Jim McHenry coming?" Emil fiddled again with his tie.

"Of course. He's your paid minion. He wouldn't dare decline."

"He's a dependable workhorse. He looks after my papers conscientiously."

"I don't doubt it, but to my mind he's only your lawyer, Emil. There's no reason to be involving him in your social life with your intimate friends."

"I have a new business proposal I want to discuss with Jacob in a relaxed setting. That's why we need McHenry around."

Jacob and Felice Karakoff were also voracious collectors. Whereas Emil specialized in Surrealist work, Jacob Karakoff surrounded himself with the Abstract Expressionists of the fifties. Jacob, like Emil, was a businessman, who had amassed his fortune separately and spent on art as a hobby. He had made his money in bathroom installations, striking out from the bottom, first manufacturing porcelain sinks and toilet bowls, then gradually expanding into tiled shower units and sunken bathtubs with elaborate faucets, which cornered the higher echelons of the market. His holding company, Belle John, Inc., now umbrellaed several brands. A year ago, when he took it public on the Amex, Karakoff's own net worth had vaulted to about a hundred and twenty-five million.

Jacob was one of Emil's very few pals. Emil did not make close friends easily. There were really only two subjects he enjoyed discussing, the international finance business and art. Jacob Karakoff could hold his own in both areas and on occasion enjoyed holding a glass with Emil late into the night, too.

"What nature of business?" Susannah wobbled on her painful shoes from the chaise longue over to the mirror. She drew a couple of rapid flicks of mascara.

"Art business. Something new. Is Giulietta coming?"

Susannah nodded. Giulietta Giuliani was another of the select members of the inner circle. She ran a successful contemporary gallery in SoHo. Emil occasionally bought neo-surreal works from her. They had known one another since before his affair with Susannah. He trusted Giulietta's taste, and she, who was used to dealing with eccentric millionaires, knew exactly how far she could wield the whip and get away with it.

Emil carefully refolded his breast pocket handkerchief. "How is she?"

"Bossing everyone around as usual, enjoying herself playing the grande dame. When I invited her for tonight, she did a song and dance, wailing and hollering about how many important shows were opening downtown tonight and what-all she was jeopardizing by not being there to hobnob. I didn't pay her any mind. You know full well she'll sail in, gobble her way clear through three helpings of Wiener schnitzel, and just when we think she couldn't manage another bite, she'll ask for rum baba *and* Bavarian chocolate cake *and* kirsch soufflé."

"Susannah," he scolded, a little awed. Emil had trouble distinguishing between malice and wit. Susannah's fiery nature still tantalized him. He knew that behind his back she was not exactly leading a nun's life. Well, she was alone so much, and she was a voluptuous woman. What could one expect? He never questioned her about his suspicions, and she never flaunted her liaisons in his presence. The arrangement suited him. More and more often recently, however, as he sat sipping his wine late at night in Montreux, he wondered how different it might be to share his life with a real wife again. Susannah had bridged the twenty years since his first marriage. Now perhaps he was ready to take the plunge once more. He thought of his father, dead with the coronary at fifty-nine, and suddenly felt sorry for himself, incarcerated in his elegant villa on the shore of Lake Leman, surrounded by his invaluable collection of Dalis and Mirós and Magrittes.

"So where are Giulietta's downtown art openings tonight?" he inquired conversationally.

"Something at Dante's, something at the 313 Gallery."

"Dante's shows get worse and worse. She's better off here with our Château Margaux. Are you ready? Perhaps we should go downstairs."

He stood stiffly for her to pass him on the staircase, the marble treads half-carpeted in a fruity, plum nap.

Susannah rocked wildly in her heels and reached for the banister, not his arm.

He made no effort to steady her. "Is that young Englishman coming, too? The one whom I helped to get the job at the auction house?"

"Nick Jones? Yessir." He's another one wouldn't dare say no, thought Susannah. When Emil dug him up last summer in London, he was a penniless kid running errands in a stuffy old gallery in Duke Street. Living on fish and chips or whatever impoverished English folks ate. Before you could shake a stick, he hightailed it to New York, where one phone call from Emil got him a plum job with the most exclusive auction house in the city, working in the contemporary department. It was no wonder he jumped through the hoop when asked to dinner with her and Emil.

"He's a talented boy. He can't be much older than thirty. He could be useful to me." Emil rarely performed a wholly altruistic act.

"Anyhow, that's you and me and Delphine, Felice and Jacob Karakoff, that lawyer McHenry, and Giulietta. Seven. And your British protégé makes eight."

2

RITES OF PASSAGE

Nick Jones grew up in Wiltshire, in a comfortable house with three bedrooms and a well-tended garden. At six or seven, when the earth began to glow with its interior light, Nick would escape behind the flower beds of clematis and snap-dragons, to pore over *The Maltese Falcon* or *The Long Goodbye*. At evening, especially after rain, the pink light changed texture. The lush fields seemed to swallow the sky and then reflect it back; the land itself became luminescent. The coppices and hedges, the rows of beech and elm that dotted the fields, shivered in the breeze at the passing of Druid ghosts; Stonehenge was nearby.

A few years later he left for Oxford to study art history. Dutifully he plowed through the texts of civilization's signal critics: John Ruskin and Walter Pater from the last century, Gombrich and Berenson from this one. Most of the dons appeared to be more interested in their own careers than in the education of their students. Showing up for his weekly private "tutorial," Nick frequently found pinned to the door a note signed by his teacher that read, "Sorry. Gone to Ravenna [or Arles or Vienna]. Be back in 16 days."

There was one Cecil Rawlings, however, who took an impassioned interest in Nick's progress. Rawlings was a member of the small board of art dons assigned to grading the end-of-year examinations.

Nick, who had plans for joining either a prestigious gallery in London or obtaining a scholarship to participate in the Sotheby's training course, knew that he needed high marks in his exam. One day, shortly before his finals, he knocked tentatively on Rawlings's oak door.

"Come in," called the reedy voice.

Nick could hear the strains of Joan Sutherland singing an aria from *La Traviata.* He swallowed and opened the door.

Cecil Rawlings sat at his desk in an ellipse of lamplight. The bony fingers were writing feverishly, a hairlike scrawl in a crimson-tinted ink.

He muttered, hardly raising his head, "Take a seat, if you please. I will be with you shortly."

Nick sat stiffly on the chaise longue and watched the jerky movements of Rawlings's elbow. The don was wearing a lilac-gray shirt, with a gray scarf wound around his scrawny neck and tucked down the front.

The pen spurted and scratched while Joan Sutherland's voice warbled on. The record and the stylus needle were old. When they hit a bump and wheeled into a painful repetition, Cecil Rawlings at last stood up languorously to readjust the arm.

"So, my dear boy. What have you brought me today?"

"This week I've been doing the Sistine Chapel."

"A worthy enterprise." Rawlings coughed dryly. He smoked Russian Sobranie cigarettes nonstop. "What would you say to a cheeky little claret to accompany our perambulations across the Vatican?"

"That would be very nice."

"Speak up, dear boy. Has anybody ever told you, you mutter dreadfully. Although, I must add, you possess a pleasing profile that approaches that of the *Apollo Belvedere.*"

"I said," said Nick, raising his voice, "that would be very nice."

When Rawlings had poured the wine into the glasses, he settled himself opposite Nick on the horsehair-stuffed leather armchair, the pewter ashtray of Sobranie butts close to his right hand. Nick launched into the reading of his essay.

That was the normal pattern of an art history tutorial. The don would dispense some subject at the end of the previous week's session, such as "the role of patronage" or "So-and-so, painterly versus sculptural tendencies." Cecil Rawlings would lean his head back and close his eyes, while the student simply read his work aloud from start to finish. As his student droned to the conclusion, Rawlings would jerk his head and comment "A good effort," or "Might I suggest, the topic begs more depth." Then it would be time to go home.

So Nick read and sipped, while Joan Sutherland trilled and caroled, and Cecil Rawlings smoked and sipped and snoozed. The last cigarette consumed itself in a tube of ash. God knew, the essay was soporific: a blow-by-blow descriptive account of each of the biblical panels that constituted the famous ceiling.

Just when he seemed to be sleeping soundly, Rawlings sat up with a twitch, inhaled deeply from the moribund Sobranie, and demanded pointedly, "Tell me, dear boy, have you in fact ever visited the Sistine Chapel?"

"No." Nick was about halfway through the essay.

"Tell me, my young friend, are you unprompted by curiosity to observe for yourself what you so laboriously describe for me?"

"Of course I want to go to Italy sometime."

"That I may be able to arrange. Let us nibble on some Tuscan olives with our claret. A formidable combination, I have always found. Tell me, my dear Apollo, how would you like to begin with a few days on the notorious island of Capri?"

"Uhmm." The olives, which Cecil Rawlings had set between them, were unpleasantly wrinkled and shriveled.

"I make it an annual pilgrimage myself," said Rawlings. He stooped to refill Nick's glass and unhurriedly sat himself at the end of the chaise longue. "I am particularly attached to that infamous grotto in which the Roman emperor Tiberius is said to have enjoyed fondling the legs and private parts of small children."

Nick took a wrinkled olive and winced.

"Children of both genders, I should add," Rawlings continued. "I would like you to see also the lapis lazuli color of the translucent sea. Tell me, young Apollo, do you have plans this year for your summer vacation?"

Nick hesitated. Cecil Rawlings would be marking his exam paper within the next two weeks, and he needed a dazzling score.

"I have to start thinking about jobs and things." He forced himself to look Rawlings squarely in the eye and noticed how the gaunt don's veins protruded at his temples. "I'd like to carry on with an art career in London, that is, if I get a First Class degree."

"A First indeed." Rawlings nibbled at the wrinkles of his olive with his gleaming white teeth. They were far too white to be real, thought Nick, especially after a lifetime of Sobranie smoking.

"I want to get a really good job after university. Since I don't have any family connections, I'm going to need all the academic clout I can muster."

"Have you perchance contemplated a future in academia?" He moved a few inches closer to Nick on the chaise longue. "If you do in fact obtain a First—you may at least dispel any concerns regarding your Michelangelo paper—you would become eligible to pursue a further degree." His knee was resting lightly now against Nick's blue jeans.

Nick did not move a millimeter.

Cecil Rawlings closed his eyes for a moment, as if in profound meditation. The knee continued to brush Nick's leg. "You have a well-tempered mind, young Apollo, and your physical attributes are beyond question." His bony fingers dallied indolently with a tuft of Nick's light brown hair. He wore it in long, windswept curls while he was an undergraduate.

Rawlings's hand massaged the tendons around Nick's neck. Nick smelled the stale nicotine that the years had embedded in the skin. He willed his racing pulse to calm down. This was his big chance to ensure a brilliant exam result. It need not take all that long. Lots of the other students did it; some even seemed to like it. Once, at boarding school about five years ago, he and young Buxton had done it after lights out, under the Ping-Pong table, where they were well hidden. Nick still remembered the rush of orgasm with a certain shiver of taboo excitement. But that had been five years ago, and Buxton had been young and blond and lithe.... If he gave in once now, to Cecil Rawlings of the Sobranie cigarettes and shriveled olives, would that capitulation guarantee his exam results?

"If you are dead set on a career in the commercial world," drawled Rawlings, spitting as he whispered the word *commercial*, "I have a number of close acquaintances..."

Rawlings pushed him back firmly on the chaise longue. Nick was amazed at the old man's force. Rawlings's face was over his, and now he could smell the alcoholic breath. The liver must be long shot, too. Nick had one glimpse of the snow white teeth before he turned his head, uncontrollably, away to one side.

"Apollo is coy. Perhaps he will be bolder in Capri."

"Yes ... Capri ... August ... great."

Rawlings's hand groped at Nick's crotch now. Despite his physical disgust, Nick felt the beginning of a schizophrenic erection. He bit his tongue and closed his eyes and sought some compelling image that might carry him over to the other side of the next few minutes. He tried to count and remember the panels of the Sistine Chapel. The erection was growing and Rawlings kept trying to force his face back. How had he ever got himself into this? He wanted a dazzling career, he was intelligent, talented, good-looking. He only lacked the correct social chips. Damn it, every success in history was built somewhere on a compromise. Just one compromise, and then hopefully he would never need to compromise again.

"Oh, for Christ's sake!" Cecil Rawlings heaved himself furiously onto his elbows. Nick opened his eyes. The record had hit another broken groove, and Joan Sutherland's voice dived into an unbearable spin.

Rawlings stomped across the room to the record player.

Nick sat up straight. "I must go," he bleated. "I promised to dine tonight at Trinity."

"Yes, yes, dear boy. Of course. Do not let me detain you." Rawlings seemed to have regained his composure, as if he had awakened from a trance. He stared at Nick blearily. "Your essay this week was not bad, not bad at all. You may expect triumphant results in your forthcoming examination."

Nick nodded. Was there to be no mention of Capri? "I'll see you next week, then," he ventured hesitantly, his hand already on the inner door.

"Next week, dear me, I must forgo the pleasure of our tutorial, as I will be traveling abroad to Madrid. An impressive town. Well worth your time to make the voyage there one day. Good luck with your examination."

Cecil Rawlings was no man of honor. Nick never got his First after all, only a Third Class scrape-through. With no social strings and only his unimpressive degree, Nick was glad enough to find a job at Stumple and Stumple, an obscure gallery on Duke Street that specialized in nineteenth-century British oil paintings of cows and sheep. He earned just enough to pay for his lodging, a diet centered on bread and cheddar, and dry cleaning bills for the pinstripes he must now wear. Most low-level art jobs were poorly paid. The market was saturated by overbred women prepared to work for almost nothing in return for contact with eligible bachelors.

He sat behind his desk, answering routine telephone inquiries or hand-addressing envelopes to patrons. As he dodged the traffic in St. James's Street on his errand to the sandwich counter, where he was sent daily to collect everyone else's lunch, he sometimes thought of Cecil Rawlings. A few more minutes on that chaise longue, and he might have landed one of the coveted positions at Agnews, Marlborough, or even the auction houses.

Nick soon grew to loathe the Stumple brothers, who came from an undistinguished social background and used their art business as an excuse for airs and affectations. Hilary wore suits from Savile Row next door and sported wire-rimmed pince-nez. He drove an Aston Martin, which he parked nearby in St. James's Square. It was Nick's responsibility to remember to run outdoors every couple of hours to feed the parking meter with his stock of coins.

Otherwise his duties included answering the door buzzer (the Stumples believed that a locked establishment discouraged riffraff), greeting the client with a footmanly "Good morning, sir" (or "madam"), making routine phone calls to the insurers, the bank, and warehouse and freight companies, and researching short catalog blurbs for Victorian paintings by the likes of Thomas Sidney Cooper, Charles Jones, and Edwin Meadows.

Weeks stretched into months and years. Nick's tiny salary inched up modestly. Nick addressed Stumple and Stumple heavy cream rag-embossed envelopes to knights of the realm, Greek shipping magnates, and Saudi sheiks, inviting them to openings. The Stumples would uncork a few bottles of an indifferent blanc de blanc, while Nick's job was to remove his pinstripe jacket and hang a new "come on" painting between the windowpane and the green velour drapes.

A Friesian cow in profile, attributed to Landseer, caught Emil Papier's eye as he drove past the window late one November afternoon. He told the chauffeur to stop and wait and that he would be only a few minutes.

Nick answered the door buzzer. "Good afternoon, sir. May I help you?"

"I would like to buy the painting in the window."

Nick hesitated. "I'm extremely sorry. That painting has already been sold. Is there anything else that might interest you? We happen to have a rather fine pair of Henry Parker Ayrshire bulls just now."

Emil scowled. He needed that Friesian cow, with its uppity expression, and he would go all out to get it.

"The cow in the window—how much?"

Nick puzzled whether he should convey such information to this well-tailored foreigner. Hilary Stumple discouraged furnishing unnecessary information to unknown clients, who might turn out to be riffraff. But it was almost time to go home, and Nick did not want an argument. "Fifty-five thousand pounds," he said. "The picture has been attributed to Landseer." He added quickly, "We have a very fine Thomas Sidney Cooper for only thirty." He indicated a herd of Charolais guzzling at a watering hole.

Emil did not even look around. No, he needed that haughty cow in the window, and nothing else would do. It was his mother's seventy-eighth birthday in two weeks, and as happened each year, he had been agonizing for months over what to give the autocratic tyrant. Emil had never been able to overcome his abject terror of the harpy. Each time he doubled his millions, it did not seem to make any fundamental difference to their relationship. On the surface he played the part of the dutiful eldest son, while he peppered his respectful veneer with subtle reminders of malice. The arrogant cow in the window resembled the old lady at her most bellicose.

"Fifty-five," repeated Emil, his head cocked in the direction of the window. "*I* will give you ninety thousand pounds."

Nick hardly contained his bewilderment. Nobody could want such an ugly painting that much. "Perhaps you would care to speak with Mr. Stumple. He's on the telephone right now. If you could be patient for just a moment..."

Emil glanced at his watch. He had an appointment with a merchant banker, but the dispatch of his mother's birthday present remained the most important business on his agenda.

Nick hurried up the half flight of stairs to the cramped office, where Hilary Stumple sprawled across a catalog-laden desk. He glared at Nick's interruption. "What is it?"

Nick explained the dilemma and took some satisfaction in watching Hilary's popping eyes bulge to bursting point.

"Offer him a drink. Show him the Barker bulls. I'll be right there."

Nick returned to Emil, who was sitting rigidly on the velvet settee in the middle of the main gallery.

"We're trying to work something out. Mr. Stumple will be down in a second. May I offer you a glass of wine?"

Emil shook his head and looked back at his wristwatch, studded with tiny diamonds. He pulled out a crisp handkerchief and blew his nose.

"I'm sorry it's so dusty here," said Nick.

Emil waved away the apology. "England would not be England if it were not a little dusty."

"Do you collect English paintings?"

"Rarely. I am interested in Dada and Surrealism."

Nick looked wistful. "Marcel Duchamp and so forth?"

"Precisely."

"In London there's not much market for that sort of thing.

People here are still so middle-brow. They like armchair art. Nothing difficult, nothing dangerous."

Emil looked up at him with a glimmer of interest. "And what brings you then to Marcel Duchamp?"

"He was the greatest art genius of the century. He said a work of art could be anything one wanted it to be. He was the first person to sweep away all this." Nick nodded contemptuously around the moiré-covered walls, plastered with their jumble of ovine and bovine oils.

Emil nodded pensively. "Possibly."

Hilary Stumple came swaying down the short flight of steps like a sixteenth-century galleon, his watch chain jogging on his portly belly. He held out a milk white hand. *"Bonjour, monsieur.* Hilary Stumple. How may I help you?"

Nick knew that Hilary broke into execrable French at the tiniest opportunity.

"Good afternoon. Emil Papier. I would like to buy the painting in your window."

"You understand, the picture in question has unfortunately already been promised to a valued gallery client. *Vous comprenez, monsieur?* However, I believe you mentioned something about a substantial premium ... "

Emil glanced back at the diamond-studded watch. Despite Hilary's insistence on incomprehensible and time-wasting interjections in French, in ten minutes they reached agreement. The painting was to be shipped to Madame Papier the following morning, and Emil's purchase price of ninety thousand pounds would include incidental expenses of freight, duty, and transit insurance. Emil produced a check on the spot (most unusual in the business), drawn in sterling on Barclays Bank, and there and then filled in all the zeros. The negotiation settled, his features unstiffened visibly.

Emil looked one last time at the watch. Nick remembered that he himself had an urgent mission to execute, the feeding of the parking meter for Hilary's Aston Martin in St. James's Square. Another couple of minutes and the police would be around with their towing equipment. In all his exploited years of Stumple employment, he had never failed to nurse that meter on time.

As they stepped out onto Duke Street together, into the

clammy November rush hour, Emil turned curiously to Nick. "What you were saying before about Duchamp interested me. It's odd to hear coming from an Englishman, especially one who deals in the nineteenth century."

The blood rushed about Nick's ears. "After I left Oxford," he explained, "this gallery was my first job, and I've been here ever since. It was a kind of accident."

They stopped at the curb by a silver Mercedes. "This is my car," said Emil. "I'm on my way to the city. Can I give you a ride anywhere?"

The uniformed chauffeur sprang out to open the back door. Nick wavered an instant. Then, on a rash impulse, he lied. "That would be very kind of you. I'm going in that direction."

"So," said Emil, leaning back against the soft upholstery. "You like twentieth-century art?"

The car swept out into Pall Mall, with its imposing Regency facades of impenetrable gentlemen's clubs.

"Of course I care about Michelangelo and Raphael and Titian, too. But now I really want to work with art that's alive, not some cultural artifact. As for those nineteenth-century cows..." Nick sighed.

"Have you been to New York?"

"Not yet, but the fares are so cheap these days I thought I might go this spring."

They pulled out of Trafalgar Square, past the National Gallery swarming with hippies and tourists. Emil drew a couple of business cards from his breast pocket. "This is my number in New York, and this is my number in Switzerland. When you do decide to visit the United States, feel welcome to telephone me."

Nick took the cards. "Thank you. Could you possibly drop me just here, please?"

The driver braked smoothly and edged out of the traffic. Emil leaned over the armrest with a flash of sudden interest. "Don't forget to call me. I think I would enjoy talking more with you. Au revoir, and good luck."

As Nick watched the silver Mercedes weave through the traffic, his heart soared and he plunged into the damp evening with a lilt in his step. He had no serious expectation that his encounter with Emil would lead to anything. What really thrilled him, with a spurt of wanton and self-destructive delight, was the secure knowledge that by now Hilary Stumple's Aston Martin would doubtless have been towed by the police, and his boss would be compelled to spend hours rescuing it.

That was all ancient history now.

Three weeks ago he had arrived in New York, weary from the charter flight and tedious connecting bus rides. (Every cent counted; there was no surplus to spend on taxis.) He had checked into a fleabag hotel on Forty-third Street, recommended for its price and centrality. In his room the plaster crumbled under the naked light bulb. The plastic curtain across the "shower" (a tiny, flaking recess) was decorated with designs of copulating couples: standing, kneeling, and spread-eagled. Until dawn a neon sign winked incessantly through the blind. Finally, in order to sleep, he had to yank the cable for the nonstop loop of soft-porn video out of the wall. He pulled the thin, rough sheet around himself. Raymond Chandler. Dashiell Hammett.

Next day he called the telephone number on Emil Papier's card. He was in luck . . . Monsieur Papier was in town on a lightning trip . . . too busy for lunch this time around, but he clearly remembered the young man and the cow paintings . . . asked what Nick was doing now . . . and when Nick admitted he was looking for work, within a few minutes Emil had organized him an interview at the auction house. Then the second interview; the job offer; and the sudden phone call from a woman with a lilting, soft-spoken voice and the trace of what Nick believed might be a southern accent. She told him that Emil would be back again from Switzerland soon and that he had personally suggested Nick join them for a small, intimate dinner on Emil's arrival in Manhattan. Would Tuesday be convenient?

Susannah had mesmerized him over dinner. Nick Jones swallowed a rush of disappointment when she left the room to answer the telephone. It had never before occurred to him that a woman of her maturity could be so desirable. She had a subtle way of making him feel interesting, as she leaned over to fill his wineglass with special attention. When she bent toward him he caught a whiff of the perfume on her warm skin, which smelled more sophisticated than any other scent in the world.

Her charm helped to dilute the snubs of that bitch, the daughter. He could tell, the moment they all sat down at the dining table, that Delphine had it in for him. When he tried to flatten out those nauseating jellied egg things with his fork across the surface of the plate, she had speared him with a caustic stare from under her canopy of long lashes.

Oh, she was nice looking, little Swiss miss, with her sleek straight hair, her perfect teeth, and her tiny waist. She knew it, too.

"I hear my father helped you find a job." Her eyes never left the rubble of *oeufs en gelée* on his plate.

"Yes, he's been very kind and helpful."

"I guess you were stuck in a rut when he found you." She said "found" as one might "find" a stray cat.

"I was working for a gallery in London. We specialized in nineteenth-century animal paintings. It was small, but"—Nick struggled to find something positive to tack on—"they were knowledgeable chaps who taught me a lot."

"My father said they treated you like slave labor."

Susannah came to his rescue. "Nick has a degree in art history from Oxford University," she defended him. "He studied with the famous Professor Rawlings."

Delphine announced maliciously, "We all admire Susannah's intellectual efforts. How it must bore her to sit through our high-minded discussions."

The hostess pretended not to hear.

Nick felt the blood rush to his face, and he clawed at his linen napkin under the tablecloth. Why did the bitch hate him so vehemently, or was she spiteful with everyone? He tried once more. "What are you studying at Heidelberg University?"

She looked toward the ceiling chandelier with disdain. After a long pause she grunted, "I'm writing a thesis on U.S. imperialism in Latin America."

"That must be jolly complicated."

"I'm a Marxist-Leninist-Maoist." She lowered her voice slightly. "Of course, my father's disappointed. He wishes I'd take an interest in his business. I'd like to make him happy, but I can't give up my life to a purely exploitative activity."

"My father wanted me to go into industry, too." Perhaps at last he had located a common thread.

"What does your father do?" Again, the chill.

"He's retired. He was a managing director at a pharmaceutical corporation." That suddenly seemed so inadequate, so menial a lifework in this dazzling company. Nick himself had youth on his own side with its endless potential, but his poor father was finished, a cut-and-dried case.

The maid, in her frilly white apron, stooped to offer the fruit macédoine. Delphine waved it aside. "I have to go now. I'm meeting some friends." She reached for her evening purse, which was shaped like a killer whale and had been purchased for a thousand dollars at a Save the Wildlife event.

No one seemed surprised at her abrupt departure. When she stood, Nick noticed the slenderness of her almost adolescent thighs. She was wearing a minute leather miniskirt over crocheted lime-green tights.

She swooped over Emil and kissed him noisily on the forehead.

"Good night, little pomegranate. Don't stay out too late. You know how I will worry about you."

Then the pretty monster was gone, and the conversation resumed. Nick was finally able to sit back and relax and sneak a glance at the Max Ernst collage on the opposite wall.

The Karakoff couple, it transpired, also floated in Emil's economic stratosphere. Felice Karakoff moved carefully, as if she were skimming over glass. She had good manners, with an edge of reserve, dainty bones, and little makeup. She made a real effort to say a few words to everyone in the room. When it was his turn to be addressed, she asked how he liked New York and where he had lived in London; whether he enjoyed tea at Brown's Hotel or the Ritz; where was the best place these days to buy china; whether he ate rice pudding and treacle; whether it was safe to walk at night in Hyde Park. It was the usual string of questions he was asked five times a week here. He had already learned to smile his creamy Roger Moore smile—impeccable, with just a hint of wry humor—and answer politely.

The husband, Jacob, had a feverish, workaholic look; his face was watermelon pink, and he sweated excessively from the top of his bald head. Unlike his wife, he had no small talk. His eyes, behind their wire-rimmed glasses, glinted with a let's-roll-up-our-sleeves-and-get-down-to-work frenzy, directed right now toward Emil and the lawyer chap, McHenry.

The lawyer was a New York type Nick rapidly recognized. The Jim McHenrys of this world (there seemed to be armies of the clones) came into the preview galleries of the auction house on Saturday afternoons with their wives and live-in girlfriends. The couples would stand in front of a Twombly or Oldenburg for hours, discussing in which corner of which room of their apartment/country house in the Berkshires/Hampton beach house/Park Avenue office the piece might fit.

Jim McHenry, a washed-out blond, masticated each mouthful of his Wiener schnitzel and made no contribution to the discussion. He looked neither right nor left. When Emil or Jacob Karakoff put a question to him, he ruminated a moment before he responded, meticulously, prolixly.

The guest who seemed most interesting to Nick—other than Susannah, of course—was the art dealer, Giulietta Giuliani. Her ample bottom and bosom were squeezed into black crepe (you could not imagine such a dowager wearing any other shade), and her iron-streaked hair was pulled tightly back in a bun. She wore no jewelry but a Victorian cameo locket around her puffy neck.

Giulietta was asking Jacob Karakoff, "So what do you think of Dan Helena's sketches for the sculpture in Belle John Plaza?"

"The board is voting their final choice on Friday. Personally I'm rooting for Helena. Some of them wanted to go for the usual abstract corporate art, but I've been persuading them that Helena's figurative work makes a more powerful statement. A majestic statue of the first president of our country is perfect to exemplify the values of an all-American, democratic corporation like Belle John."

"You'll be glad you took my advice." She rapped him playfully with the back of her spoon. "Helena's the most important figurative sculptor in this country. Those abstract metal artists make fashionable corporate art these days, but a hundred years from now, most of them will be forgotten. Dan Helena, with his extraordinary gifts, will still be great. He is the only sculptor who can truly turn steel into flesh."

Jacob explained to Nick, "Belle John's a major manufacturer of bathroom equipment and fixtures. We're located in Geraldine, New Jersey. Basically the whole town of Geraldine is Belle John. We employ about four thousand people."

Emil interrupted. "Jacob and I have business to discuss." He nodded, by way of order to Jim McHenry to accompany them. "We'll have coffee and cognac in the library."

Nick followed the women into the living room, where a fire blazed in the chimney and the suit of armor cast a gothic shadow diagonally across the ceiling. The little maid set down demitasses and plates of chocolate truffles. A telephone rang. Susannah excused herself to take the call elsewhere, and a few minutes later Felice Karakoff also disappeared. Nick was left alone with the grand Giulietta.

"So you're newly arrived from London?"

Nick smiled the vanilla smile he was perfecting.

"London's a nice place for a holiday," she declared. "Of course, all English people are masochists. The houses are cold and damp, full of smelly animals running all over, and the food—for a Western country, it's beyond belief. Oh, I don't mean to insult the place. The English know how to plant a rose garden. But who would put up with such living conditions?"

"I'm enjoying New York." He wished he could learn not to sound so understated, so English.

"You will grow addicted to New York in time," she promised. "It's dirty, it's dangerous, the people are rough and rude, but this is important: you can do anything you want here and you can be free. They leave you alone. In a European city, you step out of line and people notice."

"You go back to Italy often?"

"Every summer I spend a few weeks with my niece. I've lived in New York twenty-nine years now. I wouldn't want to live anywhere else."

Nick scanned the walls uneasily. "Emil has a wonderful collection of Surrealist paintings," he remarked, his gaze roving from a cherub grown into a cauliflower to a window that opened on a window that opened on more windows.

"One of the finest in the world. He's mainly interested in dead artists, though he occasionally buys one of my boys. I sold him that one." She pointed toward the brick hearth. "Nineteen years ago."

Nick saw a terra-cotta statuette, about two feet high, of a nude woman reclining on her elbow. One leg was bent in front, the other raised at a right angle. The head, with its fountain of thick hair, was tilted back, and one arm was draped across her stomach, the hand stationed provocatively between the legs.

"Interesting," Nick said politely. It seemed a bizarre choice for this starchy Swiss millionaire to adorn his fireplace with a sculpture of a masturbating woman.

"Emil is oddly attached to that," said Giulietta. "I still remember the day he first came into my gallery in 1972—I had a space up on Fifty-seventh Street in those days before I moved downtown to SoHo in 1974—and saw the piece in the corner. He was with Delphine that day; she must have been about five or six. Cute kid. It was just after his divorce, and he used to take her everywhere with him."

Nick took a sip of Armagnac. "Who was the artist?"

"Dan Helena. Before he became so famous. He normally works in steel. The terra-cotta figure was an early piece, something he'd dabbled with in a life class."

Nick Jones had risen to his feet and was examining the terracotta statue again, more carefully. He ran a finger along the inside of the thigh, where the clay, toasted by the nearby fire, was warm to the touch.

"I told Emil I had a number of Dan's other works. But it was this piece that really seemed to grab him. He bought it for eleven hundred dollars. Those were the days."

3

AMEN, BROTHER

Susannah's first memory was learning to respect and fear Him. She knew He could be lurking anywhere, lying in wait: under the bed she shared with her sister Ellie June, crouching in the cold, stinking outhouse, huddled behind the counter of the dry goods store, coiled among the fertilizer and machine-made cakes and pouches of Red Man tobacco, or stalking like a ferret along the roofs of the redbrick warehouses over the Woodland Street Bridge. When Susannah was six, her father had fallen drunk down a farmer's well, and there the Prince of Darkness had whisked his soul away. Ever after, Susannah closed her eyes and held her breath when she passed the shaft in the ground. For she knew He was still brooding down there, waiting for prey in the icy water.

The minister pierced his congregation with glittering eyes. He had slicked-back blond hair and shiny temples, like the skin of a scrubbed butternut squash. He had a habit of plucking imaginary mosquitoes out of the air with pudgy hands, as if he were swatting at wayward souls. His warnings of fire and brimstone bellowed through the church. "You must put on God's armor, so as to be able to stand up against the devil's enticements." After the six elders had passed around the Lord's supper, first the trays of bread cubes, then the thimbles of watery grape juice, the minister would announce the latest tribulations. This one had been bitten by a rattlesnake, that one had had himself a stroke, So-and-so's son had been mangled in a threshing machine, some wretched girl had been banned from the church—officially they called it "disfellowship"—for getting impregnated. "Your lips have spoken lies, and your tongue utters untruth.... Vipers' eggs they hatch, and spider's webs they weave." As the minister preached from Isaiah, various members of the congregation gave vent to a heartfelt "Amen" or "Amen, brother." The minister stepped down from the pulpit and paraded between the pews. On either side of him, people were praying in snatches, "Lord save us sinners from the hellfires of damnation! Amen, brother." Several women were sobbing softly. The minister's baritone charged above: "Repent, or the perpetual fires of hell will be upon you. You must be saved to enter the kingdom of Heaven."

Susannah's stepfather was a church elder. The front door would slam as Zachary returned from the snuff factory, and the whole rickety house would rattle as if an earth tremor were vibrating beneath the floorboards. Her mother sprang up anxiously and wiped away the oil and cornmeal from the catfish she was preparing to fry. She ran her hands through her stringy hair (it had once been thick and gleaming like her daughters', she swore) and set her features on automatic in an expression of resignation.

Zachary read every night to the family from the Book of Job and the Letters to the Corinthians. They all feared him, her three elder sisters and her weary, flattened-out, prematurely aged mother, who had spent her youth covering up for a drunk and now her middle years drudging for a sanctimonious bigot. After supper the stepchildren assembled in the parlor for the evening's lecture. They sat with folded hands on the patched couch and stared dully at their hated guardian. Susannah pretended to listen. Step by step, street by street, in her mind's eye she traced her imaginary runaway route. She would sneak through the picket fence, hurry across the Woodland Street Bridge, past the redbrick warehouses, leaving behind the shabby, poor white district of Edgefield, and saunter into Printer's Alley, where the strippers at the Rainbow Club and the Voodoo Lounge jiggled their plump tits. At the notorious Brass Rail Stable the bourbon and rye flowed late, every patron's bottle with his name on it.

When they lay in bed together, each tugging for a wider share of the blanket, Susannah solemnly told her sister Ellie June, "I ain't gonna end up like Mama. When I'm a grown woman I aim to wear real lipstick and glasses with rhinestones and sleep in a feather bed."

Ellie June giggled. "And eat goo-goo clusters for breakfast." The gobs of caramel, chocolate, marshmallow, and peanuts were the passion of every local child.

Susannah whispered, "And I'll have me a steaming hot bath every other day. That's what I intend doing."

"Wishing won't get you nowheres." Her sister was skeptical.

"Never you fear, I ain't scrubbing for no husband."

"Hush, girl." Ellie June was shocked now. "Don't talk no filth, Susannah Maud. You know what's written. 'I had rather keep house with a lion and a serpent than keep house with a wicked woman.'" The followers of the Church of Christ interpreted the Bible literally and combed every line of the Scriptures for clear instruction on how to lead unsullied lives. The elders charged that women, the weaker vessel, were created to serve.

Life in Edgefield centered on family business and procreation, making biscuits and chopping turnip greens, listening to rumors of the neighbors' unholy excesses and gospel programs on WLAC. There were few diversions. The Grand Ole Opry, where Loretta, Hank, Roy, and Minnie performed at the Ryman, was strictly off limits. Music could lead to dancing, dancing was the devil's own work. None of the elders kept televisions in their homes, and Susannah had managed to sneak away only a few times to the movies at the Paramount and the Knickerbocker, using for her ticket the dimes she filched out of the collection platter in church.

In church Susannah hummed to herself, "Durn if I end up like Mama. Never, never, never." Her mother's breasts drooped, and the veins in her legs branched like the tributaries of the Cumberland River. Those veins were the badge of a lifetime of standing and bearing children. "Sinners, you are sadly wandering," the congregation caroled tunelessly. In accordance with scriptural interpretation, their church forbade any musical accompaniment. The resulting hymns never sounded quite right. "One day," sang Susannah, "I'm fixing to sleep in my own bed."

She had slept alone only once, for a few days when she had measles. They moved Ellie June out of the bed and onto a makeshift cot of sacks on the porch. While Zachary prayed loudly in the parlor for his stepdaughter's recovery, her mother wiped her flushed face and held her hand. When Susannah began to feel better, her mother showed her the precious box.

It was an old tin sewing box, with a picture on the lid of a pretty Confederate lady in a crinoline and bonnet. Her mother kept it hidden from Zachary, under the molasses jars and Martha White flour sacks in a kitchen cabinet. The child stared mesmerized as her mother pried open the lid. Inside lay the crumpled photograph of her vilified liquored-up father, who had stumbled into the well, clutching his bottle of Jack Daniel's, who gave up his spirit to Beelzebub, gasping in the blind, black waters, clutching at the walls of the shaft, and sounding the Rebel yell as he fell.

Her father had been a handsome drunk, tall and confident, with a wry, defiant gleam. He at least had not lived his short life in fear of Mephistopheles. "He was a mighty fine fiddler, too, the poor sot," her mother confided, "when he weren't swilling moonshine or guzzling bourbon." She lowered her voice. Zachary was still praying, a thin wall away. Fiddling was a damnifying sin. "He was ever fixing to travel north someday. He said we'd make sojourn to the big city of Cincinnati, or Chicago maybe. He reckoned he'd locate steady work in New York, maybe working the docks or erecting skyscrapers. 'There's work for all folks in New York,' he said. 'You won't believe it unless you see it.' If he hadn't done fell down that well...Lord bless his miserable soul." She shook her head philosophically.

When Susannah grew up Zachary enjoined, "Shuck back

those lascivious curls and attempt to look decent, before I get me a shears to crop 'em. And quit worshiping yourself so whole-hearted. I don't intend to say it but once." Susannah swept away the sheaf of brown hair. Zachary permitted no vanity, not even mirrors, in his household.

Susannah always sat well up in the front pew, alongside the other elders' children. She felt the minister's attention wander from his hymnal to traverse her breasts, while with his icy white teeth he beamed at her briskly, exhorting her to lift up her voice and glorify the Lord. "Though your sins be scarlet, they shall be white as snow," she sang from the pit of her lungs.

If she was old enough to toss her head wantonly, she was ready to earn her bed and board, said Zachary, so Susannah went to work at the chicken factory in Madison. She had to swallow hard every time the belt swung by, swaying with car-casses. The chickens arrived still alive each morning, rustling in the crates where they were jammed tight. The men electro-cuted them and cut off their heads. After the feathers had been mechanically plucked, the pink lumps were strung up on the belt for the women to disembowel. Each girl had her own op-eration. Susannah's job was to separate the gall bladder from the liver. Sometimes the small sac of flesh split neatly. Some-times she had to claw and pick at it with her nails through the rubber gloves.

In 1967 Nashville passed a referendum that liquor could be served by the drink, not just a fifth or a half-pint. Zachary sputtered like musket fire, "The end'll be acoming. Lucifer is raring in this town." In 1968 the Supreme Court declared un-constitutional state laws that prohibited teaching evolution. Zachary ranted, "Them sorry Yankees with their evil tribunals are doomed to destroy us all."

And Susannah's nest egg grew. She caught the Gallatin Pike bus at 6:15 A.M. each morning and took on all the overtime she could get. She hoarded every leftover cent, stuffing the dollar bills into her mother's sewing box, where they lay hidden among the flour sacks. There was time for nothing but chickens, church, and sleep. There would be opportunity for dancing later, when she escaped to New York, where Satan set folks whirling naked in an orgy of rock music and marijuana.

For Susannah was not afraid of Satan anymore. She had made her unlikely peace with him, ever since the Saturday the minister, formidable in his black, broad-brimmed hat, came to call on Zachary. He found Susannah alone in the parlor, reading a forbidden magazine that she had smuggled into the house and listening to illicit music on the radio.

"Where's your stepdaddy, then?" The minister peered cautiously up the staircase, as if the family were waiting to pounce.

Susannah slid *True Confessions* under the couch. "Gone to his brother Augustus in Smyrna to slaughter a blue-ribbon hog."

"Your mama yonder, too?" He shuffled restlessly and passed a handkerchief across his forehead.

Susannah leveled her eyes at him. He did not frighten her anymore. A volt of power surged through her. "All my kinfolk." Susannah's other sisters were married now, one to a small-time farmer, one to a garage mechanic.

The minister took a small step closer. "And what's detaining you at home, little Susannah Maud?"

"I ain't so little no more." She was seventeen and stood almost as tall as the minister. Underneath her T-shirt her chest heaved a fraction, the breasts that had been fascinating the minister for too long while he preached, and made his eyes narrow with pagan appetite.

He laid his pudgy fingers on top of her head, like a blessing. "You've grown up mighty pretty, Susannah Maud."

"My stepdaddy says a heap too pretty for a virtuous servant of the Lord." The weight of his hand ignited her with a reckless excitement. She hankered to drag him with her in her rebellion—him, the despotic, squeaky-clean minister, who ruled the congregation with the threats of brimstone. She leaned closer to him.

The minister's breath was racing hot. He used the same tone to order her as he used to command in his church. "Hitch your skirt a speck higher," he instructed bluntly.

The blood pounded in her ears. She bit her lip and looked away over his shoulders while she obeyed. She felt a tightening in her legs and a fluttering at the pit of her stomach. She was flooded with delicious shame.

The pudgy fingers grappled the skin between her legs, grabbing at the hair and wriggling between the lips. She froze.

"Don't be afeard." His fingers ventured stubbornly against the virginal membrane.

Now she grew petrified, her whole body rigid and shaking. She had never imagined that committing this sin would paralyze her with a mortal fear. A clammy sweat drenched her lower back and inner thighs. Her married sisters had told her it was uncomfortable at first but that they got used to it. Learned to like it. How could she—a grown seventeen years old—be such a coward? Her teeth chattered.

"Hush yowling, child. I ain't going to do you no harm." The busy hand prodded and stormed the armor of her body.

She took a breath. Through clenched teeth she breathed, "Preach it to me."

"What, sugarbaby?" His other hand roamed over the curve of her buttocks, stroking and coaxing her baby flanks.

Her words came in tiny stabs. "Vipers' eggs they hatch, and spider's webs they weave."

"Lord, what are you carrying on about?"

She rubbed herself, pleading, against his hand and opened her legs a few inches wider. "Preach."

His voice complied slowly. "He who eats of their eggs will die." He had roared it often enough from the pulpit.

She whimpered as his fingers edged deeper, feeling out the secret layers. Now she was rocking against the hand, sucked into the rhythm of his manipulation. The terror lifted. She was opening, petal by leaf, as his words from Isaiah hissed in her ear.

"Truth stumbles in the public place, and honesty can find no entrance." He raised her leg toward the back of the couch, unbuttoned his fly with sleight dexterity, and hurled himself upon her. With a shock she felt it assault her, three times as gigantic as she was expecting and more solid than any human flesh should be. It was impossible, she panicked, her body was surely too narrow. Her skin would rip and she would be punished for her effrontery.

Then the voice once more again in her ear, as he drilled against her. "Our transgressions are ever with us, and our iniquities we know." This time she yielded, suddenly sailing, smooth and easy, opening wider and wider to him—no, not to him, not to that man with the pudgy fingers, but to the voice that cajoled in her ear, to the mystical words.

When his voice stopped directing her, she could still hear the verses in her mind. The minister's attention was concentrated on his own climax. His hands gripped hard at her buttocks, and he came with a gurgling noise, like the slurp of percolating coffee.

He yanked out of her brusquely and looked away while he dressed. She turned away, too, hugging the tattered arm of the couch. She screwed her eyes shut until she heard his retreating footsteps. He left the house without a word. After that, when he preached on Sundays, his gaze no longer flitted over the pews toward her breasts. After his sermons, when the congregation filed out, each addressing a few words to him, he adroitly avoided speaking to Susannah.

The day before her departure, on April 23, 1970, she stole Zachary's silver snuffbox out of his bottom drawer, to pawn it on Lower Broad. By the time he discovered the theft she would be hundreds of miles short of home.

Before she returned home from the pawnshop, she stopped at the infamous Printer's Alley. She wanted to see the interior of the saloon where General Jackson once hitched his horse to the railing outside and the elders whispered, Satan himself did his nightly work among the gamblers and boozers. Secret passageways, now cemented over, linked up all the hot spots in Printer's Alley during Prohibition. Everyone knew the Brass Rail Stable was still haunted. They said mirrors fell off the wall and once in a while the half grandfather clock still bonged, although its inner springs and wheels were long since removed. Some said the ghost of a fugitive slave haunted the place, for the saloon had been used as an escape route for slaves; an underground tunnel led down to the Cumberland River. Perhaps the ghost would understand. Susannah was a runaway, too.

She slunk past the corridor alongside the bar, where the walls were plastered with photographs of celebrity ruffians and ne'er-do-wells. In the main room a pianist was playing "Blue Moon of Kentucky." Susannah chose a quiet booth, under a gilded mirror, and ordered a beer with a barbecue sandwich. Although she did not want the food, they would not serve the drink without it. She huddled in the darkest corner and spread a piece of paper on the rutted wooden table surface. Her head bowed in concentration, under the curtain of her long brown hair. She composed her runaway letter.

Dearest Mama,
    When you read this I will be far away. Do not try to find me. I aint coming home. Molly and Annie Virginia are married and have babies, and Ellie June will be soon too. So you will not be too lonely. I will miss you always and maybe one day I will write again.

                    Your loving daughter,
                    Susannah Maud Lucile Bishop XXXXX

The next morning Susannah retrieved the rest of her savings from the sewing box and slipped the creased photo of her daredevil father into the back of her wallet. Her bus left from the Greyhound station at 6:45 A.M.

When her mother was still rereading the note, and Zachary cursing the hussy for stealing his snuffbox, Susannah blinked at the spectacle of Madison Avenue, where a ratatouille of humankind scurried and churned. The streets stank of old food and fresh food and soot. The buildings towered, dwarfing Susannah's memory of the twenty-nine-story L&C Insurance Company in downtown Nashville; until today that had been her tallest yardstick. Northerners talked as rapidly as firecrackers, in short staccato intonations. The men wore no hats, and the women swished by, in pants suits with pink-and-turquoise prints, flowing paisley scarves, and hexagonal wire-rimmed sunglasses, every color of the rainbow. Instinctively she clutched at her semitransparent plastic pocketbook, which held her entire savings. If Satan didn't get you first here, surely the pickpockets would.

How would she earn a living? She had no qualifications, no education except for her profound knowledge of the Bible. Was nineteen too old or too young to find employment in this electric city? Could she wait tables, or serve at the counter in Chock Full o' Nuts, or work the cash register in a small store? The staff in the midtown boutiques were so polished, with their ponchos and vinyl boots and little crocheted chignon coverings. No one took her seriously when she inquired for openings. The manageresses looked her up and down, from her spotted bandanna to her unfashionable hemline, and shook their heads distractedly.

A salesgirl at Bendel's who took pity on her suggested that Xavier was looking for a new shampooist.

"Who's Xavier?" Susannah asked.

"Who's Xavier? Who's Spiro T. Agnew? Who's Xavier? Xavier's Xavier."

Susannah's eyes still pleaded ignorance.

"Xavier's the most famous stylist on Madison Avenue. All the beautiful people go there. You heard of Kenneth? You heard of Elizabeth Arden?"

Susannah's face fell. "He won't hire no country hick like me."

The salesgirl touched Susannah's hair admiringly. "You talk funny, but it's kinda cute. You look clean, and you've got that face." As Susannah turned away, the girl reminded her, "When you see him, just smile and wet your lips."

In the busy salon Xavier juggled with pins, spray, and blow dryers. He sizzled with activity, stealing bites from his grilled-cheese sandwich while he combed out the ladies. They never complained, his faithful, even when he ate stinking liverwurst.

"So you want to work for me, Miss Scarlett?" he chomped. His mouth was full of cheese.

Susannah nodded timidly.

"We work hard here. This is no sleepy Dixie town. We got to accommodate the regular clients at all hours. You had any previous experience in the beauty business?"

She admitted she had not. How could she, in Tennessee? The Church of Christ would never have condoned such a lewd occupation.

"Too bad." He gulped his coffee and burned the roof of his mouth. "We'll give it a shot all the same. Three weeks' trial period. If you're late or you chew gum on the job or scald their heads with hot water, you're fired. And we'd better fix you some proper makeup. Hey, Amber, you wanna step over and show Miss Scarlett how to handle a mascara wand?"

Xavier's girls streaked the new shampooist's eyelids with all the "in" shades of the season: moss green, jonquil yellow, and lily cream. They built her lashes like Liza Minnelli's and glossed her lips in Jean Shrimpton's pout. At lunch hour they took her to Ohrbach's and Mays for window shopping. Although Susannah could not afford much, there was no law against trying on. She wrapped herself in Aztec print shawls with dripping fringes, Peter Max tunics, and dozens of wigs. Everyone, including Xavier, was designing them.

But New York was swarming with Lauren Hutton lookalikes; it took more than long legs and a sexy pout to get noticed. She studied Xavier's plentiful copies of *Vogue* and *Harper's* with the same attention she had once lavished on Deuteronomy and Ecclesiastes. Rich and beautiful people, she learned, ate at Lutèce and kicked up their heels at El Morocco ("El Mo's," Xavier's clients called it), Shepherds, or the newly opened Hippopotamus.

At night she sank wearily into her lumpy bed, burrowed under the stained aqua cover, and trundled through the regulations of Emily Post and the other etiquette gurus. At the Palace West Hotel, Susannah's bed took up most of the floor space. She had no chair, only a Formica dressing table where she stored her face creams and makeup. She kept a quart of milk and a lump of cheese outside on the grimy windowsill. The advantage of owning so little was that strays were less likely to break in. Even so, sometimes late at night the loose bolt on the door rattled alarmingly. The prostitutes brought their tricks back to the hotel rooms rented by the hour, and derelict characters crept into the warm corridors from the street.

Susannah struggled to ignore the unnerving rattles and footsteps. She memorized the correct way to eat a lobster, how to write to one's son's fiancée, learned how to introduce a celebrity and arrange a wedding. She perfected the protocol for addressing foreign dignitaries. A sultan is known as "Your Highness"; "Excellency" for the president of a foreign republic; the Prince of Wales is "Your Royal Highness" and the shah of Iran "Your Imperial Majesty."

Was Zachary still cussing her for the loss of the snuffbox? Did the minister in Russell Street ask the congregation to pray for her soul, the runaway sinner, she who had been "disfellowed"? Or was her name never spoken, the memory of her short life eclipsed in its shame?

Her best lessons came from Xavier's "ladies." She observed them minutely, how they walked and dressed and gabbled about their children's schooling at Deerfield and Andover and discussed their world, far away from the smells of the subway; away from the hookers downstairs on Ninth Avenue, freezing their legs in the February chill; away from the radiator that would not turn off and blasted her hotel cell like a boiler room.

"We tried everything to make Dimitri cut his hair," wailed Mrs. Ouliadris. "It grew almost down to his waist and smelled like a rotting garbage pail. We bribed him to cut it, and you know what he did with the money? He ran away to Katmandu. Oh, Bunny dear, how was your trip to London?"

Bunny Trumpington, a society matron with strawberry-blond highlights, wrapped the zebra-patterned nylon gown over her dress. "We flew over on that frightful 747 jumbo thing. Can you imagine, they squash ten people into each row in economy class. Why, it's worse than a bus or a ferry. They'll never last, those ghastly planes."

"Tell me," asked Mrs. O. "What do you think of this new 'midi' length?"

"Too, too unwearable," said Mrs. T. "I suppose we'll just have to wait and see what Paris has to say."

Xavier never missed a word of the dialogue. He fluttered between the ladies, adding a final touch to Lucinda Cavendish's comb-out. Deaf Miss C., who was seventy-one, tended to shout. "My granddaughter Betsy went to the gynecologist last week," she bellowed to the entire room, over the hum of the dryers and the swish of running water. "She has something called herpes."

Nobody had ever heard of such a disease. The ladies all pa-

tronized the same fashionable gynecologists, pediatricians, or-
thopedists, and chiropractors. The "bites" of their children's
teeth were rendered flawless by the same orthodontist, whose
files lodged the X rays of most of the mouths of the *New York
Social Register*. Xavier held up the hand mirror for Miss C. to
inspect the back of her bob. She nodded briskly. He undid Miss
C.'s zebra robe and dusted her neck. "You're looking lovely as
ever," he promised. "Don't you go breaking hearts."

"Or catching hermes," piped up Mrs. T.

"Herpes," Miss C. corrected her.

Mrs. T. settled herself on the shampooing chair, and Susannah eased Mrs. T's neck another inch over the sink. "Just one
more lathering, ma'am, if you'll sidle up some to the faucet,
thank you kindly. Now you be sure and holler if I get the water
too hot." Her deft fingers plowed into the thinning clumps of
hair. "It'll cost me considerable, but I've taken a notion for
attending night school next spring. I'm going right ahead and
get me a real beautician's diploma." She ran the comb through
Mrs. T's skimpy strands, twisted and scooped them into the
cone of a warm towel.

While she massaged their scalps, Susannah chattered guilelessly to her ladies in her Tennessee drawl. She made them
laugh with her hillbilly expressions. The tips were generous.
How else could she have survived in Manhattan? She paid sixty
dollars a week for her room at the Palace West Hotel, with its
bleak view over the roofs of Ninth Avenue.

Xavier interrupted, his mouth full of pins and tuna fish. "Hey,
Miss Scarlett. Cut the chitchat. We're running late already today."

"Ain't he a stitch? Xavier don't mean no harm," Susannah
told Mrs. T. She patted her temples dry with the towel. "We're
busy today. Look-a-here at him, smoking like a fiend, near
crazed as a hornet in the parlor." Xavier smoked two packs of
Gauloises a day. The rancid odor blended with the fragrance
of the spray. No other salon in New York smelled quite the
same.

Xavier provided more than a weekly paycheck and a twenty-
dollar bonus at Christmas. He had appointed himself Susannah's mentor and endlessly corrected her grammar. When she

told her ladies "she should have went," he yelled at her from behind the customers, "Gone, Scarlett, gone."

After the final appointments she swept up the hair clippings while he closed the cash register. "You're a good-looking doll, but you need some class, Scarlett." He tugged at her mane of mousy brown hair. "You got a few minutes free this evening?"

"I'm doing laundry. I should have went yesterday."

"Gone. Gone. Gone. You hear me? Gone. Forget the laundry. I'm going to make you gorgeous."

And he did. Xavier was the finest colorist on the East Coast. He dyed away the mousy brown forever, replacing it with a deep, passionate red, the color of a tropical flower, whose shades grow richest at the innermost petals.

"Gee," admired Amber, the junior stylist. "You could go any-where looking like that! Acapulco or St. Tropez or drinks at the Rainbow Room. You want to come out to my folks in Brooklyn for Christmas Eve?"

Susannah made a quick excuse. Amber's family went to mid-night carols, and church was one place she did not want to be. In Edgefield the minister would be calling for repentance and Zachary would be sniffing the cranberry punch suspiciously to be sure her mother had not slipped in a thimbleful of rum.

In Manhattan the mica in the sidewalks sparkled, a dusting of snow lay on the lampposts, and the air cut like a razor. The last-minute shoppers had finally given up, and the streets were almost empty. Even the shivering whores, with their naked knees and thighs, had abandoned the doorways. Downstairs in the Palace West the toothless inhabitants in bedroom slippers were watching a variety show on TV. They turned up the vol-ume so loudly that it deafened Susannah, even when she pulled the pillow over her ears.

Susannah put on her midicoat with its wide belt and hurried through the cold to the Shamrock.

The bartender, a daytime student at the Art Institute, some-times bought her a sidecar or a grasshopper on the house and kept an eye out that the regulars did not harass her. "What would you say," he asked, "to a hot plate of stew with cabbage and boiled potatoes? Or there's a leg of fried chicken left in the kitchen."

"No *chicken.* Just coffee."

The bar was deserted. The melancholy regulars, who leaned on their elbows watching TV sports, were all absent tonight. The chain of cheap colored lights draped crookedly across the bar, and someone had propped up a ragged sprig of holly in an empty Hennessey bottle.

The bartender brought her coffee, laced for good measure with a jigger of Irish Mist. "What'd you be doing alone on Christmas Eve?" he asked kindly.

She wondered how many other waifs were out roaming tonight, people with no bus tickets or plane passage or families waiting for them. People like her, who would rather not talk about their pasts. The city caught the drifters in its meshes. Zachary and the family would be sitting down to a heavy dinner of ham with redeye gravy and pecan pie. She drank some more coffee. The bartender had put "Jingle Bells" on the jukebox, probably for her benefit. Maybe he thought she needed cheering. Wrong. She was free. She was young. Each day was a marvelous adventure. Mrs. O. had given her a bottle of "Je Reviens," and Mrs. T. had given her a ten-dollar Christmas tip. She had escaped forever from Zachary and the elders, exchanged her artless appearance for a slick new exterior. Who in Edgefield would recognize her now?

The bartender brought out some stew and grinned to see her dig into it. "You should eat more," he scolded. "You'll be wasting away in this weather. Put that away," he ordered when she tried to pay. "I'm not taking your money. You only ordered coffee. Hey, would you be looking for a chance to earn a few extra bucks in the evenings?"

Susannah nodded eagerly. "After working like a sharecropper all day, I'm perished. But I do need every last living cent for beauty school."

"They're looking for life class models at the Art Institute. A cool-looking chick like yourself could get a job in a second. The bread's not great—a couple of bucks an evening—but it's no sweat, if you don't mind lying still."

He was right. It was an easy job, and at least she was off her feet. The students at the institute arranged their easels around her in a three-quarter circle. They all dressed lightly; the studio was kept overheated, for the sake of the naked models. Some of them wore butcher's aprons; some of them had neat pinafores; one odd bird turned up routinely in a pin-striped suit and tie. There was a bearded dwarf, who perched on a high stool and squeezed his tubes of oil paint with gusto. Susannah wondered (she never dared look) how the poor stunted creature saw her as he stabbed his canvas with a palette knife.

The teacher plugged in an additional heater alongside Susannah and planned the pose, bending her elbow and spreading her legs to expose the inside of her thighs. She sensed his male satisfaction as his class looked on in their semicircle. In the silence the pastel crayons scratched and the brushes swished against the canvas. As she breathed her naked stomach rose and fell rhythmically. The teacher sidestepped between the easels and the coffee cans of brushes. He gave each student a murmured critique.

"See, you've foreshortened her head and torso, so the knee is out of proportion. . . . That breast is too big, you want to even them out. . . . The lower right quadrant of your canvas is empty; why not add a dog or a bowl of fish? A little more green on the nipples to give them contour. . . . That's nice, very nice indeed." He stopped to admire the dwarf's work.

Only one student worked in clay. He kept his distance and never spoke to anyone. The others recognized his isolation and kept their distance.

His eyes were fierce and professional when he surveyed her body. She sensed him studying the contours of her flesh. She flushed and ached between her legs. Did he guess? If the rest of the class noticed anything, she hardly cared. It was as if she were alone with him in the room. His broad hands caressed the clay. She wanted revenge, to excite him the way he had kindled her, dangerously, in front of the other students. She had seen his lips curl. He was enjoying his conquest.

From the corner of her eye, she watched his fingers, smoothing and molding. *Naked did I come forth from my mother's womb, and naked shall I return thither.* She smelled the loamy scent of the wet clay. It was more erotic than turpentine or linseed oil. She watched his hands stroke the shape that became her shoulder blades and pelvis.

The sculptor finished his piece. The following week he did not return to the institute, or the week after, or the week after that. Susannah missed the primitive smell of the clay. She could not shake the memory of the man who had made her moist and breathless when he had stared at her.

She never quite forgot him, although she began to meet more men. They bought her grasshoppers at the Shamrock, under the bartender's watchful eye; they asked her to dance at Tuesdays and Wednesdays and Fridays, where she got in for free on ladies' nights; they took her to dinner at Maxwell's Plum; she met them walking their dogs and haunting the supermarkets; the bolder ones stopped and asked her zodiac sign. She met corset salesmen and cabdrivers and bookkeepers, photographers and unemployed actors, dentists and chiropractors and teamsters. They gave her eau de cologne and teddy bears, boxes of candy on Valentine's Day, black camisoles and garter belts, junk jewelry and joints and bottles of their own favorite Scotch to keep on hand. She met a plumber from Hoboken, who fixed the leaking toilet next door to her room in the Palace West Hotel, so it no longer clunked all night to keep her awake. She met a married insurance salesman, who took her for the weekend to Atlantic City and bought her rhinestones.

For two years she thought about the mysterious sculptor she would never see again. She did not know his name, or whether he lived in New York, or whether he was a famous artist. When she strolled past the windows of the galleries on Madison Avenue, she sometimes paused before a Lipschitz or a Henry Moore, trying hopelessly to pick out a piece in the mysterious sculptor's style.

Mrs. T. noticed that Susannah was looking tired.

"I ain't been sleeping so good lately. And I reckon I'm swole up from the cortisone." Susannah hosed away the suds of lather. A muscle in her shoulder had frozen as a result of the hours of posing. A doctor had put her on cortisone treatments and ordered her to give up the institute.

"Swollen," bellowed Xavier, wielding the curling iron with a flourish. "Swollen up!"

"You mustn't take hormones," Miss C. warned shrilly. "Goodness, my dear, you'll end up growing a beard."

"Not hormones," Xavier shouted in Miss C.'s ear. "Cortisone." He gestured to his audience. "Deaf as a post. Some days."

Miss C. smiled benignly. "My cousin took hormones, and she grew hair all over. Like a gorilla. She had to have special harem pajamas designed by Worth. Everyone went to Worth in those days."

"Phone for you, Suzy." The salon receptionist called out to Susannah, mouthing the words over the hum of the blow dryers. "A Mrs. Giuliani. You know her? Is she one of our clients?"

Susannah shook her head. "I don't recall her. Does she want an appointment?"

"She says she wants to talk to you."

Susannah put down the brush she had been using to paint Mrs. O.'s curls inky black. "Pardon me, ma'am."

She picked up the telephone. "How can I help you? . . . Yes, that's my name. Would you like to come in for a cut? We have a wash and blow dry special for twenty dollars." Her voice grew hushed with astonishment. "That is correct. I once worked at the institute as a life class model, but I'm no longer in that line of business." Her voice jumped an octave in a squeak. "Who? A statue of me?" Her heart raced. She gripped the telephone. Was it possible? She had given up all hope of ever finding the rugged sculptor. "An art collector? Well, maybe a short meeting would be satisfactory to me."

Mrs. T., on her way out, brushed next to Susannah to stuff a three-dollar tip into her pocket. Susannah looked so bemused that Bunny Trumpington patted her on the arm. "Is everything fine?"

"Thank you, ma'am." Susannah touched the tip and straightened up quickly. "That lady called just now, she owns an art gallery. One of her clients, a gentleman from Switzerland, has purchased a statue of me that got made there. He wants to meet me. Nothing'll content him even until he's clapped eyes on me."

"Do be careful, dear," warned Mrs. T. "There are such weird people about these days."

She struggled to look demure while her imagination hissed, His name! Maybe you can learn the sculptor's name! "I wouldn't be surprised none if they was looking for some hussy who'd be

willing to disrobe for degrading photographs. Lord knows.
Maybe I shouldn't have spoke with her at all."

Xavier was passing by with a stack of freshly ironed zebra
robes and a half-eaten peanut-butter sandwich. "Spoken," he
rumbled. "Watch that grammar, Scarlett. When are you ever
going to learn? Oh, what will we do with our southern belle?"

4

COLLECTION

Giulietta Giuliani cradled the telephone receiver under the pouch of her double chin. She reached for another Cointreau-filled chocolate. Emil Papier had started sending her boxes of them twice a week from Switzerland, after she had mentioned to him her yearning for the liquor-stuffed confectionery, banned in the United States since Prohibition.

"I have good news for you, Emil. We've found that girl." She was getting suspicious. Emil had been calling Giulietta every day since he had set eyes on the terra-cotta statuette in her gallery. Something was up.

Emil engaged in active combat against his phobias. He was obsessed with terrorists and kidnappers. Most terrifying was his fear that the emotional responses in his brain had somehow atrophied. He remembered, when he was a child in his parents' large chalet in Gstaad, overhearing the English governess gossiping with the caretaker. "He's a clever child," she admitted, making Emil smug where he hid behind the coppice of apple trees. "And he's a wonder at sums. Bound to be another Swiss gnome like his father. But something's missing inside. He's hard as nails."

Was it good or bad to be "hard as nails"? Emil's father, a dour financier whose family had been money traders in Switzerland for two hundred years, would have been complimented. His mother, an iron-backed Prussian, would approve, too. When Emil grew into a young man, who guiltily enjoyed messing with his watercolors more than the stuffy, drawn-out banquets with his father's colleagues, he questioned whether it was an advantage to go through life with a paralyzed heart.

He tested himself, poking and prodding for some kind of response. Women, beyond the flush of physical libido, did not mean much to him. He married Delphine's mother, the daughter of one of his father's banking associates, out of deference to family expectations. When his daughter was born, Emil felt, for the first time, a certain proud thrill. Yet he had never been besotted. The only experiences that swept him out of his psychological corset were the unaccounted-for hours he spent in the great museums of Europe.

He used every business trip to snatch a few hours in the Uffizi in Florence, the Pinakothek in Munich, or the Orangerie in Paris. At the beginning he worshiped Titian, Brueghel, and Rembrandt. The burnish of a goblet, the luster of hair, and the sheen of fabric compensated for the bloodless financial ratios and equations that his karma had ordained. For all his wealth (later he multiplied his father's fortune by ten), he best understood the word *rich* when he studied those glowing, time-defiant pigments.

He made his money first by trading in minerals and later in currencies. As his net worth accreted, he gave up his own secret watercolor painting and began to collect twentieth-century art. Buying paintings and small sculptures brought him a keener pleasure than acquiring more real estate or Maseratis. He took a fancy to the technical virtuosity of Magritte and the whimsy of Max Ernst. He identified with Dali's subworld. Here was a school of art that understood what it was to spend one's life locked into the straitjacket of fear and guilt and cruelty.

Giulietta Giuliani had tucked away Dan Helena's statuette in a corner of her gallery. The moment Emil saw the terra-cotta nude, it allured him like a bait of raw flesh on a fishing line. He swept between the valuable Brancusis toward Dan's clumsily defiant figure.

"You like that?" Giulietta registered her client's fascination. "It's by a young artist of mine. Interesting fellow. Beginning to work in metal, too. So few sculptors are doing figurative these days. The art world oracles have branded realism as something obscene. This guy Helena doesn't pay any attention. He's his own man, no question about it."

Emil stared at the figure like a man possessed. Was it the spirit of the artist or the subject herself that egged him, skipping wickedly like a poltergeist among Giulietta's blue-chip array?

He bought the piece on the spot. He nestled his new acquisition possessively in his hand, rubbing the grainy baked clay against his skin. With his finger he traced the curve of the arm, down to the hand where it rested between the model's thighs.

Giulietta watched him avidly. She had a knack for customer psychology. If she had not ended up selling art, she could have dealt in canoeing equipment or baby's knitted goods or secondhand cars. She had a sixth sense for the instant of mastery and domination, that watershed moment when a client's will would start to melt and drip.

Yet Emil Papier was a tough nut to crack. He was a man who did not reveal himself easily. You could tell by the way he stiffly held his jaw, clenching his teeth like a vise, even when he smiled tightly. It had to be grueling, living inside Papier's skin. She had corroborated his credit, which was excellent, with the auction houses as well as other galleries in New York, Rome, and Milan. The dealers' intercontinental hot lines swiftly sorted out the flakes and the shams.

"Would you care to meet the artist?" Giulietta suggested.

Most collectors did. Parading the artists was a significant service of the gallery. The collectors loved to consort with the talent, ushering out the artists to a smart restaurant to hold court until late in the evening. It was as if the buyers believed the romance of bohemia could temporarily rub off on themselves.

"Perhaps." Emil grated his teeth nervously. His voice grew

hoarse with anticipation. "I wonder—I mean, would it be possible—not too much trouble . . . "

"What, Emil?" She shot him a quizzical look.

He spat it out. "To meet the model."

Giulietta wondered if he could be kinky. He looked so proper in his flawlessly tailored suit, but you could never tell. She had once sold an Egon Schiele to a Rumanian count who sodomized ducks.

She told Emil, "It's difficult. The girl might be anyone, a girlfriend, another artist, or even a hooker. Who knows?"

Emil turned to examine one of Dan Helena's crouching steel lions. Maybe if I cooperate, thought Giulietta, I could interest him in Helena's bigger pieces. She knew how fiercely collectors demanded to be stroked.

"I'll ask the sculptor," she promised. "I'll let you know next time you're in New York."

"I'll telephone you from Switzerland. Which kind of chocolates did you tell me you liked? Praline or Grand Marnier?"

When Dan Helena stopped by to show Giulietta his latest sketches for a series of steel Agamemnons, she took him into the gallery office and sat him down on the red velvet sofa.

"I don't know her name," the young sculptor told Giulietta, stretching his long legs. Giulietta presided behind the desk, surrounded by shelves of art books and file cabinets of correspondence. She had a valuable Fontana painting on the wall behind the desk, a pale canvas gashed with rips and vaginal slits. "I've no idea who she was. The models come and go in the institute. I never speak to any of them."

"Call the institute. See if they have names."

"Hey, what's the big deal? Who is the Swiss guy, anyway? I mean, he's got good taste, he appreciated my piece, but . . . "

"The Swiss liked her. Don't you get it? I know, I know, I'm in the business of selling art works, not sex, but come on, you know and I know, this is a cattle market, art's a brutal biz, and sometimes we have to accommodate them. That man has a lot of money to spend. He bought a de Chirico for twenty-five thousand last week at Sotheby's."

Dan stared gruffly at the Fontana over the desk, with its labial gashes.

"Just get her name. Maybe he'll buy one of your steel lions or your fallen warriors next time. Then we can make some real money, you and I. Have you seen the new Kounellis catalog?" She held it out to him. *Arte povera* was hot in the early seventies, launched by the Italians, who created their work out of twigs and old rope, rusty bedsprings, and any other bits and pieces of flotsam and jetsam that chanced in their paths.

The next day Emil called Giulietta from Montreux. "Have you ascertained the person's name?"

"We're working on it."

"I've been thinking. The last time I was in your gallery, I was quite struck by the chair hanging upside down from the ceiling."

"Ah, yes," murmured Giulietta. Everyone looked at those upside-down furniture pieces, but no one ever bought them.

"I would like to buy the chair for the salon in my new pied-à-terre in Zurich. Could you possibly remind me of the price?"

"Twelve thousand dollars."

"I will be sending you a banker's order at the end of the day."

The next time Dan Helena stopped by, Giulietta asked sternly, "Have you got the name?"

"I've found her. She's a shampooist at Xavier's. The beautiful people's hairdresser on Madison Avenue."

Emil was so pleased that the model had been located that he immediately bought two rubber armchairs coated with phallic vegetation. While many gallery visitors admired the surfaces of seaweedlike barnacles, no one else had been prepared to fork out twenty thousand dollars for some rubber hedgehogs you could not even sit on.

"Lovely," said Emil. "I will put them in my bedroom in Paris." He wrote out a check on the spot.

"You have an apartment there, too?"

"A small one in the seventeenth. You know the *quartier?* I have a nice view of the Seine." He added briskly, "I will be arriving in New York at midday tomorrow. Would you be so kind as to telephone the person and arrange for her to meet me at the Carlyle. The Bemelmans Bar at seven. I shall be staying in my usual suite."

"You canceled your trip to Tokyo?" Giulietta was astounded. Emil was a man of fastidious habit and routine. What compulsion could have induced him to monkey with his business itinerary?

He hesitated. "Giulietta?"

"Hmm?"

He felt gauche. "The lady, is she . . . is she—married?"

"How should I know? Does it matter?"

"No. No, of course not. Giulietta?"

"Yes, my friend."

"I need your advice. Should I wear a gray tie or a blue one?"

"Gray is good."

He wore the gray tie. Susannah showed up in a strapless black cocktail dress, scented with a trace of the Xavier aroma of Gauloises smoke and hairspray.

He recognized her instantly when she stepped into the bar. He had been waiting for months for his first glimpse of the majestic torrent of hair, but he had never expected that carnal shade of red. She paused, scanning the dark room. Then she walked quite straight, indifferent to the flutter of attention, like an emissary from a magical island.

Emil jerked stiffly to his feet. He had chosen the dimmest corner. A frieze of bunny rabbits, dressed as businessmen in top hats, romped across the walls. Emil never sat at a bar when he was waiting for an appointment. He gravitated toward a secluded spot, always arranging a clear line of vision toward the door. If any member of the Baader Meinhof or the Red Brigade attempted a public attack, he would be first to raise the alarm.

"Miss Bishop?" He held out his right hand, with its crisply starched cuff.

She examined his deceptively boyish face. His ingenuous bright blue eyes pleaded behind wire-rimmed glasses. He looked quite gentle and harmless. She held out her own hand, in a gesture that was spirited and diffident and awkward and proud. Around her wrist was an ugly string of paste diamonds, the junk souvenir of the weekend in Atlantic City.

He groped for words. The only thing he wanted to say was that she was the most beautiful woman he had ever seen; how her tropical sea of hair reminded him of the nudes of Gustave Courbet. He longed to confess how she was the first flesh-and-blood creature who had ever stirred him like this; until now he had only felt the twinge in front of certain paintings. He stared and stared at her dumbly.

When no words came, she gave him a weak, embarrassed smile and reached for a cashew nut. "May I inquire, Monsieur Papier, the name of the artist?"

"What?"

"The sculptor! Will you put me wise? The man who made my sculpture!"

With effort he forced himself to speak. "I beg your pardon. I—I was thinking of something else. His name is Dan Helena."

"Helena." She whispered the word like an incantation in her Tennessee drawl. "Helena. That's irregular. It's a woman's name."

Emil's eyes smothered her. "He is a talented young sculptor. It's an accomplished piece. But you are a hundred times more beautiful."

She had no inkling how deeply he meant it. As they drank through the Dom Pérignon, the squeezing constriction released in Emil's throat and his clammy palms dried. He needed to talk to her. The sluices and floodgates opened. He ushered her into the backstage recesses of his mind, where no one else had ever been invited.

"I was divorced a year ago," he explained. "My ex-wife never cared about me at all, I think. She was only interested in my money. I was generous with her settlement—there was my child involved. I gave her apartments in Geneva and Düsseldorf and Paris, and a house in Antibes. She gets fifty thousand Swiss francs a month."

Susannah had no idea what fifty thousand Swiss francs amounted to. So all she said was, "It must be lonesome, always traveling, even a successful, well-fixed businessman like you." Her thoughts were far away. The name sang. Dan Helena. Dan Helena.

"I have too much money, Susannah. I mean it. I meet a lot of beautiful women these days, models and movie actresses and society hostesses. Since my divorce none of them will leave me alone. But really I'm a shy person. I feel you understand that."

"Uh-huh. I reckon I understand." Oh, Dan Helena, where are you? Will I ever see you again?

They ate in the hotel dining room. Emil patronized only those restaurants in which he felt safe after years' familiarity with the maître d's and owners. His father's recent death still haunted him everywhere. He had never yet been able to discuss openly the fatal heart attack or the state of chronic shock it had induced in himself. His mother, with her military self-control, also imposed a convention of silence on the subject.

But he told Susannah. "It was shortly after the Palestinian terrorists attacked the Israeli Olympic team at Munich airport."

Susannah nodded. How could anyone ever forget the horrific news reports, the scenes of random carnage and prostrate bodies, riddled with Kalashnikov gunfire and scattered across the airport terminal that had been converted into a slaughterhouse.

"My father was always nervous about kidnappers and extortion. We're a wealthy family, and make an ideal target. After the PLO and the Baader Meinhof began huge-scale sabotage all over Europe, he got really frightened. Americans don't understand the state of siege they've reduced us to, those anarchist groups. My father fortified his house and garden. He even installed bulletproof windows in his bedroom and on his Citroën."

Susannah had never before met anyone like Emil.

"When we heard about the airport attack, we were numbed by the brutality. No one knew where the violence would end. Even in Switzerland, where we pride ourselves on our orderly lives, we had no guarantee of safety. We were neutral in both world wars, and every house in our country has its atomic bunker—but how can we protect ourselves from these crazed fanatics who roam across borders, attacking innocent victims?"

Susannah swallowed a sliver of smoked sable. She had never eaten in such an elegant place. It smelled of starched tablecloths and warm bread. The maître d' stood sentinel beside the circular buffet table, which spilled pink shellfish and luscious fruits.

Emil lit a cigarette. "My father was traveling on a short business trip to Luxembourg. There was a false bomb alert at the airport, a lot of shouting and sirens. People were crawling behind benches and trying to shield themselves with suitcases. He had a heart attack, and it killed him."

Susannah nibbled at the bitter garnish of escarole. "There was no real bomb at all? Nothing was afire?"

"Not that time. My father was the only casualty." Emil turned his face away. Just talking about it made a muscle twitch beneath his eye. "And your father?" he asked politely. "Is he alive?"

"My daddy? He died when I was six. Drunk as a coot. They found his body rolled down a well, along with his bottle of bourbon. My stepdaddy was a church elder, with the disposition of a yellow jacket. He maintained the world was created in seven days, and all them scientists that held otherwise was some kind of Antichrist."

She had become pale. Emil covered her hand gently with his own. She was equally exotic to him.

"I don't talk easy about my childhood."

He stroked her hand. "Please. Tell me. I want to know."

"He worked all day at the Bruton Snuff Factory, then he'd come home at night to our rotting house on Fatherland Street, and sit swinging on the sagging porch out front and filing his manicured fingernails." She shuddered, as if she could still hear the whisper of filing nails. "He did never touch liquor, no sir, he was too scared shitless of them elders from the church on Russell Street. Boozing and dancing and adultery, they were the four-star sins. And the Lord help you if you made love standing up. Someone might think you was dancing. He was a God-loving serpent. Hated Jews and niggers. Nor did he take a much prettier view of northerners."

"It's a terrible world out there." Emil shuddered. "I've made enough money to buy my privacy from it." He talked on about his father, in whose footsteps he had dutifully followed, sacrificing his only pleasure of watercolor painting, in order to devote himself to the art of juggling currencies.

"What happened to your watercolors?" Susannah asked.

He sniffed. "They were nothing special. I keep them hidden away somewhere. I've never shown them to anyone."

"I'd be honored to look if ever you was willing."

He nodded slowly. "I think I might show them to you."

Emil, at thirty-eight, relished the unexpected rush of libido. He hungered for her body; her legs and the cascade of her hair excited him. A week later he invited her for the evening to his suite. They ordered in room service. Susannah chose the lobster, to find out what it tasted like. Afterward, when he drew her to the huge bed with its crisp sheets and bolster pillows, she let him throttle her with wet, voracious kisses, and she moaned obligingly when he parted her legs. As he clambered across her thighs, she thought again of Dan Helena.

Emil showed up every four weeks in Manhattan. He found constant business to transact, and he liked poking around SoHo, the new art center in its infancy. One by one, galleries were relocating from the glossy showrooms of Fifty-seventh Street and Madison Avenue.

His addiction to Susannah was quickening. He took her shopping for clothes and patiently perched on a chair outside the ladies' dressing room while she zipped into butt-hugging cocktail dresses with plunging necks and a slit up one side.

He shepherded her among the latest conceptual exhibits of the era. They surveyed galleries stripped of contents, examples of so-called negative space; ice sculptures, designed to melt and self-destruct; arrangements of eggplants and potatoes, intended to putrefy, according to nature's cyclic laws. He bought her a six-volume treatise entitled *A World History of Art* and inquired each night when he phoned her how far she had progressed with it.

Yet when he suggested that "they" buy a beach house, she gaped at him, disbelieving. The only beaches Susannah had ever visited were Coney Island and the boardwalk in Atlantic City.

"I want a hideaway," he insisted. "Just for us."

He already had his villa in Cannes, but the chic Riviera was no retreat. Emil wanted an escape, an intimate corner by the sea. American real estate was a good investment, and in his absence Susannah could look after it.

They found the house on Martha's Vineyard in twenty-four hours and furnished it in forty-eight. That was Susannah's first lesson as to what real money could do. She learned that the lobster, the Valentino dresses, and the Carlyle's starched sheets were small change.

Like all Emil's homes, it was designed to look inward. The

sprawling building was ugly from the outside, three stories high, in slate gray clapboard. The multilevel decks and ramps and balustrades resembled a ski lodge more than a beach chalet. Deep in the heart of the house lay a swimming pool and several patios. The previous owner had been a Broadway choreographer. Of all the oddments of furniture left behind, Emil decided to keep a Steinway grand piano in what had once been the rehearsal room. Hardly anyone ever lifted the lid. Susannah would glance at it and wonder whether the beach house had once been full of chatter and laughter and frivolous show people, before she and Emil turned it into a mausoleum.

They ordered up eleven beds with best-quality orthopedic mattresses, seven sofas, three dining tables, thirty-four chairs, fourteen chests of drawers, patio furniture, and a Ping-Pong table for Delphine. Emil scraped together an assortment of his less valuable surreal bric-a-brac. He sent up anatomical lamp stands and coatracks and a recent find that had taken his fancy— a fur-lined bathtub.

Susannah watched with awe as he assembled an entire household like a shopping list. His vast resources gave him authority. He became a magician, a superman who could make anything materialize or happen simply by flicking a push-button telephone.

"You like it?" he asked as they sipped morning coffee next to their new swimming pool.

She nodded, wide-eyed. Was he going to let her just go on living here, soaking up sun and wandering aimlessly around their seventeen rooms? Or would he tire of her by the autumn and send her back?

They never used to venture out on the beach until dusk. Although terrorists posed little risk at the Vineyard, the crowds and families, with their picnics and volleyballs, made Emil shudder. He preferred to lounge all afternoon beside his own swimming pool, browsing through back issues of the *Financial Times* and the *Frankfurter Allgemeine*. At sunset he and Susannah would stroll down to the water's edge for a short walk in the sand. The roar of the glassy surf was better than taking ten milligrams of Valium. On the horizon the clouds lay low and a ribbon of airplane smoke blazed out an advertisement for vodka. Emil appreciated the heaving, thundering sea. It reminded him, as did his primeval Swiss mountains, what a speck of dust he represented in the cosmos.

He took her arm and steered her through the sand. "We'll buy an apartment in New York this autumn. You will hire the staff, pay the bills, and learn how I like my flowers arranged. I want you educated, too. We will hire an elocution instructor, who will train you to speak like a college professor. You'll learn. Don't worry. The Berlitz crash method, ten hours a day. And you'll enroll in art courses, too."

Impressionism, Cubism, Dutch landscape, Islamic rugs, she survived them all, drifting hazily while some spinster lectured the flock of disciples. They lugged their folding stools around the museums from painting to painting, from rug to rug, cramming for the best view. The sparrowlike lecturers, with their crusty voices, glared at Susannah suspiciously. She was too young and too attractive to belong to their blue-rinsed brigades. No respectable young woman had a right to that brazen hair or the provocative mouth.

The six volumes of the *World History of Art* found their final resting place in the East End Avenue study and lay dormant. Nineteen years later Susannah sometimes picked one up superstitiously, as if the physical contact with the object could open a window on the past. The book was lighter than she remembered. Everything in her life had shrunk with familiarity. Rooms had grown smaller, distances shorter, rings and bracelets dinkier.

The floor-to-ceiling bookshelves were ranged with Emil's glossy art tomes, exactingly organized by style and period. No one ever read those hundred-dollar coffee table volumes. Only the maid slid them out for dusting and shooing off spiders. Emil, whenever he flitted through a bookstore or received one of his specialty catalogs, automatically ordered three or four copies of any new publication that caught his attention: one for the palazzo, one for Switzerland, one for the Vineyard, and sometimes for the other pied-à-terres. Occasionally he would bring one out to show Jacob Karakoff an amusing illustration or to win some trivial drunken argument with him.

Emil opened yet another package of Benson & Hedges Light 100s and leaned to refill Karakoff's glass. Lounging in his library, surrounded by his surrealism books and his prized Giacometti on the coffee table, drinking with his best friend, this was the closest he came to an hour's contentment. Jacob Karakoff's cigar overwhelmed the room with its acrid fumes, but Emil did not care.

The lawyer McHenry sat up poker straight on the edge of his chair, tight-lipped and all too obviously still on duty. McHenry's puritanical nature was embroiled in some inner struggle to mask his disapproval of the whole scene: the gaudy luxury, the art, the alcohol.

"So what do you think of my Englishman?" Emil asked Jacob.

"He's presentable. His accent will be an asset in the art business. Looks like a go-getter."

"He's ambitious. He's dissatisfied, restless. He'd like to be rich. That's why I found him a job and invited him here tonight."

"What do you want with him?"

"I want to put him to work."

"You? You're a currency trader."

"I'm slowing down, Jacob. I'm tired of spending my whole life on the telephone, selling marks for yen and pounds for lire and shorting dollars and taking out index options. I've been doing it for thirty years now."

"And you're the best." Karakoff shot a swift glance at McHenry. He wondered why Emil had needed this outsider to schmooze with them.

"We're the same age, more or less, Jacob. You know what I mean when I say there comes a time when you have to start taking stock of your whole life. We haven't got forever."

Jacob nodded. "My cholesterol's way up. That Wiener schnitzel of yours will be my undoing."

Emil stubbed at the cigarette guiltily. "I want to have some fun, before it's too late. Get into a business I'd really enjoy."

"You not thinking again about starting a gallery." Emil had been babbling for years about opening his Surrealist collection to the public.

Emil shook his head. "I am more realistic these days. My collection would not have sufficient general appeal. If I had a museum, it would have to achieve the status of the Frick, the Gardner, the Saatchi, or the Thyssen collections. After what I've done with my career as a trader, I would not be happy doing anything unless I were the best."

Karakoff nodded. It was impossible for the president of Belle John to imagine starting out completely fresh, without the backing of his retinue. He too hated to be beaten. "My doctor's at me to take off forty pounds," he grunted. It was so much easier to market a new and phenomenally successful line of low-consumption flush toilets.

"What I'm good at," Emil continued slowly and deliberately, "is trading commodities. Currencies are the most difficult and unpredictable of all, and I can do that. So why not paintings?"

"What?" Karakoff sat up an inch. Even the lawyer's eyes flickered a trace in his waxy face. "For your own account?" Karakoff looked toward the desk, at the elongated Giacometti figure of a goddess, with arms outstretched, as if in welcome. She pointed with one finger, not accusingly, but rather as if she were singling him out. Giacometti had stripped away everything material; he, who cared for nothing but his art. Emil recalled the dramatic moment at Sotheby's when he had outbid his rival collector von Tislowicz for the piece.

"Never. A recipe for disaster in business. Taste clouds the judgment. I'm thinking about an investment fund."

McHenry dared to interrupt. "You mean like for real estate, only art?"

"Exactly. Or oil and gas exploration. We capitalize, we buy artwork, we hold it a few years, resell at a profit, and distribute a handsome return to the investors, retaining a percentage as our management fee."

Jacob hesitated. "The market's collapsing."

"It will settle in the long term. We needed an interim correction. Everyone realizes that. Fresh profits will be there for the buyers who hang in."

"An investment fund can't wait for decades. We'd have to show steady returns."

"If we have enough inventory, we can turn it over gradually."

"Those attempted art funds so far never fly." Karakoff blew a smoke ring. "Chase Manhattan and Citicorp have been kicking the idea around for years. Only the Artemis group in Brussels sort of pulled it off. And with what size war chest? About forty million? What can you buy for forty lousy million? A few pencil sketches and watercolors."

"Wait! Don't forget the British Rail Pension Fund," Emil insisted. "The real return on that fund's money, after inflation, was twelve percent. They'd have made less than eight percent investing the money in the stock market. We're talking a substantial return on investment, Jacob."

"British Rail made the big return on the Impressionists. It's too late to pull that rabbit out of the hat again. That market's overshot itself."

"Forget Impressionists." Emil stared at his friend invitingly. "We'll stick to our own bailiwick."

"Twentieth-century."

"Precisely. I know Surrealism, that's the twenties and thirties, and you're the man for Abstract Expressionism, that's the forties and fifties. Between us we cover half the field."

Jacob looked worried. "What about the later half? Sixties, seventies, eighties? How about Pop and Minimalism and Pattern and Photorealism and New Wave, and all the other newfangled avant-garde stuff?"

"Warhol cereal boxes and Beuys old snow shovels; Lichtenstein comic strips and Flavin neon lights. We'll invest in those, too."

Jacob gnawed on the cigar. It was a tantalizing notion, maybe too tantalizing. "It's never really worked before," he repeated.

"Why not?" Emil leaned forward avidly. "Because the previous efforts—and they've all been nickel-and-dime operations—were run by dealers. The dealers kept the best art for their own business and dumped the dross in the fund. We're not dealers, Jacob. We're managers. And we're blessed with a depressed market."

"We're back at the initial problem, though. How do you acquire enough inventory to keep on producing capital gains in a slow-moving market?"

Jim McHenry polished his glasses meticulously with a corner of his handkerchief and ventured obsequiously, "You mentioned a forty-million-dollar purchasing budget. . . . "

"That was Artemis." Emil stared straight ahead. "Supposing we were looking for five hundred million?" he asked.

"That's a sizable sum," McHenry gasped. "You'd need a huge number of limited partners."

"We'll find them," Emil promised. "Ivan Boesky put together a billion dollars with less than ninety-nine investors. We're going after the new money. Entrepreneurs from Iowa, tycoons from Tacoma. Guys who made it big in the eighties' creation of new wealth, and don't know by themselves how to put that extra million into culture. Cowboys who want to be able to say, 'I own one-thousandth of a de Kooning.'" Emil lit another cigarette. The last one still smoked. He was too bent on his theme to notice. "Art has become a commodity. Like pork bellies and coffee futures. The Western world has created an entire new social class, by the manipulation of financial instruments. That new money needs respectability. Buying art has always been the best shortcut to aristocracy. It's a lot quicker than breeding your daughter to blue blood. We can find the right investors, Jacob. We're self-made men, too, in our way. The difference is, we started learning art a couple of decades earlier than these bozos." Emil turned sharply to McHenry. "How could we do this? Do we incorporate?"

McHenry nibbled at his lower lip. "Unlikely. I would recommend a limited partnership structure."

Karakoff wiped away the gathering driblets of sweat from his temples. Why did Emil always keep the apartment so damned hot? he wondered. He turned to McHenry. "How would a limited partnership work?"

McHenry coughed. "You and Mr. Papier would, I presume, become the general managing partners. You would arrange some sort of advisory panel for the acquisition of the art works, and then sell shares to your investors, whose liability would be limited to the extent of their specific investment."

Jim McHenry shivered slightly, as he sensed the reproof of the four eyes upon him. He had already answered their immediate questions; his presence was clearly no longer required for the more intimate details of their discussion. Smoothing the wrinkles in his suit, he edged toward the library door.

Even after the door was tightly closed, the two seasoned businessmen sat a moment together in silence.

Karakoff finally looked up. "You're talking about putting together a lot of money." He looked toward the door, where McHenry had just left them. "I thought he was going to piss in his pants when you said you wanted half a billion."

"That's just to begin with. I'd like to go higher eventually, maybe even a couple of billion. As big as an equity fund, like Dreyfus or Magellan or Fidelity."

"We're rich men, old buddy. We've both got healthy businesses, healthier than our cholesterol counts. We've been able to collect the kind of art we like for ourselves and plaster our walls with it. What do we need this new headache for?"

"You're right. You can only sleep in one bed at once. It's no longer the money. Now I want power."

"Power?" echoed Karakoff. The word had a resonant, metallic, seductive ring to it.

"I care about art. More than almost anything. Of course I care about my daughter, too."

"And Susannah."

"Susannah is another story. I care about art, and before I die—I've been thinking about that more, my father's coronary and so forth—I want to exercise real power. There's only one way left to do that."

"Forget it. You can't play at being Peggy Guggenheim anymore. Twenty years ago, maybe. Now it's too late. Everything costs too much."

"Exactly, exactly. You and I are multimillionaires, but we can't even make a dent with our personal money any longer. That's why we need a deeper pool of resources. A pool that we control."

"Hmm."

"This is the age of the money manager and the financial megainstitution. We know that."

"Yeah, yeah, but so far all the gigantic mutual funds have

invested in some kind or other of paper, stocks or bonds or commodities."

"We'll break new ground. So far no one's had the guts or the sophistication or the client list to pool that kind of money for buying collectibles. We'll throw ourselves into the cultural cocktail circuit for a few months, all over the U.S. and Europe and Tokyo. We'll each donate a couple of good art works to some major museums, and get big publicity from it. We'll call in a few favors, throw a few lunches at Le Bernardin here and Taillevent in Paris."

"How can we prove our track record? Why should they come to us? We're competing against a lot of heavyweight dealers."

Emil leaned back contentedly. "Nick Jones."

Karakoff made an unconscious gesture of looking around the bookshelf-lined walls, as if for a second he had wondered if their conversation might be recorded. "The auction house," he replied slowly.

For a couple of minutes neither said anything while they relished the prickling thrill in knowing that their cerebral impulses were racing down identical synapses. It took a certain kind of brain to make their kind of money.

Emil sat up straight. He spoke quickly and matter-of-factly. "Nick Jones will pass us enough inside information to outbid the competition. We'll learn ahead of time how many order bids have been prelogged, the highest price limit an absent bidder has authorized the auction house to place bids on his behalf. We'll know the strength against us and exactly how much money they're laying on the line."

"That's the most classified list." Jacob puffed.

"That highly confidential information is the price of Nick Jones's career. And that's not all. We'll also get the secret reserve prices the house attaches to each object, the rock-bottom amount the seller is prepared to accept."

"Very useful. A lot of art goes unsold when the bidding never reaches the reserve. If we knew for sure how high we needed to go, we could be certain not to let any important piece slip our net."

"And not overbid, either. Through my young protégé, with his Oxford accent, you and I are going to sweep the floor with our old rivals." Emil gloated at the thought of Baron von Tis-lowicz.

"Will he play, the Englishman? Will he undermine the auction house?"

Emil chuckled. "You know how much they pay him there? Twenty-eight thousand dollars. He's living in a fifth-floor walk-up on Ninety-ninth Street. He likes good food, he needs good suits. I've got a hunch he likes attractive women. Don't you worry, I'll take care of him."

"You old devil." Jacob was beginning to enjoy himself. He had not had such a good evening since the last time he had cheated and pigged out on bacon chili burgers.

5

THE MOST CHIC ELEVATOR

WEST OF COLOGNE

*U*pstairs, in Emil's bedroom, Susannah was showing Felice the catalog for the latest Whitney biennial. Those painters and sculptors whose work was selected by the museum's curators became household names. Their prices shot up like bullets.

Felice flipped through the pages. "The nineteenth-century Paris salons kept out the Impressionists. So much for official approval. Nowadays who remembers or cares who was the public favorite in 1880? While Monet and Degas and Renoir were being laughed at."

Susannah nodded absently and rearranged a couple of the decorative apples in the Venini dish. Emil liked them symmetrical. Susannah's mind was not on biennials or salons or Impressionists. She wondered how long Emil and Jacob would closet themselves in the study for their business parlay. Would Dan remember to telephone her before it was too late? Maybe she was taking a risk, answering her lover's phone calls when

Emil was in residence. All the same she did not discourage Dan from calling. A few gruff words gave her a private joy to hang on to, to steer her through the tedious hours of Emil's financial dinners or the prickly evenings with the truculent Delphine.

"What's this?" Felice fished out an invitation from the pages of the catalog, where it was serving as a bookmark.

"Careful with that!" Susannah flipped over the engraved card crested with a golden gun. "It's for the big bash in the Egyptian temple of Dendur at the Met. The gun lobby people are hosting it in May. It'll be the smash event of the season. Emil's flying in special from Switzerland, so I reckon he's got some business to attend to. Everyone who's anyone will be there."

Felice frowned and nibbled her lip. "I guess Jacob will want me there as well. I'm no good at these flashy affairs. I never know what to wear."

"We'll find you something. How about my new Saint Laurent? I was thinking of wearing it myself, but I'd much rather give it to you." Susannah was generous with her bounty of material goods. She would have freely given away her entire wardrobe and jewelry. Her designer dresses no longer brought her pleasure. On the contrary, they had become the uniform, the reminder of her entrapment in Emil's palazzo.

Felice shook her head. "Only you can carry it off, Suze. I'd look a fool in that low-cut back."

"If you say so." But all the same she wished Felice would accept. Giving away was more satisfying than accumulating.

When the light on her private phone line flashed, the two women glanced at each other awkwardly. Felice long suspected her friend was seeing a man, although Susannah told her nothing directly. Was he someone from their own world, somebody important? When Felice hinted gently, Susannah clammed up and withdrew, as if they were treading in sacred territory. Could it be mere sex? Susannah normally spoke so frankly about the subject, it made Felice blush. Which did not take much.

Felice jumped up. "I'll go downstairs, okay, and see how the men are getting on." Susannah smiled apologetically and reached for the phone.

"Having fun?" Dan's voice growled. He knew the strain Emil exacted.

"Jacob and Emil have gone off to talk shop in the library." She sounded weary. "You miss me?"

He ignored the question. "What about Jacob? Did he mention my commission?"

"Is that why you called?" Now she was piqued.

"I just wondered. It's the biggest I've ever had."

"I—I wasn't paying attention."

"Hey," he murmured softly. "Don't be mad. You were great this afternoon in the subway. I want to do it on the platform next time."

Susannah, hearing a noise outside, hung up quickly. Was Emil on his way upstairs to the bedroom to check up on her, or had he forgotten something here? Did he experience odd twinges of jealousy when he realized his mistress was sharing his bed? Although he avoided the subject, she knew he knew. Knew there was *someone*. Not that it was Dan Helena, the wild man, Giulietta's protégé. Not that Susannah's affair had already lasted nine years. Not that Susannah betrayed him in thought every waking moment, while she went through the empty motions of her padded life.

It suited Emil, Susannah reflected, not to know too much. Paying the bills meant nothing to him, and where could he replace his finely trained housekeeper, who aged the apples for the Venini bowl, who arranged the lilies and birds of paradise and straightened any crooked picture frames? How he hated pictures askew. Unless, unless . . . Perhaps he *could* replace her, maybe he already *had*. Had he found someone who did not need to touch up the roots of her hair, someone who was young and brash and confident as Susannah had been confident when she had given up her life to Dan Helena?

She had first officially reencountered Dan shortly after Emil had installed her in the palazzo. Giulietta was relocating her gallery from midtown to SoHo, and Susannah and Emil were attending the reception to mark the occasion. It was early days; Susannah still agonized over social events. Although Emil supervised her wardrobe and shunted her into tame conversation with the least intimidating people, suppose she should disgrace herself with some faux pas? Every remark was a trap for the unwary. Or suppose she were to run into one of Xavier's customers at these monied events? How was she to explain her new life? When Xavier's "ladies" had been kind to her back then, she had never dreamed of becoming their peer. Now she lived in super-luxury beyond *their* dreams. Mistresses, she discovered, were not popular with anyone. The society women disdained them as gold diggers, the career girls resented their easy money; the Eurotrash sniggered, and the outwardly liberal-minded were surprisingly shocked.

At the reception Dan Helena was sloshing around a glass of Perrier, looking bored and lurking near the door for a quick escape. As Susannah set eyes on Dan, all her social jitters condensed into a much worse panic. Sinking. Engulfment. Watching him, she was arrested by inexplicable helplessness. Would he recognize her, after three years, dolled up in her Bill Blass, with a Céline purse under her arm? Would he remember the skin tones, the shape of her body under the expensive new wrapping? Yes, it was the same man all right, who had modeled her body in clay, studying the proportions with an insolent half smile.

"Dan! Miss Bishop! So good of you both to come. Hope you're enjoying the party. Try some stuffed mushrooms." Giulietta bustled up, the indomitable hostess. "You know one another, of course." Giulietta glanced swiftly from one's frozen expression to the other's. Did she guess something was amiss, Susannah panicked, the crackerjack dealer who never missed a trick?

Dan nodded silently. His eyes swung away, to the other side of the room, as if he did not want to look at Susannah directly. Had he heard rumors about town, Susannah wondered, of Emil Papier's bizarre eccentricity, transporting a little shampooist from rags to riches? Or did he look aside in order to mask the hungry-wolf gaze, impermissible in Giulietta's presence?

Susannah stood rooted in her tracks. She had no idea how to crack the silence. If only Emil would come and rescue her. No, not true. She would have gladly preserved that awkward, jagged silence for hours. At last Dan Helena spoke, more to himself.

"You were really something then," he said.

She bristled. "And now?"

"You look like a dressed-up chimpanzee." He jerked his head contemptuously toward the clusters of guests. "They all do. But you were better than that."

They ran into one another from time to time. They hardly spoke, no more than a few sparse comments. Dan rarely ventured into art world gatherings unless Giulietta insisted. When Susannah would glimpse him across the room, she stepped quickly out of sight, behind a column or a sculpture. Their short, strange meetings drained and discomfited her.

Ten years later one rainy night, she bumped into him coming out of the Knoedler gallery.

"Where are you going?" he asked.

The intimate, sluicing curtain of rain emboldened her. "Home. Emil's away in Europe. Would you like to come with me for a drink?"

"No. Let's walk a bit, though."

"You want to march about? It's pouring."

"Is it? Who cares? I like this weather."

For ten more blocks he did not speak again. He set the pace, a long-legged stride. She followed meekly. She had to strain, on her high heels, to keep up. She and Dan were isolated. The damp smells and puddles and swollen gutters, the squealing brakes and horns and parades of umbrellas, stopped existing.

A newborn guilt invaded her, a premonition that she must somewhere pay for this deviation. She was starved for the wild man. She needed him as an ally to help her resist Emil. Yes, that was it! Like a twitching larva, all of a sudden she wanted to break the chrysalis, the golden mummy case Emil had set around her. She required Dan Helena because he was the only creature Emil's money could not buy. The rest of them—Giulietta, the Karakoffs, the lawyers and businessmen and aspiring artists—would sell out at a given point. Emil had taught her that. When the soul does not respond, he instructed, we simply increase the dosage. Sooner or later they all crumpled under his economic weight. But not Dan Helena. He seemed so sterile, incorruptible, a sort of holy idiot. She laughed aloud in the rain at the idea. If there was anyone, anywhere, who might help her escape from the labyrinth, it was this half-baked, psycho sculptor.

She wondered, Is he really deranged? They call him some kind of genius when it comes to heavy-metal sculpture, but those unpredictable creative types are the wackiest.

They were mounting the flight of concrete steps that led up over the FDR Drive. She took a deep breath. "What's with you, Dan Helena? What do you want from me? Why do you always look at me twisted?" And what are we doing here in the pelting rain? she asked herself. Yet she already knew full well.

He put his hand on her arm. Fiercely. "Shh. Don't talk now. Later."

"I ought to be home. Emil phones me every day when the market closes. It'll drive him crazy if he can't find me."

"I guess he's going to be one crazy guy tonight, then." Dan Helena stopped her on the middle of the bridge. "Look down." He stood close behind her, so that she could feel the warmth of his body against the back of her thighs and the unmistakable pressure of his erection.

The dusky sky had darkened early, and they could hear the whine of the rubber tires of the traffic on the wet highway underneath.

She protested weakly, "Not here."

"Why not? It's better this way."

The three lanes of FDR traffic were beginning to clog, moving in stately progression. To the south, along the bend of the river, Susannah could make out the cables of the Brooklyn Bridge indistinct in the mist. It was the end of rush hour. The whole city was thrusting homeward, pounding with frustrated energy. Up above the highway, commanding the empty pedestrian bridge, she and Dan were in control of their lookout.

"Lean over."

He pushed her so that her forearms grazed the granulated concrete of the bridge. She glimpsed the red and gray and silver cars below, jerking and squelching in the flooding water.

Her hair was getting wet, not to mention the Valentino jacket that was supposed only to be dry-cleaned. Yet she no longer cared. He spread her legs apart like a prisoner's splayed before a wall. With one hand he cupped her breast; with the other he gripped her thigh. The foaming wave of excitement gathered within her.

She did not resist. When she finally felt him penetrating her, she did not even care if they were discovered, exposed ... or if Emil should learn. Dan Helena was the only man she had ever really hungered for. *Our transgressions are ever with us, and our iniquities we know.* The dormant erotic energy burst its dam. For years she had been waiting to feel Dan Helena deep inside her.

Now she rocked slowly back and forward on the bridge, balancing on the balls of her feet while he thrust. Thawing, melting, like a warm bath running in. This was the only true liberty left, the last defiance, carrying on atop the slow-moving streams of traffic. This was the airborne liberation of a pilot taking his plane alone through the clouds, only a reckless second from oblivion. Take me there, take me with you, she begged in her heart, take me all the way. Pulverize me, make me dissolve, give me my freedom by taking it away. Nothing else matters. If I had to die for this frenzy, if you were to hurl me into the East River, if they were to drag out my waterlogged body, one more useless statistic, I could not stop now. *He who eats of their eggs will die, and the egg that is left uneaten will hatch out into an adder.* Long buried sensations. As she felt the whirlpool funnel her down, sucking her under with its deliriously sweet, slippery ripples, she used her last breath to beg him to go on. And on. And on. "Don't stop, for mercy's sake, don't stop. Please don't stop!"

Dan waited, his groin thrust tightly against her. "Quiet! Someone's coming by."

It was a homeless bum, who shuffled hastily beyond them, clutching a bottle wrapped in newspaper and a sack of empty soda cans.

When he had gone, Dan ordered, "Get down."

She shivered. "Right here? In the rain? Anyone might come along. And what about my jacket?"

He took the Valentino off her shoulders, with its padded satin shoulders and matador slashes, and spread it on the wet ground. She did as he told her, automatically, heedless of the hard cement against her back and the rivulets of rain trickling down her face and legs. It did not last long, that interlude, but while he lay covering her, doing his best not to crush her too violently, she was free, and she bought right out of time and place.

When they finished and stood up, he inspected the jacket slightly sheepishly. A seam had been ripped, and the satin was blotched with patches of mud.

Susannah shrugged. They walked down the steps silently toward the river. When they reached the railing, she tossed the bundle of rag lightly into the eddying water.

From then on, her padded life took on a new value. Should she have bestowed it unquestioningly on Emil? What had she to show for her years of fealty but a handful of trinkets and clothes and baubles?

She resolved that she needed a real contract, a binding legal assurance that Emil could not abandon her penniless. The adventure with Dan infused her with a rush of courage to make the demand. Emil had listened, nodding docilely. She never knew when he was shamming, like a praying mantis in camouflage that might rear up alert.

It was too late to backtrack anyhow. She stumbled on, "If we're going to stay an item, you and me, I must have something—something—some piece of paper to spell out all the fine things you promise me."

Emil, who normally controlled his people as if they were marionettes, had actually agreed.

Dan left Susannah in the taxi, wiping her smudged lipstick and readjusting the Dean & DeLuca grocery bags. He vaulted down the subway stairs at the Hyatt Hotel entrance and hurried past the concessions with their comforting aroma of sugary doughnuts. He imagined that Susannah would soon be getting dressed for Emil's welcome-home dinner party. Had she crumpled up the oyster panties, or would she wear them all evening as a tribute to him? He felt good. Good about taking her in the subway entrance at Delancey, good about forcing her skillfully painted mouth down on him in the backseat behind the leer of Jose Ortega, filling her throat just until he felt her gag. He reached into his pocket for a token.

A couple of black kids, who must have been six feet six at least, with shiny ebony faces and an array of chunky finger rings, got on at Astor Place with a ghetto blaster. One was wearing a skull-and-crossbones sweatshirt and clenched a half-smoked cigarillo between his teeth. Their rap music singed his eardrums, and they stood so close that he could smell the sauerkraut and onion on their breath. He looked straight at the pair. Some animal signal passed between the three of them. The two giants moved away submissively. Dan leaned back and closed his eyes.

The projection of his unflinching authority attracted some people and repelled others. Even as a teenager, in Anaconda, Montana, something about the way he moved caused the most massive smelters and miners to give him a wide berth. He was tall, although slender by comparison with those mammoths, whose exaggerated forearm muscles looked like a normal man's leg. They were never comfortable with Dan, never quite welcomed him into the fraternity. They sensed his uncontrolled energy and kept their distance.

Dan had not been back to Montana in sixteen years. He sometimes thought he would like once again to see the sawtooth mountains, the yellow pine, red fir, and tamarack, and the primeval glacier lakes, glinting thousands of feet below. When he grew frustrated with Manhattan concrete and asphalt and the claustrophobic village mentality of the SoHo art scene, he hankered after the mountains of his childhood.

A professional woman with an expensive streaked hairstyle and a Gucci briefcase got on at Bleecker. Her eyes were weary from a long office day, and she wore no wedding ring. Dan stared at her, registering her sexuality, and caught the response. She shifted her legs and pulled her briefcase closer to her chest. Usually the yuppies and overgroomed Madison Avenueites did nothing for him. He got enough of designer lingerie and insurable jewelry with Susannah. The train roared on.

He wondered whether his two brothers had stayed on in Anaconda, enslaved in the now moribund mining business. The family had all lost touch years ago. They were not a letter-writing clan. Although Dan's cursive longhand was rhythmic and almost beautiful, he still grew flushed and tight inside at the thought of composing sentences. He had left school at fifteen, and he had not learned much up until then.

At Spring Street he got out on an empty platform, shooting a parting glance at the girl with the briefcase. She was watching him avidly, of course, as soon as she figured he was not looking. He climbed up to the street and turned onto Broadway.

Maybe his brothers had stuck with the mining industry. Miners and their families were a strange breed; despite the grimness of the job, they clung to the business as if wedded. He smiled. Even he, in his own way, had never quite given up the obsession with metals and alloys. As he bent over nine-foot sheets of stainless steel in his studio, tracing the cutting lines, he sometimes thought of his father, "roasting" the copper and iron ore to "blister"; resmelting to extract the sulfur, lead, and arsenic; refining out the nickel and cobalt, the silver and gold.

He had visited the smelting furnaces where his father worked, when he was a child in Anaconda. He remembered staring up in wonderment at the copper converters, gigantic rotating kegs gushing out a molten stream of oxidized matte and leaving the ninety-nine-percent-pure blister copper. His father had proudly pointed to the sample ingots, solidified from the bath of metal, and explained the necessary expertise for continuously testing the brittle red surface, as it was refined to a silky sheen.

Dan stopped at 418 West Broadway and joined the small group waiting for the elevator. The cast-iron building housed the most prestigious conglomerate of galleries on the street, a blue-chip nest in the funky, ephemeral SoHo art world. The porters downstairs always looked half-asleep and fixed you with a glazed stare. As for the elevators, talk about taking a slow boat to culture.

A sweaty woman leaned her Picassoid hips against Dan as the pink-and-gray art deco elevator inched up its ascent. She was wearing square enamel earrings. The left earring depicted an Andy Warhol electric chair, the right earring the straw chair by van Gogh. She was doused in a powerful perfume, a violent hybrid of disinfectant and gardenia.

A girl in no-heel black button boots and an ankle-length cotton skirt asked an acne-scarred man with a black Chinese pigtail, "Didn't we meet at Castelli's?"

The elevator lurched and halted. The door did not open. Dan

felt the wedged bodies stiffen around him. The woman with the Warhol/van Gogh earrings thrust out a flabby arm with urgent jabs at the "Door Open." Nothing happened.

"Try pressing some other floors," suggested another female in an adenoidal voice. She sported an original Lichtenstein silk-screened shirt. This one was overperfumed, too; hers smelled of musk and artichoke.

A blond boy with buckteeth obligingly punched the buttons for seven, eight, and nine. Nothing stirred.

"Don't do that," roared the chair-earrings woman. "You'll screw up the mechanism."

The boy shrugged at her apologetically. He was wearing un-laced sneakers and creased baggy pants, today's semiofficial uni-form for the creating class. He had a bright-eyed, immature look; he was probably about twenty-five.

"Try ringing the alarm bell," volunteered the pockmarked man with the Chinese pigtail. He was perhaps an artist, too, Dan decided. He knew that type. They smeared lurid, foment-ing, runny pictures, an expression of painterly macho.

The blond buck-toothed boy obediently tried the alarm, which gave out a muffled whimper, like a far-off miaow.

The artichoke-smelling woman studied the ventilating fan above them and the absurdly small square that must open as an escape door in emergencies. "It's getting hot," she muttered. No one else wanted to say it. "Try 'Door Open' again."

The earring woman's voice quavered. "Try the emergency alarm. Maybe it rings outside the building." The buck-toothed boy hesitated. There were so many orders to execute now, flying at him fast and furiously. "Push it," the artichoke woman squealed. "Right now, push it." Dan noticed that drops of sweat were gathering around her upper lip and temples.

"Have you tried the 'Up' button?"

"Try all the buttons."

"I'm never taking an elevator again!"

"Somebody must find us soon."

The chair-earrings woman was beginning to hyperventilate.

"Keep ringing it, don't stop."

The boy's hands fluttered.

Dan leaned his muscular frame hard against the door.

"Don't do that," shrilled the earring woman. "We might be between floors."

Ignoring her, he pushed again. Minutely, centimeter by centimeter, he felt the metal slide, yielding against the weight. He eased the door halfway open. They all let out a breath. The elevator box had stalled level with the floor.

The traumatized crew surged past him, an ashen-faced group of frantic and fashionable people.

"Phew," said the boy. "That was hairy. I thought for a minute those women were going to rip me to shreds."

"You did fine," said Dan. "What's your name?"

"Caspar Peacock."

"You an artist?"

"Antiartist. Art's dead, as we know it. Died in 1971. I do performance stunts, too. How about you?"

"I work in steel."

They entered the gallery, where a packed crowd had already gathered. Dan's elevator group clustered around the table where the California Riesling was being poured into plastic cups.

"You like this minimal stuff?" asked Caspar.

Dan glanced at the walls. The pictures were all seemingly identical. There must have been at least forty dotted along the white walls, monochrome rectangles of dense orange pigment, undifferentiated by any perceptible surface variation. Dan had once fallen into conversation with the artist at the late night delicatessen. She had told him that she produced them in layers, superimposing dry pigment and resin on thin sheets of aluminum, as many as sixty levels of it. Painstaking work, Dan considered, for a monotonous result. Did she never get bored, he wondered, stamping out her stylistic insignia over and over? She had been producing those same orange squares for years.

It was a goodly turnout for any downtown opening. The usual cross section: scruffy artists, some dealers in pinstripes, a few eccentric women, already passé in their oversize earrings and joke jewelry (that East Village look had really gone out by the late eighties), the ubiquitous baby carriages, a couple of dogs, and the sprinkling of Germans you found embedded in any art gathering these days. They were taking over in New York as the master race of the avant garde. Black was the "in" color.

Except for the businessmen, everybody wore it: sweeping black skirts, boots and black Reeboks, black sweaters and shirts and scarves and knapsacks and stockings. Even the babies, Dan noted, had been scrubbed and diapered and swaddled in black. Only the Germans—you could spot them by their faces, since they never looked as if they were having any fun—interspersed in browns and tweeds.

Dan pointed to a solitary figure, huddled in an oversize sweater, a leather skirt, and sneakers with bobby socks. "That's the artist."

She seemed to be the only person in the room, other than a few isolated Germans, with no one to talk to. An intense and obsessive creature, she rarely raised her voice above a whisper. To utter more than a couple of simple sentences seemed to cause her pain; had she not been showing with one of the most respected SoHo galleries, she would have been judged autistic. She stared bleakly out of the window, over the roofs of SoHo.

Dan stepped over to her. "How's it going?" he asked. "Sold much?"

She blinked at him in an agony of confused shyness and mumbled something. Her hand muffled her mouth.

"What?"

She held up four fingers. "Paint," she whispered.

"What?"

"The act of painting. You can't separate the paint from the act of painting. The paint is the definition."

"Sure," said Dan. He backed off rapidly and returned to Caspar Peacock. He asked, "What kind of stunts did you do?" He did not warm to people easily, but this kid had a kind of spunk behind his goofy buck-toothed look.

"I rode around on the top of Manhattan busses for a while. I once stayed up on the Madison Avenue M-four for fifty blocks before they pulled me down. That kind of thing."

"You get in trouble?"

"I got arrested once, for a staged holdup at the Guggenheim admission desk."

"Why do you do it?"

"I'm an artist. I wanna make money. I need publicity."

"How about your artwork?"

"That comes later. This is the 1990s, man. If I get a little famous first, I won't have any trouble marketing my stuff. Would you believe it, a couple of years ago I was holed up on Wall Street, selling junk bonds. Now the junk market's shot, I figure I can do better selling my own original creations."

"You got a dealer?"

"Not yet. Have you?"

"Yeah. Giulietta Giuliani."

Caspar looked faintly impressed. "She's big-time. I need someone who's got real business savvy. Someone who's prepared to inflate the prices of my work, and keep pushing it."

"What kind of work exactly do you do?"

"I'm an umbrella artist."

"What's that?"

"I create collages on umbrellas. I don't believe in picture painting, obviously. Sculpture's better, but it's still too earth-bound for me. This is the new thing. Art that you carry around with you. Like a cordless phone."

"You think there's really a market?"

"You bet. That's what I'm in it for, the bucks. I'm hip. I don't go for any of that starving bohemian art for art's sake. I tell you, I've got my finger on the pulse. What are people buying these days?"

"Just about everything."

"Yeah, sure, but what do they really dig? Koons, Kiefer, Salle, Schnabel, Warholiana. Brassy, gaudy, kitschy stuff. That's how my umbrellas look. And you can flash them around, show them off to all your friends without even asking them over to your house."

"There's a guy," said Dan, pointing at a figure newly arrived on the scene, "who passes himself off as Russian to half the world. He's really Polish, I found out, but since Russian art's the peak of fashion these days, he figures most of this bunch here can't tell the difference. Hey, Oleg, what's up?"

The closet Pole joined them. He was dressed in a black suit over which he had appliquéd a constellation of unfathomable Cyrillic graffiti.

"This is boring," said Oleg. "This monochrome thing is twenty-five years old. Went out with Yves Klein and Ellsworth Kelly."

Dan seized a familiar arm. "Luke, meet Caspar. Caspar Peacock, Luke Elliot. Luke's a Neo-geist. Caspar does performance stunts. And this is Kitty." He indicated the pale girl who slunk at Luke's side. "Luke's wife."

Luke looked irritable. "It's not Neo-geo," he insisted. "Dan's always labeling me that." He scowled. "It sounds so old-fashioned."

Caspar asked Kitty, "What do you do?"

She looked depressed and suspicious. Her bones were sharp and her skin was papery, which gave her a spiritual quality. Dan preferred earthy women.

"I'm a waitress," she said.

"Where?" asked Caspar.

"At the Siamese Twin."

Dan and Luke had an odd friendship. Dan was a few years older, taller, and much more successful. Luke was educated, however, and that made a difference. Luke had an MFA from Cornell. Dan, who had difficulties expressing himself on any subject except art, and then only instinctively, kowtowed to Luke's superior class culture.

About Luke's artwork, he was more skeptical. Luke painted vertical stripes, bands of color a couple of inches wide, on muddy backgrounds. The paint strokes were uniformly applied. No critic could accuse him of sneaking sentiment, via gestural brush stroke, into the purity of the geometric canvas. And the colors! Luke labored long hours over his palette to concoct the most offputting combinations of bile greens and fecal browns; woe betide a decorative, eye-pleasing hue. Keep the paint strokes opaque and the colors repulsive, and no one should doubt that the art work stood for any purpose but its own existence.

Dan Helena was constantly trying to help Luke find a gallery to take him on. He had spoken several times to Giulietta Giuliani, brought her Luke's slides, and even persuaded her to pay a short "studio visit" to examine Luke's originals. She proved intractable. Not even to humor Dan, who was the most prom-

ising talent in her litter, would she represent his friend. Luke's
work, she snorted, was garbage.

To find a top-notch dealer in SoHo was easier said than done.
Although a plethora of galleries had opened their doors since
the mid-seventies, only twenty or thirty carried any real clout.
A gallery of stature generally abstained from representing more
than a dozen or so artists. The famous dealers were swamped
with the slides of hopeful aspirants, as it was well nigh impossible
for artists to make a serious living without the support of a
gallery. But the dealers too needed a constant supply of fresh
blood. Their artists often defected to other galleries, or went
out of vogue, or never fulfilled early promise. As a dealer you
had to be prepared to take some risk on newcomers. The space
and promotion for a four-week one-man show cost about thirty
thousand dollars in SoHo and as much as a hundred in midtown.
You gave them a show or two, and then, if they proved fruitless,
you dumped them. Despite the highfalutin cant they all self-
righteously proclaimed, a successful gallery was only a business.
You sold what the market sucked up.

"Forget this shit," Dan suggested. "Let's move on to the 313."

"What's there?"

"Mummified animals. Guinea pigs and cats and squirrels."

Caspar agreed to join them, so the three artists and the waitress tramped off down West Broadway. The garbage cans were
already filling up with the plastic cups discarded after the openings, sometimes still half-full of white wine.

At Gallery 313, a Texan couple (she in a white lynx, he in a
ten-gallon Stetson) gazed at the motley zoo of mummified pi-
geons, rattlesnakes, woodchucks, and one giant spider.

"Whaddya think, Mrs. Milholland?" asked the husband, temporarily removing his hat.

"This artist is maturing, pussycat." She caressed her own coat.
"You like the spider?"

He leaned forward to take a more careful look. "Ours is
better—our small spider in the breakfast room."

"We could buy him this fellow to be a big brother."

"Naw. Not today. We already bought the Chia and the Serra."

Caspar winked and led his group two flights of stairs to another gallery, where a friend had an "earthworks" opening. His friend fashioned hard-caked muddy mixtures, incorporating slivers of pebbles and tiny twigs into patties, like hamburgers. He did not restrict himself to earth; there was a pyramid of salt and a mattress softly layered with flour.

"Oh, earthworks," said Luke. "Who's still doing these?"

"They're so ugly," Kitty said. "I mean, what's the point, really."

Luke looked at her patronizingly. She should know better. "The point is not that they should be pretty. The point is that they should have impact."

Dan turned sharply to Caspar, who was discreetly scraping away at a moist patch of a thirty-thousand-dollar muddy wedding cake. "What are you doing?"

The kid was pouring a stream of seeds from a small envelope. "Bean sprouts," he said.

"Bean sprouts! You can't do that."

"Why not? It's Bio-art. We'll come back next week and see if they grow."

"Let's get moving," said Dan. "It's nearly eight. You want to eat?"

Luke nodded vigorously. There was nothing he and Kitty appreciated so much these days as a sponsored meal. Dan was inclined to be generous. Luke keenly looked forward to some hearty meat and vegetables, cooked and arranged on a real plate. He was accustomed to living for days on nothing but cocktail finger food, hot dogs and chocolate bars, and whatever ethnic leftovers Kitty brought home in foil cartons from her waitress job.

They spread themselves out at a table at the Metropolitan Bistro and studied the menu. When Kitty announced that she was not feeling hungry, her husband shot her a poisonous and reprimanding glare.

"I'm so tired," she explained. "I've been working double shifts. Or maybe it's some exotic additive they put in the pork *pla lad prig*. I've really gotten to detest Thai food, but I can't afford to eat anywhere else."

"Things'll improve if I can get a dealer," promised Luke. "If only I sell a few paintings, maybe we could get away to Europe this summer."

"Maybe we first should think about fixing the leak in the ceiling, and paying back the money we borrowed for the phone bills, and getting a new mattress to sleep on." Kitty sounded strained. She explained, "The stuffing seeps out."

"Luke's always an optimist," said Dan.

Kitty sighed. "We've had some close scrapes. Last December, when I got fired from the Steakhouse and couldn't find another job for a couple of weeks, we were right down to our last three dollars and forty-one cents. They were about to cut off the phone, and we both got sick with strep throats and needed antibiotics. You were away in Mexico, Dan, and we'd already borrowed from everyone we knew. If the drug dealers next door hadn't come through with a loan for us, I don't know what we'd have done."

Dan asked politely, "How are you making out now?"

"We're scraping along. The tips at the Siamese Twin aren't exactly great, but . . . "

Caspar asked, "Does Luke work, too?"

Kitty shook her head philosophically. "If he goes back to being a janitor, he'll never get time or peace for painting."

Caspar grinned at Kitty. "Are you really just a waitress? You don't write or paint or dance?"

"I wait tables. Are you really called Caspar Peacock?"

"Not exactly. When the great Leo Castelli saw his first Jasper Johns target painting in 1957, you know what really impressed him? That a man with a name like 'Jasper' would make a painting that was truly two-dimensional. If Jasper Johns did it, Caspar Peacock will, too." He turned to Dan. "So what's your real name, then, man?"

Dan shrugged. "Hey, that's my private business."

Dan Helena had come of age in the sixties, when a score of artists, like Judy Chicago and Robert Indiana, were all adopting places as surnames. Dan chose Helena. Not only did it serve as his rugged western trademark, but he liked it also because it was a woman's name. All true artists, he said, must be genderless.

The waiter brought a bottle of champagne.

Luke looked pleased. "Hey, what are we celebrating?"

Dan leaned back and announced in his deadpan style, "My most important commission yet."

"No kidding! What is it?"

"A thirty-foot sculpture outside the headquarters of Belle John."

"Why, that's great," exclaimed Caspar. "Corporate art's the future of our industry. They can really afford us."

"It's not the money. It's the opportunity of creating a major, major site-specific work."

Luke dug into his veal chop in Calvados. "Have you signed a contract?" he wanted to know.

"I've made the preliminary sketches for the approval of the board. When they accept them, I'll start buying materials."

"This is very nice of you to invite us, Dan." Luke chewed greedily. "As soon as I find a dealer, we'll be able to pay you back your various loans."

Knowing Luke was an unpluggable drain on friendship. He never showed any shame in asking for yet more money. Maybe they taught you how to do that at Cornell, along with theories of negative space and iconography.

Luke suggested, "Shall we move on to Lucky Strike now? Or get some Irish coffee at Le Zinc?"

"Later." Dan stood up. "I've got a phone call to make."

He disappeared downstairs to the phone. As he dialed Susannah's number, the line Emil never answered, he wondered whether she was still wearing the oyster panties.

6

STRINGS ATTACHED

*E*mil telephoned the following week.

Nick was surprised, proud, and relieved. He was surprised that Papier should phone him directly; proud that such a prestigious call should boost his standing at the auction house. He was relieved because it gave him an excuse to escape the clutches of Georgia.

Georgia Cavendish was manager of the auction house's bid department. Her job was to coordinate the advance bids collected by the telephone clerks before a sale. The phones rang fast and furiously all day long in the bid room. The five clerks entered the details: name, address, lot number, identifying description (*Cézanne apples; Warhol Marilyn*), plus the price up to which the buyer was authorizing the auction house to bid on his behalf. At the end of each day, Georgia assembled all the pink slips and entered them in lot order on photocopied forms in a looseleaf notebook. That innocuous-looking notebook became the highly confidential "auctioneer's book." Guarded under lock and key, it was brought up to the auctioneer's pulpit shortly before a sale commenced.

Georgia had graduated from Smith College, written a doctoral dissertation at Yale on sixteenth-century Flemish tapestries, and worked in the auction house ever since. She was not flashy enough to start out at the front desk. She worked initially as a secretary in oceanic, later as an assistant cataloger in silver. She made a lateral move into Art Deco. She had ended up running the bid department, making a humble salary for her conscientious and meticulous responsibilities.

Although Nick Jones respected her connoisseurship, he found himself glazing over every time she brought her coffee upstairs for a midmorning chat. Georgia had a broad and profound knowledge of art history, but she looked like a horse. She was too tall for her own good, and obviously there had been nothing any orthodontist could do about her enormous teeth, which thrust her jaw forward and stretched her upper lip.

"Excuse me, Georgia." He reached for his telephone. She scuttled away, to weary someone else. Nick wished he could find a way to get rid of her without being unkind. She had latched on to him from his first day with an unrequited devotion. Never mind that he was penniless and far too young for her. All that was exonerated by his green eyes, the wavy hair, and above all, the English accent. For Georgia would not brook philistines, and Nick Jones spoke the language of Laurence Olivier.

Emil sounded strained on the telephone underneath his impeccable formality. "I was wondering if you might be able to join me for an early lunch."

Nick had already invited one of the sexier blondes from the estates department for a hamburger. An invitation from his new mentor took priority. "Love to."

"Meet me in forty-five minutes at Les Pleiades."

On his way out of the building, Nick stopped in estates, to beg off. The blonde was waiting for him, cross-referencing newspaper obituaries from all over the world. She was really too pretty, Nick considered, to be involved in such a ghoulish job. The function of her department was to liaise and maintain relationships with the most important trusts and estates attorneys around the globe. In reality the auction house often took a more aggressive role. The major business of any auction house is death, and no one could afford to be squeamish. The estates department followed not only the news of the newly deceased, but also who was on their way out. They had highly confidential connections at hospitals and nursing homes. The last gasps of a powerful collector rarely took them by surprise.

Nick smiled apologetically at the blonde. "Something's come up. Will you take a rain check?"

She shrugged. "I'll eat at my desk. It's been a busy morning. Death's been good to us today."

Nick hurried on downstairs, waved cheerily at the glossy girls at the front desk (privately known among the other employees as "the stewardesses"), and galloped down the street for his meeting with Papier.

Les Pleiades did a brisk lunchtime business. It was located opposite the Carlyle, at the nucleus of the uptown art world. The same regulars had been patronizing it for years. The service was always pleasant, and when the maître d' heard that Nick belonged to the Papier reservation, he gave him an extra-mellow smile.

"Right this way, monsieur." He led Nick through the red leather upholstery chairs and banquettes, past the floor pillars with their sconces and little red shades and the tableaux of Dutch orchards and seascapes. Emil was already waiting at a corner table at the back of the room.

He greeted Nick with unexpected warmth. "So good of you to join me at such short notice. Alas, I must fly back to Switzerland tonight."

"It's a pleasure. It was very kind of you to invite me. And thank you also very much for dinner last week."

"I'm glad you could come, and see my Magrittes and meet my daughter. I hope you had an interesting talk with her. She is so serious about her studies. It's good for her to meet young men. So what will you start with? I always have the consommé and then the sole amandine. I've been eating that for twenty years." He raised his glass. "So, here's to your new job with the contemporary department. Are you enjoying it?"

Nick was beginning to relax. "It's like a dream come true. Everyone who works there is so knowledgeable, so well educated, so attractive . . . "

"And well connected. It's a service industry."

"That too." Nick chattered on enthusiastically. "It's such a privilege finally to be working with the best." His eyes shone.

He buys in, thought Emil. He's lapping it all up.

"When you sent me for my first interview," Nick added guilelessly, "I have to admit, I never expected I'd get the job. Most people do start at the bottom, however good their educations are, and here am I, already a senior cataloger in my first few weeks."

Nick's department included the vice-president, or "expert," as all the department heads were called, the assistant vice-president, Nick, another cataloger, and a departmental assistant. As a cataloger, Nick was responsible for writing the copy for the sleek brochures and researching the histories ("provenance") of the art works included in forthcoming sales: who had owned the work, in which museums it had hung, and through which galleries it had passed. Often he was shunted off downtown to the printer for the tedious task of checking proofs. Or he was sometimes dispatched to cosset the marginal sellers who brought their more mundane pieces into the auction house for inspection. He occasionally paid house calls. He assessed the object with reference to the *Auction Index,* the volumes that listed all recent auction prices. Someone had to show up, murmur some soothing words of appreciation, and arrange for the consignment to be packed off to the storeroom pending sale.

The expert had no time to deal personally with all the small fry, let alone those optimistic sellers whose objects Nick apologetically rated "NSV" (no salable value). The blue-chip paintings, of course, the Pollocks, the Bacons, and the de Koonings, were appraised by the expert. The rest of the time the expert busied himself reinforcing connections with the track-record collectors at parties and dinners and country weekends. He had been meeting on and off for years with Papier and Karakoff, for lunch in the auction house's own private dining room.

Emil glanced away from Nick to the vase of red carnations

between them. "Let us just say that it is essential to be introduced through the appropriate channels."

Nick's first impressions of the auction house had over-whelmed him. He would always remember the white-gloved doorman, two men soaping the marble steps, and someone else polishing the door knocker. Inside, the carpets were so thick that it was like walking through a meadow. Despite the flurry of activity behind the department doors, the hallways remained silent. Nick could hear no voices and no telephones as he fol-lowed the glamorous "stewardess" on the winding route to his interview with the contemporary expert. Each time they passed through another set of doors she flicked the combination of the computerized lock with ease of habit. Even the most venerated strangers were never allowed to roam alone in the corridors. Nick turned his head sharply as they trotted past the odd mish-mash of paintings that decorated the halls. He noticed a Turner watercolor and a Chinese scroll and an Italian stone cherub. He loved the notion of such intimate chaos, the way antique trea-sures awaiting auction were casually dispensed to hang over the water fountain or next to the men's room. He had wondered if he too would ever flick as expertly at the combination locks as his leggy guide.

Now, after a few weeks' employment there, he did. Nick took a mouthful of his crab salad. "You've been so helpful to me. I wish there were some way I could thank you."

"There does happen to be a service you might perform for me. Naturally, I intend to compensate you handsomely. We might call this a retainer."

Puzzled, Nick unfolded the check Emil slid across the table-cloth. It was drawn on Chase Manhattan for the sum of twenty-five thousand dollars. The paper fluttered in Nick's hand.

"This," said Emil, "is a private matter between the two of us. Confidentiality is the essence in the art business, as you well realize."

"Yes, yes, of course." Nick's face looked as though he were plummeting into the depths of a deep black well. Twenty-five grand was a sizable sum for someone who was constrained to take subways home at 2:00 A.M. and choose the cheapest items on menus in the cheapest sawdust-and-burger dives he dared suggest going to with his new yuppie friends. For Emil Papier, on the other hand, the money was surely a bagatelle. But did even Swiss gnomes hand over such checks without strings?

"New York is an expensive place," Emil murmured. "Not a city to be enjoyed in poverty. There'll be a lot more money for you as our business relationship matures."

Nick swallowed. "What must I do?"

"By now you are doubtless familiar with the auction procedure. In that tiny village we call the 'art world,' when a famous dealer spends a few million on a work, that secret takes between three and five days to get out on the grapevine."

Nick had a sudden glimmer. "Do you want to guarantee your own anonymity for bidding? I'll be glad to help you with that. I can arrange to be on the telephone team for any contemporary sale in which you've a special interest."

At an important auction, four or five silken-haired stewardesses were assigned to "man" the phone lines to clients who were bidding from out of town. It was considered a routine job. The catalogers from the applicable departments also rotated on phone duty, usually dealing with the touchier clients. The more temperamental bidders would book their call days in advance, often requesting such-and-such an employee to take care of relaying their bids.

Emil shook his head slowly and took a small sip of the ninety-five-dollar bottle of Bâtard-Montrachet he had ordered for them. "No, thank you. I am no longer concerned with my anonymity. In fact, *au contraire,* I soon expect to be courting some degree of publicity. I intend to be buying a great deal in the next few months, and not only for my own account."

Nick took a final mouthful of the flaky sole amandine. It had not been well cooked, but at least it was a square meal. Perhaps he had landed a lucky break. Papier was gearing up for an art-buying spree and wanted a sympathetic ear inside the contemporary department, someone to grease the wheels, set up lunches with the expert, summon attention at short notice.

"I'll be delighted to do anything I can," promised Nick.

"Good. You're familiar with the so-called auctioneer's book?"

"Naturally." Nick thought of Georgia, with her equine teeth, the custodian of the looseleaf book of order bids. "Potential buyers place orders in advance, authorizing us to bid up to their limit for them."

"I understand it's kept under lock and key," Emil continued. "After the names of the anonymous bidders are filled in, no one sees it again except the department expert, until it's sent up to the auctioneer."

"Yes, they make a big palaver of it."

"Right. When the next round of contemporary sales comes up, I want to know the name and price of every bidder in that book."

"What!"

"I know, I know, it may take you a while to get access to the sacred book. When you do, though, there'll be another check for you. A bigger one. Only do me one favor. Spend the money discreetly. Nothing too obvious, to draw attention to our arrangement."

Nick scowled at the check. It looked so innocuous, so innocent, a scrap of paper fluttering between them. Was it possible ever to buy out of the endless chain of compromise that seemed to dog him in whatever he did? Each time the invisible monster came back in some new guise to mock him.

He wet his lips. "I do want to help you. But if anyone ever found out . . . it would be a flagrant breach of employee confidence . . . a sort of industrial espionage. I'd be sued. I signed some bit of paper my first morning, saying I would be personally liable for any breach of client information."

Both looked at the check, still waiting, like a gauntlet between them. Emil had tucked it next to the vase of red carnations. "Nobody will find out," Emil declared. "You will be discreet. And incidentally, I have another request. I wish to know the identity of any well-known collectors who pass through the viewing rooms prior to the twentieth-century sales."

"How can I find out? I can't spend four workdays loitering around the viewing galleries to see who comes and goes."

Emil's lips twitched into a tight smile. "You have a lot to learn. What happens to the old tapes from the video security monitor?"

"They keep them a few days and then tape over."

"Exactly. You will find out where they are kept, and from now on you will examine those tapes and report to me who has been in."

Nick sighed despairingly. He seemed to cave in at each new twist. The monster, which had now taken on the human shape of a beautifully tailored, soft-spoken Swiss gnome, could fly or swim or hurtle through any moral barrier.

"You'll move," Emil purred. "You can get yourself some smart bachelor apartment on the forty-ninth floor in some high rise in midtown or on the Upper East Side. You can take a house in Southampton next summer. You want a BMW? You want a jeep? Most important, I'll see to it that you meet the right people. This is your big chance to get ahead in the art business. There are only two rules. Don't draw attention to the money, and"— Emil's face clouded—"absolutely no drugs."

Nick nodded. As they both knew, the trust fund babies, the bratpack who worked at the museums and galleries and auction houses these days, were heavy users of cocaine, and many of the kids dabbled in what they called "recreational heroin."

"I never do drugs."

"Sensible." Emil looked deceptively benign. He needed a stooge he would be able to rely on. He could not afford to experiment with any immature, spineless thrill seeker who, after the first flush of new money, would be out all over the rug. He wanted someone hungry for the good life. Ambitious. Not too scrupulous. He had a hunch that Nick Jones had latent grit in his nature, buried below that educated, and slightly effete, Oxford accent.

While Emil was staying in New York, Susannah awoke at dawn each morning, in good time to brush her hair and apply a dash of mascara before he should see her. She would then stumble downstairs to the kitchen to supervise the presentation of his cold cuts, *muesli*, and yogurt. There was no reason that the maid could not have equally well performed the task. Once or twice, however, the salami had been sliced too thick or the cheese dry around the edge. Ever since, Emil demanded that Susannah play high priestess at the breakfast ritual.

Today he was absent, back in Montreux, leaving her to sleep late and luxuriate alone under the goosedown duvet. She opened her eyes at ten and smiled at the world. She spread her arms wide across the bed, like a child playing angels in the snow. Emil would not be back for five weeks, in time for the much anticipated museum party at the Temple of Dendur. And even better, in a couple of days that exasperating, surly Delphine was leaving too, to return to the university in Heidelberg.

Susannah rolled over and buzzed the intercom to the kitchen to let Iris know she was ready for her morning cup of hot chocolate. It would be less fattening to drink coffee, she supposed, but somehow it never seemed quite important enough to make the switch. At least she was perfectly proportioned, and her legs would always win the day. Anyway, Emil was too preoccupied to notice if she had gained a pound or two. Of course if Dan Helena had objected . . . One day he had found her, in T-shirt and socks, lying on her back with her legs in the air.

"What the fuck are you doing?"

She panted, "Waist, hips, ass."

He sat down next to her and slapped her backside.

"Get up. Your ass is fabulous. Some people aren't meant to do exercises. You're one of them."

She persisted. "I remind you it was nine years ago that we got acquainted on that bridge, Dan Helena. I'll never be so young again, is all."

He took her small hand in his big, muscular paw. (These days the veins in her hand tunneled just under the skin. They only disappeared when she raised her arm to let the blood run down.) He chuckled. "You really believe if I met you for the first time right now it would be any different between us?"

She shook her head. Iris was arriving with the newspapers and hot chocolate on the art deco breakfast tray. While Susannah scanned the headlines of the arts section (geopolitical events could wait), the maid drew the curtains to let in the April light.

"Any phone calls yet today?" Susannah skimmed through a review of the latest homoerotic photography exhibit. The bestiality suite (young boys and mountain goats), although described by some major critics as "compellingly beautiful," was setting off a flurry of scandal.

"Lu called to say she'd be a few minutes late for your manicure. Her little girl's got a cold."

"Again? She needs a dose of sugar and turpentine. That child
doesn't dress warm enough. Find her a couple of our electric
blankets to take home."

Susannah took an interest in the family lives of her "elves,"
the Vietnamese manicurist, her Rumanian masseur, and the
young man from Kenneth's who set her billowing hair every
other day. They were well compensated for their journeys to
the palazzo. She paid the elves three times the going rate and
tried to throw in some household article or useful gift when she
learned of their needs. She would never have considered going
out to a crowded, noisy salon. Better to avoid the malicious
gossip her position attracted and let her elves minister in the
security of the palazzo.

"Breakfast will be ready in fifteen minutes, ma'am. I've made
eggs and fritters and all your favorites." Discreetly Iris swept
up the pile of yesterday's clothes, where Susannah had let them
tumble in a neglected heap.

"Lord, I'm starving. Afterward we'll go through the household bills for the week."

Running the palazzo took a lot of administration. Susannah
marshaled a constant stream of marble layers, plumbers, up-
holsters, insurance appraisers, framers, security alarm engineers, extra caterers, antique furniture restorers, window
cleaners, bookbinders, phone engineers, deliveries of food, fire-
wood, and birdseed, photographers from *Art Insider,* and electricians to rewire the chandeliers. Since New York roaches did
not distinguish between the territories of the humble and the
mighty, there were occasional exterminators, too. There was
always some task to attend to. Emil insisted the apartment be
maintained in flawless condition. Even the spinet, which no one
ever played, must be kept tuned. He had once picked out a
scale with one finger. When he struck a sour note his face
creased in fury.

Susannah worked hard for her bed and board. If Emil ditched
her, would her replacement attend to the Vineyard swimming
pool and sauna, the two Mercedes, Emil's multiple fax machines
(which always broke), the nurture of the tropical plants in the

conservatory? Susannah had a gift for organization, as well as nineteen years of training. Surely no one could automatically step into her shoes.

Or could they? She determined to call that bloodless lawyer at Whittaker & Blessing. She must ask him to explain the details of the contract that promised her security. At the time Emil had drawn it, the terms seemed generous consideration for the mere renunciation of her life. Now she was no longer certain. When she sensed Dan's unspoken contempt for her trappings of inventory, she pondered the roads not taken. Yet it was easy for Dan to be aloof. Susannah, who was not impractical, had to live somehow.

"Oh, and the worm man is coming at three," Iris reminded her. "Mister P. was not happy when he found that hole in the wood paneling."

Downstairs in the dining room Delphine was buried in a newspaper, grunting over the capitalist atrocities of the hour. She stretched her legs and propped her stained sneakers on a brocaded chair cushion.

Susannah found her eggs steaming under the silver dish cover. "Would you kindly remove those filthy sneakers," she suggested. "You know full well how incensed your daddy gets. If there's anything he hates, it's when you mess up the cushions with utter disregard."

"So what? You can always get them cleaned. That's your job." Delphine glared. A dark shadow cut sharply across the promise of the day.

"Maybe I'm busy," Susannah replied coolly. "Maybe I've got something better to do than clean up after you." Why couldn't they stop bickering and call a cease-fire for once? Since childhood Delphine had engaged in making her father's mistress squirm. She kept a sharp lookout for any chink in Susannah's self-control or any opportunity to pick a squabble. Whenever Susannah timidly complained to Emil, he airily dismissed his daughter's impudence. "She's going through 'difficult years,'" he would murmur vaguely. "The divorce was hard on her." Delphine's "difficult years" had extended right through adolescence and now well into adulthood.

"You? Busy?" Delphine snickered into her napkin and fenced

around for a nasty swipe. "Are you taking those French classes again?"

Susannah laid down her fork. She was losing her appetite for the fritters. Delphine knew how she had engaged numerous tutors and once even enrolled in that hated semester at the Alliance Française. The grammar foxed her; her tongue got twisted in knots.

"We can't *all* speak six languages." Susannah managed to make the retort sound a little barbed, although it was perfectly true that Delphine did, and fluently.

"Yes, we do all have our particular talents." Delphine flipped her head in the direction of the bedrooms upstairs.

Doesn't she ever guess, Susannah wondered, what a travesty my infrequent sex with Emil has become? How rarely he ends up rolling against me, plunging heavily and blindly inside, when the alcohol has not rendered him impotent? Yet how could Delphine know, unless Emil had actually confided in her. For the father and daughter shared some astonishing intimacies. At times Susannah was quite startled to see them acting more like husband and wife.

When the three of them went out to dinner, it was Delphine, not Susannah, whom Emil consulted on the choice of wine or dishes. The last time they had all been together in Geneva, they had left the chauffeur and walked through the steep streets of the old city. Wrought-iron lamps jutted between the shutters. Delphine explained patronizingly to Susannah that it was here in the Grand Rue the philosopher Rousseau was born, while Emil said nothing.

"If my father only knew about all the goings-on here in New York behind his back." Delphine smirked knowingly.

Susannah tried to disregard the unending cattiness. "Let's not dispute it." She struggled to keep her temper. "Especially your last few days in New York. Can't we make an extra effort this once to keep off each other's toes?"

"You can't wait for me to leave, can you? You're delighted that Papa's gone, too. When the cat's away the mice will play. Is that right, Susannah? Do the mice play?"

Susannah took a final stab at the fritters and bit down hard on the fork. Don't let her provoke you. That's what she wants, to goad you into an explosion. Ignore. Be ladylike. Remember: she's led a zany, twisted-up life, too. Emil reared and spoiled her with every indulgence, like a foie gras goose, like those Japanese cows they massage for better beef. No surprise she resents me, no wonder she hates to share her exclusive relationship with her father. The exclusivity I ceased invading long ago. Doesn't she suspect how far I've been pushed out of the picture?

"Got a date tonight, Susannah? Don't tell me you're planning to curl up with a book. That doesn't sound like you."

Don't answer. Don't give her the satisfaction. Don't let her suspect for a moment that you *do* have a date indeed, the very best kind too, worlds away in Brooklyn with Dan.

Switch tack. Cut and parry. "And what are you doing this evening?"

"Nothing you'd understand. There's a rally in Washington Square. Mineral exploitation in the Antarctic."

Roll with the punches. "Why, I think that's a fine and worthy cause."

Delphine scrunched up her nose. "You don't understand shit about the problems we're trying to solve in the world. You're too busy shopping at Adolfo's to know or care. Have you ever seen those villages in El Salvador—Suchitoto, Quetzaltepeque, Guatjigua, Nejapa—after the slaughter? Can you imagine no food, no electricity, no bandages? Have you noticed the homeless beggars downstairs here on the street? Have you watched them wheeling their shopping carts into the park next door at one in the morning on cold winter nights?"

The chain snapped.

"That's enough! Quit sassing me and shut it, you prissy little hypocrite. Don't give me that saintly smirk. What do you know, girl, about hunger and poverty? Did you grow up in a two-room shanty with a wood stove, sharing a bed with your sister? Did you gut chickens for a dollar twenty-five an hour? A smidgen of experience would take the starch out of you right quick. You think anyone gives a fig for your living room limousine liberal claptrap, your trust-fund-baby bullshit? I declare, you're transparent as a snakeskin. You're a shiftless, spoiled brat, and it's time you grew up and pitched out your everlasting commie hogwash. 'Soak the rich.' Lord, who do you reckon the rich are? You are, sugarpie. That's right. You, you, you."

Susannah ran out of breath. They sat and smoldered at each other, until the tap on the door broke the silence. How long had Iris been shuffling outside, listening avidly to her employers' skirmish?

"Lu's here for the manicure, ma'am. Whenever you're ready."

"Right away." As Susannah swept from the dining room, she indulged in a parting shot. "And it's no wonder you can't even find a decent boyfriend. Why, no normal young man could possibly want to put up with your lip. Except to get his hands on your money, that is. Oh, sorry, I clean forgot. Soak the rich!"

After Susannah slammed the door, Delphine rested her clammy forehead in her palms. Her proud little face crumpled up with shame and humiliation. How could she have been so naive after all those years of the finest education? She, who had won a medal for junior Olympic downhill skiing, who had collaborated on a new annotated edition of *Das Kapital* and had been photographed dancing with the king of Sweden.

Even now, months after the affair had ended, she still winced at her memories of the Montreux public swimming pool.

That was where she had met Rudi, in the golden Indian summer. For Delphine, a public swimming pool was already a highly charged and almost erotic adventure. Had her father suspected she went there, he would have been mystified and furious. He would have pointed out that she was taking an unwarranted security risk. What was the use of his going to such lengths to guard his own life and person, if his only daughter roamed at large in Europe, offering an easy target to kidnappers? She could swim in her own luxurious pool any day, he would protest, among the invaluable underwater assortment of tubas and sea serpents.

So she had sneaked into the noisy, overchlorinated public pool in the town, where she was surrounded by beach balls and rubber tires, Radio Luxembourg and ice cream, snotty children and fat women with varicosed legs. She felt like an Amazonian explorer as she sauntered past in her black string bikini, tanned and spaghetti thin, her hair swinging boldly behind. At last she was no longer Papier's Daughter.

She brought her research material to the poolside and unfolded her beach blanket. While she soaked up the August sun, she absorbed statistics of Sandinistas slain and contras abetted, of seventy thousand El Salvadorans killed in a decade of civil war, American furnishments of aircraft and ground missiles, hundreds of villages razed and demolished. When she finished her list of the Spanish jungle towns—Mejicanos, Ciudad Delgado, Escalon, and San Benito, poor steam-rollered villages with their romantic-sounding names—she flexed her long legs and jackknifed balletically into the aqua water.

She surfaced for air in a veil of bubbles and gulped.

"Hello, mermaid," said Rudi, treading water.

He was tall and well built, with muscular thighs and prematurely receding hair at the temples, which gave him a prophetic look. And this young man, this shepherd of the people with muscular thighs, had no idea she was Papier's Daughter.

They swam together. The sun was hot and she felt like an ordinary person. Rudi could do good somersaults underwater and stand on his hands; Delphine could swim many meters below the surface after all her childhood practice between the Dada snakes.

Then they sat at the edge of the pool and he played with her toes in the water while they talked. He told her that he came from a simple family. His father was a mailman in Lucerne. Rudi had studied medicine in Geneva before he decided to dedicate himself full-time to his political activities. He organized some kind of splinter group, called Friends of the Feeble, which devoted itself to various creditable causes: industrial toxic pollution and the abolition of U.S. air force bases from Western Europe.

It seemed so natural that he should be sitting beside her and stroking her toes. Whatever would this political activist think if he discovered he had been inadvertently chatting with Papier's Daughter? So she spun him a yarn, about how her father owned a small *pâtisserie* in nearby Lausanne and came from a long line of *pâtissiers*. She told him that her mother was dead (the rich divorcée was actually on a cruise in the Maldives) and that her brother (nonexistent) was a village station master. She did not mention her polo pony, Liebknecht.

It was head spinning and liberating to pretend to be someone else. How ashamed she was of her real life and how she hated her pampered isolation. She never knew whether people were really interested in her for herself. Rudi clearly found her physically exciting and also seemed impressed by her incisive grasp of the Central American political equation.

They met every afternoon at the swimming pool. They flip-flopped around in the water or lay in the grass and talked about everything: the fish dying in the Rhine and the Ruhr, and the seals in the North Sea poisoned by the swill of polychlorinated biphenyls; the urban air dense with ozone, hydrocarbons, and nitrogen oxides; American support of corrupt officials in the jungle shanty towns.

They strolled in the nearby castle of Chillon, where from 1532 to 1536 François de Bonivard was chained to a pillar in the dungeon. Rudi's eyes gleamed as he thought of Bonivard, a real prisoner of political conscience, a Reformation freedom fighter. They admired the outline of his footprint in the rock wall, as well as the pillar inscribed with the poet Byron's—another freedom fighter—hewn-out signature.

"I'd like to help your organization," Delphine suggested timidly as they climbed out of the dank cells into the cobbled courtyard. "To do something useful for the Friends."

He turned around slowly and peered at her. "You really want to help? Your motivations are pure?"

"Of course. I was thinking I might write public relations copy or articles or pamphlets, or liaise with the international organizations . . . or even lick envelopes."

"We are not that kind of organization." He took her hand.

The headquarters of Friends of the Feeble were in nearby Geneva, located, Delphine wrongly assumed, in some obscure back street. Yet the next day they were speeding past the colossal fountain and the sign for Kuwait Airways and the panoply of flags along the water's edge, directly into the enemy territory of the international banks. They stepped into a gleaming lobby.

Rudi, who had become all efficiency and slick since the night

before, ushered her smartly through the reception area of the
Compagnie Financière de Tripoli, S.A.

"Where are we?" She swung around, bewildered.

"This is where I work. Headquarters."

"What about Friends of the Feeble?" Was she dreaming?

"We have a couple of offices and our own fax and coffee
machines. I'll take you around in a minute. But Feeble is just
one of our many corporate enterprises. It's useful as a cover,
too."

"You mean a front for Tripoli?" Everything was turning upside down and inside out.

"Exactly. Now, if you're ready, it's time for our appointment
with Sheik Yasif. He came in yesterday from Libya."

Sheik Yasif was waiting for them in the boardroom, impecc-
ably dressed and heavily drenched in Aramis after-shave.

The sheik held out his hand. "Good morning and welcome,
Miss Papier," he greeted her briskly. "A pleasure to meet you
at last." His face was deeply furrowed, like a newly plowed field,
and his teeth glinted with gold.

"Sheik Yasif is a cousin of our illustrious Colonel Qaddafi,"
announced Rudi. "We are deeply honored that His Highness
has condescended to meet with us today."

"I understand, Miss Papier, that you are anxious to assist our
organization," continued the sheik.

Fear gripped Delphine. Ashen-faced, she stuttered, "You
know who I am, then?"

"Certainly. You are Papier's Daughter. That is why we are
interested in speaking with you. We would like you to inter-
mediate on our behalf with your father."

"My father!" That was it. The nightmare scenario. Emil's
paranoia had not been groundless after all. They wanted ran-
som money.

"We have a business proposition we believe might interest
him." The sheik must have spotted the terror in her face, because he changed his tone abruptly, with a trace of irony. "We
are businessmen, too, you know. We have our own requirements, such as the procurement of certain, er, military equipment."

Chemical weapons, that was it. They wanted weapons for biological warfare.

"My father is a currency trader. He can't help you." Her throat felt like sandpaper.

"We have a lot of currency. We have billions of oil revenues that we would like to turn into marks and dollars. Quietly, without attracting attention from the demonic Western governments. Now, Mademoiselle Papier, if you are sincerely interested in aiding our cause, we would like you to propose to your father that he act as our financial agent in our banking requirements."

Delphine's entire world was unraveling before her. "What about your environmental activities? Dismantling the U.S. air bases?" She tried to steady her voice.

"We are aligned with many causes of conscience and endeavor in every respect to counteract the iniquities brought about by filthy Western capitalism, and in particular the satanic United States. We have many arms and legs. Terrorism, like everything else, is big business."

The sheik was unwrapping a cigar.

"Look, I'm really sorry." She flushed. Her courage was dribbling back. "I'd like to help you myself, licking envelopes or writing Marxist copy or whatever would be useful. But my father wouldn't be interested. For one thing, he's shamefully pro-American."

"May Allah, in His wisdom, help him to see the error of his ways."

Rudi spoke up. "Let her go, Your Highness. She has taken enough today of your valuable time."

The sheik nodded in a friendly way and brought his fingertips together in a gesture of farewell. He did not seem angered by her refusal. "May the peace of Allah be with you," he offered politely. "And may your offspring be multiple."

Delphine bowed her head. "Thank you, Your Highness."

One of the secretaries escorted Papier's Daughter down the fluorescent-lit corridors, where the telex and fax machines ticked and throbbed, to the elevator. Outside, the sun shone weakly. Her pulse raced as she left behind forever the headquarters of Compagnie Financière de Tripoli, S.A., where it was business as usual.

When she returned to Heidelberg University, she threw herself frenetically into her thesis. She labored over microfiche of foreign periodicals, studying the $350 million voted by Congress to the Contras, the $1.6 billion to Honduras, and unspecified amounts of Irangate back-door funding.

Rudi sent her a short, cordial note, typed on Friends of the Feeble letterhead, with a post office box address. He wrote that he was sorry her departure from Geneva had been so abrupt. He hoped she would not resent his oblique approach to her father and pointed out that she had consistently deceived him as to her haute bourgeoisie origins, even by fabricating a village station master brother, when she was an only child. He reiterated that Tripoli and Feeble channels would remain open for negotiation with Emil if she should reconsider her stand.

Delphine tore the stationery into a hundred tiny pieces and flushed it away.

She tried to block out the sorry incident. She hated herself worse than ever, then remembered that she really did not know what that "self" was except a confused jumble of other people's expectations. She took long solitary walks and asked herself over and over, How can I have been born so rich and pretty and privileged, and yet carry this miserable worm around inside me that blights whatever I do? On the surface she behaved normally except that she nowadays went out of her way to avoid attractive young men or, if forced into proximity with them, as with Nick Jones, became extraordinarily rude and churlish.

7

EXTRA HOT AND SPICY

That's one order of pla-pa-muok, one tom yom koong, a ped krob, not too spicy, and a gang ka-gop." Kitty bowed her head over the order pad. Why, for God's sake, couldn't they order in English (the menu provided translations) instead of this Alice in Wonderland Thaispeak?

The girl with the half-shaved head interrupted. "Wait a sec, what's gang ka-gop?"

Kitty smiled ingratiatingly, which she knew she did badly. These people did not look like decent tippers anyhow. "Frogs' legs sautéed in coconut milk. How would you like that? Hot and spicy?"

"Frogs' legs!" The girl, who reminded Kitty of some rain forest insect, looked appalled. "That's disgusting."

"She'll have the mu gra-tiem prik-Thai," dictated her companion. He was a beefy type, with spiked leather accessories and dangling earrings.

"Pork with garlic," Kitty clarified. She hated it when they sent the dishes back capriciously. Fair enough when that group found the duck's head that had made its way into the ped toon soup, but it was annoying when the customers simply had not read the menu properly.

Kitty tried to move gracefully in her sarong as she took the order back to the kitchen. She did not want to lose this job. The Siamese Twin, frequented by the parade of East Village exotica, was within walking distance from home, and the tips were fairly decent. Her customers weaved out into the night with beatific smiles on their faces. Many of them were normally high on something or other. Then one night Kitty had tasted some shrimp tamarind, from a bowl not intended for the staff. Within moments a light-headed euphoria swept her, as if she had been freed from gravity. The chef was sneaking grains of opiate into his giant woks.

The tranquil atmosphere made a refreshing change after her previous jobs at the steakhouse and the lesbian bistro. At the Siamese Twin the arpeggios of gamelans—Javanese xylophones—tinkled softly, and Buddhas smirked between the lotus screens. The guests were invited to take their shoes off at the door. They lounged sideways at the low tables on padded cushions, propped up on an elbow. There were no Western tables and chairs.

She readjusted the sarong to reveal the correct expanse of bare midriff. She was always nervous it might fall off altogether. The Oriental girls seemed to be born with a knack of keeping the material wound snugly. Kitty knew she would never master the mysterious skill of draping. It was not in her blood. She had been reared in Teaneck, New Jersey, and had majored at college in poststructuralist feminist cinema. She had written her senior-year term paper on phallocentricity, the study of civilization's signifiers to describe woman-as-castration-fetish in a male-dominated society.

Kitty sent out a string of résumés to the avant-garde cinema journals and took a job at a vegetarian cafeteria while she waited for something to germinate. Serious cinema jobs were not easy to find. Between various waitress stints she signed up for unemployment.

It took several weeks to establish a claim. Kitty did not really mind spending all morning in the hushed line. She was required to return every Wednesday, sometimes for three hours or more, and dribble along with the crumpled souls, inch by inch, between the snaking ropes. The clerks at the row of desks up front plodded dully, bringing procedures to a frequent standstill each time they came up against one of the many claimants who spoke no English at all.

On her third Wednesday, Luke Elliot, her future husband, was inching right ahead of her in line. She noticed curiously the way his light brown hair was brushed straight up, like a hedgehog's. It gave him an almost European, and definitely cultural, look. Her stare traveled down his back. She saw the paint-splattered jeans and the book he was reading with such pure attention.

Kitty drew in her breath. His book was entitled *Implosion of Meaning in the Meaning,* a heavyweight treatise by Jean Baudrillard, one of her favorite French philosophers.

As she realized that this paint-splotched unemployed young man was clearly a thinker too, a strange thing happened. Unconsciously she put her hand up to her runaway hair and wished 1) that he would look up from his Baudrillard book and 2) that she herself were more attractive.

For Kitty had the kind of fierce looks that some people found interesting, and occasionally riveting, and other people considered downright ugly. She was bony and dusky-skinned, with big eyes and untamable black hair that she scraped back with a barrette into a bushy ponytail.

The line sprinted ahead. Out of her grimy carry-all New York Film Festival totebag, Kitty whipped the copy of Lacan's *Feminine Sexuality,* which she had been carrying around for months.

She tried to zero in on the phallus as central signifier and the subversion of woman to the masculine standard. Meanwhile a row had broken out at the front of the line. A woman who spoke an unintelligible language had gotten into a dispute with the clerk over her entitlements. The woman burst into a hysterical barrage of gobbledygook. The commotion caused Luke to raise his head from the text. Kitty looked straight into his eyes. They were topaz-colored, with a dancing gleam.

With an impatient flick of his Timex watch he remarked to Kitty, "Goddamned morons they employ here. Are they going to keep us waiting all day? Some people have lives to lead."

She nodded sympathetically.

"You signed on before?" he asked her.

She replied she had not and asked him what kind of work he had been doing. He explained, with a gesture toward his paint-spotted pants, that, yes indeed, he was an artist; during the past year, however, he had worked as a janitor emptying wastepaper baskets. In combination, the two activities struck her as wildly glamorous.

He stepped closer and provocatively removed her thumb from the title of her book to see what she was reading. His own fingernails were rimmed with charcoal.

"Hmm," he said. "Lacan was instrumental in developing today's theories of scopophilia."

"Of what?" For an instant she wondered if he might be referring to some crude sexual deviancy.

"Scopophilia, as Freud called it, the voyeuristic pleasure of looking. Postmodern artists today are trying to deconstruct our preconception of woman as physical object."

She noticed how his eyes lit up from within and wondered what he would be like in bed.

They met in line each Wednesday after that. They filtered along to sign their official claims with the stubby pencils provided by the Department of Social Security. Afterward they would go together to the nearby coffee shop and exchange life stories. The first time, Luke made a big issue about picking up their tab for $3.45. Thereafter, she noticed, he always let her pay.

She learned that he came from a wealthy Virginia family, who had left him several hundred thousand dollars in trust. The nest egg enabled Luke to devote his twenties to painting, while he squandered his entire capital on expensive rented lofts in SoHo and lobster lunches ordered in whenever he felt like it. At the age of thirty-four he was compelled to take stock of his eroded fortune and figure out a way to earn a living. The janitor job was the first attempt. All evening he would vacuum the corporate offices and boardrooms, empty ashtrays, and soap the bathroom floors. He continued to paint mornings. So far he had sold nothing, but Kitty was mesmerized by his blind confidence in his own talent.

He was fired from the janitor job when they caught him reading a book by the philosopher Foucault instead of sudsing the floor of the john. He confessed that he suspected from the beginning his work days would be numbered. Once they had found him napping on the sofa of the director of human resources; another time they had caught him filching Scotch tape from the supplies cupboard.

Kitty looked forward all week to the coffee shop discussions on Wednesdays.

Luke explained to her that he was living at the moment in the studio of his friend Dan Helena, who happened to be in Alaska. Dan traveled all over the world, Luke described with a touch of envy, to South America and India and Santa Fe or on trips up and down the Northeast in his flatbed pickup truck, scavenging or purchasing steel. In his absence he was glad to have Luke there as dog sitter for his Great Dane, Judd.

They went on going out for coffee and Danish, while Luke devoured her greedily with his eyes (what was it he had called that—scopophilia?). One afternoon he invited her to join him for a real drink at Valhalla, his own hangout on East Houston Street. Kitty fumbled in her totebag to make sure she had enough cash to buy them a few rounds.

Valhalla turned out to be a mecca for the local painters, whose own violent work adorned the walls. There were three-dimensional sculptures cut out from grocery boxes, mixed-media canvases incorporating amputated baby dolls, erotic photography describing sadomasochistic acts, and lots of kindergarten-style finger painting. The bar itself was the last place left in Manhattan where everyone still smoked cigarettes. The lock on the ladies' room door was broken, several flies buzzed perpetually around the toilet, and every inch of wall space, even the toilet seat, was inscribed with graffiti.

Luke put Billie Holliday on the jukebox and ordered a vodka on the rocks. It was 2:24 P.M.

Kitty glanced along the length of the bar. On her left two

girls dressed in long baggy skirts and brogues were discussing the neighborhood.

"That gas explosion last week, that was no accident, that was landlord sabotage."

"Fernandez bombed his own tenement?"

On her right two men were drinking Rolling Rock and hotly debating the sanctification of the Artist.

"I don't call myself an artist," said one. "I call myself a 'visual scientist.' The genius of Duchamp lay in showing that the act itself of painting was no longer necessary. When he found what he called 'readymade' objects, like the famous urinal, and called them art, he was showing that it was enough just to point at something. You needed only the eye, not the hand, to do the job."

His friend looked like an ancient Norse hero, with flaxen tendrils of hair crowning his massive shoulders. "Bullshit. Cézanne, Picasso, Pollock, the big three, they all believed that the artist should be a magician." He pounded the bar with his Rolling Rock bottle.

Luke lit a joint and passed it to Kitty. She had started smoking again since she met him. "Having fun?" he asked.

"We were mugged on the corner of Houston," said the girl on the left. "It was bad this time. Three guys with knives."

"How much did they get?"

"Fifty bucks. A week's grocery money."

"It's worse on the corner of First and Ninth. The whole block's swarming with crack dealers."

A tall woman appeared in the doorway, pushing a shopping cart with a couple of canvases strapped on it. She had short straight black hair, cut like a pudding bowl, and two black front teeth, which gave her a macabre smile.

She kissed Luke on the mouth. "Hey, Luke," she said. "What's up? You haven't been 'round."

"I've been broke again. The usual story. I can't even afford to drink. Meet my friend Kitty."

Kitty shook the gigantic hand of the Amazon, whom Luke introduced as a major activist of the seventies.

The girl waved off the homage. "That's all through. So I was one of the original organizers for the Anti-Imperialist Cultural Coalition. And where's it all now? A decade of Reaganomics and who cares anymore about minorities and Central America?"

"You're still involved with Eco-art," said Luke. His tone carried respect.

"I participate in the Sisters of Sodom, it's true. But what's that? We run a small press, a storefront on Delancey Street, and we're putting together a co-op gallery. We've done some mural painting in the South Bronx, using paroled grade A felony teenagers. But it's not like it was."

"What's Eco-art?" Kitty asked.

"You read the papers? You hear the news? You heard of the greenhouse effect and global warming going on all over this planet? I'm out of here. On my way to Fort Apache. See you 'round." She gave Kitty an icy stare. "Nice meeting you, too."

As she wheeled her shopping cart away, Luke slid his hand around Kitty's knee. "I'm sorry she was rude to you. Maybe she's a little jealous. We were seeing each other for a while once. Some time ago."

"You used to go out with her?"

"She was a major name in the seventies. When the activist thing was still big." He pulled Kitty closer.

The girls alongside were still talking neighborhood politics.

"It's like, where do you go now, to get away from yuppies? They've invaded Alphabet City, they're swarming over Tribeca and the Lower East Side, it's worse than the cockroaches."

"Outer boroughs. Long Island City, Brooklyn. Set up an artists' colony in Staten Island, maybe."

Kitty felt Luke's mouth on hers as he squeezed his body up against her. Had he no inhibitions, in the middle of the afternoon in this greasy joint where he knew everyone intimately and had probably had affairs (or whatever these people called their entanglements) with most of the women?

But all artists were narcissistic, right? You had to be, to do the job. And what was wrong with spontaneity? How was she going to get anywhere in the circles of downtown bohemia encumbered with the bourgeois scruples of Teaneck, New Jersey? Anyhow, she liked feeling him pressed against her. His whole body felt vitally warm, as if his temperature were racing. He ran a hand across her backside and down her inside thigh and ordered another vodka.

The Wagnerian Hero was complaining about the abuses of his dealer.

"You know what Peter Dante has the nerve to tell me? That he's blocked in his own painting. Here's this dealer, raking in money, works three days a week, spends the other four in his house in Woodstock, owns a couple of horses, Jesus, and I'm trying to figure out how to pay my heating bill. Peter Dante, he has the gall to talk to me about how he likes to paint as an amateur. I don't want to hear this guy's problems, you know?"

"They're all like that," said the Visual Scientist. "They try and get palsy with us. They're shit scared we'll take our friends to the gallery next door."

"All I ask is a little respect, okay? I mean, another ten grand to get me through the season would not go unappreciated, but you know Dante, he'll never advance anything."

"So who advances these days? They used to once, but now you're lucky if they pay your forty percent commission before you die of hypothermia. I tried to trade a painting the other day, in return for my dentist bill. My dealer hears about it, and next thing he's on the phone demanding his sixty percent cash."

Luke explained softly to Kitty, "The dealer gets his commission, somewhere between forty and sixty, on every single thing his artist sells, whether it's the dealer's own sale or not."

"Is that fair?"

"It's fucking outrageous, but the galleries claim they spend a lot of time and money all year long promoting their artists, so they're entitled to all and any follow-through."

"Artists are pawns in this city." The Visual Scientist picked up the thread. "There are a hundred thousand of them living in New York, you realize that? And maybe a couple of thousand of those support themselves from their art. The dealers ride right over us."

The Hero held up his Wagnerian hand for attention. "That is, until the artist gets famous. Then he can call the shots. Then it's his turn in the sun. He sells his stuff for a hundred grand or two, he gets any dealer he wants."

The Visual Scientist nodded gravely. "Like a rock star."

"Just like a rock star."

If Luke ever got that famous, Kitty wondered impulsively, would he still be interested in someone like me?

Luke drained his vodka. "Come back with me today to Brooklyn."

Luke and Kitty took the F train across the river to Plymouth Street.

"My friend Dan's crazy about this place," said Luke. "It's quieter than Manhattan, better for working. They call it Dumbo—Down under Manhattan Bridge Overpass."

Kitty looked around Dan's studio, up to where the motes of dust hung in the timeless air. "What's he like, your friend?"

"Dan left home when he was fifteen. He roamed around the country doing casual labor, ranching cattle, racing motorcycles. He got some training as an auto mechanic and worked a while at a filling station in the middle of the Arizona desert."

Then she saw Dan's unfinished sculpture. She stood rooted and petrified, wishing she could run away. Was it the sheer size of the thing, a twelve-foot monster of steel, that panicked her, or the unholy aura created by the dust and light?

"I'll show you some of my own stuff," said Luke.

He turned to a stack of canvases piled against one wall near an open plastic drop sheet. She stood back while he lifted the first painting by its stretcher.

After the rush of adrenaline produced by Dan Helena's creature, Kitty was not ready to look at anything else. She blinked and refocused.

Luke's signature stripes partitioned the picture into a sickening clash of mustard and beet purple, executed in clean strips of color. She wished she knew more about art theory. Luke's was difficult work, no question; some people would call it austere. The longer she looked, the more ignorant and uneducated she felt.

"You like this?"

He held up another, in stripes of puce and shocking pink, like a cheap picnic blanket. "This painting is titled *Won't*. The most important thing you have to understand is that a painting is a two-dimensional object. The best paintings are those that reduce line and color to their simplest expression."

She nodded weakly.

"The reason you find my colors repellent is that I have annihilated every reference of prettiness. Let's go to bed."

They spent all evening and then all night on the futon. They made love six, seven, eight times, until they were both sore, and found they still did not want to stop and that the raw bruises added a new round of sweetness. Finally Luke got up before midnight to go out for more cigarettes and walk the Great Dane. Kitty gave him her last five dollars to bring them back some pizza.

Dan's sculpture would not let her sleep. While she waited for Luke to return, she sat crouched and huddled on the edge of the futon. She had seen movies of Egypt, those god-size limestone pharaohs and sphinxes that guarded the religious secrets of Karnak. She could not imagine what kind of man would produce such a creature.

Weeks later, when Luke proudly introduced them, Kitty disliked Dan Helena on first sight. His macho stare gave her a weak, dizzy feeling. She hated his defiantly half-shaved stubble. She had always been faithful to Luke, since that first night on Plymouth Street; yet she had an instinct that if Dan chose to, he could atomize her fidelity in a second, use her body, and throw her out when he was through, and that he would do it with faint amusement, not caring a bit.

Recently he had come into the Siamese Twin, on his own. "Hey, Kitty, I thought I'd finally check your joint out. So what do you recommend?"

She smoothed the sarong over her hips. "How about the shrimp in red curry and coconut."

"Make it extra hot and spicy."

When she served him she had to kneel down to arrange the dishes on the hot plates on the low table. She looked up, and Dan was laughing at her.

"That's how I like my women," he said. "Obedient."

She bit her lip and did not answer.

Two days before Dan returned from Alaska, they had discovered the walk-up off Avenue C. The six months' cash flow of unemployment income was nearing its end, and neither Kitty nor Luke had any job prospects. Luke heard in Valhalla (Kitty suspected the tip came from his bony activist ex-girlfriend) that there were still some city-owned squats empty on Avenue C, dilapidated tenements whose occupiers had died or drifted away. If you could stand a few months without electricity or hot water, you could live rent free; it was July, so why not try? Moreover, if you were prepared to take some trouble and renovate, a few years along you could even buy your apartment back legally from the city at a fraction of its restored value.

They went to look immediately. Alphabet City was still a wasteland at that time, a bombed-out devastation of crumbling facades. The population lived the airless summer months on the stoops or huddled in menacing groups and glared at the intruders.

The streets were awash with garbage. Kitty waded ankle deep through fast-food wrappers and old newspapers in Spanish, English, Cyrillic, and Korean. As she and Luke hurried past the crack houses and boarded-up delicatessens, Kitty heard a violent shattering of glass behind her. Luke tugged at her arm. She turned her head. A group of kids, ten or eleven years old, were laughing. One of them held up another bottle menacingly, ready to throw.

It was frightening sometimes, living as trespassers on the grace of the barrio, but the moment Kitty saw the two-room "apartment," in the rotting building next to the Funeraria Santa Maria, she determined to test her courage.

The abandoned building preserved a scarred, stubborn beauty. Molded cornices and columns framed the windows. A fire escape of exquisite wrought iron clung to the flaking wall. The front door hinges were broken and the surface smeared with graffiti: "I hate it all," "Dirty Kikes," "Jesu salva," "Kill the yuppies," and "class warfare."

Luke examined the large room, streaming with light through the gouged-out windows. One pane of glass was still left, a sort of symbol of endurance. "I could use this room as my studio," he announced. "I must have privacy to paint."

They slaved all summer long to fix up their new home and make it marginally habitable for winter. Although Kitty would come back from her job exhausted, to start scrubbing and painting and hammering, those were the happiest days of her life.

She loved working on the apartment more than anything she had ever done. She planted a window box with petunias and trailed festoons of ivy down the walls and across the fire escape. Luke did his best to coopt various artist friends into helping with the electrical wiring and plastering. He painted the baroque fire escape in aqua. He even managed to trade a painting (an unprecedented event) in return for some professional plumbing. They were living on nothing, as usual, but her tiny wages and the doggie bags she used to sneak home. Her family in Teaneck would have been horrified to see her, surviving on cornflakes and skimping on laundry detergent. She combed Orchard Street for scraps of linoleum and oddments of furniture. She actually enjoyed hoarding from her wages of nothing to buy glass windowpanes and a gleaming, new, unstained Belle John sink. They attached a hose and spray nozzle to a cold faucet and euphemistically named it a shower. Luke built a set of bookshelves, even though they had far too few secondhand books to fill them. But the freshly painted walls blazed with color. They hung his unframed stripes on every surface.

Opposite their apartment, some neighbors had turned a vacant lot into a wild and overgrown garden. Stolen street signs clustered between flower beds planted with faded roses and tomatoes. A huge sculpture towered in the middle, adorned with East Village junk: tires, empty food cans, crushed bicycles caked in paint drips, and a big toy gorilla on top.

August was sticky. Their secondhand fan seemed to produce more noise than breeze, but every night, as Kitty's exhausted legs gave out under her, she fell asleep contented. Luke was never too tired for sex. Unlike Kitty, he slept late each morning. After hosing off the evening's sweat with the spray nozzle, Kitty would crumple down on the lumpier side of the lumpy mattress. She was so wiped out that she could have slept on rocks and never noticed. Luke would reach out for her, like a young puppy, quivering with libido, covering all her skin with eager kisses. He was a sperm factory, able to go on for hours. In the hottest nights of summer his body throbbed like a furnace. Despite the burning weight, and the lumps sticking into her back, Kitty fell asleep while he was still inside her.

She found another job, with better money, at a Ukrainian

dive on St. Marks. By then she had given up looking for work in cinema. Those film jobs were so few and far between, and you probably had to sleep with someone to get them. She could not imagine being unfaithful to Luke. Once, in Valhalla, the Visual Scientist (she knew him now; his name was Irwin and he came from Kansas City) had drunkenly confessed to a secret infatuation. While Luke was squandering quarters on the pinball machine, the Scientist revealed that his erotic fantasies of Kitty had inspired his recent collage, displayed prominently over the bar. Kitty looked up. The work consisted of a bra and slashed panties pasted over a stick rendering of a woman.

Kitty brushed aside his proposition.

"You'll be sorry," said the Scientist. "Luke Elliot's a grade A prick. He thinks being an artist's an excuse for fucking over his girlfriends. You know what they all call you here, behind your back? Saint Kitty. You're better than that. What's more important, his work's crap. He'll never get a dealer if he sticks with those boring, Neo-geo stripes."

Kitty defended him staunchly. "Luke believes in the denial of all referential signifiers," she responded haughtily. "Naturally, it's difficult art."

Luke was still making efforts to launch his career, hawking the slides of his stripes all over downtown. It was a depressing campaign. Most of the dealers, he groaned to Kitty, did not even bother to look at them. Storming the commercial art world without an entrée was like battering on an armored tank. Kitty nursed a pang of pity when his topaz eyes clouded over with despair. She did not dare scold if he purloined from the peanut-butter jar where she stored her hard-earned tips.

At the end of the summer, a ray of false hope struck. The Wagnerian Hero agreed to get his dealer, Peter Dante, to take a serious look at Luke's slides.

"Well?" Luke asked eagerly. He had just bought the Hero a Rolling Rock.

"Yeah, well . . . Dante likes them. Maybe he'll come by your place soon and pay a studio visit."

Luke was optimistic. He was ready for a break. It would only take a dealer like Dante who understood the importance of nonreferential ugliness.

Luke bought himself another vodka and turned around to Kitty, his topaz eyes dancing.

"Let's get married," he said.

"Okay," she agreed.

So they did, in a judge's chambers. The license cost twenty dollars, and Dan Helena was a witness. Nothing changed. Dante never paid the studio visit.

Luke kept bugging Dan Helena to get him some attention from the prestigious Giulietta Giuliani, he kept dipping into the rainy-day peanut-butter jar and assuring his friends at Valhalla it would not be long now before he struck due recognition. Kitty went on paying his bar bills and trying to admire his latest mayonnaise and neon violet stripes. He was producing plenty of work, painting through stacks of canvas (although with canvas at ten dollars a yard, she wished he were less prolific), while she hurried from kitchen to customer with steaming plates.

She was kneeling now, in front of the girl with the shaved head, scooping up the half-eaten dishes. She felt the edge of the sarong soak up a pool of the garlic sauce.

"Kitty! Psst!" It was one of the other waitresses. "Is that your table, number four, leaving?"

"Yeah. So?"

They were a couple of very stylishly dressed men, who had eaten their fried broccoli noodles without complaint and tipped handsomely. Now some kind of a rumpus was going on.

"What's the matter?"

The blond one was hopping up and down excitedly at the gilded door. "I can't believe it. How could you let this happen? Someone's taken my shoes."

"Oh, my God."

"Nine hundred dollars those cost me, from Susan Bennis Warren Edwards."

"Are you sure they're gone?"

"Let me tell you, this restaurant is going to pay up or else."

"Nothing like this has ever happened before."

"Or else I sue. My friend here's a lawyer."

Kitty was down on her knees and stomach now, scrambling among the cowboy boots and thong sandals and Reeboks.

"It's ridiculous," bleated his lawyer companion. "Who ever heard of a restaurant where you take your shoes off? Think of the diseases you could pick up."

Kitty held up a pair of green jodhpur boots. "Could these be them?"

The man wrinkled his lip in disgust. "You think I'd wear something like that?"

"Hold it!" interrupted his friend. "What's that bronze bowl there?"

"That's an antique begging bowl," Kitty said. "From Tibet, sixteenth century."

The other man pounced. "Well, whatever it is, I don't know how my shoes got into it." He fished out a pair of iguana-skin loafers.

Kitty sighed. The evening was still young, and hours were left to go before she could pack up the remains of the gai masaman to bring home for Luke.

Her husband was also getting tired of eating cold Thai food night after night. She sometimes hauled the leaking paper bags up the splintering stairs to their fourth-floor apartment, only to find he had slunk out already to Valhalla or the Sidewalk Cafe, taking the telephone bill money with him. Kitty would wistfully wedge the gai masaman into the corner of their small, empty refrigerator, behind the ketchup and the mustard bottles.

8

SCAVENGERS

*J*im McHenry stared out of the window at his "view" of the building opposite. Even when he leaned back in his padded chair he could not see a glint of sky. He had to meander down the hall to one of the other partners' offices to learn what kind of weather was going on outside.

The middle-aged executive who worked across from him in the adjacent skyscraper used to pace up and down while he talked on the telephone. When he thought no one was looking (he did not realize that McHenry commanded a direct line of vision) he would take off his jacket, get down on the rug, and do his air force exercises. One afternoon McHenry had seen him come back jauntily from a late lunch, with a woman in a tight dress. They drank coffee together out of polystyrene cups; the executive kissed her strenuously. She pretended to resist at first, but from where McHenry sat, he guessed she was shamming. She was hot for it, too. He saw his neighbor's tie fly across the room; then they pulled down the window shade, and that was that. The incident seemed paradigmatic of McHenry's entire life: a brief glimpse into the adventures of other people, then an abrupt door shut or window blind slammed down.

When had life begun to pass him by? He had never had a serious involvement with a woman, never been intimate enough with any of his odd dates that he could have broached the subject of marriage without making them burst out laughing. As he approached forty, he begrudgingly admitted he was becoming persnickety about his sterile apartment and more and more prissy about his dates: this one was too tall, that one mispronounced words like "chef d'oeuvre" and "sotto voce," another one was pretty but had bad posture. He had taken a pathologist from Cornell Medical Center to dinner last week. She had referred three times to a current Broadway production as the *Merchants of Venice.*

If only he could shoot a bolt of electricity through his overeducated brain. He craved an active involvement, just for once, in the drama, instead of his outsider's obsession with the affairs of his clients. He shuffled irritably through Papier's Limited Partnership Agreement, which lay in front of him on the blotter. Papier and his flamboyant southern mistress, for example. They invited him to dinner and then they looked right through him, as if there were nobody sitting on his chair.

Papier and Karakoff were growing increasingly excited about the fund. They had codenamed it PAP (Papier Art Partners), and decided to market the units at one million dollars apiece. Hearing the price, McHenry had paused for breath. "That's high."

Papier had dismissed such trepidation. "We only want the big boys. As soon as word gets out in the right circles, their friends will be beating down the doors to buy five, ten, twenty units for themselves."

It was true. They were capitalizing already at a frantic clip. Papier and Karakoff raced toward their goal of five hundred million in the kitty, as they located investors to be limited partners. The final agreements could not be signed until all the money had been found and the pie carved up, each investor's percentage of the enterprise established according to his number of one-million-dollar units.

Two weeks ago Papier announced they had passed the hundred-million-dollar mark. They had made up those hundred units among just thirty-two people. Some of the investors bought only a single unit apiece, others five or a dozen. One tycoon from Arkansas, who ran a trucking company, came up with twenty-three million dollars.

Jim McHenry had never known an entrepreneurial client to perform with such velocity. Papier explained matter-of-factly that the whole formula depended on the "snowball effect."

"There's a trick to this kind of business," he stated. "First, you choose a specialty area. Art's ideal. It's a small world of big-time collectors. A knows B knows C knows D. You tell A that B's just put in a lump, and C's about to, and soon you have A breaking down the doors to be there, too, with his friends. It doesn't even matter if B's lump is small. A will never ask you exact details. That would be an admission of ignorance on his part."

Papier made it sound easy, but how the blazes did he find B and C so fast?

During the past six weeks Papier had flown in three times from Switzerland, making a couple of coast-to-coast fund-raising tours, with stop-offs in Amarillo, Wichita, Sioux Falls, South Bend, Pittsburgh, and Tallahassee. Billionaires lived in the damnedest places. As for Karakoff, he was busy hopping between breakfast meetings, lunches, and evening galas at the Met, the Whitney, and the Museum of Modern Art. Gossip mushroomed of the newest investment vehicle on the block.

Yesterday they were up to two hundred and thirty million dollars, and Emil was expecting another fifty units to roll in any moment, courtesy of a Filipino mogul who owned large real estate holdings in the United States and needed to park some cash, no questions asked.

McHenry flipped through the clauses of their sixteenth, and hopefully final, draft of the agreement.

> The parties hereto wish to form a limited partnership pursuant to the laws of the State of Delaware of which the parties designated in Schedule 1 hereto will be the Limited Partners, Emil Papier will be the Managing General Partner, Jacob Karakoff will be a

General Partner, which parties together with two in-dependent expert directors will comprise the Advisory Board....

The purchase of Works of Art shall be within the sole and absolute discretion of the Managing General Partners with the consent and approval of the Advisory Board. The Partnership will limit its purchases to Twentieth Century Works of Art, and will invest solely in those Works of Art which are of the finest quality and in good condition. The expenses relating to the operation of the Partnership may include picture fra-mers, photographers, customs brokers, restoration and conservation, shipping, storage, vaults, packaging, travel, and office expenses. Such expenses shall be de-ducted pro-rata from each Limited Partners' Capital Account....

The switchboard buzzed through. "Call from Switzerland for you, sir."

McHenry reached for the receiver. Out of deference to Pa-pier's paranoia, he never, ever put him on the speaker box.

"Good evening, Jim. We got it."

"Pardon me?"

"He's in with us. Juan Gomez, fifty mil from Manila."

"Congratulations. That's splendid."

Papier sounded revved up and feverish tonight. "You keeping track of the arithmetic, Jim? What's that now? Two hundred and eighty million?"

"Indeed it is," McHenry answered weakly. "We've faxed you our latest draft of the agreement. First question: Who are the two members of the advisory board? We need to list them on schedule two."

"Ah. Giulietta Giuliani will be one. She's well known in the business. I believe you met her at my apartment recently. And the other is Sam Harrison, a close friend of Jacob's."

"Is he a dealer, too?"

"Sam? He couldn't tell the difference between a Landseer and a Lichtenstein. Sam owns most of eastern Wyoming."

McHenry cleared his throat nervously. "Er, in that case how do we justify him on the advisory board?"

"Sam has visibility when it comes to art money. He bids a lot at auctions. He doesn't know what he's doing, and he buys plenty of turkeys, but everyone sees him waving his paddle around. My dear fellow, haven't you read anything in the newspapers about the new Harrison wing of sixties Pop and Minimalism?"

McHenry shifted on his chair. He did not read the reviews or cultural sections of the newspapers.

"Don't worry about him," ordered Emil. "He'll do exactly what Jacob tells him. What's your other question?"

"In the partnership agreement we should address where you intend to warehouse the inventory."

"You mean where will we keep the art?"

"Yes. In your house, for instance, or in the Belle John offices?"

"Alas, no. Insurance premiums have rocketed these past years. To store it at home would be a frivolous expense. Besides, Jacob and I have so many pieces already, we hardly have extra wall space left."

McHenry suggested, "Would you consider museum loans?"

"Ditto, same insurance problem. And even if the museums covered the insurance costs, we don't want auditors regularly poking through our inventory. Maybe it's sad to deprive the public of art treasures, but that's the reality. Our works will be safely stored in reinforced concrete vaults with steel panels, four-way bolts, and electronic time switches. Fireproof and explosion proof."

"Like Fort Knox."

"*Voilà*. And by the way, keep next Thursday evening free. We've an appointment a week from today with a senior loan officer from North American Bankers' Corp. I need to be able to leverage with large sums."

"You want to leverage on top of half a billion dollars?"

"Wake up. Think big. If I can raise half a billion myself, I can borrow another billion on the strength of it, using the assets of the fund as collateral. We're taking the banker out to a swanky party at the Metropolitan Museum. The fireworks of the season. Poor little fellow, we're going to blow his mind."

"We?"

"I want you there, too. Put it in your diary."

"Very good, Mr. Papier." He could never quite bring himself

to call his client Emil. He looked out the window. The man opposite was no longer alone. There were two other men in that office now, sitting on the sofa and looking stony-faced. Some kind of serious meeting was taking place. McHenry had an intimation his neighbor's career was in jeopardy.

"Excuse me a moment. My other line's ringing and my secretary's gone home."

"Take the call," said Emil. "It's time for my dinner anyhow."

McHenry changed lines.

"This is Susannah Bishop."

"Susannah, what a surprise." He had no trouble using *her* first name. "I was just speaking to Monsieur Papier."

He sensed an instant's hesitation. "I hope I'm not interrupting."

"Absolutely not. What can I do for you?"

"Jim." She sounded weary. He had a sudden image of her rich cascade of hair. "Jim. If you've got some time tomorrow, I'd like to make an appointment to come into your office."

"Sure, sure. I'll squeeze in some time." What could she possibly want? She had never called him before, except to ask him to dinner on Papier's orders. Had she got a parking ticket, or was it some dispute with Bergdorf's or her furrier?

"It's about that old contract in your files Emil and I drew up all those years ago."

McHenry stiffened. "Does Emil know you're calling me?"

"No. . . . Does that matter?"

McHenry's blood froze. Like hell it mattered. If Papier ever discovered McHenry had been advising the mistress, it could be the end of his most important single client and a fortune in legal fees kissed away.

He stammered, "Um, I'm looking at my schedule for tomorrow, and I notice I'm out of the office all afternoon. . . . "

"Please, Jim. I'm in a pinch. Just a few questions is all. I'd be much obliged."

He thought again of her hair and her winged mouth. It was out of character for Jim McHenry to allow sentiment to prevail over common sense.

He glanced up, divided. Some kind of bitter argument was going on in his neighbor's office; the man looked boxed in and scared. Poor guy, thought McHenry. I'm sure he's about to be fired. It was crazy, but he knew he was going to miss him.

Susannah Bishop was still waiting for his answer. Bizarre, a woman like that, needing a waxwork like him, even for a short consultation. "All right," he agreed impulsively. "Tomorrow at four-thirty."

Nick Jones finished composing the description of Claes Oldenburg's sculpture of a wedge of blueberry pie. "Muslin soaked in plaster over wire frame, painted with enamel; 10 by 20 in. 25.5 by 51 cm; executed in 1961; estimate $125,000–150,000." It was six-fifteen, time to go downstairs and look for Georgia.

He passed through the halls, by the various departments: American folk art, Islamic, pre-Columbian, Judaica, paperweights, and glass. The crowded files and reference books lay jammed between typewriters and computers. The intimate workplace of an auction house, the organs and capillaries the public never saw, resembled the accounts offices of a department store. Of course it was a department store, Nick was beginning to realize. Once you penetrated beyond the theater of glossy lobbies on every floor, the long-legged stewardesses at reception, the sale rooms, and the neoclassical dining room (with its own adjacent kitchen where they prepared the poached salmon for their guests), the backstage area was nuts and bolts. Space was always short, inventory got jumbled, and no one cared how much mess was made. Secretaries taped daily memos onto Attic vases and glanced up at Second Empire clocks to see if it was time for lunch.

Everybody spoke well and read the right books, but cachet aside, this was retailing with a Harvard (or Bryn Mawr) accent. Most of the chiefs, particularly the English ones, came from impeccable lineages. And some of the Indians, like Georgia, contributed both their sweat and their blue blood.

He found her in her tiny office adjacent to the order bid room, filling out the looseleaf notebook with the day's harvest of pink order slips. She glanced up at the unexpected visit. All the clerks had gone home at last, and the telephones had finally stopped ringing.

"Am I interrupting?"

"Not at all. I'm almost done." She ventured hopefully, "You want to go out for a drink?"

He stood close to her, brushing her sleeve lightly. "That's a very pretty spring frock. You should always wear yellow."

She blushed all the way to the roots of her hair. "Why, thank you. Thank you for noticing. I made it myself." She scribbled faster than ever in her eagerness.

"You're quite a mine of hidden talents, aren't you? You do that beautiful needlepoint, you sing in the St. James's choir, you play the oboe, and you know more than anyone I've ever met about tapestries from the Low Countries."

"I like to keep busy." She flashed him a smile like a grinning skull. "I'm done now. Shall we go?" She slid open the bottom drawer of the Regency Carlton house desk, a genuine antique they had allowed her in her office. It functioned as receptacle for sacred auctioneer's books.

"I wish I could." Nick tried to look wistful. "I've promised to have a drink tonight with a boring old queen from the Guggenheim. I'd much rather be going out with you."

She looked mildly crestfallen. "Never mind. Another time." She bent down to pick up her bag, which was an old and battered Gucci, an almost identical version of those rip-offs they were selling this month on every New York street corner. Georgia's had seen better days, but it had been bought at a store. Trust old Georgia to carry nothing but the real thing.

She fished through it absentmindedly. The key she used to lock up the drawer was a sturdy modern one, with an octagon-shaped head. The desk drawer lock had evidently been refitted.

"Wait! Don't move!"

She blinked at him innocently.

"There's a lash on your cheek." He leaned close to her face, brushing the skin with a feathery touch. Her eyes were screwed tightly shut. She drew in a breath, and her body muscles tensed.

"I've nearly got it." He pressed closer, feeling the shudder of her compressed excitement. With one arm he reached behind her, frantically probing the cavern of the open Gucci bag for the key chain. With the other hand he cupped the nape of her neck, tilting her head back.

He fumbled around the contents of the bag, groping among cosmetics and pencils and a perfume aerosol. Ah. His fingers closed on the metal ring. There it was, his treasure, his baby.

"Georgia," he murmured in her ear. "Oh, Georgia, what are you doing to me?"

Her lips parted and she drew him closer.

With tremulous fingers he slipped open the key chain and withdrew the octagon key.

Her tongue explored the warm crevices of his mouth.

He pulled her away gently. "Not right now," he whispered. "We must behave like adults." As soon as he got rid of her, he would strike out for the nearest locksmith to cut his own copy. Over tomorrow's coffee he would slide the octagon original back in Georgia's Gucci purse.

She straightened up coyly. "Oh, Nick, what came over us?"

He glanced at his watch. "You're a temptress, Georgia. I'm already late for my appointment at the Guggenheim."

Susannah was late, as usual.

Felice Karakoff glanced around the Sign of the Dove, anxiously searching out a secluded corner where she could wait in peace. It was a genial spring evening, and the glass doors of the bar were flung wide open on the streets of Sixty-fifth and Third. Every table was already occupied.

As she approached, the barman nodded toward one of the remaining empty barstools.

"What'll it be, ma'am?"

Felice awkwardly hitched up her white linen skirt and climbed on the stool. She wore a simple Chanel dress and no jewelry but a single gold chain around her neck. She hated waiting alone in bars for Susannah, even though strangers rarely approached her. The men took one sneaking look at her upper-class face and were swiftly intimidated by its iciness.

The Sign of the Dove had been Felice's choice. The customers were successful businessmen in dark suits and sophisticated, well-dressed women of her own age. Susannah teased her gently about her taste for "stuffy" cocktail bars. "The airport lounge," she called it. "The kind of place I'd take Emil." Susannah herself was equally happy stepping into a pair of blue jeans and a (fourteen-hundred-dollar) sequin-studded denim jacket and striking out for that disgusting downtown dump, Valhalla, or Saigon, where no other women came, only men playing pool under red lights.

Felice once dutifully followed Susannah to Valhalla because she did not know how to refuse her. She had sat clutching her Campari and soda and avoiding the whirlpool of cigarette smoke. She wished she were invisible. She tried to hide out in the ladies' room for a few minutes. The buzzing flies and forest of graffiti sent her scurrying back to the bar. Yet all Susannah had to do was ask and she would have followed her to even more fetid and decadent holes than Valhalla.

Felice did not feel guilty about her unbridled passion for the other woman. She accepted it calmly, with the same resignation she accepted her failed marriage. She knew her own limitations and did not question her inadequacies. For example, after she and Jacob had been married for ten years, one day she realized—without fuss or regret—that she was frigid. Although she sometimes found men attractive, and even liked thinking about the more romantic aspects of lovemaking, when it came to the moment of sweat and pumping on the squeaky bed, the sooner that was over the better. She was not so crazy about the male anatomy, either. She considered it ludicrous how boyishly proud her husband was of his eight-inch erections (quite wasted on her, she reflected philosophically), and she could never learn to like the odor of those sticky juices that secreted with his excitement.

She never came. She could not help wondering what it might be like, whether the whole business was not just some kind of myth. Then, that peculiar evening last year with Susannah in Valhalla, she had found herself gazing at Susannah's fingers, heavy with gaudy rings, and she had suddenly wanted those fingers to storm her modesty, to touch her in the intimate places she cringed from touching herself.

Felice caught the barman's eye and blushed. Could he have any idea what she had been thinking about? Did it show, like a mark of Cain, that she was besotted with this illicit lust?

The bartender slid her a bowl of peanuts down the bar and smiled extrovertedly. Don't be sorry for me, prayed Felice.

Please don't try to start a conversation to keep me company. She slid out a paperback of Thomas Aquinas's *Summa Theologica,* translated.

Felice's church going perplexed them all. It made Jacob, who attended Bar Mitzvahs and observed Yom Kippur and Chanukah, downright uncomfortable. He never criticized her openly as she set off every Sunday for St. James's, yet she read in his eyes the reminder of the gulf between them. As for Susannah, at any mention of religion her animate face would darken and become almost frightening.

Felice pretended to read another page. St. Thomas Aquinas promises there is a divine purpose running like a thread through our lives.

Felice came from a disdainful *New York Social Register* family. She had deliberately gone out to shock them at the age of twenty-four by marrying a Russian Jew from the furniture trade. Her family, who had previously espoused safe, liberal causes, immediately turned up their noses. Her marriage became her crusade. Felice finally returned to Greenwich for a semiconciliatory weekend with her family. For the first time since the wedding, she took her horse on her favorite ride, through the beech wood and alongside the stream. The motorcycle leaped across the path, backfiring, from nowhere. The animal whinnied in terror and reared. Felice fell between its legs. The horse she loved, in its own panic, kicked her hard around the groin. For several weeks, while she lay in Greenwich Hospital, Jacob and her family were terrified she might die. She pulled through. Fragile in appearance, she came from fighting stock. She only lost a kidney. Years later the doctors finally decided it was the kick that had made her infertile.

She and Jacob occasionally considered adoption. One or the other always withdrew the enthusiasm at the crucial moment. Their marriage was too insecure. They were both guilty about their own relationship, which neither knew how to improve or abandon. They paid for their guilt by denying the child, the only thing they still both wanted.

"Are you mad with me? I'm sorry I'm late." Susannah quickly kissed her mouth when the bartender was turned away. She wore a black dress, slashed up one side, and stockings appliquéd

with a pattern of seed pearls. It was too late in the spring for
black. There could be no excuse but sheer exhibitionism for
her black hat with its daredevil red rose. Felice could feel all
those crowded tables of sedately dressed men and women staring at them.

"That's a pretty necklace. Can I take a peep?" Susannah
leaned over Felice's shoulder to unclasp the chain behind her
neck. The touch of fingertips on her skin made Felice draw in
a breath.

Left to herself, puritan Felice considered it a shameful waste
of money to squander several thousand dollars on a designer
dress or jacket. Since Jacob had been pitching such efforts into
the PAP Fund, he implored his wife to show some public dazzle.
He complained about her entertaining, too. Felice's Yankee notion of a dinner party consisted of a pot roast with peas, or
maybe lasagna.

"What, are you trying to embarrass me?" Jacob stormed as
he turned up the air-conditioning, which she turned off automatically, along with any other unnecessary electricity. "We're
aiming to raise a half a billion dollars here, and you serve Juan
Gomez spaghetti bolognese?"

"I'm sorry. I never thought—"

"Call Le Périgord. Call La Côte Basque. Call the Parker Mer-
idien. See if anyone'll deliver. Dammit, Felice. Susannah Bishop
may be a little loose in the morality department, but at least
when Emil needs it, she can put together a dinner for grown-
ups."

It was true that Susannah had no problem spending money.
She bought clothes and cars and rented out Mortimer's for an
evening party as if it were all nickels and dimes. Felice knew
she would never be able to splurge with such aplomb, just as
she would never in a thousand years have been able to come
out wearing that hat with its scarlet rose.

"So where's Jacob consorting tonight?"

"He's got a black tie dinner at the Auction House. Eleven
hundred bucks a plate, raising money for cystic fibrosis. There'll
be a lot of big collectors there."

"You didn't elect to go along?"

"I told him I had to stay with Ezekiel the Third. He barks when he's left alone." Felice pampered and spoiled her entire dynasty of Akitas. And she used their neuroses in rotation with her own migraine headaches as an excuse for staying home. "Actually, I think he'd rather go alone. I get in the way when he's signing up his investors." She sighed. "I'm so unhappy again. Maybe we should get a divorce."

Susannah took Felice's hand. Felice wore only the slimmest gold band as a wedding ring, restrained compared with Susannah's diamonds and sapphires, which dazzled from every finger except her fourth. "Have you all had a fight?"

Felice shook her head. "We don't fight, ever. I'm too bottled up inside. I don't even know how to express my anger. I'm trapped with him. But if we did split up, I don't know what I'd do, or where I'd go."

Susannah stroked the slender forearm. "Is there someone else?"

Felice shook her head vigorously. "No, no one."

"If you want my opinion, maybe it would be better if there was, while Jacob's busy attending to *his* business."

"I can't. I'm not like you. I mean, I wish I were more like you." Although Felice smiled weakly, there was an unbridled adoration in the smile. They made an unlikely pair.

Susannah suggested, "Do you hanker for a career? You're blessed with the smarts to do it."

"What could I do? I've had no experience."

"Could you make do with museum work? Jacob or Emil could get you something in two shakes. Lord knows they've donated pieces to all the major institutions in New York. Or publishing? I venture to say, if worse came to worst, Jacob could buy you a company."

"It wouldn't help. And I'm sick of taking courses. At Hunter, at the Y, at the New School: Norwegian literature, Gestalt theory, calligraphy, cheesecake making. I think I want to be by myself for a while. Suze, can I tell you something?"

"Yes, ma'am."

"Jacob and I, we haven't . . . made love . . . for years."

Susannah dabbed at her lipstick. "You miss it?"

"No. No, I don't. A couple of weeks ago he moved into another room. It's better. Before, he was sweaty and restless, and he snored."

"Don't do anything rash." She gently moved a few strands of the blond hair out of Felice's eyes. Her hand lingered a moment on the temples and traced a line down the jaw, toward the throat. The delicate pulse beat quickened. Her hand grazed the milky skin of the neckline. Felice, not moving, breathed deeply and let the air escape with a sigh.

"Maybe we should go away for a weekend, you and me," Susannah suggested.

"Would you do that with me? Really?"

"Sure." Susannah turned away, her attention diverted. "Hey, see those guys next to the piano?"

Felice peered. A couple of middle-aged men were deep in conversation. "Don't stare at them," she begged.

It was too late. The bartender was already moving over with another round of drinks for the women. "Compliments of an admirer."

Felice pushed the Campari away. "No, thank you."

Susannah raised her vodka martini brazenly, with a nod to the men. "It's just a drink," she said.

Felice changed the subject. "How are things with Emil? Any better?"

Susannah shook her head. "Worse. There's some monkey mischief going on in Europe. I know it, plain as a pig on a sofa. He doesn't call me every single afternoon anymore. For nineteen years he's been calling till now, every day, every last one."

"It's all this PAP business. Jacob's gone batty over it, too."

"If only that was all. I'd feel a heap better." Susannah fished in her Fendi purse and drew out a pillbox studded with diamonds and sapphires. She opened the lid and extracted an aspirin.

"Pretty box."

"You like it? It belonged to Alexandra, the Romanov empress. Emil gave it to me for my thirtieth birthday. He taught me who the Romanovs were, too." She hesitated. "Oh, take it. It's yours."

"I couldn't possibly do that."

"It's no use clinging to the past." Susannah opened her hands in a fleeting gesture of despair. "Leastways not the trinkets.

There's an old Hank Cochran song about that. The girl gets to keep the letters and the records and his class ring. But she loses the guy."

"You haven't *lost* Emil."

"You can lose a person and go right ahead on living with them for twenty years. The relationship's shot, whether he phones or not. That's how I figure it. Emil's a difficult case, Lord knows. Fussy, egotistical, chilly. Sometimes he seems more a fish than a man. And he'll never rate more than a three and a half in the sack."

Felice harpooned a cube of ice with her cocktail stick. She did not want the discussion to drift in such a graphic direction. "Yet you still care," she murmured.

"Sure, I care. I'm Cinderella, remember? Time was, I succeeded in touching Emil's cold, fishy heart. He saw fit to talk to me. He really liked to talk with me, and that's the truth. He didn't mind that I was naive and ignorant. He kinda liked it that way."

Felice sniffed. "His control fixation."

"Doubtless it was. The point is, no one else ever talked to me that way, smooth as honey. Don't get me wrong. There are other things to do with men besides talk." Her gaze wandered across the room, and she half smiled to herself. Felice guessed she was thinking of the mysterious lover, the one whose name was never spoken. "And I don't just mean humping," Susannah added, and shook her head. "I'm crazy as a loon tonight. Why, Felice sugar, does it have to be so complicated?"

Although Felice did not enjoy seeing her so distraught, she relished the privilege of confidante. Susannah was wandering from Emil's orbit to spill her emotional guts with Felice, if only temporarily. She patted Susannah's wrist. "You're conflicted." Her own shrinks had been telling her that for aeons.

Susannah took a dim view of Felice's "psychobabble." She called it another form of religion. She changed her tone brusquely. "I managed to get an appointment to see the lawyer tomorrow. I gotta find out what all's in that contract."

"Don't worry, please don't worry. You know, if you ever need help, or somewhere to live . . . "

"You're a treasure." Susannah slid from her barstool and

reached in her purse for a credit card. As she scribbled the signature, she flashed the men a good-bye glance.

"That's Papier's broad," said the president of United Upholstery. "They say she hooked him years ago, but now he's on the prowl for fresh meat."

"Great legs," said his Venezuelan friend. "I wouldn't mind a shot. Even secondhand."

"Better not mix it with business," advised the furniture king. "PAP's the hottest item on the street. They've pushed up the initial investment requirement. Won't take less than five units now."

"I was thinking of putting in five million," said the Venezuelan. "Art's safer than real estate nowadays."

"Did you hear how that Filipino Gomez came up with fifty?"

"Does Papier mind doing a little laundry? We used to keep the—er . . . profits—in Panama, but that's not secure any longer."

"Hey. Papier's a Swiss. He's discreet. The only reason they've kept this show onshore is that they've got a lot of legitimate U.S. money. The market's still booming here, and everyone wants to buy class."

The Venezuelan shook his head philosophically. "The Swiss has got together an odd circus," he reflected. "Pension funds, airline owners, chain store moguls, corporate chiefs, and third world racketeers." The drug lord reached for the check. "The drinks are on the company."

Dan Helena leaned over his chalk outlines and directed the hissing oxyacetylene blow torch to bite deep into the metal. The fountain of sparks gushed red through the window of his visor. Then he hacked off the slag with the peen hammer. The clang of striking steel would have been enough to drive any other man mad.

Dan's workshop on Plymouth Street was like a small airplane hangar, about three stories high. It housed an impressive array of tools and instruments for shaping steel: gristly-toothed saws and welding electrodes and the blow torches. An array of hoists and pulleys dangled from the ceiling beams like hangman's nooses. By day the elongated windows grudgingly let in a veil of light. He worked until evening, using the shadows to penetrate the obscurities of the half-inch "black" steel planes. Finally he would turn on the two bulbs and continue by their dim glare.

In one small corner, the "living quarters" consisted of nothing but a futon mattress on a frame, a gas ring for cooking, a sink, and a small refrigerator. He sometimes heated himself a can of tamales in his single cooking pot. Otherwise he and Judd would live for days off the remnants of cold hamburgers he brought home in doggie bags from the coffee shops where he ordered food and then hung out, noticing and absorbing, long after midnight.

He stood up stiffly from the metal tracing and rubbed his lower back. He ought to go downstairs and untie the Great Dane. Judd's delicate eardrums could not tolerate the din of the hammer, so Dan used to let him roam on a long lead about the empty building site by the river.

He stepped back a few feet from the new piece. He had been battling all afternoon against the weight of the steel, using all the strength of his own body, as a mountaineer tackles a precipice. Dan Helena, when he worked, nurtured his body like an athlete. He was still almost as powerful at forty-one as those copper miners in Anaconda. In another ten years or so he might no longer have the brute strength to harness the steel by himself. Heavy-metal sculptors, with their toil and stresses, tended to burn out faster than other artists. His own hero, David Smith, had died tragically in a truck crash at fifty-nine, after living recklessly, working and drinking and racing cars, to let off pent-up steam.

The sheer joy of heavy-metal sculpture was its physicality, a total involvement of eye and mind and muscle. It took both strength and exacting skill. When Dan Helena created human ligaments or delicate folds of drapery, applying the precise degree of force in the press, he realized there was probably no one else in the country who understood the resistance of steel as intimately as he did, after twenty years of self-ordained apprenticeship.

Dan could well afford to employ several assistants, as many of the other famous sculptors did. He chose nevertheless to do most of the work himself. He demanded absolute solitude and detested the notion of sharing his studio, even for a few hours, with anyone. Moreover, he wanted to continue to cut and weld. The look and feel of the metal—an act as simple as hammering in a nail—prompted him to new discoveries.

He wished he could have completed the larger sculptures alone, too, instead of sending off his designs and Styrofoam mock-ups to the fabrication company in Connecticut. It was physically impossible, however, to assemble a thirty-foot piece, not to mention the engineering expertise required to be sure the tons of metal would not collapse under their own weight.

With a satisfied look at his evening's work, he stripped off his heavy gloves and goggles and left the building. At ground level, massive iron bolts sealed the doors of the neighboring ware-houses. The crack addicts would break in anywhere these days to steal welding equipment and sell it for a ridiculously tiny sum to a contractor on a building site. Some of the windows were blown out, leaving hulking holes. The streets were empty, except for a couple of swollen rats that scampered across a vacant space littered with tires and rubble.

When he reached the river, he squeezed deftly underneath a barrier of barbed wire. The dark water slapped ten feet below.

"Good boy, good dog, I'm back." Judd was tied to a rusty post, with ample leash to snuffle around the weeds and sandy dirt of the empty building site. Dan loved this barren spot and dreaded the fatal day some gentrified high-rise condominium was doomed to rise here, tyrannosauruslike. Wall Street was only one subway stop over the water, and its armies of labor craved lebensraum.

Judd slobbered all over him and raced in circles of excitement around his master.

"You hungry, boy? What's that you've got there?" Dan ex-tracted a splintering chicken bone from between the animal's teeth. "That's bad for you. You mustn't eat those. They get stuck in your throat." Dan hurled it away into the river. Recently he had found several such festering carcasses, one of them shud-dering with maggots. He knew where they came from.

At the other end of the vacant site a curious pattern of small rocks and pebbles was laid out across the asphalt in the formation of a star. Once he came across the gang of kids, practicing their crazy voodoo, which included the slaughter of chickens and some bizarre sexual rituals. He watched from a distance, hidden behind the building. He could see, by the illumination of the full moon, that the girl was naked. He felt a stirring of interest at the sight of her skinny hips and pubescent breasts. She could have been no older than fifteen. For a moment, seeing the jet of dark blood gush over her thighs, he wondered if she were being raped. He sprinted forward instinctively. He was un-afraid—perhaps ill-advisedly, he reflected later—even of malev-olent gangs. He always carried an illegal switchblade with him wherever he went in the city, and he knew exactly how to use it. Then he realized that the blood was in fact spurting from the neck of a chicken, which one of the boys was waving over her. Dan stepped back into the shadows. Everyone in this sleepless city, rampant with desires, had their own quirks. He had seen many peculiar sights and knew to live and let live.

The moon was waxing tonight, swelling like a pregnant woman, and Dan wondered whether in a few days the black magic crowd would be back again. He pulled Judd's sleek body down beside him. They sat quietly together for a few minutes, in Dan's favorite place, looking up at the moonlit outlines of Manhattan Bridge. An endless string of boats passed by at all hours, barges and tugs and speedboats and the evening cruisers, floating globes of tiny lights. By day you got a more impressive view of the belly of the structure. The immense steel slabs slashed the sheet of powder blue sky with a painterly precision. If you half closed your eyes, you would think the gray metal lay all on one plane in an impasto of air.

Judd nuzzled timidly at his leg.

"I know, boy. I know you're hungry. Let's go."

They returned home. The nightwatchman was hunching over a foul-smelling petroleum fire, where he had erected his shanty, with a corrugated roof and a couple of old sofas. He and Dan exchanged their usual jerky wave. Although they rarely spoke, Dan sometimes brought him a bottle of fortified wine, a pouch of loose tobacco, or a few cans of soup.

Back in the studio, he checked the refrigerator for leftovers for himself and Judd. There were none but a couple of stale doughnuts. He ate them himself and filled the dog bowl with dry cereal for the Great Dane. He had not left Brooklyn for almost a week. He had not glanced at a newspaper and had heard only a couple of snippets of the TV newscast from the television in the Angel's Kitchen, the local dive where he took an occasional break for a game of pool and a beer.

It had been worth the effort and confinement, though, he considered as he reexamined the giant hunks of metal. During the fifties, sixties, and seventies, most artists of the avant garde had rejected out of hand the slightest return to representational painting or sculpture. Nowadays, as the erudite Luke Elliot liked to explain, with his fancy vocabulary of "ologies" and "isms," art was evolving into a many-splintered "pluralism," more concerned with destroying all the antiquated cultural symbols of previous culture. Today's postmodernists juxtaposed (Luke called it "appropriated") images culled from the Romans, the Renaissance, and Renoir in an exercise geared to question (Luke called it "deconstruct") age-old symbols of power and violence, repression and prejudice.

Although Dan Helena found it interesting to listen to Luke's expositions, he had little reverence for current art fashion. Dan was concerned only with finding expression in the tensile strength of the steel for the ideas that drove him. Dan was interested in relationships of authority, between man and woman, between man and man, between men and gods. He was obsessed with erotic urges, with religion and brutal superstition, and matters that could not easily be discussed with civilized people.

But now it was time to sally a few hours into the world. Once more he left the studio, sliding into place the twelve-inch bolts and padlocks he had made himself to protect his fortress from the marauders. He turned into the York Street station.

The garishly lit subway platform, with its all-seeing television monitor, was empty. Dan had a fantasy that one day he would bring Susannah out here and would force her to lean over, opening her legs to him, in front of the camera's eye. He would slide his hand between her thighs, spreading the creamy folds until she relented, right there in front of whoever was studying that monitor.

The train roared in, and Dan took out his sketch pad. He

drew a lot on the subways and in coffee shops. People sneaked him curious looks. They rarely approached. The nearness of his huge body, pinpointed with absorption, kept them at bay. Tonight there was an old man with only two teeth and torn pants, sleeping and burping and snoring; a couple of teenage girls, fleshpots with obscenely painted lips and weighty dangling earrings; a man missing a chunk of his earlobe, who was watching the girls and massaging his crotch; a Hispanic woman immersed in a religious booklet. Dan worked quickly, shading with the broad edge of the pencil lead.

He got out at Lafayette. It was almost midnight. Luke's wife would be closing up shop at that pretentious Thai restaurant where she worked. Still, the curried shrimp last time had been spicy enough, and he owed the girl a visit.

She was kneeling at one of the black lacquered tables, writing out some final checks. He called from the threshold, "Hey, do I have to take my shoes off after hours?"

She looked up, startled, and overturned an egg-size cup of green tea. "Oh, it's you. Have you eaten? The kitchen's closed, but maybe I can get something. . . ."

"Don't bother. How have you been?"

It amused him the way she flushed when he let his stare travel from her smallish, mango-shaped breasts down across that patch of dark bare skin at her waist. The flesh was too taut, the way it stretched across her lower ribs.

She yawned. "Our ceiling at home has been leaking again. Otherwise, things are . . . the same. Did you get my message?"

"Yeah, you phoned." He studied her face curiously. The call had surprised him.

"Thanks, Dan, for stopping by." She sat down opposite him, cross-legged, at the low table, and carefully hitched up her sarong across her breasts and shoulders. "It's about Luke."

When she said her husband's name she glanced away toward the feet of the gilded Buddha, where a couple of jasmine incense sticks smoked. She really is in love with him, Dan thought. I might be able to have her body, but it would not change anything important. She's always going to love him, despite everything.

"How is Luke?"

"Very depressed. Did you hear about the robbery?"

"Jesus, you got robbed? Did they take much? That's terrible."

"No, no, not our apartment. Valhalla."

"They broke into the bar?"

"They broke a window late one night and got a few hundred bucks out of the till. It was weird, though. They took all the art on the walls, too. I mean, Dan, most of those East Village artists can hardly even sell their stuff. Why would anyone go to all that trouble to steal it? I know, a couple of them have gotten famous recently, but these burglar guys didn't differentiate. They cleaned the place right out."

"Is that why Luke's so down? He only had a couple of paintings hanging there. I remember those grasshopper green stripes."

"Dan, it's so embarrassing." She rested her forehead a moment against her hand. "That's the whole point. They stole everybody else's art *except* Luke's. The only thing they left in the place was the grasshopper stripes."

"They took *everything* else?"

"I'm afraid so. They even took those collages made of Tampax wrappers and the photos of the enlarged cockroaches."

"And they left Luke's?"

"It's humiliating. Naturally everyone in the East Village knows by now."

"Gee, I'm really sorry."

"It's all too much sometimes." She sighed. "It's bad enough always living on the edge, scraping by, eating garbage, being hot all summer and cold all winter, always looking through windows at other people eating in fun restaurants and wearing new clothes and pushing baby carriages." She stopped short. "Sorry to lay this all on you. But I get so sick of every gallery sending back Luke's slides without having even looked at them. It's been such a battle, and now this. It's like the ultimate insult, the last twist of the knife."

"Poor guy. I wish I could help. You need some cash?"

"Not now, Dan. We already owe you so much." She looked at him hesitantly. "Please, could you try talking to Giulietta Giuliani once more?"

He reached across the table and plucked a thin strand of

noodle out of her hair. She froze like a statue. "I'll ask her," Dan promised. "But don't expect too much. She always says the same thing. She doesn't want those stripes."

Kitty nodded wearily. "Thanks anyhow. We'd better get out of here. Everyone else is gone." She led the way to the doormat. Her battered sandals were the last remaining shoes. Suddenly she asked him, "What is the trouble with Luke's stripes? Why does no one want them? You think they're good, don't you?"

He hesitated. No one had ever asked him before straight out. "Luke is a smart guy. He knows a lot about art, and I admire him for that."

"But has he got real talent? Tell me he has talent. Please tell me."

What could he say? Dan Helena's loyalty was granite solid. Luke Elliot was his friend; instinctively Dan defended him. What did it matter if Luke was a bad painter, maybe even a truly dreadful painter? Among today's artists talent was no longer even the issue. Making a statement was deemed enough, and it could be practically any kind of statement—about oppression, materialism, superficiality, corruption . . .

Kitty was still imploring him for confirmation. "What do you think? Truly?"

He shrugged. "What does it matter? I'll talk to Giulietta again. You want me to walk you home?"

"No, no, there's no need." Her voice quavered.

Dumb broad. Does she really imagine I might push her into a doorway, thrust her down behind some overflowing garbage pail? Doesn't she realize that she's inviolable? I would never say aloud that my friend was a bad painter, and I would never seduce his wife.

New York was crawling, anyhow, tonight as any night, with real women, sluts who smelled of sex, with hips made for riding and ass you could knead like fruit. Dan made no excuses or apologies for his preferences. He knew what he wanted from steel, and he knew what he wanted from flesh.

---— 9 ——---

THE WINGED URINAL

*E*mil dialed the general house number at East End Avenue for the third time. The answering service picked up again.

"Pappier residence." They rhymed it with "happier."

"This is Monsieur Papier. And it's pronounced like 'papier-mâché,'" he barked.

Emil hung up irritably. Where did they get these rotating imbeciles he paid to answer his line? When he dealt with New York, he felt like just another number, another account, cut down to size. In Europe the insulation of his money still procured a gush of respect. Too many megarich people were concentrated in New York.

Besides, where was Susannah? When he called her private line he got no answer either. Emil, creature of habit, was used to telephoning from Switzerland at ten o'clock local time, as soon as the market closed in New York. He lived an orderly life, punctuated by the schedules of the global currency markets. He rose every morning in time to realign his portfolio in accordance with the previous day's financial activity in Hong Kong and Tokyo. Until the close of trading in New York, he did not slack off for a moment. In his windowless study (a picture-postcard view of the mountains and lake might have distracted his keen judgment), he followed the currency fluctuations in London, Paris, Frankfurt, Zurich, and Milan. Then, after hunching over the telephones and computer console for so many hours, he would move stiffly through the empty chambers of Mirós and Magrittes, into the living room, where the maid set out his decanter of wine and laid a fire.

Two kilometers from the castle of Chillon, his house perched against the hillside above the village of Villeneuve. You would never have guessed the secrets of its interior from the white walls and brown-tiled roof, the four-pointed turrets, the window boxes and stenciled balconies spilling with geraniums. The dominoed window shutters resembled a Hansel and Gretel gingerbread cottage, with licorice timber beams and jellybean flowers and sugar frosting lightly powdering the roof, where in reality a shower of May apple blossoms had sprinkled.

The interior was designed by Raoul Epinard, a precocious Belgian surrealist, who in his early thirties succumbed to schizophrenia and spent the rest of his life incarcerated in an asylum.

Symbolic phobias of the subconscious frescoed the main living room. A woman's body grew into the head of a grasshopper; the tail of a fish smoldered like a cigar; forms of birds, close up, turned out to be grotesque leaves, veined and chewed ragged by caterpillars. In the middle of the floor the tortured Epinard had designed a black acrylic lake, like an inky plastic puddle.

The furniture was not without some dark humor. Lamp stands were shaped like ears or noses with ominously dilated nostrils, table legs turned into gnarled human toes, and the grand chandelier tapered in bronchial extensions into glowing penises.

Here Emil stretched out with his wine in front of the fire each evening and made his string of personal calls to New York. Among all his far-flung properties, this was his favorite room and the one he had considered turning into a museum. Susannah, when she visited, was guardedly noncommittal. She bridled her disgust at the Epinard self-portrait over the fire, of a man with four arms and a crushed eye. Delphine was more direct. She informed Emil that she would be ashamed to invite any of her university friends back to witness such a spectacle of capitalist display. Besides, they must conclude that her father was doggone crazy when they saw in the courtyard the winged inverted urinal by Marcel Duchamp, no matter how often Emil proudly explained it was a "fountain."

Emil dined late. He liked to wait until the servants went to bed. His years of solitude had engendered in him a pathological irritation at having them around while he ate or relaxed and tried to obliterate the symphony of yen and marks from his wound-up, overstimulated brain. He needed to be completely alone with his phantasmal collection of half-human eyes and hands—all the paintings and murals and sculptures that came alive in the eerie firelight.

The staff left prepared food for him next door in the dining room. The tureen of leek soup simmered on the hot plate, the slices of dried smoked beef and pork knuckle lay neatly wrapped in plastic, the bread nestled under a linen napkin in the basket. He had been eating almost the identical menu every night for twenty years, while he drank his Chasselas wine from the local Vaud region of Switzerland: Mont-sur-Rolle or Chardonne.

He stubbed out his cigarette and tried Susannah's number again. Where the devil had she gotten to on a Friday afternoon?

He managed to locate Jacob Karakoff. "I've been trying to reach Susannah. Have you any idea where she is? Is she seeing Felice?"

"Not today. Felice is out at her existentialist philosophy course on Fridays. I've been shut up with the board all afternoon," Jacob puffed and panted. "They've finally greenlighted Helena's sketches for the statue in Belle John Plaza. It's going to be one of Dan's best, I think. An imposing seated figure."

Emil was sick of hearing about the Belle John commission. "How about the new PAP Fund investors?" he interrupted.

"I've got the chairman of Pizza Palace, a couple of rich widows, and a guy who's huge in the lawn mower industry. Another twenty million bucks all together."

"Good work." Emil beamed. He fantasized fondly that soon he would enjoy the exquisite satisfaction of outbidding all his old rivals for the highest-priced art treasures. He would soon even old scores with von Tislowicz. For Emil relished the warfare of auction with the same glee that ancient heroes hacked their way across the battlefield and their modern counterparts sprayed napalm and AK-47 shell fire.

"The catch is, they all want to know how we're going to turn the inventory over fast enough. That's always been the problem with the other art funds, our diddly squat predecessors. They could never promise their investors sufficient short-term capital gain. It could take years to resell at a profit."

"Ah, but we've got Nick Jones."

"The miraculous Englishman? What can he do?"

Emil chuckled contentedly. "He's already got himself a duplicate key to the precious auctioneer's book."

"How exactly does that help us?"

"From now on, when I go into an auction, I'm going to know precisely who's bidding against me, and how many of them there are, and how much they want the art. I'll know exactly where there's a real market, and where a cluster of competitive collectors will be waiting next year, when I'm ready to unload. That way I won't get stuck with duds, those white elephants like the overpriced van Goghs."

Jacob vouchsafed him a short silence. The simple brilliance of it took his breath away. "In other words," he recapitulated slowly, "we'll be able to sit down before the sale and figure out which items are attracting widespread attention and which are yawns. We'll be able to budget our funds with scientific precision."

Emil was rarely so lighthearted. "Nobody else, not a soul, has that information. Even the auction house itself, when it decides months ahead on the estimates, doesn't know for sure which will be the really sought-after pieces. By the time all the order bids have been received, it's too late for the auction house to readjust the estimated prices without giving the temperature away."

Jacob experienced a twinge of nerves. "That Brit had better be reliable." Inside information in the art world? A mere variation on the arbitrage scandals of the eighties? The trials of all the Wall Street moles rose fresh in Jacob's memory. The fates of Levine, Boesky, Milken, and their accomplices recalled the perils of industrial espionage.

"He's perfect. Middle class, greedy, intelligent. And we'll know," Emil concluded, "when the competition's real or not. Whether there really is competition or the auction house is just 'bidding up.'"

Jacob and Emil were well aware that all the major auction houses were guilty of the "bidding up" practice. The skilled auctioneers would keep an auction afloat, wafting to higher and higher levels, as they appeared to pull new bids out of the air. It was a scam. The house was playing against only one purchaser. Once in a while the house got burned, too, stuck at an elevated level that no bidder would cap. That was rare. Auctioneers were wizards at knowing precisely when to stop.

The noise of a door closing downstairs made Emil jump. In spite of the armed watchman who patrolled the garden and ground floor every hour with two Alsatians, Emil twitched at the least alien sound. After midnight the man and dogs snoozed lightly outside Emil's bedroom door. One had heard the most gruesome tales of people assaulted and butchered in their own homes. Although Switzerland was generally a safe place, his business acquaintances reported stories of robberies in the Riviera and West Germany. They relayed shocking accounts of kidnappings and terrorist ambushes. The new generation of the Red Brigade and the Baader Meinhof would have a field day with Emil and his priceless collection.

"*Bonsoir, Papa.*"

He had forgotten that Delphine was visiting for the weekend from Heidelberg University. "You frightened me, little pomegranate." Instinctively Emil's hand flew to the left side of his chest. "Be careful, you could give me a heart attack." Into the telephone he told Karakoff, "We'll talk Monday. My regards to Felice."

He turned back to his daughter. She stood by the door, her brown hair dripping water over the floor. She wore nothing over her slender legs but a T-shirt decorated with scenes of nuclear devastation.

"You've been swimming?"

"I nearly drowned. What on earth is that *thing* in the middle of our pool?"

Emil grinned with pleasure. "You mean my new soft sculpture? It's by one of Giulietta's Neo-surrealists."

"I got caught up in the tentacles," Delphine pouted. "They're all over the pool."

"They're only foam rubber. Where else was I supposed to put such an art work? It's too big for the garden."

She shook the water out of her ears, scattering a spray of drops. "It's always been a pain in the ass swimming in and out of your underwater sculptures. Now, with this disgusting octopus, it's nearly impossible."

Emil himself rarely ventured into the sixty-meter indoor swimming poor. He thought of it more as an artistic aquarium, an aquatic grotto for his sculptures of fish with human legs and tubas that twisted into the bodies of sea serpents. His queasier guests declined to dip among the menagerie, but Delphine had grown up paddling in and out of the malevolent flora and fauna.

"Let's eat," said her father. "I'm hungry."

He led the way to the dining room. Through the window, at a distance, shimmered the thirteenth-century castle of Chillon, once the inspiration of Byron and Shelley. Twentieth-century floodlights now illuminated its walls and ocher-tiled roofs.

"Nice evening?" asked Emil.

"Okay. I went down to the casino to watch some clips of the jazz festival. You should go out sometimes, too, Papa. It's not good for you to sit holed up here alone every night."

"Umm. I don't want people to notice me."

They sat down at the table, where the prepared supper awaited them, taking care to avoid the Man Ray "nail" chair. The several rows of spikes planted in the seat had come close once or twice to causing Emil's guests irreparable damage.

The dining room windows embraced a slice of the lake shore. Emil's eyes were gently refreshed by the diadem of lights from Montreux below. He lifted the cover of the soup tureen and ladled out the bowls. "I can't get hold of Susannah," he grunted. "I don't know why she's not taking my call."

Delphine looked down at her fingernails. "Some new flirtation."

Emil looked annoyed. "I wish you two got on better."

"It's true, Papa. Didn't you see the way she was leaning over that greasy English boy you invited to dinner?"

"He's not greasy. I want you to be nice to him."

"What's he got to do with me? He's just another one of your parasites, another leech trying to use you."

"No, petite." Emil passed her the bread basket, which she waved aside. "Au contraire, I am using him."

She looked up sharply. Her hair had almost dried now and floated over her shoulders.

Emil put down his soup spoon dreamily and stared at the ancient Alps, the Dents du Midi, just discernible in the moonlit sky. They were his reminder, those primeval crags, of how short life was and how minuscule the reach even of his wealth and power.

He did not want to talk about Nick Jones right now, so he launched into his favorite lament. "Today's prices are ridiculous. People will buy anything. Art's become a commodity like soybean futures or pork bellies."

"Yes, Papa." She had already heard this diatribe, many, many times.

"Art used to have spiritual meaning. Now it's become nothing but a gambling chip, like the tokens they give you in that casino." He pointed out the window in a dramatic flourish in the direction of Montreux.

"But, Papa, I thought you believed in Dada and Surrealism and all that anarchic stuff." She flashed him a little girl smile, a trick she had discovered usually worked.

"Even Dada had meaning: negative meaning. It was invented in Zurich in the middle of World War One. The Dadaists were disgusted with the conventional dogmas of the age, clichés that had no relevance to a world ripped apart by a brutal war."

"Yeah, yeah, you've been telling me since I was two." She began absentmindedly to braid a skein of long hair. "Marcel Duchamp was the bigshot, right? He did that awful upside-down urinal with wings we've got in the courtyard here."

"Fountain," corrected Emil patiently. "He did the original famous urinal in 1917, and now it's in the Museum of Modern Art in New York. He did ours in 1919."

She fiddled with her napkin and looked bored. Her father's repetitious line of bombast had nothing to do with the real problems of the world: nuclear threat, deforestation, or exploitative regional conflicts.

Her father was a man of such bewildering complexity. She tried sincerely to navigate the murky areas of his psyche. She disapproved of his anal accumulation of wealth, yet she admired his bookish, intellectual side, the way he would retire among his paintings or into his libraries, away from the vanities of commercial life.

He was still blathering on about the apocalypse of the art business. "There's only one way to prove that the emperor has no clothes. It's to be richer than anyone else. Richer than all the rest of them combined. So rich it would be possible to corner the market, to create and destroy superstars at will."

"Anyway, I still don't see why I should be nice to that slimy Nick Jones."

Her father did not answer her.

"Have some dried beef." He lifted the lid off the platter, where the cold meat lay in its usual unappetizing heap. The lid, modeled on a design by Magritte, was shaped like a woman's breast with a network of blue veins and a glaring raw-red nipple. Delphine tried not to have to look at it.

He served her solicitously.

"Enough, enough."

But he added another withered slab. "You're so slender and frail. I so wish you could find some man, someone reliable and tough and solid, to look after you."

"I look after myself. Anyway, you're here."

He shook his head gloomily and thought of his own father, dead at fifty-nine with the coronary. "I worry about you, little pomegranate. I'm so afraid you might end up like me, rich and envied and all alone."

"You're not alone. You've got Susannah in New York." She could not help hissing the name.

Emil clucked. She had reminded him again that Susannah was missing. He reached to the side table for a telephone. "She's still not answering." He scowled. "I hope she's all right."

Delphine scoffed. "Why do you bother, Papa? Don't you realize she's leading you a dance?"

"I've ruined her life."

"You? You've ruined her life? You found that penniless nobody, that lowlife, and you dressed her up in beautiful clothes and gave her money and wonderful apartments to live in . . . "

"I found that red-haired spirit, who had no education or money or breeding, but she looked like the wild nudes of Gustave Courbet. She was different from other girls. She made her own rules. An original. A submissive rebel. I had a compulsion to stamp out the rebel and make her all submission."

"She's using you. She's making a fool of you."

"She's unhappy. That's why she sometimes does . . . bad things. It's my fault. I gave her money and clothes, and I broke her spirit. I wouldn't marry her and I wouldn't let her have a child. So what has she got? A big wardrobe of Christian Dior."

"She could leave."

"She has nowhere to go. I've made it too easy, too luxurious, for her. She can't match me with anyone else, some accountant or actor or bond salesman. They couldn't maintain her as I do, and even more important, they can't give her the cachet she gets from being my mistress."

Susannah had been his toy. Gradually he had tied her drifting soul in knots, using the money as bait. He had watched her grow attached to her new comforts and advantages. Sure, she someday might sacrifice the clothes and apartment, the lunches at Le Cirque and Doubles. She still had enough spirit not be chained by all that. What she had grown addicted to, however, was the "fuck you" money, the swath carved out by so much ready cash, which liberated her from anyone's hassle or intimidation. Except Emil's.

"Why do you stay with her?" asked Delphine. "You don't love her anymore."

"I care for her in a way. I don't want her to be unhappy. No, I'm not in love with her, not hypnotized the way I was."

"So why keep her?"

His mood shifted abruptly. "She keeps the apartment going for me in New York after all, and I hate staying in hotels." He looked up earnestly at his daughter. "Do you think it would be foolish of me to have another child, at my age?"

"What?" Delphine caught her breath.

"All those years you were growing up, I never wanted to. I thought it might come between you and me, and I was always guilty about the divorce from your mother. Recently, though, I think about my own father"—his hand flew unconsciously to his left side—"and I wonder if a baby son might be a comfort."

"You can't! It's crazy! Susannah's getting too old, anyhow."

"There are other women."

That had never seriously occured to Delphine. She swallowed nervously. "Like anyone in particular, Papa?"

"No, no, no, no, no one special. Some nice young girl, I was thinking, someone innocent and good-natured."

Delphine scrutinized him. "You've met someone."

"All right, I'll tell you. I did see a girl last week—I hardly even met her, just shook her hand and said two words—but she struck some chord in me."

"Oh? Last week you were at the tulip festival in Morges, donating that Miró painting to the town."

"I met her at the festival. She goes all over Switzerland, appearing at cheese and flower festivals, carnivals, and the first night of *William Tell*, that kind of thing."

"Whoever is she?"

"She's a beauty queen. She's already been crowned Miss Gruyère. This year she's in the finals for Miss Switzerland."

"Papa, how could you?"

"I haven't done anything except notice her. She looked so soft and blond in her apron and clogs and traditional costume. Her name's Helga." He twitched guiltily. "She's twenty years old."

"She's younger than I am."

"Yes, I suppose it is foolish of me. There's no fool like an old fool, right? Why should she want anything to do with me, anyway? She probably has some young boyfriend of her own. Let's forget about it for tonight, okay, little pomegranate?"

Once more he reached impatiently for the telephone. "Where

the devil is Susannah? She knows I expect her to be home at the end of the afternoon to talk to me. After the phone call, she can do what she likes."

"You're a real sweet to see me," said Susannah. "I know you're busy."

Colorless McHenry flushed. No one had ever called him, of all people, a sweet. But then, no one as flamboyant as Susannah Bishop had ever sat in his office before, on the corner couch where he invited clients to describe their predicaments. When she shifted her behind on the sofa, it set off a twinge of inexplicable excitement in the starchy attorney. Just sitting there, she gave the room an aura. He hoped he would be able to remember later, when she was gone, back to her exotic, scandalous life. Maybe a trace of her perfume would remain a few hours in the air. He needed time to digest at leisure the image of this flaming creature.

"Is that the contract?" When she gazed at him pleadingly, he relished another little spurt of power.

"Yes. I haven't had time to review it."

The weight of her anxiety hung between them.

She bowed her head demurely. Today the ocean of hair was swept away with a ribbon. It made her look younger, he thought, needy and vulnerable.

He shuffled through the five stapled pages, reluctant to give up a shred of his new authority. Once he handed over the short agreement, she would glance through it, ask him a question or two, look relieved, stand up, adjust her jacket, shake his hand, smile politely, and leave his office forever. Something compelled him to detain her, to prolong her visit another few minutes.

"I take it you may have some concerns regarding your present domestic arrangement; that you would like to know the precise nature of your rights under this document."

Her answer took him by surprise. "Jim, I reckon you've heard some stories. I've led a whacked-up life. When I met Emil, I was twenty-one years old and the sorriest little hick you ever did see. I've got no schooling like you. I was by my lonesome in New York, miles from home, with no money and no real talent and nothing but"—she looked away modestly—"interesting looks."

McHenry nodded at her encouragingly. He consciously softened his stern expression. She was so different this afternoon from the last time he had seen her at dinner, when she had swept like a bird of paradise among her captivated guests as they choked on those digusting jellied eggs. That evening she had awed and mesmerized him. Today she seemed helpless and frail.

"I loved and trusted Emil," she went on. "He demanded I give him my whole life, and that's just what I did. He bought me, just like he buys another painting by Magritte. He drew the checks on the same old checkbook. Can you imagine how that feels, to be a slave, to be a human work of art?"

McHenry shrugged apologetically. He could not begin to imagine.

"Later I wanted a child, someone of my own to care for and keep me company. He always made vague promises. He always said 'Later, when Delphine grows up.' He used Delphine as an excuse. He claimed he was broken up with guilt over the divorce. Emil loves to feel guilty."

McHenry looked away, out of the window. It was compromising enough that he had allowed her to come to his office. He refused to be lured now into some implicit condemnation of Papier.

A couple of moving men were clearing out his neighbor's office. His instincts yesterday must have been right. Sure enough, the man had obviously been canned, with one short chop of the ax. It crashes so swiftly, he thought, when it falls.

He skirted the danger. "Let's take a look at your contract."

"Yes, yes, of course. I know I'm using up a heap of your time, jawing and jabbering. I don't know how to say a thing but to say it. I want to explain why I'm so—scared. I've got nothing, Jim. I'm uneducated, untrained, useless as crowbait. And I'm not getting younger. You know how it feels, Jim, to be a woman who's too old to have children? No, of course you couldn't know that. I'll tell you. As long as you can still bear 'em children, men'll follow you like cats go for catnip. Afterward, you're on your own. That's the surest thing I know."

"Why the sudden concern?"

"Emil is bored. He's ready to pitch me away, like an old pair of shoes. He wants young flesh."

"Has he said so?"

"It's the truth. If I'd been a painting, I'd get more valuable with the years. But for a woman it's the other way around."

Whatever she claimed about feeling old, McHenry wanted to reassure her that she still looked a head and shoulders better than anyone else who had ever walked though the forbidding lobby of Whittaker & Blessing. He did not know how to express it without sounding impertinent, so he hurriedly glanced at the contract.

"You don't seem to have anything to worry about, even in the most extreme scenario, which is at this stage apparently mere supposition."

She leaned forward. "What do I get?"

"Let's see. In the event that Emil should remarry—someone other than yourself, that is—or predecease you, or effect a constructive abandonment or voluntarily choose to enforce the obligations of this agreement in lieu of your current financial arrangements, you will receive . . . hmm, let's see . . . you will be entitled to free and unencumbered title to any U.S. properties in which you have hitherto been resident."

"You mean, I can have the co-op on East End Avenue? It's worth a couple of million now, at least. *And* the beach house at the Vineyard, too?"

"Yes, it looks that way."

"And what about cash? How will I keep up the maintenance?"

She takes it for granted, McHenry noted astringently, that she should go on living in that spacious duplex. A thriftier woman would sell the extravagant real estate for cash. Not Susannah. "In addition you are entitled to choose any twelve paintings or three-dimensional works of art from that part of the Papier collection that is permanently stored in the United States."

"So I can have me anything from East End Avenue? Anything? We've got a Matisse and two Picassos and more Surrealist tripe than you could shake a stick at."

"We may safely assume you will never starve."

"And supposing he didn't actually remarry? Supposing he just found a—a replacement companion?" Her voice faltered slightly.

McHenry did his best to concoct a benevolent expression. "Such a relationship would doubtless constitute 'constructive abandonment' on the part of Monsieur Papier."

"You mean if he took up with another woman, all that money could be mine right quick?"

"If he were to enter into a long-term relationship, or at least demonstrate his intention of so doing . . . "

She was fishing for any snippet of information he could dole out to her. "What if it was the other way around, Jim? What if I was to leave Emil, before he left me?"

"In that case, according to these terms, you would receive nothing."

"He could dump me out along with the trash any time?"

"I'm afraid so." It irked him to see her frown. "Surely you must have realized that over the course of so many years."

"I never did pay it much mind. Emil and I were an item, even when we went through stormy spells. I live in the present, Jim. I've never had any sense of the future, and as for the past, it's done and gone."

"Maybe this is another stormy spell."

"Maybe. Maybe not. Can I take a quick peek anyhow at my contract, before I depart?"

He slid the papers across the table.

"What's this? An endowment to the Department of Fine Art at Yale University."

McHenry scanned the papers she passed back. "It's a tax-deductible pledge. Dated the same day as your contract. It must have gotten in the file by accident."

A look of horror came over Susannah's face.

"What's wrong?"

"Look, Jim! He never did sign my contract."

"What? Let me see."

She handed over the unexecuted contract. Her hands fluttered. He flipped to the final page:

IN WITNESS WHEREOF, the parties have executed this agreement this 21st Day of December, 19—.

Underneath Susannah had signed her own name in a bold scrawl. The line over Emil Papier's name was blank.

"Good heavens," McHenry gasped. "You're right. He never signed it." How could he have missed it? Well, he never doubted that Emil was a cunning devil, that old son of a bitch. "Hmm. Let's not race to precipitous conclusions." McHenry's gun-metal gray voice reeled out his professional platitudes.

Susannah gaped at him. Did nothing faze this paper pusher, this soulless custodian? He reminded her of Emil's early Picabia (it hung in a guest room) of copulating, courting machines. She could imagine McHenry constructed in two-dimensional metal disks articulated with wire and hose. She looked away, toward the skyless view of the brick facade, lest he read her impatience and disdain.

McHenry laboriously scanned the clauses again. "Is there perhaps a duplicated and fully executed copy of this agreement with your own attorneys?"

"I don't have my own attorneys. Emil would never countenance such independence. I reckoned my contract would be secure here with you all."

"At Whittaker and Blessing, our probity and integrity are beyond question."

"Yes, yes, I'm aware of all that." She could not contain her urgency much longer. "What does it mean? I get nothing?"

"Without his signature it's unenforceable. Worth the paper it's written on."

She clung to the edge of her chair. "Jim, please, help me."

"I wish I could." He meant it, too. "Have you any family who could help tide you over?"

"No kin but a couple of sisters I haven't heard from in twenty years." And short shrift they'd give me, too, she thought, if I showed up on the doorstep. Me, the runaway, who made good in the big city.

Who could blame their envy and suspicion? After Emil took her in, Susannah used to send money home to Edgefield, ten or fifteen thousand dollars a year out of whatever loose cash she salvaged. Her mother wrote back occasionally, letters of misspelled acknowledgment and blessings. Embarrassed, Susannah hastily threw away the illiterate correspondence, before

Delphine or Emil should find it. When Susannah was twenty-six the misspelled letters stopped. Later her sister Ellie June sent her the sewing box, with a brusque note. Dead. Pancreatic cancer. Susannah slipped the crumpled photo of her drunkard father back where it belonged in the sewing box, which she wrapped in tissue paper and hid in a Bergdorf hatbox.

The tap on the door interrupted her reminiscences.

"Pardon me, Mr. McHenry." A paralegal with darting eyes quivered at the threshold.

"What is it, Debbie? As you see, I'm in a meeting."

"I'm sorry to interrupt, Mr. McHenry. We can't find a copy of the banker's draft. . . . The client's phoned three times from San Diego. . . ."

"Okay, okay." Jim stood up impatiently and crossed over to a file cabinet in the corner of his office. Whipping through the manila folders, he compiled an armload of documents.

Susannah meanwhile lifted an old April *New Yorker* from a neat stack in the magazine rack and mindlessly riffled a couple of pages. With flamingo pink nail tips she strummed on the desktop, trying to collect her thoughts. How could Emil have failed to sign the contract? Was it some mistake, some simple screw-up? And yet, and yet . . . Felice often remarked how Emil thrived on control. How he wanted to keep Susannah (and all his minions) a chain jerk away. That was why he had bought her off with a few baubles, her Romanov pillbox and her necklaces, and an accordion of plastic in a Vuitton credit card case. The bills came in every thirty days. She was a month-to-month tenant.

Her eyes slid back to the tax-deductible pledge to Yale. It lay facedown. Even through the opaque rag paper she could make out the strokes of Emil's spluttering signature on the reverse side.

Jim and his paralegal were still searching frantically through the sheaves of files, their heads bent over the squeaky metal drawers.

Susannah touched the edge of the Yale pledge with her fingertip. She thought, It's dated the same day as mine, right? Identical as two clothespins on a line. And just suppose I managed to substitute the signature page for the last page of my unsigned copy at home and add my name? It wouldn't take but a staple. But what if Jim figures out what all I've stolen? Never mind, I'll fix him later.

McHenry mumbled, "I'll be with you in a second, Susannah." She heard the thud of a file drawer being shut.

With an imperceptibly deft movement, she sandwiched the Yale pledge between the pages of *The New Yorker* and leaned back.

One moment later Jim located the errant document and added it to the stack under which his paralegal was buckling. Still clucking his teeth over the interruption, he returned to his desk and Susannah. To his relief, she seemed to have regained some composure.

"Actually, there is another copy in my safe at home," she murmured. "I must have clean forgot about it. I'm sorry for coming here and wasting all your time this afternoon...."

"Don't worry about that. If there's ever anything I can do to help." On a wild impulse, he blurted out, "Susannah, would you let me take you to dinner sometime? Just us, without Emil? Maybe we could figure out some alternative game plan for your life."

"That would be delightful." She could imagine nothing drearier, but she smiled bravely. She couldn't have Jim mentioning to Emil her unexpected office visit. What better way to insure his silence than to compromise his self-styled integrity? Her mood seemed to toughen as she stood up with resolution. "You've been a real pal, talking to me today, and listening to me run on with all my babble. I'd love to have supper with you. Emil's coming to New York next week for the Met party. Let's do it before then."

"Sure."

"We won't say anything about it to him. This'll be our private date."

Jim McHenry found himself agreeing ardently, before he knew what he was doing. He had never met anyone like Susannah Bishop before, so spirited and vulnerable at the same time. What she required was guidance. A dose of healthy normality. He wondered whether it was feasible to take her away, once and for all, from that decadent arrangement with the Swiss megalomaniac. That was surely what she needed, an ordinary, decent, straightforward kind of guy, someone she could learn to depend on and share things with. He wondered whether she liked chamber music. Next time he saw her he'd mention his subscription at Alice Tully Hall.

"I'm obliged." She held out her hand. He took it limply at first, then on second thought made a determined effort to squeeze it cordially. She asked, "Will you call me tomorrow?"

"Definitely."

When she was gone he sat down heavily at his desk, his thoughts racing. He was so flustered by the unexpected turn of the day, he had not even noticed how she had carried out a copy of *The New Yorker* under her arm. Of course, had he seen it, he would have assumed she wanted to finish browsing some article.

They had stripped bare his neighbor's office now, taken out the file cabinets and desk and chairs. McHenry wondered what the next executive, the replacement, would be like. Yet it no longer seemed as important as it had been yesterday. Jim McHenry had had a whiff of a real life of his own. It was almost unthinkable that he, the sterile waxwork, had invited out the siren. Hardly imaginable, yet suddenly possible, that she might accompany him to his evenings of Bach and Vivaldi, in place of his career girl dates who mispronounced words like *liaisons dangereuses* and wore colors that clashed. He and Susannah would start with a concert and a light supper afterward and then...

Across the way, the moving men trundled out the last file cabinet and turned off the fluorescent light.

The ax falls fast.

MYSTERIES OF

THE TEMPLE

*E*mil scanned the gallery for Joe Kominski, senior loan officer from North American Bankers' Corp. Keeping track of Joe in the melee was turning out to be a full-time nanny's work. Emil was glad he had asked Jim McHenry to come along tonight. Joe had latched on to Jim right away, like a drowning man in a sea of wreckage. Although Joe's poker face did not give much away, he was clearly suspicious of the avant-garde art crowd. Only in Jim McHenry he recognized a kinship. They chatted quietly together about recession and a soft landing for the U.S. economy, while the expensive horde buzzed around them.

Emil had planned out this evening's itinerary with care. The objective was simple. By pulling out every stop, he was already confident he could soon raise five hundred million dollars in equity from the limited partners. He needed Joe's authority at the bank to leverage another half-billion-dollar loan in debt. Emil intended to razzle-dazzle Joe, unimpeachable husband and devoted father of three, sterling loan officer of twenty years' standing, Yankee fan and staunch Republican, member of the Fort Lee Volunteer Fire Brigade.

The triumphant highlight of the evening was to be the much touted party at the Metropolitan Museum. The paparazzi would kill for an extra ticket. Emil wondered whether Joe appreciated the privilege of such an invitation. After consultation with Giulietta, Emil planned out a whirlwind crawl of fashionable downtown gallery openings as hors d'oeuvres to the entrée. Susannah and Giulietta and Felice were all with him now, Felice in a beaded beige chiffon by Herrera (Jacob had insisted she spend the twenty-five hundred dollars) and Susannah in red-and-white polka dots with puffed tulle sleeves and elbow-length black satin gloves. Giulietta wore her usual dowager's black. Following Emil's instructions, the women were doing their utmost to cosset honest Joe. Although the banker responded politely, he was obviously happier nattering financespeak with McHenry.

Whatever turns him on, thought Emil. If they could entice him into proposing their loan, the PAP Fund would be ready to launch with all the fanfare of a space shuttle. The equity money was surging in now. They had passed the three-hundred-and-fifty-million-dollar milestone. As Emil had explained to McHenry, the more funds you attracted, the easier it became. Word was out crackling in the investment community, and everyone who had any conviction in collectibles was taking an interest.

They kicked off at the latest conceptual show at the 313 Gallery. Perhaps it was rash to plunge honest Joe quite so quickly into the vortex of the avant garde. The eyes in the poker face bulged visibly at the sight of both art works and art crowd. Joe was baffled. "Why a shovel? Why a bottle rack? Why an earmuff? Why a garbage pail?" He turned to Emil in puzzlement.

"These are Duchampian 'readymades.' Ordinary day-to-day objects the artist has picked up for no special reason and decided to turn into art."

"They call this 'art' now?"

Emil cleared his throat. "Presentation is everything."

They clambered back into the waiting car and sped down the street to Dante's, where a muscled blond, the Wagnerian Hero, was showing his famous vomit suite. These dramatic oil impastos offered vivid examples of today's Expressionism. Emil noted how Joe studied the price list with care. Next to the columns of prices ($60,000 to $100,000), the little red dots indicated that most of the paintings had already found buyers. Joe perused the titles curiously: *Mexican Dinner, Chinese Dinner,* and *Burger King.* The banker blinked at *Mexican Dinner,* recognizing the blobs of guacamole, the smears of enchilada, and the streaks of pimento.

Peter Dante greeted Emil effusively. The dealer was a noisy character, who sported an 1890s walking stick and never removed his homburg.

"Good to see you, Papier." Dante pumped his hand vigorously. "This show's a real sell-out. We expect to get a deal on every one of the vomits by the end of this evening. We've only got a couple left 'on reserve.'"

The galleries allowed their regular clientele the privilege of putting certain works on reserve for a few days, while the purchasers made up their minds to part with eighty or ninety thousand dollars. Sometimes the collectors liked to return again to stare at their potential acquisition and see how it grew on them. Or the dealer might even let them take it home, to see how the art blended into the bathroom or guest room or den. Of course, such treatment was only vouchsafed to the big spenders.

"We've just sold *Morning Sickness.*" Dante motioned to a ninefoot tableau streaked with coffee and orange acrylic, which formed a dynamic backdrop for the daubs of lox and bagel. Arabesques of onion slivers punctuated the surface.

With some misgiving Emil introduced the banker. "I'd like you to meet Joe Kominski. We're trying to give Joe a bird's-eye view this evening of the potential for capital gains in today's contemporary work."

"You'd better believe it!" Dante swung around, like an aircraft carrier performing a maneuver in open sea. "You see that *Burger King?*" Rectangular French fries and elliptical pickles swam in a foamy sea of pink shake. Dante lowered his voice to a stage whisper as he leaned toward Joe and Emil. "I just shook hands on a sale for a hundred and fifty thousand."

Joe swayed dizzily on his feet. Emil did not know whether it was the shock of the prices or the vista of such blazing color or the bodies packed so close. Most of the galleries, including Dante's, were poorly ventilated. A crowd quickly used up the oxygen.

"Another drink, Joe?"

"Not for me. Maybe some fresh air...."

They took their limousine up to the Metropolitan Museum. Emil switched some tinkling Mozart on the stereo system and broke open a bottle of Dom Pérignon. Emil put Joe on the third seat with Susannah and McHenry. He and Giulietta, who needed extra seat space, rode behind the driver. The Karakoffs followed in their own limousine.

Emil gave their names to the guards with the guest list and ushered his party into the fray. He had the glorious impression that a constellation of eyes was suddenly upon him. He was indeed the man of the hour, the mysterious Swiss currency trader who had had the guts and vision to strike out for a billion-dollar art fund, an idea that was so obvious someone surely should have carried it out before, and yet somehow no one else had gotten around to it.

Emil had been confident that the Semi-Automatic Association would put together a dazzling spectacle. He was not disappointed. The gun people had taken over the temple of Dendur on the ground floor of the museum and arranged the supper tables all around the two-thousand-year-old monument. The temple had been transported stone by stone from the upper Nile. Floodlights illuminated the sandstone slabs, carved with legends of Isis and Osiris and jackal-headed Horus. Behind the two lotus columns, you could just glimpse the walls of the inner shrine, protected from the public's prying eyes by the squat walls. For thousands of years the Nile had washed right up to the foot of the columns. The priests and pharaohs, who alone were privileged to converse with the gods, would have entered the temple by boat at the side door. Tonight the narrow door was roped off from the party. The rustling crowd, even in their Nipon and Roehm and Missoni finery, were not allowed to set foot in the ancient sanctuary.

The Venezuelan was lounging with a sinister slouch against the hieroglyph-hewn temple wall. He greeted Emil deferentially.

"Evening, sir. I hear you're getting close to capitalization. I spoke with your lawyer last week about making a small investment."

Emil took an oyster tartlet off a passing tray. "When you say small, I presume you mean in the range of, er..." His voice trailed away. Numbers were so relative.

The Venezuelan beckoned. "Come with me a moment inside the temple. It's empty there and no one can hear us."

Emil twinkled. Who had ever heard of bugging the temple of Dendur? With a quick glance to make sure no one was noticing their trespass, he followed the South American behind the rope that barred off the narrow door and into the temple itself.

The Venezuelan's voice rang slightly hollow. "Only five units to start. You understand, we have some obstacles in moving substantial sums of cash. Until recently we operated freely. Now it's more risky, with so much political cannon fire aimed at the laundry."

"We'll take five million," Emil agreed. "But I want it now, in escrow."

"Will you take a money order drawn on a Bogotá bank?"

"We don't like Colombia. It's too unstable. We'd rather have Bermuda or the Caymans. Give McHenry a call in the morning at Whittaker."

The two men stepped out of their hiding place. Outside, the women fluttered like butterflies in lace and feathers, Tiffany's, Van Cleef, and Harry Winston diamonds. A man bore down on Emil.

"Why, it's old Papier, God bless you, fella, good to see ya. Remember me? Billy Berrymouse. Berrymouse Biblical Theme Parks. I had the pleasure of bidding against you last year at Christie's for that John the Baptist." Berrymouse took off his jacket, rolled up the sleeves of his dress shirt, and loosened the magenta cummerbund.

"Ah, yes." Emil now recalled. He had let Berrymouse outbid him in the end. He had not cared deeply about acquiring the painting of a bloody head on a plate. It was not worth going over a couple of hundred thousand dollars as a mere provocation for his mother's dining room. Billy Berrymouse was small fry. Against his old rival von Tislowicz, Emil might have carried on bidding . . . up to damnation. But Tizz always got his blood boiling.

"That was one fine painting you let slip the net." Berrymouse was still reveling in the afterglow of winning in one-to-one combat. "I've got it hanging now in my own office in Salt Lake City. Now tell me, what's all this I hear about your new partnership?" He winked. "You believe all those soup cans and cereal boxes and barbed wire are here to stay?"

"Without question."

"I tell ya something, Papier. Just so happens I need a tax loss for the next few years. We've been expanding our parks and marine worlds again. We sell participations to the public, get a lot of the evangelical flock. It's all perfectly legit. Folks put in twenty grand, they can come and spend a weekend in our Exodus or Genesis or Gethsemane theme parks the rest of their lives. Anyhow, point is, I'm sitting on a pot of cash right now, and I wouldn't mind parking it with you culture people."

"That could be arranged. Lunch tomorrow?" Emil passed him a card. "See you at the Four Seasons? By the way, Billy, how did you end up at the party here tonight?"

Berrymouse proudly pointed to a small gold tie pin. "See that? I'm one of the organizers. Assistant treasurer of the Semi-Automatic Association, yep, that's me, ol' Billy Berrymouse. Ya didn't know ya had friends in such high-up places."

"Congratulations," Emil responded vaguely. He surveyed the crowd again. Where was honest Joe?

A galaxy of candles lit the cavernous gallery, with its panoramic windows across Central Park. The vases on every table brimmed with lilac sheaves and paper white "iceberg" roses. The buffet food was all top-notch: crayfish claws and cold *vitello tonnato*. Eurotrash princesses chattered over the swing-time rhythms of the band.

Susannah and Giulietta huddled together at the Papier table. Giulietta had slipped her shoes off, under the tablecloth. She welcomed a chance to sit down and rest her monumental body.

Her feet always swelled from standing around at parties and openings, the more so because she insisted on squeezing them into tiny Ferragamo shoes with satin bows. The shoes were her last vanity.

They hardly looked up as Emil approached. Giulietta was busy showing Susannah some snapshots of her grandchildren, between bites of charlotte russe. They were a large clan, her own bambini, and then their bambini, spread among Manhattan, Scarsdale, and Rome.

"Has anyone seen Joe Kominski?" Emil made a small bow to the women.

"He's still with McHenry," answered Susannah. "They're arguing about corporate profits."

Giulietta reached for his arm and pulled him onto the chair. "Leave them alone. The banker is happy. Now I want to show you a cute picture of my new grandson, Luigi." She flashed him a snapshot of a baby's diapers being changed.

Who was that, talking with Susannah, his long legs jutting insolently from under the table? Of course, it was Dan Helena, Giulietta's protégé whose work Jacob had commissioned for the new Belle John Plaza. Emil had not seen Dan in a long time, and never before in black tie. But he recognized Dan's wayward cool, even when it was stuffed into conventional evening clothes.

Dan was saying to Giulietta, "I want you to take another look at my friend Luke Elliot's work."

"Those wretched stripes. How can I sell that garbage? Imagine the reviews in the press! My gallery will become a joke."

"Give the kid a chance. Put him in a summer group show. There's safety in numbers."

"You've always had real taste, Daniel. Why do you support this incompetent minimalist?"

"Luke's having a rough time. No one wants his stripes. He's broke, he's depressed, hell, he's just recently gotten married."

"No one wants those stripes 'cause they're abominable. They're sloppy. They've got no message, no impact, no meaning, no statement, no originality. They're boring, boring, boring. You hear me?"

Giulietta leaned back. Dan Helena was her prize racehorse,

and dealers liked getting their artists' recommendations. But the experimental decades were over. Gallery space cost thirty dollars a square foot, and she could not afford to dabble in losers.

"Yeah, I know." Dan gave up. It was no use defending Luke's painting. "Okay, okay, I know Luke's no great talent. But he's a nice kid and an old friend, and I thought maybe you'd give him a break."

"You're too loyal to your friends, Dan. That's your trouble."

Dan rumbled, "Artists gotta stick together." Under the table, he felt Susannah's ankle wrapped around his leg and her hand working its way toward his crotch. He shook her off. There would be time for that later. He accused his dealer, "You've changed a lot. When we first knew each other, you loved to promote young artists. They all called you 'Momma' and you got a big kick out of it, remember? You used to feed us, have us all over for lasagna verde, let us sleep on your spare mattress, loaned us money when we couldn't pay our rent."

Giulietta sighed. "It was different then. Art wasn't such big business. People became dealers because they really cared about the art and wanted to be part of a creative business. Now there's so much money it's out of control. Tell him, Emil. Maybe he'll listen to you."

"You weren't like that before," Dan protested. "Remember the summer you rented the house upstate and invited a whole group of us out for weeks? We painted, we barbecued, we went skinny dipping, we did a few drugs. You were a real momma then."

"For once and for all, Dan, I'm an old lady now and I've learned to be realistic. Those days are through. The other dealers will bullshit you—excuse my language, you know I talk straight—about how they only promote what they believe in. Forget it. That's their line, okay, art's high-class marketing."

McHenry led Joe Kominski back to the group's table. The banker was beginning to looked faded and more than a little dazed.

Giulietta, opposite, was waving gaily at an old friend. "*Cara,* come and sit with us. Have you tried this magnificent dessert?"

The friend was dressed in crepe de chine pajamas, yellow with brownish markings like the hide of a giraffe. Two spindly giraffe horns poked out of the turban that covered her skull.

The two women kissed loudly. "Princess," said Giulietta. "Meet my friends. This is Emil Papier, from Switzerland. Meet the Princess Paluzzi. And this is Joseph Kominski, our special guest tonight."

Joe took her hand as if he were not sure whether to shake or kiss it. He had never before met a real flesh-and-blood princess.

Dan removed Susannah's fingers from his fly. "Join me outside the door in two minutes," he ordered. He stood and strolled from the table.

McHenry was leaning over her, panting down her neck. "I've got an extra ticket for the B Minor Mass on the twelfth," he said. "Will you be able to come?"

"We'll talk about it another time, Jim."

She left the table and wove between the guests. Dan was waiting at the exit, next to the statue of Horus.

He took her arm roughly. "Walk fast. Don't turn around. The guards aren't looking."

She followed him past the mummies and sarcophagi, through a discreet door.

"Where are we going?"

"You ask too many questions."

He hurried her down another flight of steps and then another. They had to be right under the museum. He stopped her on the landing, forcing her back up against the wall, and kissed her hard. His rough skin scratched her face. She open her mouth wider, drawing his tongue deep inside. Her whole body felt like a leaf.

He pushed her forward abruptly. "We haven't got much time."

He led her into the labyrinth of corridors beneath the museum, the secret catacomb of rooms where the paintings were stored and repaired, the bricklayers' and electricians' and stonemasons' workshops, the eerie armory of medieval helmets and breastplates, the storerooms and all the other supplies of the netherland beneath six city blocks.

"In here!" He pushed her toward yet another door and down a final flight of stairs.

"We're going down farther?" These stairs were steeper and more airless. Susannah had no idea the museum's foundations reached so deep underground.

"To the basement storeroom. This used to be part of the city's old sewer system. Hardly anyone ever comes here."

They had to bend their necks to crawl out of the stairs and onto the deepest floor. The air became thin here and unnervingly hot, as if no one had breathed it in years.

A sheet rustled around her with a whirring noise, making her jump. Dan took her hand. "Don't be frightened. It's only a wind machine."

Now that her eyes were growing accustomed to the faint light, she could make out the weird shapes of a higgledy-piggledy junk heap of forgotten art treasures. There were gilded Buddhas and Renaissance ceramics, marble gargoyles and fluted columns, Arabian scimitars with sickle blades, and primitive Icelandic hatchets. Dingy oil paintings lay stacked against a clavichord. Propped beside a Tiffany lamp, a head of a goddess with wavy hair and blank, blind eyes surveyed the jumble. Dust sheets draped the abandoned medley, flapping and whistling softly in the current of the fans.

"It gets even hotter farther in," Dan warned.

She shrugged. When he was next to her, she was never spooked.

They crept down the aisle, between the baroque assortment of antiquities, a more bizarre collection than anything dreamed up by Emil's Surrealists.

"What's that noise?" She stopped. Something was definitely alive in this necropolis of dead things.

He laughed. "It's only crickets chirping. They're always here."

When they came to an overstuffed armchair, he made her kneel, like a felon before the scaffold, and coaxed her legs open from behind. It struck her what a bizarre pair they made, she in her red-and-white polka dots ballooning over the Dior garter belt and gossamer stockings. Only two stories upstairs, behind glass, the soft paste porcelain figurines posed delicately, Harlequins and Columbines, musicians and shepherdesses and blackamoors, couples and groups caught for eternity in their antic dance.

The air was so scant, and she felt faint with her head down, until a moment later he was filling her again, sweeping her away into that state of submission where nothing mattered but his will to dominate and her desire to please. She was plunging fathoms, swimming in the sweet, sticky sea.

When he felt her shaking subside he pulled her up. "Let's get back to Emil. Don't forget your purse."

Susannah bowed her head as they clambered up the stairwell. "Dan Helena, I'm in bad trouble. Emil hasn't said anything yet, but I have a premonition . . . I don't know what I'll do, I don't know where I'll go."

"You'll get by. You're still a good-looking broad."

They had almost reached the ground floor now. "Would you ever let me come to Brooklyn?" she cajoled. "For a visit?"

"I ramble around all night, I sleep all day. What would you do in Brooklyn, anyway?"

"At least can I come and see the Belle John maquette?" It would be an excuse to visit his studio.

"No one's to see it until it's finished. The fabrication company's making progress. I drove up to Connecticut last week to look. It's the best thing I've ever done."

They could hear the strains of music drifting down the corridor. "You go first," he ordered. "We shouldn't get seen together. Anyhow, I'm outta here. I'm meeting Caspar Peacock at Valhalla."

She found Emil in a flap. "Where have you been so long? We've all been waiting for you. Joe keeps yawning. It's time to give him a change of scene. Do you think he's enjoying the evening? Do you think he'll give us the loan? Where have you been?"

She prevaricated. "Let's go downtown, Emil. The party's over here."

"We're going to Mortimer's."

"Stuffy old Mortimer's," she pouted. "Let's do something right fun. Let's go to Valhalla."

"How about Joe? Will he like Valhalla, that's the question."

Susannah glanced at Joe, slumped across the table. He had worked his way through a steady series of Jack Daniel's, while he and McHenry dissected the recent contractions in the credit markets. Now his eyes were glazing over, and his collar was crumpled.

"Sure, he'll like it. We'll be providing him with fresh experience. Those East Village artists are the real thing. One day they're drinking and cavorting in Valhalla, next thing you know, they get picked up by some swanky SoHo establishment, all ready to transform 'em into the latest high flier, a new Jean-Michel Basquiat."

"Is it safe there? In that neighborhood?" Emil never forgot his anxieties over the security of his person.

"Sure it is, sugar. Sometimes you've got to live a little. Be venturesome." Susannah was determined. "Tonight we're going to find the real artists, is all. You ever been to Valhalla, Giulietta?"

The grande dame pulled a face. "That dirty place on Houston? My dear, if you ever have to go pipi, you are in bad trouble. The *toiletta* is disgusting."

Susannah accused Emil. "You're turning into an old fuddy-duddy."

He winced. Maybe Miss Gruyère would find him prissy too. When he had taken her to dinner last week at the Palace Hotel in Gstaad, her forget-me-not blue eyes had skipped and roved around the restaurant.

He took Susannah's arm. "Agreed. We'll go to this notorious Valhalla."

They took their limousine downtown. Giulietta, Felice, and McHenry begged off the excursion. Giulietta was losing the battle against her pinching shoes. Anyhow, she was never at home, with her huge dimensions, on a barstool. Felice muttered something about one of her migraine headaches coming on. Jim McHenry remembered he had an early breakfast meeting scheduled with the president of United Upholstery. Joe hesitated. Without his new friend McHenry in tow, he cringed at yet another circus of these artsy weirdos. But the whiskey had softened him up, and when Emil slapped him jovially between the shoulder blades, he obediently clambered into the backseat.

Emil pondered. Had they won the banker over yet? That princess friend of Giulietta's had turned out to be a useful trump card. The proximity with royalty stirred Joe on a level the vomit paintings had not.

Susannah led the way into Valhalla. The bar was hopping with chatter. Jacques Brel crooned on the jukebox. Caspar Peacock and Dan Helena were discussing the recent Richard Serra show with the Visual Scientist.

Emil ordered a round of drinks and leaned heavily against the bar. His head was beginning to clear again. Next to him an elderly black man jabbed his elbow.

"Cigarette?"

"No, thank you."

"You got a cigarette for me, mister?"

He had misunderstood. Hastily he passed the man a whole pack. "Keep them."

"God bless you." The man eyed him knowingly. They took him for a drug dealer down here. Emil, in his impeccable pinstripes, always looked like a stiff fish out of water in the East Village or Tribeca.

Emil examined the walls, plastered with a range of the local regulars' work, freshly reassembled since the recent robbery. There was an old refrigerator door, hacked and lacerated; a childlike spaceship drawing twinkling with dime-store sparkles; a painting of a skull with a long red detachable tongue; a three-D cascade of kitschy plastic tomatoes; and he even recognized one of the famous vomit paintings (*Sashimi and Green Tea*), loaned by the artist to the owner of the bar, in remembrance of unpaid tabs before the artist became famous.

Emil turned around to make sure Joe was settled. Jacob was haranguing their banker again, invoking the lists of record-breaking prices at auction.

"Picasso, de Kooning, Bacon . . . trick is to get into the action now, Joe, while there's still loose cash around. Specially from Japan."

Joe closed his eyes. He was looking very bleary.

"You having fun?" Emil interrupted anxiously. "We can go somewhere else if you like, Joe. Would you rather meet some attractive women?" It was lucky Felice had gone home. She always put a damper on their late night safaris for lonely, easy flesh.

Joe Kominski shook his heady indifferently. Was it the garish bar light, or had his skin turned an unhealthy yellow shade? The banker opened his eyes and groped for his glass, spilling a splash of whiskey on the bar. "It's been a long evening," he apologized. "I'm not much of a party man."

"But did you have fun?" Emil and Jacob's eyes crossed meaningfully. They were trying so hard to butter up their banker.

"Well, it was...different. Some of that art, though, boy, I can't believe anyone would even think of it. Morning sickness, Mexican dinner..." His voice trailed off wonderingly.

Emil soothed him. "It's difficult to take it all in at once."

Jacob waved at the barman and pointed at Joe's empty glass for a refill.

"Not for me," the banker protested weakly. It was too late. The ice was already clinking.

"So tell me," Jacob urged placatingly. "What kind of art do *you* enjoy?"

"It's my wife you should be talking to, really. She's the art expert in our family. She knows about all of them, van Gogh, Rembrandt, you name it."

Emil nodded thoughtfully.

"Don't get me wrong, fellas. I can appreciate some of the modern stuff, too. A nice, upbeat design and some bright colors to liven the place up, nothing wrong with that." Joe took another swig and half slithered off his stool. He lumbered back heavily. "You want to know the very best painting we've looked at this evening, gentlemen?"

Both Jacob and Emil leaned forward avidly.

"Now this may surprise you, but I'll give you my opinion here for free. You see over there, that one hanging behind the pinball machine?"

The two collectors' heads spun around. There was hanging the most singularly unappealing painting they had ever seen in their lives. It consisted of plain vertical stripes of unequal width, in the colors of dried blood and green pea soup. It was not an exciting or even a shocking picture, or one so brilliantly disturbing that it made an original statement. On the contrary, it was so boring, so achingly dull, that you wanted only to turn your head and look in the other direction.

"You like that?" Emil repeated.

"Hmm," said Jacob.

"That, fellas, is a real work of art."

Emil cleared his throat. "Brilliant spatial relationships."

Jacob trumpeted. "A retinal triumph."

"You see?" Joe Kominski was beginning to perk up. "I know what I'm talking about."

"A real find," Jacob agreed.

Emil capped him. "A small masterpiece."

"I'd put a painting like that on my own wall," Joe proclaimed. "Right over the sofa."

Emil snatched at the opportunity. "I'm sure we can arrange that." He called out across the room, "Is that painting for sale?"

Before the barman could answer, Dan Helena broke in, shouting back. "You like it? It's by a friend of mine, Luke Elliot. The title of the work is *Isn't.*"

"How much does he want?" asked Emil.

"I'll call him." Dan Helena was already on his feet and counting his change for the phone.

Kitty picked up. She sounded exhausted.

Dan relayed the good news. "You want to celebrate? I'll meet you both at the Odeon."

"I'm dead beat," she slurred. "I've been working a double shift. Luke says he'll come out alone."

Joe Kominski was meanwhile entering into the spirit of excitement. The color seeped back into his face. His cheeks lost their yellow-ocher tinge. "Is he a well-known artist?" he questioned Emil and Jacob eagerly.

"A budding new talent," raved Emil.

Jacob added hastily, "Never mind the price, Joe. This one's on us. A small souvenir for you, to remember this enjoyable evening."

Emil gushed, "Congratulations, Joe. You obviously have the eye of a real expert. Jacob and I are grateful to you for having brought this new talent to our attention."

Caspar Peacock leaned forward. "Pardon me butting in like

this, sir. But I happen to know that Luke—that's the artist you're interested in—is looking for a dealer. You know anyone?"

"We really don't," Emil answered hastily. He would not be seen dead approaching any reputable gallery with those dreary, fifth-rate stripes.

"Yes, we do!" burst in Joe Kominski. "Sure we do! That Italian lady, Giulietta, the one on the PAP Advisory Board. She's got a gallery."

Emil swallowed. "The work is too, er, minimalist for Giulietta."

Jacob grimaced. "Anyway, Giulietta's not taking on anyone new."

Joe was adamant. "Are you guys serious about your business or what? We all agree that I've made some kind of discovery tonight, a potential genius, maybe, an unknown master with real class. Don't we want to get in at ground level? Isn't that the name of the game?"

"But it's Giulietta's decision whom she represents."

"Hey. You put her on your advisory board, right? That's a pretty big honor. Now she can do something for us. Are you with me, folks?"

He raised his glass, and the other two reluctantly followed suit. Dan came back and sprawled across the bar. "I called Luke. You can have it for three thousand," he said.

The barman whistled quietly to himself. Nothing in Valhalla cost that much. The kids who put their stuff up on the walls here were over the moon to pick up a few hundred dollars once in a while. Luke Elliot and Dan Helena were milking these uptown geeks for all they could get.

"No problem," replied Jacob. To Joe Kominski he announced, "The painting's yours."

Dan added, "Luke says would you mind leaving a check here for him tonight? He's slightly strapped for cash right now."

"Fine. We'll take the picture with us."

"You carrying it out like that?" asked the barman. "We haven't got no crates or nothing here."

"We'll put it in our car," said Emil.

Dan turned to Caspar. "Help me get it off the wall."

Caspar stood up and joined him to heave it to the floor. "This sure is Luke Elliot's lucky night. I told them Luke was looking for a dealer. They're going to fix him up with Giulietta."

"Giulietta's seen his slides already. She won't touch him."

"Don't be so sure. Those friends of yours are out to impress that schmo. They promised they'd talk to Giulietta."

Joe Kominski was thrilled as they all piled back into the car for the journey home. His new painting, *Isn't,* was wedged securely behind the backseat. He wondered what his wife would say when she saw it, particularly after he'd explained to her that one day it could be worth zillions. They were nice people, those PAP Fund partners, fishing out three grand like that for him without the blink of an eye. They deserved to get their bank loan. He would do his utmost to maneuver it through the loan committee. He smiled to himself in the dark and felt sanguine about his first acquistion. The parties, the vomit paintings, and his encounter with the princess were all forgotten in the flush of unearthing an undiscovered genius painter. It was fun being a collector.

STEALING BASES

*E*mil stubbed out his twentieth cigarette of the morning and switched on the limousine television to the latest financial news. The traffic was jamming up on the East River Drive, and he was running late for his appointment at Giulietta's gallery.

He had a hectic schedule to cram in today before his five forty-five Swissair flight to Geneva. Already this morning he had knocked off three investor meetings, including breakfast at the Marriott with Bill Berrymouse, morning coffee in the 1080 Fifth Avenue apartment of an eighty-one-year-old dog-food heiress, and an hour in the offices of United Upholstery. After his date with Giulietta, he had a late lunch scheduled with Nick Jones at Les Pleiades. Then it would be time to leave New York. Since he kept complete wardrobes in all his homes, he never had any luggage to worry about. He jumped aboard the Concorde to Paris or the overnight Swissair flight with less fuss than other people climbed on a bus.

Helga would be waiting for him at arrivals when he stepped off his plane tomorrow morning in Geneva. It would restore his mood to see her rose-petal skin again and her pert little nose. She would take him by the arm and parade him downstairs to the curb, where the chauffeur would be waiting, lolling against the Mercedes. They would glide into the fresh morning, picking up the autoroute for Montreux. Helga would caress the back of his hand with her pastel shellacked nails. Should he give her her new earrings while they were still in the car, or should he wait until they arrived at his villa? He felt in his pocket for the small Van Cleef box, holding the fourteen-carat sapphires wrought in the shape of forget-me-nots.

"Sorry about the traffic, sir." The driver interrupted his reverie. "It's snarled up all over the city. It's the UN again. The president of Zimbabwe or Zambia or Rwanda—one of those places—is in town."

Emil did not answer. He did not like exchanging unnecessary conversation with servants, and he had little interest in African presidents. They sometimes invested in bullion, and they loved buying airplanes, but he had yet to meet one who collected de Koonings or Rauschenbergs.

Ah, they were moving again at last, exiting the drive at Houston. He began to feel better. The June sky was a brilliant azure, and he had lined up four hundred million dollars. Who else could have rallied so much big money so quickly? Certainly not von Tislowicz. It had taken Emil persistence, phoning around the world at all hours, keeping his manner crisp yet bullish. They had struck the right chord, he and Karakoff. The funds were flowing in like molten lava. Only another hundred million to go before blast-off. He chuckled to himself. Only.

Then there would be double cause for celebration. For the day they amassed their half billion dollars, the provisionally executed investors' pledges became binding, and the North American Bankers' Corp. was ready to enter into a loan for a further five hundred million. Joe Kominski spearheaded the team of bankers assigned to number crunching. The loan committee had convened and finally ratified the transaction and lined up several other major institutions to join the financing syndicate.

The car turned onto Spring Street, where the gay banners outside the galleries fluttered like a regatta of sailboats in the wind. The fruit and flower stores dotted the sidewalks between the cast-iron columns. It was peony season. The swelling pink and white globes nodded over the peaches and strawberries. Emil ordered the driver to pull up, just past the Zen bookstore, and to return for him in thirty minutes.

The staircase climbed deep into the bowels of the building, to Giulietta's gallery on the second floor. The girl behind the desk was wearing dangling earrings woven from human hair and teeth, and a tiny miniskirt. Giulietta trained her reception girls to look even snootier than their counterparts at Dante's and the other rival SoHo galleries.

Emil hardly glanced at the current show, a sinister collection of battered gravestones, onto which the artist had fastened tubes of toothpaste and deodorant, underwear, credit cards, subway tokens, douche bags, and eclectic personal items to symbolize the transience of the deceased.

Giulietta's clarion voice penetrated the partition that screened off the office. Emil recognized her patter; he had heard it often over the years.

"If I could take another couple of minutes of your time . . . " Giulietta was wheedling a couple of her most lavish Texan clients. "I'd like to show you some etchings by the same artist. . . . These were exhibited last year in Cologne and in Basel. . . . " Emil heard the sliding of a file cabinet drawer and the rustle of tissue as she unwrapped the artwork to show her captive collectors. Emil made out a muffled reply. Giulietta sallied on, "Yes, fifty thousand, it's a steal. . . . One of these has already been purchased by the Museum of Modern Art and two by the Ludwig Museum, which, as you know, is the most prestigious contemporary collection in Europe. . . . " She knew exactly how to flatter the buyers with her saleswoman patter. Before they knew it, they were coaxed into believing in some newly acquired gut feeling. Wily Giulietta, disarmingly bighearted, had once or twice nearly sold the Brooklyn Bridge.

Emil tilted his head through the open door. The portly husband in his ten-gallon hat asked, "Whaddya think, Mrs. Milholland?"

Mrs. Sanford Vincent Milholland III slid another inch of her white lynx coat off her shoulders. It was hot in New York in late June, and the snobbier galleries still resisted air-conditioning. "I think it's a no-no, pussycat. We got to maintain our lofty standards." MaryLou Milholland explained to the hovering Giulietta, "My husband and I have assembled a real bouquet of Reinhardts, Newmans, and Clyfford Stills. Next year we're loaning out the Sanford Milholland Collection on a traveling tour all over the world. We're sending our beloved family—we always think of our paintings like children—to the Museo de Arte Moderno in Bogotá, the Contemporary in Houston, the Phillips, the Fine Arts in San Francisco, the Stedelijk in Amsterdam, the Beaux-Arts in Brussels, and the Whitney here in New York City."

"We're partial to new painters, too," added Mr. Milholland. "But we got one rule of thumb. Nothing but the best."

Giulietta wagged her head wisely. "I never, never try to influence the taste of a collector. A piece of art is like a human being. Some you respond to, some you do not. It is an emotion you must feel inside." She gestured toward her wide diaphragm. Although she was approaching the climax of her marketing momentum, seeing Emil, she broke off instantly, and excused herself to the Texans. "Would you forgive me for five minutes? My dear friend Emil Papier is leaving for Switzerland this afternoon, and we have a couple of matters to discuss."

MaryLou was impressed. "That isn't *the* famous Papier's PAP Fund Papier, is it, pussycat?" The Texans backed off discreetly to the far end of the gallery.

Giulietta turned to Emil urgently. "About this Luke Elliot—we must talk."

"Have you got the slides?"

"They are unspeakably dreadful." She rattled a file cabinet and drew out an envelope. "I don't get it, my friend. I've known you for twenty-five years, and never, never until now have you asked me to take an interest in such a fifth-rate artist." Giulietta maintained an uncanny grasp for the individual taste of her collectors. Like a grand maître d' who never forgets the favorite dessert of his regulars, she sensed unerringly whom she could tantalize with what. "How can I sell this excrement? How do I price it? And imagine the reviews in the trade press! My gallery will become a joke." She snorted. "Emil, you're out to lunch. Why are you doing this?"

"Let me see those slides."

He held them up to the light, one after another. He winced at the clash of hospital green with mustard, a shade reminiscent of infant diarrhea. The stripes were clumsily executed yet could not even enjoy the redeeming label of faux naif.

"You want to look at them on the projector?" asked Giulietta. She wondered if seeing their glaring banality enlarged might jolt her old friend to his senses.

"Not today. There's no time. Giulietta, I'm sorry to do this to you. Joe Kominski, our guardian angel from North American Bankers' Corp., has fallen head over heels with this bilge. We have no choice. We must keep Kominski sweet. He's putting together another half billion in loans for us. The future of the PAP Fund depends on him. I wouldn't ask you to help, my dear, if it weren't essential."

"All right, all right. I'll take three or four of these noxious stripes and tuck them away in the summer group show."

"Bless you, Giulietta. We're all grateful."

"Everyone will say I've gone off my rocker. Never mind. After this, you owe me one, my friend. Ah, Mr. and Mrs. Milholland, do let me introduce you to Emil Papier."

Emil held out his hand. "*Enchanté.* I am a great admirer of the Milholland Collection, particularly your superb Twomblys and Stellas."

"We're proud of our babies, too, ain't we, pussycat? We sometimes feel just like parents sending them off to visit in museums all over the world. You looking at something interesting this morning, Mr. Papier?"

A loud gurgling erupted from Giulietta's middle. She was getting irritable; lunch was overdue. She broke in maliciously. "Emil is taking a special interest in a young artist called Luke Elliot."

MaryLou held a hand coquettishly toward the transparencies. "If Emil Papier has made a discovery, it must be worth looking at." She held a slide up to the light and squinted, blinking her fan of artificial lashes. "Whaddya think, pussycat? Do we want a front seat on the bandwagon, too?"

Her husband grunted. He was getting hungry, also, and he had seen enough art for one morning. "How much, Giulietta?"

The grande dame raised an eyebrow toward Emil. "Nickels and dimes. Ten to fifteen."

"Ten thousand bucks?" Mr. Milholland III guffawed sonorously. "I think we can afford a few of those, don't you, Mrs. Milholland? Let's have two of the tens and two of the fifteens."

Giulietta gasped. Much as she relished making sales, she was accustomed to a more conservative inspection. "You haven't even seen the paintings!"

"What's good enough for Papier is good enough for us. Right, pussycat?"

"We'll pack 'em in with the collection. Send 'em round the world a few times with the Stellas and Reinhardts. It's good to support a new artist every so often. Like having a little baby brother."

As usual, Nick and Emil ordered the flaky sole amandine.

Nick was looking sprucer. Emil's stipend had contributed to shopping excursions at Paul Stuart, FR Tripler, and Dunhill.

Today Emil did not have much extra time for chitchat. "How's Georgia?"

Nick sighed. "I paid a stiff price for that bloody key. Last week she cooked me a romantic candlelit dinner, made me listen to the whole of *Gotterdämmerung*, and cornered me onto her sofa, where she crawled all over me. I don't know how much longer I can keep her from jumping my bones."

"You be nice to her. I don't care if she's ugly. I want to make sure I get a thorough look at the auctioneer's book for the big November sales. That will be the PAP Fund's maiden voyage." Emil slid out a fat envelope and propped it next to the vase of red carnations. "Perhaps this will put you in better spirits. Put it somewhere safe. There's twenty thousand in there, in hundred-dollar notes. That should get you through the summer."

"No check?" It was the first time Emil had paid him in cash.

"We must be more careful. I don't want you involved in any IRS investigations. The PAP Fund is really taking off now. I want no bad smells."

"I can't deposit this?"

"Absolutely not. You're an overworked, underpaid, generally exploited young cataloger. You will keep a low profile. You can hide your money under the mattress. There's excellent security in that yuppie Versailles you've moved into on Central Park South." Nick had already exchanged his dingy walk-up for a large park-view two-bedroom on the thirty-seventh floor in the Trump Parc. Each day he sauntered home past the doormen and concierges and hallmen in the lobby hung with tapestries, through the electric-eye glass doors, and into the elevators that reminded him of moving jewelry boxes.

Nick grinned. "The mattress isn't safe. I have a cleaning lady now. Twice a week."

"The sole seems marginally better today," remarked Emil. "And so, to business. Your order bid lists were excellent. Exactly the information we needed."

Nick had managed to make photocopies of the auctioneer's books, going back three years, for all the contemporary May and November sales. Emil swiftly discovered which museums and collectors were ardently thirsting after what, and where they might make a quick profit by acquiring and reselling after only a year or two.

Emil's eyes narrowed. "That beach house you've rented in Quogue. It must be quite expensive."

"Twelve thou till Labor Day. But it's nice. We have our own pool and tennis court." Nick patted the swollen envelope of hundred-dollar bills, stowed safely in his pocket. Today's remuneration was going to cover his extravagant weekends. After English summers, Nick found the scorching New York heat detestable. He craved that shady clapboard house and the nearby ocean with its salty tang. He liked the parties, too. Every Friday night, after the three-hour bumper-to-bumper drive, there were cocktails in somebody's garden or around the pool. The conversation was of deals and cars and boats and condos; the girls were tanned and athletic.

"As they say in this country, there are no free lunches. Having fun is expensive," Emil reminded him. "I need to know about those telephone bids."

Emil never changed the tone of his voice, yet something about his frigid smile was making Nick uneasy. At first their arrangement had seemed like an honest to God windfall. Now Nick was discovering that it was not so straightforward plying a living as a spy. Yet having made the initial leap from life in a crummy walk-up, he could not stomach a return to holy poverty.

Emil's demands for information were unquenchable. By stealing Georgia's key and sneaking into her office after hours, Nick considered he had well earned that first twenty-five grand. Then Emil came up with a slew of further questions. What were the names of the undisclosed underbidders last May? Had the auction house arranged any prefinancing for major purchases? Emil expected to be informed of all significant "reserve" prices, the unrevealed floor price beneath which the art may not be sold. He also insisted that Nick investigate any pending guarantees. Sometimes the auction house would agree to take a consignment off the seller's hands if the bidding did not reach a certain level. Where any such promise existed, Emil wanted to know.

To ferret out business secrets required constant snooping. More than once Nick had rifled the expert's own desk, snatching spine-chilling opportunities when all the department were out to lunch or attending someone's retirement party down the hall.

Meanwhile, Nick's legitimate career was progressing. The clients liked the well-mannered, clear-spoken young Brit. He hit the right note between deference and disdain. The flicker of irony, the occasional prickle of cultural superiority, went over well, too. The expert had called him in last week to congratulate him on the influx of good reports. While Nick listened modestly, the expert's secretary had rapped on the door.

"Baron von Tislowicz is here early for his lunch appointment. Shall I ask him to wait next door?"

"No! I'll meet him myself in reception." The expert hurried out, his attention abruptly diverted. Nick took advantage of the five-minute hiatus to peep at the open file lying by the blotter. He shuffled hastily through the pages. It belonged to Sandy

Pike, an Australian tycoon who had amassed a fortune in distilleries.

There were contracts of sale, bills of lading, insurance policies. Nick skimmed an interchange of correspondence. As he flipped to a startling item, his eyes popped out of his head. Here at last was something to tell his spymaster. He tried to memorize as much as possible of the list.

Emil drained his last dregs of Corton-Charlemagne. "Please excuse me if I skip coffee today. I'm due at the airport and my schedule's tight."

Nick took a deep breath. He was still a debutant at the rules of barter and enticement. "I've been thinking it's time I got a car of my own," he remarked chattily. "I'm sick of cadging lifts out to Quogue from my friends."

"Good idea." Emil hardly listened. He was busy flagging down the maître d'.

"I've fallen in love with a certain Porsche."

"Too flashy. Stop throwing money around." Emil glanced indifferently at the check and left a thirty-five-dollar cash tip on the table. They gave him credit for the rest of the check, kept a running tab, and sent him a bill every few months to East End Avenue.

Nick tried to look tough and venal. "I need thirty."

"You want more money, you have to earn it."

"I have earned it. I looked at Sandy Pike's file last week. You'll be interested to learn he's unloading."

"He's selling! He has the largest contemporary collection in Australia. If he starts dumping major painters, it could be cataclysmic for the market. Why didn't you tell me right away?"

Nick began to enjoy his momentary advantage. "Do you want to know what he's selling?"

"Of course." Whenever an important collector dispensed with an artist's work in bulk, the market went haywire. There was nothing as detrimental as a surfeit of available work. Often the going price for such an artist plummeted on the news.

"I remember some of the list. He's selling some Calders, some Motherwells, a Rothko, a Noguchi, an Artschwager, a Judd, some Hockneys, and some Kiefers."

"That's too vague. I need to know exactly what he's selling." Emil looked flustered. Why had Nick Jones waited until the last minute to lay this egg?

"And *I* need thirty thousand dollars."

Emil rapped on the tablecloth. The precocious young Englishman was becoming too big for his boots. Who exactly did he think he was to start driving deals with his mentor?

Yet he wanted that list. The Australian's divestiture might drive down the price of anyone, and Emil could not afford to be caught holding a brace of turkeys for the PAP Fund. Moreover, if Emil approached Sandy Pike privately, the billionaire might be persuaded to sell some paintings directly to the fund rather than sending them all the auction route. There were advantages to private sales. Keeping a work away from the marketplace allowed a purchaser to resell it more easily and sooner. Art commanded a special cachet the first time it appeared at auction, fresh from the private vaults.

"All right. You can make a down payment on your miserable Porsche. But I want to know exactly which pictures Sandy Pike is selling. And for that list you get twenty thousand from me," he stipulated irritably. "Not a penny more."

The traditional Bor au Lac hotel suited Emil. Conversation was hushed in the spacious dining room, where everyone minded his own intimate business, and the service was impeccable. The food was perfect, of course, too, although Susannah had always complained about coming here. "The ghouls in the graveyard," she nicknamed them, tossing her head around the walls where self-effacing businessmen huddled.

Rose-skinned Helga was a child, and one did not ask children their restaurant preferences. She spent longer in the bathroom getting ready than any other woman Emil had known; beauty, however, was her trade. When she emerged, spellbinding in a backless Ungaro, the Van Cleef forget-me-nots twinkling in her ears, Emil tingled with the same thrill he relished from acquiring an exquisite Paul Klee or a Fabergé egg.

Sandy Pike, a rough-and-tumble business maverick of about his own age, was bound to feel a flicker of masculine envy. Emil factored that in. When a man feels outclassed by his rival's dainty young girlfriend, how else should he compete than by boasting and bragging about his treasury of art? And Emil had his eye on that treasury.

"How was New York?" Emil inquired conversationally.

"Hot and humid," replied Sandy. He was a well-built, sinewy man and a sailor well known for his driving ambition to carry off victory in the Americas Cup. "I had a nice weekend up in Newport with Juan Gomez. He sends you his best regards."

"Ah, yes," murmured Emil. His favorite Filipino investor in exile sailed his schooner *Esmeralda* at thirty-six knots and used her bridge as a floating office.

Sandy Pike turned jovially to Helga, who looked bored. "Do you enjoy art, too?"

When she simpered back, her perfect teeth reminded Emil again of the Fabergé egg. "Emil is teaching me everything. He has taken me to the Louvre and the Uffizi and the Tate. We have seen so many paintings, I get them mixed up."

Sandy leaned to extract a golden thread of Helga's hair that had fallen into the mushrooms. Emil flinched possessively.

When Helga excused herself over coffee, Emil knew she would be away from the table for a while, remaking her face and perfecting the sweep of her blond pageboy. He took the opportunity to remark to Sandy Pike, "Our PAP Fund will be making a number of acquisitions over the next few months. I happen to mention this, in case you were thinking of divesting anything."

He said it so breezily that he might have been talking about collecting old clothes or soup cans for the Salvation Army. Officially, the forthcoming sale of major Pike holdings at the auction house was still a close secret.

"Hmm," said Sandy, whose entire concentration appeared to be directed at clipping his cigar. "And if I were thinking of selling—I'm not saying I am, mind you—why should I choose to go the private route?"

"Your fiscal situation is your private business, Sandy. All I know is that if you take a major capital profit at auction, the whole world is going to be watching, let alone your revenue people. On the other hand, if you do a deal with me directly,

I'll transfer the funds into any offshore haven you name. You like Vanuatu or that tiny atoll, Nauru?" Those small Pacific islands, east of Australia, were the latest fashionable garages for covert transfers.

Sandy Pike bit the cigar. "How much art do you want?" He did not ask *what,* only how much.

"Thirty million dollars, give or take. If that suits you."

"Thirty." Sandy counted rapidly on his fingers. "Let's see, for that I could sell you a couple of Mirós, a nice Chagall, a decent de Kooning, two good Rothkos, maybe a Frankenthaler, a smallish Kiefer, a Donald Judd I never was cuckoo about, and several Beuyses that have shot way up in value." He could have been a grocery clerk, measuring out a pound of tomatoes, a half pound of coffee beans, and a small bunch of bananas.

"We can iron out the details later," said Emil. "It's a pleasure doing business with you, Sandy. Really."

"Mutual. By the way, if you're ever down under in my part of the world, I'd love to take you out on my boat." He added quickly, "You're a pretty rum bloke, Emil, laundering Picassos and whatnot."

"No, no," Emil interrupted hastily. "Laundering isn't my business at all. I am running the largest art fund in the world, and that's a respectable job. I happen to have spent thirty years of my life trading in currencies. I've put together a valuable roster of banking connections. Once in a while I utilize my contacts to keep the wheels spinning."

At that moment Helga returned, scented and prettified, bewitching Emil and the Australian as she stepped through the hushed room past the dessert trolley. The impeccable waiters twitched at the sight, while even the ghouls in the graveyard twisted their rigid necks.

Jim McHenry stood at the threshold, clutching a cone of pink roses and baby's breath, like a shriveled shield, to his chest.

"Why, I declare, how romantic of you! Come on in." Susannah offered a cheek demurely to his lips. McHenry was sweating profusely. His armpits were already damp, and the premature lines in his forehead glistened. "You poor sweet, look at you, all hot and bothered. It must be ninety-five degrees in the shade. First thing you'll be needing is a long, cool drink and a spot to put up your feet."

She led him past the statue of three-headed Cerberus, through the wood-paneled living room. It was all very well for Emil to entertain his investment bankers in that room, where the shadow of the suit of armor gave them the creeps. So much the better if they escaped from the palazzo awed and a trifle discomfited. Next day they would show up all the more malleable for business. But Susannah intended to lull Jim McHenry into a very different state of submission.

He was here to be compromised and corrupted. She needed to guarantee the secrecy of her theft. In case Jim should notice the disappearance of the pledge to Yale—not at all likely, as Emil made so many diverse bequests to museums and educational institutions, as the whim moved him—nobody must connect Susannah with the vanished document. Her plan was to land Jim McHenry so deep in it, he at least would keep his mouth shut.

In the adjacent conservatory the air-conditioning filtered deliciously through the curtain of leaves and fern fronds. Susannah arranged a nest of cushions across the wicker bench. A fan of lilies bowed in a canopy overhead. A rare orchid (gift of a junk bond fund manager) tickled her face whenever she and Dan slid off the cushions and onto the flagstone paving.

She swept aside a spray of honeysuckle and invited McHenry to sit. In the background Willie Nelson's voice murmured of loneliness and love easily shattered.

"What can I bring you to drink? A nice cool Margarita? A Seabreeze? Or shall we dip into a bottle of champagne. We have some good Krug eighty-two."

"Not for me." McHenry loosened his tie a half inch. "Have you some diet Coke or ginger ale?"

A violent screech and cackle erupted behind them. "Harder, baby. Give it to me."

McHenry almost jumped out of his skin. "My God, what's that?"

She laughed. "Pay no mind. It's only Gauguin. The parrot."

"What on earth did it say?"

"Nothing," she assured him hastily. "Nothing at all. Here's your Coke."

"I'm glad you asked me here tonight," said McHenry, jiggling the ice cubes around. "I've been thinking about you a great deal over the past few weeks, and your situation, and I'm glad we have a chance to talk."

"Have you been thinking about me? Really?" She put a delicate tremor in her question.

He looked away. "A great deal. A very great deal, in fact."

"Suck my balls," squawked Gauguin.

Susannah flushed. "Maybe we'd be more comfortable next door."

"I can't figure out what it's saying," McHenry pondered. "Is that English or is it just gibberish?"

"Gibberish. So you've been worrying your head about me? Oh, Jimmy. Whatever is going to become of my life? When Emil departed for the airport this afternoon, I could read in his eyes his patience is wearing thin."

"Are you interested in travel, Susannah?"

She blinked. "We've done a heap of traveling, me and Emil."

"I know someone who runs an agency and needs a new clerk to train. They'd be willing to take you on without any prior experience."

She blinked. "You mean to work?"

He fixed her sternly. "That's what you need. To be independent. To make a living for yourself for once."

"I don't know. . . . It's mighty thoughtful of you to go worrying about my prospects." She stood. "Time to change the music. You like Randy Travis? Reba McEntire?"

"You got any Bach or Vivaldi?"

She shrugged apologetically. "I'm shamed to say I don't. Emil and I have ever been art people more than music people."

"It doesn't matter."

"I'm coming," shrilled Gauguin. "Baby, I'm coming."

McHenry swallowed the rest of the diet Coke. "It is speaking English. I understood that."

"Forget the bird. It's most important we talk. Yessir. I want to talk to you so bad."

"I'll never be able to compete with Emil when it comes to

material possessions. But I live comfortably enough. I have a two-bedroom co-op, and I've been thinking for some time about buying a small farm in the Berkshires or maybe Columbia County."

She was utterly confounded.

"I've been thinking this over and over." He leaned forward earnestly and covered her hand with his. "I do realize that you and I have lived very different lives, yet I still believe that in time we could find much in common. I want to teach you, share with you. About music, for example. Chamber music in particular."

She swallowed. Was the waxwork offering her a refuge from Emil and lessons in musical appreciation, just as the Swiss had once sent her to courses on Cubism?

Slowly and deliberately, she moved over to where he sat. She took both his hands in hers and laid her cheek next to his smooth face. Now he was on his feet, and she caught a whiff of the drying sweat on his shirt. She pressed her pelvis up against him.

"Susannah, poor, lonely Susannah." He ran his fingers, with their Princeton signet ring, through a sheaf of her hair. This wanton creature ("courtesan" was his secret label), with her ghastly taste in music, was the most exciting woman he had ever encountered. She was everything he despised and feared, and she was the only person who had ever made him feel vital. He knew he risked losing his most important client. Yet who, he asked himself suddenly, could turn away from the sun?

"Come a little closer," Susannah whispered. "Take another cushion for your back."

"Maybe," he said, "I'll change my mind, just this once, about that champagne."

"Good idea. I'll bring the glasses. And don't you pay attention to that filth-squawking bird. He comes out with the damnedest foolishness. Why, who knows, maybe we can teach him some new nonsense tonight."

Emil shifted restlessly and readjusted his pillows. Chronic jet lag played havoc with his biological clock. Half a liter of Mont-sur-Rolle hardly helped. He crumpled into a wine-heavy sleep, only to reawaken a few hours later.

Two A.M. Three A.M. The lonely hour of the wolf. That desolate time when the most trivial shopping list can assume a monumental importance. Emil reached for a sip of Perrier and knocked the glass against the dish of musty apples. Damn fool housekeeper. Why couldn't she learn to arrange the bedside table? Susannah would never have stuck the Venini dish at such an obstructive angle. Imbecile servants.

Susannah. He was going to miss her if he married Helga. Was there the remotest chance she might consent to see him from time to time? Soon he was going to have to spill the Helga beans. He could not put off the confrontation forever. He shuddered at the thought of Susannah's reaction. Would she take it coolly, or would she become hysterical? How Emil detested emotional scenes with women. His mother had thrown a tantrum at her last birthday party, which had made Emil so upset he checked into the hospital the following day for an electrocardiogram.

He heard a distant thud, like the noise of a falling book or a paperweight. It must be the nightwatchman, who slept directly outside the door. Cretin. How often had Emil told him to move carefully when he patrolled the villa on his intermittent nocturnal rounds. One day the clumsy oaf would stumble into some priceless art work as he stomped drowsily from room to room.

The curtain parted a fraction in a draft. Emil tossed fitfully. There should be no drafts in his shuttered, sealed bedroom. How he hated the tricks of insomnia, the ghostly murmurs and glimmers that teased him like will-o'-the-wisps. When he was a child he had been afraid of what lurked in the great oak wardrobe. He had never liked sleeping alone. Yet here was an irony: he had spent most of the last twenty years wrestling in solitude with his own nightly demons. He, who in theory could have anything and anyone he wanted. Helga was capitalizing on beauty sleep under her duvet in Gruyère, and Susannah was probably preparing for bed, far away in New York.

He thought he must be dreaming when he heard the Alsatians howl in unison. They had never set up such a racket before in the middle of the night. They were too well trained to misbehave. One bayed and one barked, in a grisly counterpoint. Emil sat up straight, his heart thumping, and groped for the button behind the headboard that would set off an alarm at the police station.

The dogs became suddenly quiet. Emil held his breath. Was it safer to investigate or to stay put? He wished he were in New York or London or Zurich or Cannes, or any of his other bedrooms but here.

The nightmare rolled on its inexorable course. Slowly, quietly, the bedroom door opened. Under the door frame stood a tall, menacing figure in black clothes with a benevolently crinkled Halloween mask of ex-President Reagan. It was the ultimate surreal vision.

Emil's limbs stiffened rigid with terror, and he thought he was going to faint dead away from fright.

---- 12 ----

THE PEACE PIPE

*S*usannah sat at Madame de Pompadour's dressing table and wondered what to do next.

Manhattan was home. She could never return to Tennessee. She had no family, no heritage, no life there. She had thoroughly scrapped all associations with her youth, except for a few old Patsy Cline forty-fives, which brought back memories of wistful evenings sneaking around the stage door of the Grand Ole Opry, after her stepfather went to bed.

Vipers' eggs they hatch, and spider's webs they weave. She had called the shots that long-ago afternoon, metamorphosing the minister into a rutting hog. Jim McHenry reminded her of the minister. The attorney jumped to accommodate Emil's every whim—all the while doing the mistress after hours. They were kinfolk in fraud, Jim and the minister, two sanctimonious pillars of the community. When that runt McHenry ogled her, his ego ballooned at the notion that he and his master, Papier, laid claim to the same fancy flesh.

She was paying a fair price for the stolen signature. The occasional episodes of ho-hum sex were the least of it. He took her out to tedious evenings of Beethoven string quartets and bored her catatonic with his expositions on the S&L crisis and interest rate swaps. Susannah listened to him drone, nodded patiently, and caressed him with expert attentions under the fronds in the conservatory. When he kissed her he tasted of detergent and rancid milk. Never mind. She could endure a few bilious kisses for the sake of that invaluable signature.

Now they were partners in crime. Jim would never mention her visit to his office, and Emil would never figure out how she had simply stitched two documents together. The forged signature might mystify him, but it would not dawn on him that she had stripped another agreement.

She picked a bottle of Monsieur Rochas off the dressing table. Emil's after-shave had wandered by accident into her own perfumes. She sniffed at it curiously. Yes, it still evoked for her the faraway provider, powerful as a force of nature. Long ago the scent would have stirred her emotions, caused her to miss his all-knowing, starched security. Now the whiff fortified her with a kind of rage. He had taken her like a chattel from Edgefield and recast her as an art object, a sex object, his personal mannequin. All of which would have been fair and equitable—she repeated the phrase to herself—had he played straight. If he had only signed that contract.

It was exhilarating to feel anger again after long subjugation. The worm turns. She unscrewed a flamingo pink lipstick and scrawled across her mirror, SONOFABITCH.

If only she could find another ally. Dan Helena played his part, offering short-term anesthetic from her misery. It wasn't quite enough. She needed someone who would be there for her, someone wholly on her side. Dan was immersed in his own work, sweating and grinding in Dumbo. He had no air-conditioning, since he hardly noticed the scorching August heat. Every few days he would drive the pickup truck or the Moto

Guzzi out to Connecticut to check on the Belle John sculpture coming to life at the fabrication company.

Although she admired his single-mindedness, it was no use expecting him to sacrifice one iota of his precious, conserved energy on her problems. All artists were that way. She was an authority on the breed. Beguiling and empathetic when they have time to spare, but don't expect moral support once the work bug stings them. Artists were jealous of any encroachment, paranoid that anyone might come between them and their obsession. Which was all fine and romantic until the chips were down and you needed help.

Susannah sighed, dipped a tissue in cold cream, and wiped part of the mirror. Now it read ITCH.

Face it. I'm on my own.

The squeak of the opening door made her start with alarm. The maids were forbidden to interrupt her upstairs in the evenings. Was it an intruder, breaking in to steal Emil's Magrittes?

"It's me. I didn't mean to scare you."

"Lord, you had me crazed with fright."

"I tried to call this afternoon. There was no answer." Delphine took a step into Susannah's fluffy dressing room. She had a ragamuffin allure, in her frayed cutoff shorts, the ripped and shredded "Anti-Ozone" T-shirt, and her sun-lightened hair swept up in a ponytail. She carried a canvas sports bag over one shoulder.

"What brings you here?" asked Susannah. "I thought you were at school in Heidelberg."

"I flew in this morning. I'm exhausted." She grimaced. "I came to see you."

"To see me?" Delphine had left for the airport without even saying good-bye, after the quarrel last May. Packed her rucksack and slammed the white-and-gold front door, full of venom and hatred.

Delphine let the canvas bag slide onto the rug. "We must talk. It's important."

Susannah stared at her in astonishment. Why should Delphine ever want to talk to her? Could Emil have dispatched his daughter as an emissary to break the bad news of the rupture or the other woman, whoever she was? Surely not, when he knew how Susannah and Delphine fought like cats and dogs.

"I don't understand," repeated Susannah. "You flew all the way from Europe, and then came up here, to see me?"

"Something terrible has happened with Emil."

Susannah grabbed harder at Delphine's arm. "Has there been an accident?"

"Nothing like that. Papa's guilty about you. He says he ruined your life. Maybe he'll listen if you beg him. He's furious with me, and I need you to intercede."

"Me?" It was stranger and stranger. "What can I do to help you? I've got no influence left with your father."

Delphine slumped on the edge of the chaise longue, looking young and exhausted and bewildered. She gazed up at her longtime enemy and thought how strained the older woman had become. She noticed the shadows under Susannah's eyes. Her father's mistress was still beautiful, however, even in her old kimono and the frayed bedroom slippers, even if her skin sagged a fraction around the neck. What happened to arch enemies who grew old and tired and lost the zest for battle? Delphine felt inexperienced.

"What happened?" Susannah finally asked. "Why is Emil so vexed?"

"A couple of days ago someone tried to kidnap him. They broke into the house in the middle of the night, got as far as his bedroom door, and knocked out the armed guard who was napping."

Susannah gasped. "Was Emil hurt?"

"No. Luckily the dogs barked and Papa had time to ring the alarm by his bed to the police station." Delphine crumpled back against the shell pink cushions. "The police arrested one of them as he tried to slip away. I left Heidelberg straight away for Switzerland when I heard the news."

Susannah took in the string of events. "How did they manage to break into the grounds? How did they know which room he slept in?"

"Rudi planned the whole thing. He was a former boyfriend of mine. Just a stupid mistake. Someone I haven't seen since last year. But when Papa found out, he went crazy. Like a lunatic. I've never seen anyone so angry before."

Delphine was no longer the spoiled superbrat as she trembled and huddled in the pink cushions. She was a dejected child wrongly punished. Susannah, wanting to comfort her, laid a tentative hand on her shoulder. Delphine hardly seemed to notice the unfamiliar touch.

"I reckon Emil's furious with you at the moment. It'll pass, though. It's no wonder he's in a state of turbulence, with his worst nightmare coming true. Why, he's more afraid of terrorists than anything but his old mama."

"You don't understand. He's convinced it's a plot and that I've been organizing a Marxist conspiracy against him. Oh, how I wish I'd never set eyes on that anarchist slime." She choked on the words. "The last few days have been horrible beyond belief. I had to talk to the police as well. At least *they* believed me."

Susannah yawned. She had more than enough problems of her own. Something, however, about Delphine's wraithlike figure touched her—Delphine, who was young and dazzling and had every advantage of life before her, while she, Susannah, faced a blind alley.

"We'll talk it over carefully tomorrow. Get some sleep. You'll take a rosier view of things in the morning. You must be near exhausted, and with that long airplane trip, too. We'll figure a way round this dumb mess. I've never seen the fix yet there wasn't some way out of."

Delphine moved to the door. "Anyway, now you know why I need your help. Papa threw me out, just like that, without a penny. He's canceled my charge cards and frozen my bank account. I used all the cash I could scrape together to buy my plane ticket. I've got nothing."

Susannah floated on her back like a water lily as she drank in the afternoon sun. The crimson hair spread like a profane halo in the water.

The giant pine tree that shaded the roof dipped a branch into the patio. When the breeze blew, its slim reflection leaped across the clear water. A mosaic of crayfish and squid, designed by Raoul Epinard, decorated the bed of the pool. Emil had had it transplanted, nugget by nugget, from Juan-les-Pins. The glazed urns around the pool spilled marigolds and pansies. Susannah had replanted them herself at the beginning of the summer. To the gardener's confusion, she had put on some rubber gloves and uprooted all the convolvulus planted years before, under Emil's orders. The gardener hastily offered to help. She shook her head firmly.

Susannah had sent the maid and gardener away for a few days' privacy. They were all living in a temporary limbo, she, Delphine, and Emil, a suspended lull. Susannah had whisked the prodigal daughter away to the house at Martha's Vineyard, pending the gathering storm. Manhattan was sweltering in the August heat, and Susannah needed a respite from the weekly sex and (worse) daily phone calls from Jim McHenry. If she had to endure one more lecture on Vivaldi or the money supply . . . she told him she was skipping town for a few weeks' isolation and rest.

So she and Delphine, locked in an unlikely and somewhat rickety truce, had flown up here together, away from the blistering city. They always swam and sunbathed nude ("naked as two snakes," Susannah called it), only pulling on their T-shirts when the sun got too strong or if they strolled into town to buy newspapers or a club sandwich.

Delphine kept begging her to intercede with Emil. Reluctantly Susannah agreed. She would have preferred to leave it to father and daughter to resolve their own squabbles.

When she did at last call Switzerland to argue Delphine's cause, the housekeeper informed her that Monsieur Papier was away on business.

Susannah swallowed. It was the first time he had traveled without keeping her abreast of his itinerary.

She hesitated. There was nothing more humiliating than ferreting information out of servants. "Until tomorrow? Or the next day?" She kept the question as light as possible.

The stubborn Swiss housekeeper, who understood English perfectly, became suddenly obtuse.

"*Monsieur est parti,*" she repeated sourly.

Susannah could have howled with frustration. "To London? To Geneva?" she probed. "To Cannes? To Tokyo?"

"Monsieur est parti."

Susannah slammed down the telephone in fury. Had he left instructions that Susannah should not be told of his where-abouts? Was this her entitlement, nineteen years a mistress, to be sneered and mocked at by servants?

Delphine tried to calm her. "It was my fault, Susannah. I shouldn't have bugged you to call. Papa can be such a tyrant sometimes."

Susannah glowered back miserably. Delphine, who looked like a sea nymph in her Anti-Ozone T-shirt and her hair caught up like an Iroquois, could not imagine how it felt to be cruelly disengaged, day by day, gesture by gesture. To be fired, not swiftly, but by degree, insult upon humiliation. To know one's life was trickling away like ham gravy. What would happen when Emil softened and forgave his daughter, and Susannah found herself squeezed out once more?

Better for now to keep to neutral subjects, discussions of fashion and gossip and current events. By tacit agreement they avoided the prickly sore points: the disintegration of the Com-munist bloc and the disgraces of the Sandinistas. Susannah stuck to the Amazonian rain forest and Antarctic mineral exploration. Delphine answered her inquiries effusively, taking care never to patronize or express intellectual disdain.

Each evening they prepared dinner together. Since they were both erratic cooks, Susannah suggested they hire somebody to produce something more palatable. Delphine grew hysterical. "No! No one else here. It's too dangerous. Supposing my father called...."

"He can't eat you up, sugar. He's three thousand miles away." But Susannah understood the panic. Even at a distance Emil's shadow hovered. "We'll have truffles on toast tomorrow," she soothed her. "That won't be too bad."

Delphine looked surprised. "It's only August. The fresh sea-son doesn't start until November."

"We've got an emergency supply of whole ones in a glass jar."

The next night they scrubbed them gently with a new tooth-brush under cold water, sliced them thinly, and spread them on toast, sprinkled with sea salt. The singular flavors, washed down with Château de Beaucastel, brought back shared, incommunicable memories.

"Remember my thirteenth birthday?" asked Delphine.

"When your daddy hired the elephant and you rode all over the garden."

"And my fourteenth?"

"When he hired the airplane and he bribed the flying instructor to let you fly it yourself. It was a right shameful thing to do."

"It was the greatest." Delphine took a bite of the thickly buttered toast. "That bribe must have cost a bomb. The instructor could have lost his license."

"Or got himself sent to the pen."

"These are good." Delphine licked a morsel of truffle off her upper lip. "Papa must have enjoyed bribing the pilot. It's what he likes best, buying people's lives."

Susannah glanced away toward the empty chair, where Emil's ghost at times seemed to spy on them. "That was the year we bought the villa on Cap Ferrat," she said.

Susannah had enjoyed their villa on the fashionable peninsula, where the bluest of turquoise water washed up to the slabs of iron-rich cliffs. Everyone on the Riviera lived barricaded behind elaborate security systems. The neighboring villas—Les Palmiers, Les Oliviers, the Villa Tiberius—were peach- and lemon- and cream-colored fortresses, with metal grilles behind their flamboyant shutters. Emil's villa was cappuccino-colored. It was named L'Artiste Affamé. The Starving Artist.

A few weeks after buying it, Emil changed his mind and put the twelve-room cappuccino house back on the market. Cap Ferrat, he decided, was simply too dangerous. Already the owners of Les Citronniers and Cherie had been robbed in one season.

"Don't fret. Your daddy can be mule-headed, but he'll come round, give it time." He'll take you back, thought Susannah, but what about me?

Delphine seemed to decipher her thoughts, for she reached across the table. "We're going to see this thing through together. It's the only way we can stand up to him."

Susannah studied her earnestly. Delphine radiated conviction. She was always intense, whether she was on your side or against you. Once she took a position, she pitched in wholeheartedly. How long would she preserve that uncompromising clarity of youth in a fickle world?

It was time to broach the sensitive subject. "The other woman," Susannah said quietly. "I want to hear about her now."

"What other woman? What are you talking about?"

"Quit stalling. I know there's someone. I've got to learn the truth sooner or later. Is she very beautiful?"

Delphine faltered and riveted her eyes on Emil's empty chair.

Susannah pushed on doggedly. "What's her name?"

"Helga." Muffled.

"Who is she?"

"A typical Swiss petite bourgeoise. You take one look at her and you know the only thing that interests her is having a few chunks of gold to sew inside her mattress."

Susannah's throat tightened. "Is he set on marrying her?"

"He talks about it. But you never know with Papa. He's a slippery fish. He says one thing, he does another. He wants a brood mare, and Helga's the fertile type, you can tell just looking. But the girl's a beauty queen, and of all things she's got her heart set on becoming Miss Switzerland. So she can't get pregnant yet or even get married before the next competition. I think he likes the idea of marrying a floozy with that ridiculous title. He keeps mentioning how the CEO of Sotheby's married a Miss Israel."

Married . . . *married a Miss Israel.* Susannah's thoughts flew to the forged contract. Each afternoon, as she splashed over Epinard's crustacean mosaic, Susannah planned how she would refurbish the properties if the gilt-edged title deed were transferred to her name. She would tackle the labyrinthine beach house, load up a van of surreal bric-a-brac, and dispatch it to the auction house.

She felt an eddy of water wash beneath her as Delphine surfaced and jackknifed away, her narrow hips and rump like a dark bullet, evenly tanned. "I've had an idea!" Delphine bobbed for air. "Let's sell the fur-lined bathtub upstairs. Papa won't notice. He hasn't looked at it in years."

"Who would want it?"

"Some kook. Sarah Bernhardt used to sleep in a coffin. We could always try Baron von Tislowicz. He collects all that shit, too."

The telephone rang. Susannah glanced at her waterproof Baume and Mercier watch. It was 4:01 P.M. They both gulped. Susannah scrambled out at the deep end and lunged for the nearest phone behind the sliding glass doors.

"Emil! I was swimming. . . . Where are you? I called the house-keeper. . . ."

"I went to consult my cardiologist in Zurich. A terrible thing happened here last month. I was afraid I might have suffered permanent cardiac damage."

"Delphine told me. Honey, we are so terribly anxious for your health, but all the same you must stop taking it out on the poor child. Maybe she once did a little courting with that anarchist trash, but it's long since over. . . ."

"Delphine told you?" he repeated furiously. "Have you seen her, then?"

"No, no, of course not. She called from Germany."

"Have a tracer put on your phone lines. She is never to call you again. She is a dangerous criminal."

"You haven't but one daughter. And she meant no harm."

"She shall never set foot in any of my houses, you hear me? If you dare to harbor her, I will consider you an accomplice."

And a handy trick, too, thought Susannah, to swipe two birds with one stone. "Hush now, don't go on so. Why should I help her?" He can't suspect me, she decided. He thinks Delphine and I loathe each other.

"I've warned you."

She tried to distract him. "How's the PAP Fund?"

His voice immediately grew less menacing. "Remember Luke Elliot?"

She remembered the incident in Valhalla. "The one that painted those miserable stripes?"

"We've bought up his entire back work. We got sixty paint-ings."

"That trash? For how much?"

"Ninety grand. Nothing to us. It's a long shot, and they're

probably worthless. But remember they paid twenty-four dollars and a string of beads for Manhattan. Buy low, sell high. I'll call again in a while. Maybe not for a few days. I'm very busy with the fund."

After he disconnected she stood pensively, the phone in her hand, the drops of water still trickling down her flanks and thighs.

Delphine burst through the sliding doors. "Was it Papa? What did he say?"

"He says he wants you to stay clear of all his houses. And that if I shield you, he'll pitch me out, too."

The girl's mouth fell open. "He can't mean it! He can't still be so angry."

"He's in a vile humor. I've never heard him thunder on so."

Delphine took a couple of steps back and clutched at the door handle. "I—I'll have to leave. I don't want to get you into any worse trouble. Can you lend me some money for a while?"

Susannah considered fast. They would ride out the storm somehow. They would simply have to trust the servants in Manhattan not to tattle. She could not send the once so proud heiress, cowed and alone, into the streets.

"You're not going anywhere, sugar. You'll be staying right here under my roof, and we'll see this thing through together. Isn't that what all you said yesterday?"

Delphine's face lit radiantly from within, like a burst of early sunlight on the ocean. "You're a real freedom fighter," she said. "Like Malcolm X. Like Che Guevara." The ultimate compliment.

"We'll hang in there." Susannah made a Black Panther fist salute.

During the summer the galleries operated at half-mast, padding out the weeks with retrospectives and group shows. The real season kicked off right after Labor Day.

Luke took Ecstasy before he went to art openings. The little pale blue pills rendered the whole excursion extra mellow, saturating him with lovely, melty, squashy snugness. The drug made him want to rub up, like a young puppy, against the

exploitative dealers, the full-of-it critics, and the cutthroat painters who were his competition.

He sauntered down West Broadway, wearing his old paint-
spattered jeans and beat-up sports jacket. A new spirit animated
his narrow frame. After his decade of obscurity, the flush of
success was affecting his personality. He stood straighter. His
lips curled with full-blown derision; gone was the envious pout.
Kitty remarked that his eyes were different, too. The topaz
gleam had misted over. "Like Dorian Gray," Luke joked. It
might have been the ennui of success, or it might have just been
drugs. Who cared?

"How's Kitty?" asked Caspar Peacock.

"I told her to quit the Siamese Twin. I figured the windfall
from the Milhollands was some kind of fluke, but after the PAP
Fund threw me ninety thousand bucks for my back work, I
couldn't decently let my wife go on waitressing. Whatever would
people think?"

"So where is she tonight?"

"She's gone to a seminar on male narcissism in poststructural
cinema. You want to look in at the 313 Gallery?"

"What's there?"

"A new animal activist show. The fur people are taking over
from the feminists." The gallery drifters paraded in gaggles in
the warm September air. Luke caught sight of his own reflection
in the window of Mary Boone's gallery. He was becoming a
somebody, with his new air of downtown celebrity. "By the way,
Caspar, I've been talking up your umbrellas with all the dealers."

"I'm not doing umbrellas anymore."

"What happened?" Luke asked sharply. In the scramble for
attention, no aspiring artist had the luxury of switching styles.
The public bought a trademark, a recognizable imprint.

"It's not like I got pissed off with the umbrellas or anything.
I still think they're a powerful statement. But, man, we're approaching the year 2000, and the whole world is our marketplace. Specially the Japanese."

"The Japs like umbrellas. They love umbrellas. Those umbrellas are your shtick. You can't tangle with it."

"Yeah, well, maybe. Now I've gone two-dimensional. Neo-
Johns. I'm painting a flags series."

"You're painting the U.S. flag like Jasper Johns did in 1960?"

"Forget the Stars and Stripes. Johns proved that the canvas and the subject matter can be one and the same. Seventeen million dollars later and a quantum jump in art theory." Caspar gave a mock yawn. "Mine ought to sell for double. I'm painting the Japanese flag!"

Luke whistled. "You're painting the Rising Sun?"

"You got it, man. Dozens of 'em."

Luke and Caspar mounted the steps to the 313 Gallery, where a brazen sign read Smoking Encouraged. The fur show was packed. Every season new styles and movements were conceived and born, evolved, matured, wasted away, and perished to oblivion. Nineteen eighties postmodernism had opened avenues of expression for a host of subjugated groups, known in artistic jargon as the "Other": women, non-Europeans, homosexuals, primitives, schizophrenics, and all the other exploitees of capitalist subversion. At last it was time for furry creatures to register a silent howl in the jaws of mandarin culture.

The exhibiting artists tacked pelts, still crusted with blood, inside out on wooden stretchers; swirled cabernet and lobster red with black acrylic to express yowls and whimpers; they assembled a photomontage of minks and muskrats squeezed into pens and awaiting certain death, and foxes caught in merciless traps. The superimposed captions, cut in block letters from newsprint headlines, read, MINUS THIRTY DEGREES IN MINNEAPOLIS and AN AMERICAN IS WORTH A HUNDRED NICARAGUANS IS WORTH A THOUSAND BANGLADESHIS IS WORTH A MILLION MUSKRATS and THEY DIED FOR THEIR COUNTRY.

"This is hot stuff," Caspar predicted.

Luke pointed to a couple of women examining a gory rabbit pelt. "You see that curator from the Whitney? She was wearing a thirty-thousand-dollar lynx all last winter. And that photographer with her, wearing the ivory necklace? A month from now she'll be in her Blackglama again."

Stephen Hollis from *Art Insider* waved hello. "I hear," he told Luke breathlessly, "that your paintings have been traveling all over Western Europe with the Milholland Collection. I'd like to do a full-length feature on you for the magazine. When are you showing in New York?"

"Next month at Giulietta's," Luke replied grandly. The pale blue tablet washed him with prenatal contentment. The warm flood dribbled down to his fingertips. "You'll have to speak to Giulietta Giuliani about an article. She handles all my publicity."

He turned away. A blonde with Caribbean blue eyes and a body to die for was tugging at his sleeve.

"Are you really Luke Elliot?"

He gave her the Dorian Gray stare. "Do I know you?"

"You don't know me. I'm no one. I just wanted to say I saw your painting in the Milholland show in San Francisco last month, and I think it's fabulous, really fabulous, the way you've held out for the purity of modernism and your unapologetic colors."

"You like the ragweed green?"

"It blew me away."

"You an artist?"

She nodded shyly.

"I've got to turn out a slew of new paintings in time for my show next month. I'm hiring a couple of assistants. Would you be interested?"

The girl's lip trembled. "In working with you? Of course, but I'm just—"

"Don't worry about that. It's as easy as painting a wall. Easier. You slap on a couple of base coats of gesso and one coat of enamel. I tape in the lines for the stripes and mix up a can of paint for you. All you have to do is dunk the roller in the color and fill between the strips of tape. We pull them off like a Band-Aid and we've got a painting."

"Wow. I could do that."

"You got any pretty girlfriends who like painting? We're going to need a small crew on this."

"Maybe a couple."

Luke took her to supper at 150 Wooster. Then they taxied east to the Pyramid Club, where the action was coming alive. Luke glanced at two transvestites go-go dancing on the bar. They both were sexy, beautiful even, and at a distance more glamorous than any real woman ever could be. The dancer in gold shorts and bra, with shiny wet-look boots, matched the gold Egyptian mural on the wall. The other, a Marilyn look-alike, narrowed his eyes at Luke and dragged on a cigarette in a haughty, feminine gesture.

Luke led his blond artist into the back room, where a band in palm tree T-shirts was performing a hybrid of funk and reggae. The dark walls decorated with moons and stars matched the glittering chambers of Luke's mind.

"What kind of art do you make? Are you looking for a dealer?" Luke yelled to the blonde. He really did not care—with those tits who needed to be a genius, and besides, he was only interested in his own stripes—but the Ecstasy steeped him in a glow of empathy.

"Peter Dante's paid me a couple of studio visits," she roared back. "He keeps vaguely promising me a group show. It's probably a play to get into my pants. They're all like that, the dealers. They string us along. You notice how few women artists ever get anywhere?"

They danced between the strobes and the lights of moving stars that streamed like a comet's tail across the floor.

"Do you want to come back with me?" Luke screamed.

"To your apartment?"

"No, my wife's there. It's a shit heap, anyhow. We'll go to my new studio."

They wandered out to Avenue A. "Was it tough?" asked the blonde. "I mean, you know, making it?"

Luke thought of his janitor job, of emptying the wastepaper baskets sticky with pizza remains, cigarette and cigar butts, old newspapers and files and dirty Kleenex; of drowning his disappointments at Valhalla each time a dealer sent back his transparencies unopened or refused to return his phone calls; of surviving for weeks on cocktail party food, guacamole and cheese cubes with crusty edges, or whatever was free at shows or loft parties.

"It was no big deal," he grunted airily. "If you've got the talent, sooner or later you surface."

She kissed him lustily in the cab, as a tribute befitting a maestro. He held her loosely in the darkness. He felt her hand exploring his crotch and the skin of his fingers around his wedding ring. The Ecstasy was wearing off all of a sudden. He needed something else to fill out that hollow, weary feeling.

The driver pulled up to the curb outside Luke's new loft space on Mercer Street. Luke reached down for the fare into his sock, where these days he always carried five hundred dollars in cash.

They took the grinding freight elevator to the fourth floor.

"Wow," said the blonde. "This is all your space? You work here?"

"I rented it last week. That's why it's kind of empty." So far he had bought nothing but an Italian leather divan and a glass table to fill up the seven thousand square feet. The bathroom (heart of every lavish SoHo loft) was already imperial, with its gigantic sunken tub and vulcanized rubber sculptures around the medicine cabinet. A regal flight of steps, outlined in neon tubes, mounted to the toilet.

Luke kicked off his boots. "There's some Rémy-Martin in the cupboard if you want it. I'm going to smoke."

He poured a few flakes of marijuana into his rolling paper and added some white grains from a small plastic bag.

She asked him curiously, "What's that?"

"Heroin. It'll make you feel good. Give me your lighter, beautiful."

Luke leaned back on the divan, inhaling deeply from his joint. The blonde watched him as he slithered out of the clammy hole into a lake of tranquillity. It was peaceful at the center of the lotus where no winds come. Somewhere from far away he could hear the clean crystal ping of a music more simple and godly than anything of this earth. The girl was standing now. He wanted to smile at her fleetingly, to show that he understood her leaving, but smiling took too much effort. The very idea of smiling floated away like a lilac cloud.

The blonde must have been gone for some time when the telephone rang. Once, twice, four times, six times . . . The ringing sound was in its way quite beautiful. He had only to roll on his side to pick it up, but he decided not to. He knew it must be Kitty. Nobody else would call here in the middle of the night.

When the ringing finally stopped, he drifted again, weightlessly, deep into the velvet womb of the lotus.

13

STARS AND STRIPES

*T*he commander in chief of the Colonial forces slept lightly in November 1776.

In August General Howe inflicted a crushing defeat and massacre on the patriots, routing them from Long Island to Manhattan, across the river, and into the hinterlands of New Jersey. Those were the darkest days of the American Revolution. General Washington worked late into the night, strategizing campaigns to recover his lost Hudson River forts. Would they be able to hold out against the British until spring? He sometimes despaired of ever fishing the Potomac again or entertaining his friends at balls and clambakes in his beloved Mount Vernon.

Two centuries later the small town of Geraldine, New Jersey, still commemorated the autumn night George Washington spent in their village, resisting the enemy while he plotted his forthcoming victories at Princeton and Trenton.

Jacob Karakoff scheduled the unveiling of Helena's statue

and its attendant ceremonies for the first weekend in November, to mark the anniversary of the leader's historic encampment.

Jacob, with butterflies in his stomach, woke early and snapped open the blinds of his bedroom, where he slept alone. God had sent him a crisp sky of a perfect day. He allowed himself a curtailed session on his gymnastic bicycle and a couple of extra slices of breakfast lox, since it was a special occasion. Felice emerged from the guest room where she slept, with a martyred face at the prospect of a corporate function. The chauffeur picked them up from their Sixty-ninth Street brownstone at nine sharp.

They reached the town and drove past the old-fashioned pharmacy and the village hardware store. Jacob remembered when Geraldine was little more than a cluster of clapboard and shuttered houses around an eighteenth-century church. The incubation of Belle John, Inc., changed all that. Karakoff's company had brought jobs and prosperity to the area, while it had also cost the village its quaint atmosphere. Many of the older inhabitants still treated the toilet manufacturer with disdain.

Jacob hoped that Helena's sculpture would salve their resentment. He was counting on the statue to produce a wellspring of good feeling. As a patron and collector, Jacob believed devoutly in the communicative power of the aesthetic object. For that reason he had encouraged the board to commission Dan Helena, one of the most respected steel sculptors in the country, to produce a symbol for their headquarters to last in perpetuity.

Jacob Karakoff had far-reaching ambitions for his company. Lofty standards of management, integrity, and unremitting diligence were the hallmarks of his corporate culture. Those qualities, he knew, would nose Belle John into the ranks of Westinghouse, General Electric, Exxon, Sears, and General Motors.

They rounded the drive between the manicured hillocks into Belle John Plaza. His headquarters rose like a gleaming citadel, a sleek glass cube of open floor-plan offices.

The plaza, a somewhat grandly named concrete stretch, was dotted with a few picnic tables, where the clerks and secretaries brought out their lunch sandwiches and the *New Jersey Ledger* on warmer days. Jacob encouraged the local community to use the plaza. The whole town was invited to celebrate July Fourth with free beer and hot dogs and a modest fireworks display. Once a year local potters, watercolorists, vegetable growers, and pedigreed junk-store proprietors set up their wares in the plaza for the benefit of the Geraldine Barber's Emporium: in a ramshackle hut a local dentist had attended to George Washington's rotting teeth.

Never before had a plaza event been planned on today's scale. The picnic tables were replaced by three long trestles, draped gaily in red, white, and blue. After lunch all eyes would turn to center stage, where Helena's thirty-foot statue was waiting patiently outside the main doors of the lobby, swathed in its vast, saillike sheath of canvas. The covering, decorated in the pattern of the "Continental" flag of 1776 (thirteen red and white stripes and the Union Jack), would be parted by Karakoff's tug on the rope when the cymbals and trumpets sounded the fanfare.

Jacob stepped into the lobby and took the elevator up to his own corner office. The guests were not yet due. As he leaned back at his desk, he took in with pleasure from the floor-to-ceiling window the view of the Jersey woods, a rolling blaze of autumnal fire.

He had put all this together himself, the glass cube they worked in, the 18 percent return on equity, the $400 million in after tax profits, and now finally Dan Helena's visionary monument, awaiting its birth out there under its Continental flag. Eight percent of homes nationwide contained either a Belle John toilet, sink, or shower installation or a combination of the three. Sales were galloping in the South and Southwest. Not bad, Jacob thought to himself contentedly, for a small-time Jewish bookkeeper from Sheepshead Bay who had worked his way through night school at City College and made his first dollars running errands for the kosher butcher.

Under his breath he repeated to himself, *Barukh ato Hashem Elokeinu melekh haolom shehekhiyanu vekiyamanu vehigianu lazman hazeh.* Blessed art thou, O Lord, King of the universe, who has kept us alive, sustained us, and brought us to this day. The recitation brought him comfort. As if in direct acknowledgment of his prayer, God suddenly flooded the whole fiery woodscape with a double-voltage burst of sunlight. Jacob sat back, reassured. The golden weather was bound to hold, gracing the al fresco lunch and the afternoon unveiling.

The catering vans began to arrive at eleven and soon after, the first guests. Felice and Jacob greeted wave after wave of dignitaries. Belle John had invited presidents, CEOs, and chief financial officers from all over the country. Domestic equipment suppliers, retailers, advertisers, builders, bankers, journalists, and congressmen and their families were all represented. At last tally the guest acceptances, including families, totaled five hundred and twenty-three.

Susannah, who arrived with Delphine in tow, was dressed in designer cowboy boots, buckskin pants, and a jacket emblazoned with gold patches. She kissed Felice on the cheek. "You're looking pretty as a peach tree."

"You too."

"God love you for a liar. I'm a total ruin. Look who I brought along, though."

Felice turned to Delphine. "You're not going back to college?"

Susannah took Felice by the arm and led her away from the crowd. "Delphine's holing up with me for a spell till her daddy calms down. Emil still swears he'll have her gizzard and fry her blood for consorting with that crackpot anarchist that came to kidnap him from his bed."

"Emil has no idea she's in New York?"

"And there's no cause for him to learn so don't you or Jacob tell him. When he comes to New York next week for the contemporary auctions, Delphine can take some sheets and go sleep in the co-op across the street. It's hers anyhow. Her daddy would never think of looking there."

Delphine chimed in, "I research my Ph.D. in the library at NYU. When I sort this mess out with my father, I'll go back to Germany to finish up." She linked an arm through Susannah's. "Suze and I are having a wonderful time. We've never had fun like this before. We go shopping, we go to galleries, we go to restaurants and night clubs all over the city. Last night we had a couple of bottles of Château Margaux at dinner and ended up downtown in Valhalla."

Susannah quickly assured Felice, "Don't you fret over my finances. Emil's still paying the bills. Praise the Lord, the beauty pageant bitch is in no rush to get herself pregnant."

A further pack of guests were swarming into the lobby. Felice turned to play hostess.

Delphine pointed across the plaza. "Isn't that Luke Elliot, Papa's new discovery? What's wrong with him?"

Luke's eyes were drooping and bloodshot and his pale skin, like almond cake frosting, creased with puffy rivulets. He wore a new Day-Glo green jacket, and his spiky punk hair had been cut by a fashionable downtown salon.

Susannah peered at the bedraggled figure. "He sure looks like he could use some sleep."

Jacob Karakoff was at their elbows, all smiles. His butterflies had worn off with the touch of morning frost. "Hope you're hungry, girls. We've ordered up two hundred pounds of fried chicken to feed all these people. Plus a hundred gallons of coleslaw and potato salad, and a hundred and eighty pecan pies. Don't look so horrified, Susannah. You need to put some weight on those skinny ribs of yours anyhow."

The down-home menu, in keeping with the patriotic spirit of the occasion, had been Jacob's own idea. While his conscience whispered that fried chicken was no friend to high cholesterol, today was a once-in-a-lifetime excuse to binge.

When Dan Helena whooshed up on his bike with a squeal of Moto Guzzi brakes, Jacob gave the signal to herd the crowds to the trestle tables. Over the microphones he bellowed, "Good morning, ladies and gentlemen, friends of Belle John, Inc., and your families. Now that we are lucky to have with us the gifted artist who has made it all possible, it's my pleasure to welcome you all with a mimosa cocktail to Geraldine, to share with us this historic occasion." He waved toward Dan Helena, who was slouching in black leather against his motorbike and whispering something to Susannah. "So dig into our fried chicken and *bon appétit!*"

The local school orchestra was assembling. Their specially constructed stage was draped in billows of red, white, and blue streamers. They tuned up under a tricolor forest of balloons. While the company filtered across the plaza, the orchestra thumped into "Hail to the Marines." The squeak of the trombones and the drum rumble drowned out the commotion as parents and children of all ages shoved to take their places at the paper plates laden with Unveiling Day souvenirs: Korean watches, totebags, souvenir pens, Belle John stickers, and shoeshine cloths.

Jacob found himself wedged between a congressman's six-year-old daughter and the president of United Upholstery. Felice, to her dismay, felt the portly rump of Billy Berrymouse sliding up beside her and the sticky grip of his fingers on her arm. Giulietta held court between Mr. and Mrs. Joe Kominski.

"Do you like Monet?" Mrs. Kominski asked Giulietta. "Do you like Botticelli? Do you like van Gogh?" The banker's wife chattered on, nonplussed. "What do you think of Luke Elliot? My husband, Joe, made that brilliant discovery."

"Luke is making progress." Giulietta choked on her coleslaw. Although Luke's stripes had already garnered her thousands in commission, the dealer still resented having been bludgeoned into representing him.

Halfway down the table, Luke was staring glumly at his chicken leg. He wished he were back in his new Mercer Street studio, directing the brush strokes of his two voluptuous female assistants. With a solo show coming up, and several canvasses as yet unpainted, he had no business taking off the afternoon. Besides, that hollow feeling was stalking him again. It was a struggle to focus his concentration. Wiping his greasy fingers on the tablecloth, he patted the Day-Glo jacket and felt for the small plastic bag that contained a few grains of white powder. Maybe when Kitty was not noticing, he could sneak off to the bathroom for ten minutes.

He peered down the row of chomping jaws for his wife. She had ended up next to Dan Helena, who was trying to reassure her. "Luke'll be better after his show opens," he promised. "He's under a lot of strain getting so many paintings together so fast."

Kitty ran an anxious hand through her flyaway hair. "You don't get it. Luke hardly paints at all anymore himself. He's hired these two bimbos—Cher and Madonna, I call them—and when they're not all getting stoned or drinking or probably screwing my husband in the Jacuzzi, it's the bimbos who are busy painting in the stripes between the lines. Luke says it's the modern trend. He says none of the hot artists do their own painting any longer."

"What's this with the Jacuzzi?"

She groaned. "Oh, yeah, he's had one installed in Mercer Street as well as a new video system, and a water bed and a volleyball net and a Turkish steam bath."

"He's going to run out of dough."

"Oh, Dan." She turned her wan, wretched face on him. "It's great getting rich. After all our struggles, it's paradise. Luke wants to move out of our apartment on Avenue C and get some yuppie co-op in SoHo or the Village. He says our walk-up's a slum, and he's right, but I've gotten used to it. It's our neighborhood."

"So keep it. And get a co-op, too."

She took a sip of her mimosa. "I'm scared. What's happening to him? Do you see the way he looks?"

Dan nodded. He had run into Luke the other night in Valhalla, sweating and ranting and babbling. Luke was doing a "speedball," a heroin cocktail to take the edge off the cocaine. Dan had watched sadly. Some people were better off poor and unsuccessful.

"It's a miracle," she said. "It came out of the blue. First we sold the picture to the banker Kominski in Valhalla, then Giulietta agreed to be Luke's dealer, then those Milhollands wandered in, and now Luke's being bought up by the PAP partners, the most prestigious fund in the world."

"I hope *you're* getting something out of all this."

"At least I never again have to serve curried shrimp with coconut. I bought a new coat and a new sofa and some tiles for the bathroom. I don't know. I've got so used to scraping by, I hardly know what to do with the money. That sounds stupid, doesn't it?"

Dan studied her melancholy face, with its thin nose and sunken eyes. She reminded him of a forest animal, a beaver or a squirrel, scampering through the leaves. He would never want her physically. But maybe one day they could even be friends, of a sort. Dan Helena had never had a woman friend.

When he touched her cheek lightly, this time she did not flinch. He said, "Don't let Luke drag you down."

The band started up again, pitching and tossing through the "Battle Hymn of the Republic." Dan glanced at the enveloping sheet, which rattled against the sculpture in the gathering breeze. Was there time, before the ritual unveiling, for a quick one with Susannah in the Belle John elevators or the bathroom? Or could they get away with it in one of the offices or boardrooms? Maybe not. That whole damn building was one transparent window.

A couple of the butterflies returned to jitter in Jacob's stomach. He was really too nervous to enjoy his sinful fried chicken. How many more minutes until the band would sally into "America," which was to be the signal for his unveiling speech?

The president of United Upholstery, seated on Jacob's left, hummed along quietly, "And crown thy good with brotherhood from sea to shining sea." Over pecan pie, he brought up the PAP Fund.

"Next week we're sinking some money in Australia," Jacob responded vaguely. They were under no obligation to reveal to the limited partners the sources of their purchases. "Then we expect to build up major inventory at the November auctions."

The six-year-old child on Jacob's right tugged annoyingly at his sleeve. She had corkscrew blond curls, chubby cheeks, and a dopey expression.

"What is it, Jennifer?" The congressman's wife smiled apologetically. Jacob labored to look benign.

"What do you do here?" demanded Jennifer. She only took her thumb out of her mouth to smear her food over her pinafore and the tablecloth and her mother's cashmere sweater.

The girl's mother broke in. "Shh, sweetheart. Don't wriggle like that. This gentleman here makes potties."

The doltish girl's eyes flickered with mild interest. "You do?"

"And bathtubs," Jacob said breezily. "And basins." He wiped off his jacket sleeve where Jennifer had managed to spew coleslaw.

The president of United Upholstery inquired, "Where's Emil today? Why isn't he here, too?"

"He's buying a Magritte in the Riviera. He'll be over for the contemporary auctions next week on November eleventh."

Jennifer was poking Jacob's ear with a fork. She pointed at Dan Helena's thirty-foot draped hulk. "What's that?"

"It's a beautiful statue," said her mother. "In a few minutes they're going to lift off the cover and you'll see it."

"I made a mushroom in art class," Jennifer said.

Jacob pretended not to hear. At last the band was reaching the final cue. The cymbal crashed, the drum rolled. Jacob stood up and reached for the microphone rigged up by his plate.

"Ladies and gentlemen, friends of Belle John." The microphone squawked. He reached to adjust it. A company photographer crouched down while another inched up on his belly, flashing Jacob frantically. It was a mitzvah; the brilliant blue sky had held. The photograph would make a nice centerfold for the annual report to stockholders.

"We commemorate a year of record sales by the erection of this noble statue as a symbol for future generations of Belle John management and employees of our corporate coming of age."

Jacob took a deep breath and surveyed the sea of audience. His rhetoric had stilled them. The children temporarily desisted from their food fights and subterranean scampers under the tables between the legs of unsuspecting adults. Even cool Felice was watching him avidly.

"On this happy occasion I salute all our shareholders, both those absent and those among us who have given their hearts and spirits to the pioneering business of our company."

Jacob, aware of a rustle in his audience, looked up. Luke Elliot, in his Day-Glo jacket, was stumbling and edging his way past the tables. He looked seasick, groping for the edge of the building as he lunged for the lobby.

Their PAP Fund had invested a paltry ninety thousand dollars in that seedy artist's stripes, thought Jacob. Emil had suggested they might piggyback on the leverage from Luke's incorporation into the prestigious Milholland collection. But the sallow artist, with his hedgehog punk hair, did not look healthy. Jacob wondered whether Luke Elliot would last out the season.

He plunged on. "The business of a great corporation is to

grow, to enjoy the fruits of profit and contribute to American excellence. We at Belle John strive to achieve those objectives and more."

A loud squabble broke out in front. Embarrassed parents hurried to quiet their toddler, who had just been attacked by the plastic fork of the congressman's daughter. Little Jennifer glowered triumphantly.

Jacob cleared his throat and continued. "Er, strive to achieve, er, these objectives and more. Each day, as we go about our work, we are privileged to look out at the Jersey woods and recall that on this very site the father of our country encamped two centuries ago."

"Jennifer!" rapped the congressman's wife. "Stop kicking that boy, do you hear me?"

Not only Jennifer, but the whole plaza heard her. Jacob sensed the focus of attention drift away from his speech. He trotted nervously toward his conclusion.

"We at Belle John aspire to the values of our Colonial forefathers: quality, innovation, dependability. We are gathered here to honor a contemporary masterpiece..." The drums rolled solemnly. Jacob stepped up to the rope that held fast the covering canvas. "I give you our first beloved president."

Jacob reached for the dangling rope. "Give it a good yank," Giulietta had advised him. He tugged with all his strength. The canvas parted as smoothly as a curtain.

A gasp from the crowd went up. A benign George Washington sat up at concentrated attention on a general's military camp chair. This was a George of action, dressed in full battle regalia, the steel brilliantly welded into sash, cravat, and epaulets, the long nose and hooded eyes pointed keenly toward the Jersey hills. With one hand the figure grasped a loosely rolled flag, draped in artistic defiance to the steel's rigidity. Never had metal so skillfully imitated a roll of soft material.

Jennifer's demonic voice piped up, shattering the awesome hush.

"Who's that man?"

"Shh!" her mother implored. "That's George Washington, the president of the United States. He governed the first Congress, the same place where your dad works."

The child removed her thumb thoughtfully from her teeth. Raising her voice fifty decibels, she whined, "Why is he sitting on the potty?"

A crushing silence followed, and before the band could gather their wits and reprise "My Country 'Tis of Thee," Jacob had the mortifying impression that every eye out there was glaring at him in rebuke. The board had ratified the preliminary sketches and maquettes. How was it that none of them had noticed the commander in chief's ambiguous pose? Or why, oh why, couldn't Belle John have dominated the market in refrigerators or microwaves or VCRs instead of bathroom fixtures?

It started as a whisper in the audience, like a hiss of autumn leaves. A pulse throbbed at Jacob's temple. The whisper crescendoed into a titter, rippling gleefully through the crowd. From seething eddies, left, right, and center, rumbled outbursts of muffled laughter.

Jacob struggled to smile gallantly as someone uncorked a magnum of champagne. A sudden patch of grisly clouds scudded across the sky, and a stinging gust of wind reminded him that winter was soon due.

"Now you can't say that I never take you anywhere." Emil beamed, glancing around the ivy-covered walls of the outdoor terrace, where an original Léger mural peeped out at the lunchers gathered under the yellow canopies. The sun mottled the tablecloths in delicate shadow and warmed the parapet overlooking the hillside of St. Paul de Vence. He never wearied of this view of silver olives and Provençal tiled cottages.

"It's very nice here," Helga agreed deferentially. Her eyes looked blank and bored. She scanned the tables of manicured, middle-aged French women, indulging their inseparable poodles and bull terriers and dachshunds. Lulu and Tonton and Minouche scrambled on the cushions of the wooden chairs, curled in laps, or snuffled at their mistresses' feet. Helga was more interested in comparing the Chanel jackets and Nina Ricci suits than in listening to Emil's recitals of the history of this famous restaurant.

"The Colombe d'Or was always a popular haunt of artists in

the Riviera. Picasso used to eat lunch out here often. When he was inspired he even made quick sketches on the napkins or tablecloth."

Inside, the walls were plastered with Calders, Mirós, Picassos, and oil paintings by the owner, Roux. The worn Provençal tiles, the nursery chairs and menus scrawled in oversize childish cursive, brought back Emil's memories of waiters feverishly attending to Susannah's whims as the light from the carved wood fireplace ricocheted on her hair.

"I used to bring Delphine here for the weekend when she was little. The niece of Raoul Epinard—his only living descendant—had a villa down there." He pointed toward a pink stone villa, tucked behind a cluster of terraced poplars. "She sold me some of the most valuable furniture in my house, including the chandelier in the living room."

"How fortunate," said Helga. She wondered whether it would be less fattening to choose the asparagus vinaigrette or the fish soup.

"Delphine used to race up and down the steep streets of the village and hide in the doorways." The miniature stone houses of St. Paul de Vence interlocked like a jigsaw puzzle. In between, shafts of sunlight sprang out of nowhere. It was a child's paradise.

"Charming," murmured Helga. Some ill-behaved urchin had nearly knocked her off her feet this morning as she wobbled across the cobblestones on high heels. She was in no hurry to see Emil kiss and make up with his only daughter. As long as the Papiers were at war, there would be only one channel for all Emil's millions. Helga.

"I wonder what's become of Tizz." Emil looked at his watch. "Why can't these Austrians ever be punctual?"

Papier and von Tislowicz found the Côte d'Azur a mutually convenient rendezvous for their business discussions. The baron kept a villa in nearby Antibes; for Emil it was nothing to charter the Cessna for the forty-minute flight from Montreux. He had only to get up half an hour earlier than usual. He and von Tislowicz were negotiating a simple, straightforward exchange: the baron's Magritte of a dislocated bowler hat to be swapped for Emil's Epinard sketch of an amputated foot.

It was a chance for Emil to show off his fiancée, too. Von Tislowicz collected spouses almost as voraciously as he assembled Dalis and was right now recovering from his most recent expensive divorce. Emil relished the notion of parading his young girlfriend, up here where the perfumes of jasmine and wisteria lulled the senses in Picasso's and God's country. That would surely kindle an ember in the Austrian's lascivious, crinkled eyes.

"Ah, Tizz! There you are." Emil looked up across the courtyard, where the rotund figure in a Loden jacket was marching toward them. "We were wondering what had happened to you. Does this table suit you?"

"Splendid. Excellent choice. Picasso used to sit here and sketch, you know. At this very table, in fact." The baron bowed low to Helga, clicking his heels together. "Madame, my apologies for being late. A small traffic accident. I have the bad habit of driving too fast in these mountains."

Emil automatically looked over the parapet. An overactive imagination turned his face the color of dirty water. He himself never allowed the chauffeur to exceed thirty kilometers on the sheer hills and instructed him to honk his horn with fanfare at every hairpin curve.

Von Tislowicz turned back to him. "May I congratulate you, Papier, on your enchanting new fiancée. Ravishing, dear fellow. Quite a masterpiece. You must bring her to the auction next week in New York. You will be attending, I presume? Let's order. I'm starving. They make the best rabbit cassoulet on the whole Riviera here."

Susannah was busy arranging the cauldron full of asters and dahlias. Iris ushered in the visitor.

McHenry bustled past the three-headed stone dog. "I'm sorry I'm late. Emil phoned me in the taxi. He had a string of questions on offshore fund transfers. I had to keep the cabdriver parked downstairs while we finished talking."

McHenry took his radio phone with him everywhere. Only Emil, Jacob, and Giulietta had that secret number. When they called he would attend scrupulously to their business, wherever he was, in the bath, at Carnegie Hall (he would slip into the foyer), or even in bed with Susannah.

He planted a noisy smack on her lips. A dose of irreverent sex with Susannah had wrought a deep-sea change. He had stopped fussing over his low-carbohydrate diet and learned to drink champagne. It was true that he still flossed his teeth with religious discipline, cycled around the park each frigid morning, and would only eat water-packed tuna fish, but all in all the waxwork had loosened up.

She led him into the conservatory. "How's the PAP Fund?"

He sparkled. "We bought another of Luke Elliot's stripes today. Buff and pickle green. That was one smart move of Emil's, buying up the whole miserable batch lock, stock, and barrel last summer."

Susannah noticed the way McHenry recently referred to all PAP transactions in the first-person plural, as if the fund were as much his own as it was Emil's. His passion for the PAP Fund fed off the exhilaration produced by his affair with Susannah, and vice versa. There was no doubt that the tides of fortune came and departed in runs. Success bred success; failure nurtured fresh despair. McHenry greeted each day with anticipation. He could hardly believe he had turned the corner after forty sterile years. All he had covertly wished for was a spark of adventure, and now that adventure had found him in spades.

He slid off his jacket and loosened his tie. He had learned to make himself very much at home here. He had almost grown to thinking of the palazzo as his. "I've brought you a present."

"Why, Jim McHenry, to what do I owe the honor?"

He produced a square box covered in tissue paper, and her heart dived. She shook it playfully, as if she could not possibly guess its contents, and ripped off the tissue paper seductively, with the same abandon she had used to undress when she first bewitched him, as she let him tear through her silk dresses with a wanton, hissing noise. Afterward she laughed and threw them away. She had so many closets full. It had made him feel wealthy by association.

"We can listen to it tonight," he volunteered eagerly, holding up one of the four compact disks comprising *Favorite Haydn Symphonies.* "It's a kind of good-bye gift. I won't be seeing you for a while."

Her spirits lifted. She had been racking her brains for a diplomatic way to disengage from the lawyer.

"Mind if I take my shoes off?" He inched up on the sofa and pitched forward, trying to bury his nose between her thighs.

She closed her legs and held him off at arm's length. "Where are you headed?" she asked vivaciously. Tokyo or Australia or Singapore, she hoped. A long way away.

He twitched and gazed panic-stricken around the tropical foliage, avoiding her eyes.

"Sit on my face," cackled Gauguin.

"We must do something about that infidel bird, I declare. Felice takes her Akita to the dog psychiatrist to teach it not to yelp. Maybe they could clean up this parrot's mouth. So, where are you traveling? Somewhere sunny, I hope."

He avoided the question. "Susannah, you know how much our relationship has meant to me."

Sotto-voce, Gauguin squeaked, "I've lost my socks. Have you seen my socks?"

"Shut it, you mean, disgraceful bird. Jim, what is it? You look like you swallowed a mad dog. Spit it out."

"I've never known anyone like you before. Anyone so—warm and spirited and . . . well, let's be honest, so, er, sexy."

"Much obliged, sir."

"Now you're laughing at me." The Haydn-loving waxwork clenched his fist and, with pent-up violence, broke a swatch of greenery with a yellow bulbous blossom.

"Honey, that's a lollipop plant, flown in from Peru. It's a valuable orchid."

"I'm sorry. I'm just so—so—the point is, Susannah, we can't go on seeing each other anymore."

She waited calmly with folded hands.

"The point is, Emil has offered me one entire unit of equity in the PAP Fund, in compensation for ongoing legal services."

"Why, ain't that swell of him. One unit, you say? That'd be worth a million dollars, or am I mistaken?"

"Yes, that's correct," McHenry babbled. "It's small fry, compared with the other limited partners, but it's equity. It was more than generous of him. You see why I can't go on deceiving him like this."

So he bought you, too, she marveled. And only for a million bucks. I had actually imagined your price might have been higher. After all, you're a successful lawyer. Yet it only took one miserable unit to bedazzle you. Your unit gives you the illusion of having crossed over the line. You uppity flea. You think you've jumped from a professional workhorse to the international elite.

"Come here." She reached for his tie. "Let's say good-bye properly. We'll have us some champagne and listen to your Haydn. Your treat."

She meant it. With its borrowed signature her contract was safe. Should McHenry ever suspect, he would not breathe a word. He had too much to lose, after his un-earth-shattering affair with Susannah. Sometimes she turned it over reverently in her hands, as if she were holding an illuminated manuscript. Five pages, including the signatures, executed in navy ink, duly dated and witnessed, and stapled together as good as new. If Emil jettisoned her now, in exchange for his callow beauty contestant, come hell or high water the American real estate and contents would revert to Susannah. She was finally secure. In her own right she would be stinking rich.

"Pieces of eight," said Gauguin. "I'm losing my erection."

14

UNDER THE HAMMER

Nick Jones was flattered. On the telephone Delphine sounded so friendly and familial, in marked contrast with the last time she had scoffed over those jellied eggs. His ranking must have shot way up, he decided, if the boss's haughty daughter saw fit to socialize with the poor beholden émigré. He deluded himself.

Impulsively, he suggested dinner. Delphine snapped at the invitation. So he took her to one of the hippest, noisiest restaurants in the city, down on Gansevoort and Greenwich, where the brightly lit dining room reeked of garlic and even with a reservation the fashionable baby boomers had to wait over an hour for a table. Nick frequented the place and was in good odor with the maître d. He sometimes brought the pretty blonde from the estates department here and several of the other finely groomed stewardesses he went out with in rotation.

His patronage paid off tonight. He and Delphine were forced to endure only thirty-five minutes' crush at the bar before they were shown to their table. The lanky waiters careened past, balancing a terrifying quantity of dishes, swearing at the customers in French and Italian. The steaming plates of fettucini Alfredo and shiitake swordfish wobbled dangerously, borne aloft above the naked backs of the women in their cutaway dresses.

Delphine had made a big effort for a Mao-Marxist-Leninist. She was wearing a white Gianni Versace miniskirt, skating boots, and a heavy pearl dog collar. Envious, appraising eyes followed them as they squeezed through the aisles to their table.

It was hard to believe she was the same spoiled daughter of the house who had goaded him about his middle-class origins. Tonight she dispensed charm over the first course of goat cheese on radicchio and inquired effusively about his job at the auction house.

She was sleek, like a polished, precious stone, yet not far beneath the surface lurked her father's single-minded determination. She was obviously accomplished; she spoke all those languages and she had won all those skiing championships. What fascinated Nick, however, was her isolation. She seemed so out of touch for someone her age, as if she had been imprisoned all her life in a hothouse.

"Do you miss your friends in Europe?" Nick asked conversationally.

"I actually don't have many friends." She toyed with a mouthful of her braised pigeon in raisin-nut strudel. "I have a hard time getting to know people."

"You! You, who have everything?"

"When I was little every second of my life was mapped out. I had tutors in every subject to make sure I was the best. My father really wanted a son. He decided I should become an investment banker, so he sent me for all my vacations to America or to Tokyo to perfect the languages. I spent every summer in math or computer camp. I hate math and I don't understand computers."

"Now you're grown up, you can do what you like."

"It's not so easy. People find me intense. And the ones I truly admire, the environmentalists and political activists, stop taking me seriously the moment they find out that I'm Papier's daughter."

Nick marveled at this mixed-up exotic princess. The boss's daughter was disarming him. Until, over the rice pudding with kiwis, she revealed her estrangement from her father.

"I want you to sell this for me." Delphine raised her voice over the din of the restaurant and pointed to the triple-strand pearl choker around her neck. "My father gave it to me for my sixteenth birthday."

Nick Jones had been wondering all through dinner whether such large and lustrous pearls could be real. Now she took him by surprise. "If it was a present," he protested, "you shouldn't sell it."

"I need the money. I can't keep borrowing from Susannah. How much do you think I might get?"

"I don't know anything about pearls. I'll take it down the hall to the jewelry department to have it evaluated for you. But why? Can't you ask your father for money?"

Then the whole story came pouring out, and Nick Jones kicked himself for having been inveigled into dinner. This meeting smacked of collusion.

Nick's first instinct was to grab the check, shunt her into a cab, and escape as far away as possible. He would never understand these Papiers, with their obsessions and power lust and family vendettas. No normal blood and plasma coursed through their veins. But his job was to steal art secrets, not to finagle in their politics.

"Look," he grunted, waving for his check, "I've been thinking about that pearl necklace of yours. I'm in contemporary paintings; I've no connection with the jewelry people. I'm the wrong person to ask."

She eyed him piercingly. "Why are you so frightened of my father?"

"Me? Frightened?"

"He helped you get a job. Big deal. You aren't eternally indebted."

Did she suspect? He bluffed. "I'm sorry about your problems.

If you need some quick cash, I'll lend it to you." Damn. Why had he said that? He wanted no connection with a pariah. What would Emil think if he ever found out that Nick was in cahoots with his outcast daughter?

Delphine replied frostily, "Forget the necklace. I'll find a way of selling it myself. And thanks about the money, but no thanks. I won't drag you into my family squabbles. My father's obviously got some hold on you."

"Rubbish," Nick protested weakly as he hurriedly signed the imprint for his platinum card. "It's been a long day. I hope you don't mind if we make it an early evening."

She held her ground. "Don't let him destroy you. He's dangerous. Underneath all that cultural blather, he's an armored tank. He'll roll right over you."

"I don't know what you're talking about." It would be rude of him not to escort her uptown, but maybe he could come up with an excuse. He shuffled on his chair. "I wish I could help you. Sorry. There's nothing I can do."

"There is one thing." Fixing him with her level Papier gaze, she made her final pitch. "My father's on his way to New York for the contemporary auctions next week. You'll be working on the night of the eleventh at the big sale, right?"

"Of course. We're frantically busy. What with cocktail parties every day—the countess of Lochcairngowrie is hosting the gala Monday night reception—and people withdrawing their consignments at the last moment, and mistakes in the catalogs, and keeping track of our regular customers, making sure they've been through the viewing rooms . . ."

What no one knew was that each night, after the parties, while the crowds milled in the lobby and reclaimed their furs from the coat check, and the waiters rounded up the glasses and cocktail napkins, Nick Jones crept downstairs. In the basement security office they stored the gallery videocassettes, recorded during viewing hours. In the event of a theft or incident, the cassettes provided useful evidence. Otherwise they were normally taped over the following day. With diverse exhibits in four galleries three hundred days a year, it would have been impractical to warehouse a million miles of magnetic tape.

Nick simply substituted a virgin cassette in the chief security officer's video recorder. He stuffed the used cassettes deep into the lining of his overcoat and hastened from the building.

He spent half the night in his bachelor aerie, fast-forwarding, pausing, freezing, and replaying. Emil wanted to know who had been in and over which art works they had lingered. The following morning, on his way to work, Nick sent the list of the visitors by Federal Express to Switzerland.

"I want you to help me bump into my father after the auction," said Delphine. "Accidentally on purpose."

"Why?"

"I must try to talk to him. To explain. He's crazy, Nick. Believe me. He's so paranoid that he won't even speak to his own daughter."

"Have you tried?"

"Many times. Whenever I phoned him on his private line, he hung up. Now he's had the number changed. He doesn't answer my letters."

Nick suppressed a shudder. If Papier could treat his only child with such ruthlessness, he would quickly stamp out a paid informer if Nick's mission somehow misfired.

"But why at the auction?"

"I want to approach him when I know he'll be in a good mood. He's always jolly when he's just spent the amount of the GNP of a third world country. He gripes over having overpaid, but he still feels heroic about beating out the competition."

"How can I arrange a meeting?"

"All I need to know is exactly where and when to find him after the bidding. Will he be in on the bidding in the main gallery?"

"No, the boardroom." Star bidders were occasionally allowed to watch the whole proceedings from the window in the secluded boardroom, which overlooked the auction hall. It was a rare and distinguished privilege, permitted only to a select handful of regular clients who had already spent, or were about to spend, record-breaking millions. Invisible, and yet granted a bird's-eye view of the crowd below, they could phone in their own bids to the expert, who stood cupping a telephone receiver at the auctioneer's right hand. It was the ultimate discretion, to see and not be seen.

"Which means he'll leave quietly by the back. He won't mingle with the crowds on the staircase."

"Exactly."

"Can you make sure I'm waiting in the right spot? I only want to talk to him for a moment." She opened the palms of her hands and spread the fingers in an appealing gesture. "That's all."

Nick hesitated. He would be desperately preoccupied during the auction. He was assigned to one of the telephones, to field the long-distance bids, together with the stewardesses and the expert. Nick had a full complement of bidders, from London, Buenos Aires, Bombay, Kansas City, Yokohama, Honolulu, and many other cities. Everything depended on split-second timing.

He guided her toward the door, where the throng still awaited their tables. Her request seemed innocent. Perhaps it would be diplomatic to accommodate her. Sooner or later, after she was reconciled with her father, she could become useful. "All right, I'll help you. This once. As long as your father never finds out it was me."

"Thanks, Nick. One day, somehow, I'll repay your help. You'll see."

Those Papiers were a deal-driving breed.

People said the art market was unpredictable. Interest rates, deficit financing, and sluggish corporate growth made paper investments risky. Some institutions and individuals felt safer owning canvas, wire, stone, anodized aluminum, polyester resin, latex, and ragboard. Each year, at the May and November sales, the press gleefully reported the levels fetched by living artists and the ironic prices achieved by dead ones, many of whom had eked out lives in dire penury.

The major auction houses scheduled their contemporary sales for the same week (on alternate dates), thereby enabling the prime patrons of the world to assemble in New York all at once.

Athletes, movie celebrities, rock stars, corporate hitters, movers and shakers, and plain old billionaires vied for precious tickets; journalists and dealers alike waited breathlessly to see how high this year's Pollock or de Kooning would catapult.

The event began at seven P.M. Customers flooded inside the lobby and up the main staircase. The men were mostly middle-aged or older. In pinstripes and crisply tailored dark suits, they already sported deep walnut-stain suntans tonight, although it was only November 11. The wrinkles in their faces had set exactly where battle scars should be. The hooded eyes flickered as piercingly as their gold neckchains and bracelets from Cartier *pour homme.*

Their ornamental women wore the French and Italian couturier suits of the season: perennial Chanels, Diors, Ungaros, and Valentinos. Coats were discreetly *lined* with fur; it was fashionable not to emphasize the mink and lynx too ostentatiously. This year's hair was slicked back. All afternoon hairdressers had sleeked and twisted ponytails, ropes, and chignons. Blond, as usual, was stylish. Jewelry was chunky and metallic. The youngest, who had yet no rubbery wrinkles, favored wide gold necklaces reminiscent of their primitive ancestors from Ur and Babylon.

This gathering affirmed the intimacy of the art world. They all knew one another. The regulars flocked, the famous dealers, who juggled other people's money; the museum curators, struggling to compete with the commercial buyers; and the corporate art scouts with their endless purchasing power, especially the Japanese.

Giulietta greeted the Milhollands. Up and down the staircase the packed crowd heaved, like a torpid, ruthless current of lava. This group would slit your throat but in public never be seen to push or shove. "Excuse me," "I'm so sorry," *"Verzeihen Sie, Fräulein,"* *"Scusi, scusi,"* and *"Shitsurei,"* or *"Gomen kudasai"* buzzed everywhere as the stewardesses, dolled up in their finest, graciously directed the holders of the coveted green tickets toward the main auction hall.

"Looks like tonight's the big one," predicted Sanford Vincent Milholland III. "The yellow peril's out in droves. How high's the Lichtenstein going to fly?"

"Six or seven," declared Giulietta. "Easily."

"And the Pollock?"

"Sky's the limit."

MaryLou Milholland wore lime harem pants with a cherry cummerbund and matching hat shaped like a satellite dish. "There aren't enough well-to-do people left to pay twenty million for a painting."

"There's steam in the big corporations," insisted her husband. "Sony, the Mountain Tortoise Company, Aska, IBM, and AT&T—they're the new Medicis. Mrs. Milholland and myself have put together one of the finest private collections north of the Rio Grande, but even we can't keep up with the multinationals."

"You can still find bargains out there," Giulietta argued. "Luke Elliot, for example. Remember those fifteen-thousand-dollar paintings I sold you last June?"

"Sure, sure. They're still touring with the collection. The critics have been calling them the freshest new look since Serra and De Maria. *Art Insider* said, quote, 'a moving symphony of witty reductivism and austere paradox.'"

"Don't forget. I sold them to you first. There are a couple of Elliots in tonight's sale, estimated at seventy-five thousand."

MaryLou whistled. "We'd better take loving care of our early stripes."

The Milhollands inched away to register for their bidding paddles.

"Good evening, Giulietta." Peter Dante tipped his homburg hat. "You here to bid for the Pollock masterpiece?"

It was the highlight of the auction, that dense, tragic, magnificent composition in cadmium yellow, white, and russet, executed in 1950 at the pinnacle of the artist's maturity. Everyone knew it was beyond the range of any but the deepest pockets: the Annenbergs, the Getty Museum, or the irrepressible Japanese Mountain Tortoise Company.

Giulietta parried the question. "My Luke Elliot is making his debut here tonight."

Peter Dante sniffed. He and Giulietta were ancient rivals. "Flash in the pan. He'll burn out like a cinder. He tried to get into my gallery for years."

"Did you see the reviews we got for his one-man show? They wrote that he had rediscovered the mysteries of chromatics. They called him a latter-day Rothko."

"When I showed the first vomit paintings," Dante countered archly, "they talked about a new Pollock. They also compared my Wagnerian Hero to late Monet."

"*Shitsurei,* excuse me," squeaked a Japanese man as he torpedoed past them at the top of the stairs, ramming Giulietta's foot, which already throbbed, in the dainty Ferragamo pump.

With a stifled yelp, she nudged Peter Dante. "Who's that?"

"He buys for the Shining Squid Corporation of Osaka. Keep an eye on him. They say he's a contender for the Pollock. Let's get our seats before the room fills up." She glanced over her shoulder to the wide glass window with its apple green curtains that overlooked the auction floor. Emil and Jacob, she assumed, must have taken their "ringside" positions there by now. A hand drew back the curtain an inch, then let it close again.

Emil, ensconced overhead in the hidden boardroom, peeked through the drapes to see Giulietta waddle between the folding metal chairs in search of an aisle seat with plenty of room to wedge her behind.

A few minutes earlier the expert had ushered Jacob and Emil into the boardroom and invited them to make themselves comfortable. "I'll leave you two alone now." He winked. "We guarantee your privacy. No one will interrupt you. I'll bet you've got some hot items to discuss. I'd sure like to be a fly on this wall."

Emil confirmed, "You personally will be handling my phone bids?"

The expert consulted the list in his hand. "I have you booked for lots 6, 10, 11, 18, 24, 29, 36, 38, 39, and 45. I'll place the calls up here to you. All the best." He closed the door behind him.

It was a cozy nest, with room to seat twenty for lunch at the four dining tables. Tubs of dwarf mandarin orange bushes stood on the sideboard. Already in anticipation of next week's Impressionist sales, the fabric-lined walls were decked with seventy million dollars' worth of art. It surprised Emil that no one had yet gotten around to replacing the very ordinary splat-backed chairs whose cushions were stained by the excellent rémoulade sauce prepared by the auction house's full-time chef in the kitchen next door.

The portable phone in Emil's open briefcase blinked. He extended the antenna smartly. "Yes, Nick."

"This is my final chance to call you. A last minute phone line from Hong Kong was just reserved for the big Pollock."

Emil noted it. "Any nth hour changes in the reserve prices?" he asked.

"Yes, one. The Twombly is down to seven hundred thou."

Occasionally the house or seller suddenly panicked at the eleventh hour. Or some outside event of the day affected the fluctuations in value.

"Thanks, Nick. You've done good work. Any phone reservations at all for Luke Elliot's lot?"

"Sorry. Nothing."

Emil left the private phone at his elbow. Nick Jones would only use that number to call him in a dire emergency.

"There goes Baron von Tislowicz," said Jacob, peering out the other side of the curtain. "He must be confident. He's sitting in the front row. Who's that beside him?"

"That's the man from the Shining Squid Corporation," answered Emil. "Ah, here comes the expert. Which means they're going to start soon."

At either corner two burly black porters scouted the crowd with keen eyes. Their job, as "spotters," was to follow every twitch and ripple and convey to the auctioneer any bid he might miss in the hubbub. Nick Jones, the expert, and the five stewardesses were taking their places at the row of telephones between the audience and the stage. The girls wore high-waisted dresses with puffed sleeves and hair swept back in velvet Alice in Wonderland bands.

There were two main reasons for bidding over the telephone: anonymity or mere convenience for out-of-town purchasers. As the global village contracted, more and more bidding was conducted by the phone lines. Some brazen paddle-wavers appeared on the auction floor expressly to court attention. Big money, on the other hand, often preferred the privacy of the phone-in. Why advertise one's purchases to thieves and taxmen?

The phone bidders usually booked their calls a few days in advance of the sale. During the previous lot, a stewardess would place an outgoing call to alert them that the auction had reached their designated item. As the bidding proceeded in the gallery, she would relay the numbers to the absent client. She then communicated his responses to the auctioneer, signaling and nodding and gesturing with her fingers. It was an odd system, an invasion of twentieth-century electronics into the more primitive practices of horse trading.

"You want another drink?" Jacob helped himself from the "bar," a stack of mirrored shelves holding glasses of every shape: tumblers, brandy snifters, fluted champagne glasses, and goblets as round as a Titian breast. The lowest shelf was stocked with liquor and aperitifs of all varieties and some plastic sacks of pretzels and peanuts.

Emil caressed the empty glass in his hand and shook his head resolutely. "Not till afterward."

He sat down on the couch in the anteroom, struggling to master his nerves. He remembered the last time he had been here for a luncheon with the expert and von Tislowicz. That day, mainly for his benefit, they had decorated the wall with a Dali study for *The Great Masturbator,* which faced him at the table. After lunch he and the expert had sipped their coffee on this sofa in the anteroom, next to the Japanese Edo period screen and the side table with its ornate clock, a gift specially designed and handcrafted for the auction house and inscribed by the Shining Squid Corporation of Osaka.

Jacob lifted the apple green drapes another inch. "Emil, they're starting! The auctioneer's arrived!"

Emil's heart pounded, as if he were awaiting the crack of the pistol at the start of a race. "Quick, then, turn up the sound system."

"Where's the volume?"

"Behind the Edo screen."

Jacob adjusted the tannoy so they could hear amplified, with crystalline clarity, every cough, burp, and rustle in the hall beneath them. They took their positions by the window, each within reach of his own telephone, by which they could relay

bids to the expert, who in turn would signal to the chief auctioneer beside him.

The auctioneer was a legend in his own time. His stage presence was mesmerizing. He could make snakes swirl and sway,
pull rabbits out of hats and bids out of God knew where. He
leaned close to the mike. "Testing. Can you hear me at the
back?"

No megaprice ever ruffled him. He was everyone's favorite
uncle, everyone's coveted dinner guest, a man who could hyp-
notize buyers into parting with millions by a mere inflection of
his voice.

The audience snapped to frozen attention as the auctioneer
read out the standard conditions of sale. "Good evening, ladies
and gentlemen. All lots this evening are offered for sale according to the terms and guarantees listed in the catalog. Except
as provided therein all property is sold as is, and we make no
representations or warranties as to correctness of the catalog or
physical condition of the property. Unless otherwise announced, all bids are per lot as numbered in the catalog. We
open this evening with lot one, the Basquiat. I have twenty
thousand dollars."

The turntable at the front of the room revolved, displaying
the first lot, a graffiti scrawl of a Batman-like figure with enormous genitals and a blacked-in head, gridlike teeth, and surgical
stitching: estimate $120,000–$150,000.

The bids bubbled. "Twenty-five. Thirty. Thirty-five."

Emil had witnessed countless opening lots, yet there was
something about any first round of bidding that electrified him
with a geyser of excitement. It made no difference whether they
were bidding for a Matisse or a chipped teapot; whether they
were bidding in tens or thousands. An auction was the sport he
savored.

The bids volleyed like machine-gun fire in five-thousand-
dollar increments. The auctioneer set up the rhythm. "Sixty-
five . . . I have seventy in the aisle . . . do I hear eighty?"

Jacob shrugged at Emil. Jean-Michel Basquiat's prices for his
Halloween caricatures and childlike scribbles continued to hold.
The young graffiti artist did capture some barbaric irreverence

of the age. But had he not fatally overdosed on heroin, would the scrawls be commanding six figures?

The auctioneer syncopated his rhythm as he climbed to higher terrain. "Let's make it one hundred thousand. Who's going to give me one hundred thousand? Thank you, sir. One hundred thousand from the gentleman at the back of the room."

Emil saw curious heads swivel toward the bidder, who was Peter Dante.

The auctioneer was addressing a woman near the front. "The bid is against you, madam." That is, someone else has capped you in the blink of an eye. Your horse is no longer in the lead. "One hundred and thirty." A telephone stewardess, in a plaid velvet dress with a lace collar, raised several fingers, gesticulating to the auctioneer. "Forty. Fifty here in the gallery. Sixty on the telephone."

Jacob and Emil, who could hear every murmur filtered through the tannoy system, tensed at the hushed silence. It was only the first round, and the auctioneer had already tamed them. The old snake charmer never lost his touch.

"One hundred and sixty." The auctioneer glanced one last time across the rows before him. A perfunctory glance. This was only lot one. It was too early to pile on the melodrama. "Down it goes, then, at one hundred and sixty thousand dollars. Sold to the bidder on the telephone."

The auctioneer rapped briskly with his gavel and nodded toward a raven-haired stewardess whose telephone had relayed the winning bid. The auctioneer scribbled in his book. He and the expert kept track of the amounts and paddle numbers. The auction house also preserved the sound tape of the proceedings. Disputes did arise from time to time.

"Lot two is the Judd." Five identical boxes in galvanized iron swam into view. "Forty thousand dollars. Forty-five. Fifty? That you, sir?"

The auctioneer nodded at someone, as if he were throwing them a lifeline. He usually knew exactly who was bidding. All those old myths about sitting on your hands and not scratching your nose played no part in professional sales. If you were seated, or standing at the back of the room, or even enjoying Emil and Jacob's bird's-eye view, it was difficult to tell where the bids were coming from. Some of the regular buyers used prearranged signals. They touched an earlobe or adjusted their tortoiseshell glasses. The auctioneer rattled on so swiftly. Once he had seen a paddle raised early in the sequence, he kept that bidder in line of vision. An imperceptible flicker, or even a hand gesture, was all that was required to raise the ante to the next level.

They gained altitude. "A hundred and twenty on the phone." The auctioneer looked toward a stewardess in a Laura Ashley print. Her phone was active.

"Forty ... fifty ... sixty ... seventy." The auctioneer's voice was calm. The room was hushed. Two telephones were bidding against one another, communicated by the stewardesses, whose faces were blank. Ah-ha. The auctioneer saw a paddle wave. The action was back in the gallery now. "Fair warning, down it goes at three hundred and eighty thousand dollars. All done, sold to the gentleman at the back of the room. May I see your paddle number again, sir? Could you hold your paddle up once more, please?" The auctioneer scribbled the number in his book. The screen of the conversion board flashed the equivalents of three hundred and eighty thousand dollars in six currencies. "Lot three, the Hockney, with fifty thousand dollars ... "

The PAP Fund partners had reserved a phone transmission for lot six, a nine-by-seven-foot Franz Kline, executed in 1959. Jacob coveted the mysterious black-on-white characters, reminiscent of Oriental ideograms. He loved the magic of those naked brush strokes, like dark branches against the snow.

They had examined the stolen order bid list carefully. Emil had also noted, from Nick's smuggled videotape, that the man from the Shining Squid Corporation had come back five times to study the painting at length. There would be some serious sums riding on the outcome.

The audience was alert again, waiting for the thrill of a big one. Attention riveted on the auctioneer, who opened at three hundred thousand dollars. Emil lifted the receiver of the telephone beside him.

He heard the expert explaining to him at the other end of the line the patter they both knew by heart: "The bidding is opening for lot six, the Kline. Will you please speak loudly and very clearly, as there is very little time. We're starting at three hundred thousand dollars. Do you wish to place a bid?"

Bidding for the Kline rose by twenty-five-thousand-dollar increments. The auctioneer was taking bids from the floor.

"The bid is in the room. I have six hundred in the center. Not you, sir. Say six fifty. The bid is against you on the telephone."

"One million dollars! One million on the phone. One million one . . ." Emil and Jacob listened attentively, biding their time. Emil entered the bidding at two million two hundred thousand dollars. A nod from the expert conveyed Emil's bid to the auctioneer.

Peter Dante raised a paddle decisively. "Two million three from a new place in the room," barked the auctioneer.

The man from Shining Squid bid two million four.

The girl in the Laura Ashley waved to show that her phone bidder was going to two million five.

"Where's two million seven? Come on, let's have two million seven." The auctioneer was staring hard at the man from the Shining Squid Corporation, goading him onward. It was all a part of the skilled auctioneer's technique. He had developed it to an art form, cajoling one minute, taunting the next, feigning boredom or even contempt when the bidding hit a stagnant plateau.

"That's the spirit, sir. Two million seven." He nodded brightly at the man from Shining Squid, drawing him into the stage show as a participant. Audiences loved watching him fix on one of their number.

The Laura Ashley's phone bidder placed an offer of two million eight.

Peter Dante took up the slack for two million nine.

"Will you bid, sir?" The auctioneer was addressing the man from Shining Squid. "It's the gentleman's bid now, at two million nine. Are you going to let the gentleman take it from you?" It was standard auctioneering technique to pit the bidders against one another, like elephants in mating season. Any first-rate auctioneer knew how to turn the dollars game into a blood combat.

The man from Shining Squid slowly nodded his head.

Emil went to three one. The expert, now sweating with emotion, relayed Emil's bid to the auctioneer beside him.

"Three million one hundred thousand dollars! I have three
million one on the phone. Fair warning at three million one."
Pause. "Three million two? Anywhere? No? Down it goes, then,
sold for three million one hundred thousand dollars."

"We did it," whispered Emil. He allowed himself just a couple
of sips. The PAP Fund was off to a glorious ride.

They bought a Twombly for seven hundred and fifty thousand and a small de Kooning for nine hundred thousand. They
tried for a bronze Noguchi but dropped out of the bidding at
four hundred and thirty. But they compensated by picking up
some relative bargains—a Warhol soup can and a Calder mobile.

When Luke Elliot's puce-and-carrot stripes, entitled *Won't,*
came up at lot thirty-four, they leaned forward avidly. It was
their own consignment.

"Seventy-five, eighty, eighty-five, ninety."

Luke's reviews were already causing a splash. Giulietta poured
PAP Fund money into advertising in the art magazines; it was
a costly shortcut for making critics rave. Stephen Hollis of *Art
Insider* had written:

> Luke Elliot's perceptual ironies, brought about by
> irreconcilable color combinations, teaches us a major
> lesson about the nuances of the visual process. The
> artist's self-referential vocabulary may be read as a
> monistic spirituality. The witty and sometimes inscru-
> table geometric symmetry reminds us of the sheer joy
> to be derived from intellectual rigor.

In today's art business investors sometimes took a chance on
a newcomer who might be tomorrow's Serra.

The auctioneer was staring in the direction of Mrs. Milholland III.

"One forty on the phone."

Emil looked in amazement at the auctioneer. There had been
no order bids for the stripes and no prereserved telephone lines.
Nick Jones had double-checked. Yet the stewardess on the floor
gestured as if she were fielding a call.

The auctioneer smiled encouragingly at Mrs. Milholland III. "One sixty on the phone."

Jacob and Emil shot each other looks of glee. They were experiencing it at last, the auction house's alleged practice of "bidding up" or "bidding off the chandelier." This was the proof of what everyone surmised, that once in a while the house took a chance on driving up the price against a single bidder by faking nonexistent competition. And it was all being perpetrated over their very own Luke Elliot!

Mrs. Milholland III bid on undaunted. How high would the house nudge her? Emil wondered.

"Two hundred and eighty thousand dollars. Sold for two eighty." The gavel rapped. "Your paddle number, madam?"

"My God!" gasped Jacob. By setting an auction record, MaryLou Milholland and the venerable auction house had just turned Luke Elliot into the season's new star.

Delphine was waiting in the shadow by the freight doors, where the larger consignments were hoisted in and out.

"We must run," Nick ordered. "We haven't a second to lose."

She followed him up the uncarpeted treads of the back stairs. Her heels clattered in the hollow stairwell.

"Did my father buy much? Is he in a good mood?"

"He just bought a Jackson Pollock for nineteen million dollars. I can't imagine how that makes a person feel. He's your father. Perhaps you understand." Nick's nerves were still strung as taut as gut wire after the final duel for the Pollock.

The bidding for the masterpiece, with its indelible cadmium rhythms (which Pollock had never been able to sell for a penny in his lifetime), had been intense. Baron von Tislowicz and the man from Shining Squid had taken it up to fourteen million on the floor. The baron dropped out at fourteen and a half, while telephone lines buzzed from Tokyo, Hong Kong, Stockholm, Los Angeles, and Jamaica. The auctioneer soared swiftly through the millions. The keen shopper from Shining Squid gave up at sixteen. He had already spent his evening's allowance. Hong Kong and Jamaica followed shortly. During the final seconds, Emil was battling it out with Tokyo and Stockholm. When he claimed victory at nineteen million, the room burst into spontaneous applause, the big ovation of the evening.

Nick questioned how many of the bejeweled and suntanned buyers at that second recalled that the most the painter had ever earned in his lifetime for a single painting was eight thousand dollars.

Delphine's breath came in spurts from anxiety and running. "Nick," she panted as they reached the landing, "I'll never forget this. Never, never, never. Someday, when you need something, too, all you have to do is ask."

"Shh. We'll talk about that later. Now, listen. Stand right there underneath that Flemish gargoyle. They have to pass by this way to get out. They'll be here any minute."

"Where are you going?"

"I ought to get back to the auction. I don't want my boss to notice I've been missing."

Also, he did not want Emil to catch him with Delphine.

"Whew," exclaimed a familiar voice. "I thought for a moment that Squid was going to carry the ball."

"We'll sell it back to him next year," Emil promised Jacob euphorically. "At a five-million-dollar markup."

"My God." Nick froze. "They're coming!" He ducked out of sight behind a Louis XV armoire.

Emil and Jacob turned the corner. Delphine took a deep breath and stepped into their path.

"*Bonsoir,* Papa."

Emil's halcyon smile died away, and his jowls went purple with fury. For a dreadful instant Nick Jones thought the man might be about to have some kind of seizure.

"Watch it, Jacob! It's a trap, it's an ambush!"

Delphine moved an inch closer. "It's only me. I swear."

Emil's hand clutched at his chest while his eyes darted around the corridor, seeking out the shapes of hooded assailants. "What are you doing here?" he yelped.

"I want to talk to you," Delphine protested. "To explain."

Jacob registered Delphine's pleading face. "Good to see you, kid," he said. "Though you shouldn't scare us like that."

"Papa, please believe me. It was all a mistake about Rudi. I've had a lot of time to think about anarchists and class warfare since then. Maybe I've been naive in some of my beliefs. I want to tell you all about it, Papa, and go for a nice long walk and make you a cup of your favorite chamomile tea." She put her whole heart into the winning little girl smile, the one that used to work miracles.

It took Emil a moment to answer, as if he were gathering up his strength. When he spoke, his voice came in a monotone from far away. "Don't you dare try to follow me ever again. I don't want to see you. I've already given orders to my guards not to let you past the gatehouse in Montreux, and I have told all my servants that if they talk to you, they will be fired. If you are found on any of my properties, I will call the police."

"How can you be so harsh? I never meant to put you in danger. It was an accident. Papa, I'm your daughter."

Emil stared at her as coldly as he might appraise a forgery or a third-rate surrealist of no commercial value. "I have no daughter." He turned to Jacob. "We want to beat the journalists and photographers. Let's go."

Nick, in his struggle to stay afloat, had long since made it a cardinal rule not to waste energy on other people's misfortunes. When you were headed for the top, you ran only with the winners. But seeing Delphine blanch as she stepped aside out of her father's way, Nick felt a rare emotion. A flutter of sympathy for the girl.

15

SMOKE WITHOUT FIRE

The dollar lost six points against the lira. A cold snap was putting upward pressure on oil prices, which impacted the Japanese yen. At noon the D. mark dipped briefly, until the Bundesbank moved in to support the currency.

Emil profited handsomely by shorting dollars all day, with intermittent attention to the constant stream of PAP Fund business. He had already spent a total of eighty-five million dollars, including the November auctions, his deal with Sandy Pike, and various miscellaneous acquisitions. The excitement distracted him from his chronic anxieties.

He telephoned Susannah in New York at four P.M. EST. "How have you been?" They had not spoken for two weeks.

She made an effort to chatter normally. "I went to a benefit at the Cooper-Hewitt last night. Peter Dante sends his regards. Did you see Luke Elliot's review in the *Times*? They called his stripes 'brutally poignant.' However have you brainwashed so many folks?"

He gurgled contentedly. "They see what they want to see."

"Emil, I've been worried about you, all by yourself in that lonely old villa, without even your poor daughter for comfort. I've decided to get on the airplane tomorrow. I could be with you on Wednesday before sunup."

Whatever was he going to do about Helga? She was due home any second. They were living together now. Von Tislowicz had invited her to join his skiing party in Gstaad this afternoon. Emil, who no longer skied himself, was oddly grateful. He liked to think that Helga was getting entertainment. He often worried that she might become bored, shut up in the villa. If Tizz could distract her for a few hours (and suffer a flash of envy too, hopefully), it might keep his fiancée cheerful.

He glanced at the Piaget watch again. Helga should be back soon. Maybe she was stopping off for dinner with the baron's noisy friends in one of those roisterous, bustling fondue cellars that Emil detested.

"Susannah, you can't come. I have something to tell to you."

He should have been better prepared. All autumn he had postponed the dreaded confession. He sometimes rehearsed it in his head. He shilly-shallied, hoping to string Susannah along while Helga took the regional contests and semifinals by storm and, eventually, the national crown. Her beauty had earned her the highest marks from the judges in every category: Ferragamo bathing suit, Nipon evening gown, and Alpine folk costume. Then came the talent contest. Since she could neither sing nor dance nor yodel, she elected to answer a series of questions in her chosen field. Emil had volunteered to coach her in art history. When she was vanquished by Miss Matterhorn, for having failed to distinguish between a Picasso and the *Venus de Milo*, it was all his fault. He should have let her proffer her expertise on Alpine cheeses, a subject she really understood. Now that she was ousted from the competition, she was free to breed. They were advancing their marriage plans.

"You can't come to Switzerland right now. It's inconvenient."

He heard Susannah say gently, "Why inconvenient? Is there someone else?"

He stammered, "It had to happen, sooner or later."

"I'm none surprised."

He steeled himself for a tantrum. "It will be better for you, too, Susannah, in the end. Maybe this is your chance to find the kind of man you really need. It hasn't been working between us for years. We both knew that."

"I don't bear you rancor."

Why was she taking it so heroically? He tripped into a flood of self-justification. "Since that anarchist, that boyfriend of Delphine's, broke into my house last summer, I think every day about old age and death. I think about my father, dead at fifty-nine, and I keep wondering how long I've got. What am I to do with all my money and my paintings and my houses? I must have a son, Susannah. I must. You understand?"

"You already have a daughter."

"She's a monster. She consorts with terrorists and fanatics. She wanted to kidnap me. She'd like to blow us up, and all our friends."

"Oh, Emil, you're being unfairly hard on her. The anarchist deceived her, and took advantage of her naiveté. All her crusading with Greens and Marxists and fresh-air people is a way of getting attention. She never did mean any real harm. It isn't easy being the daughter of Emil Papier."

She surprised herself with her bold assertion. The sentences seemed to spill out of their own accord. The habitual brakes no longer served any function. She could say what she pleased, do what she liked. Her five-page contract protected her.

Emil, who detested confrontation, was mumbling how his pork knuckle was awaiting him on the supper table, and he would call her again soon, and he hoped she would enjoy the holiday season.

Susannah interrupted. "Not so fast. I gave you nineteen years. You owe me another five minutes."

"What's the urgency?"

"I need to make plans. To organize my life."

"Oh, that's what's bothering you. You've nothing to worry about. I'll take care of you, of course, and see that you are equipped with enough money to tide you over."

"To tide me over to what?"

"I imagine you'd like to get married to someone. Yes, that might be the best thing to do."

The rage exploded somewhere near the base of her spine, hemorrhaging through her limbs. His mania for manipulation rocked her. The money meant nothing to him. But he craved confirmation, as fodder to his power mania, that she would be struggling and helpless without him.

"Whoa! I think you've forgotten something."

"My soup is spoiling. We can discuss this next week, when I get back from my trip to Berlin."

"According to the contract we drew up, the houses and pictures revert to me now."

"You call that a contract? It's useless. A worthless piece of paper. No, no, my dear, you'd be better advised to rely on my generosity. I'll see you don't starve."

"You wouldn't cross a dirt road to help me. I'd rather rely on my contract." Sharp as the blade of a sickle.

During the ensuing silence she could hear him heavily inhaling his cigarette over the telephone. She felt thoroughly engaged, her nerves tuned to the hilt. Was this blood rush the same high that men experienced as they locked horns in business combat?

"You are annoying me now." He labored to sound placating. "Let's forget about that so-called contract once and for all. I believe if you dig it out, you'll find it's never been signed."

"You believe wrong. I'm holding it in my hand. And your fine signature is plain for all the world to see, with its loopy 'E' and little dotted 'i' and that mean pinheaded 'P.'"

"I'm warning you. I've had enough of your time-wasting games. If you're difficult, or try to circumvent me, you won't see a penny. You can go back to living in some flophouse with the prostitutes and drug addicts."

"I'm warning *you*. Instruct your attorneys to prepare for the transfer of title deeds on both the U.S. properties into my name. My new counsel will be Cheltenham, Arbuthnot & Crewe, located at Fifty-five Water Street. I've a notion you're familiar with them. Kindly forward the documents."

"You are insane. You should be locked up. Take some Valium.

See a psychiatrist. Whatever pitiful pledge you've got there, I shall litigate. I'll stamp you out like vermin."

"It's a valid legal document, tight as a drum and clear as vodka. I am weary of your child foolishness, sugarpie. You can't dispute this. Think of the evil publicity. If you launch an assault on me, every gossip columnist will go haywire. You'll get more press than Elizabeth Taylor or Mr. Donald Trump."

"You ungrateful tramp! I made you. I created you. *Quelle conne!* Where would you be without me now? Shampooing MaryLou Milholland's pink rinse? I taught you everything. About Duchamp, about Dali. How to speak, how to dress, how to hold a knife and fork. I practically taught you how to wipe your behind. And this is the gratitude you show?"

I had rather keep house with a lion and a serpent than keep house with a wicked woman. For you, Emil Papier, I dressed and primped and supervised the servants, for you I produced dinner parties and withered inside with boredom, for you I put up with humiliation and mockery. It takes so many years to build up a city; demolition is the work of an instant.

"Don't rattle on so. You'll do that old heart of yours a real injury for once." Hearing him rant like a bloodied bull, she almost believed he might.

"*Merde.* I can feel the pain. It's stabbing like a knife. Tomorrow I will go back to the hospital for an ECG."

"You do that." In the heat of the moment, she hardly cared whether he was shamming. "And I shall commence arrangements to ship away your horrible pictures."

"No! I forbid you to touch my paintings."

"They ain't no longer yours, sugar. Let's see. The Tanguy, the Dali, the de Chirico, three Magrittes, the Epinard, two Picassos, the Giacometti in the study . . . "

"Not the Giacometti," he wailed. Her venomed dart had hit home. He cherished the skeletal sculpture with a special sentiment. He had wrested it away from von Tislowicz at auction. His voice sank. "Very well. I'll buy it from you, Susannah. But first I want to see that signature."

She had won. She had reduced the great Emil Papier to haggling.

She took a moment to savor her victory. "How much?"

"I'll give you half a million dollars."

She laughed scornfully. "I'm not charity yet. You paid two million five."

"It was an inflated price. Tizz forced my bidding up."

"That's your problem. I'll tell you what. For two million bucks you can have it back. I never did care for it. It always looked like an old bedspring to me. That's my final, last living offer. Take it or leave it. It's a steal."

On Sunday mornings the maid was away at her Baptist service, so the Karakoffs answered the phone themselves. Felice was busy gathering her sack of knickknacks for the Christmas bazaar. She let it ring twice. Jacob would pick up.

He was finishing his breakfast downstairs on the first floor. He lavishly spread his Sunday morning treat, the bagel with smoked sable, which, to embarrass his wife, he called "Jew food." Licking a morsel from his fingers, he reached for the phone. "Yeah?"

"Are you Mr. Karakoff?" The voice at the other end was slow and deliberate and sinister.

"Who are *you*?" Jacob snapped to attention. Ever since the unveiling, Belle John had been pelted with vitriolic hate mail from various cranks and ultraconservative groups. Jacob did not take the first squall of letters seriously. How could any rational person believe that his company would deliberately commission a famous sculptor to portray George Washington on the john? The convex structure upon which the president sat in full battle regalia was incontrovertibly an eighteenth-century military campstool. Jacob instructed his secretary not to bother to answer the ludicrous complaints or even to file them. Just throw them away.

The tempest broke when Stephen Hollis from *Art Insider* published a lengthy critique on the new Helena masterpiece. Helena's statue, the art critic wrote, broke fresh ground in a decade of deconstructional antiestablishment site-specific sculpture.

"Dan Helena," raved Hollis,

has given the town of Geraldine a symbol for late capitalist society. With one blow, he has blasted our iconography of corporate, governmental, and educational
institutions. For this president, uniquely posed in the
execution of a bodily function, challenges centuries of
artistic lip service to the hegemony of the Caucasian
male.

Jacob, skimming through the heap of his monthly art sub-
scriptions, had been stooge enough to smile.

The critic's panegyric impressed few beyond the intimate circles of the avant garde who made up *Art Insider*'s subscription
base. The farce would have petered out, had not the incident
been scooped by a national magazine and a major New York
evening paper.

"Helena's Washington," explained the national magazine,

is what is known in contemporary art parlance as "site-
specific," i.e., a work designed for and inseparable from
its location. Today's sculptors who attempt site-specific
work inevitably address the larger social and political
framework of the art's surroundings. Their goal is to
call into question the ideological meaning of the site.
No context can be neutral. Helena's controversial piece
is a kick in the rump to the complacency of corporate
America.

This time, glancing through the magazine, Jacob frowned
and ordered his secretary to put through an immediate call to
Jim McHenry. Was the magazine article provocation for a lawsuit?

It was later, when he turned to the gossip page of the evening
newspaper, that he realized with a nauseated feeling that the
squall was whipping up into a tornado. The nugget went:

Flush with record growth and profits, Fortune 500 Jacob Karakoff, president and CEO of bathroom equipment manufacturing giant Belle John, Inc., finds
himself sucked into a cesspool of shareholder discon-

tent. Stockholders question the acumen of squandering one million dollars in retained earnings on a 30-foot Dan Helena sculpture of George Washington caught in a glimpse of er, um, private activity. This sculpture of a pooping president, while critically acclaimed by intellectual heavyweights, has provoked an outcry of obscenity and un-Americanism from local community spokespersons and national patriotic groups. Oops, Karakoff. Better be more careful next time you decide to dump on a beloved symbol of democracy.

Since that day the bitter correspondence had been arriving in armloads. Jacob instructed his secretary to open a new file. He also engaged a public relations firm to handle the replies to the rabid shareholders. Belle John's share price had tumbled 29 percent since Thanksgiving.

Every evening Jacob came home feeling like a beaten cur. Felice even sacrificed her Scandinavian literature class to dine in with him on his low-sodium, polyunsaturated menus. For the first time in years they would sit together afterward in front of the fire and talk. His town house on Sixty-ninth and Fifth became his sole refuge from the jackals. His only comforts were the Rothkos and de Koonings, the Barnett Newman over the dining table, and the unexpected sympathy from his icy, shikse wife.

Hearing the muffled voice on the telephone so early on a Sunday, he swallowed a lump in his throat. The bloodthirsty pack was finally penetrating the fortress of his town house.

"Who are you?" he repeated. His hand was shaking, and a spasm of gastric acidity banished any pleasure in finishing the smoked sable.

"My name is Roosevelt Jackson, and I am a spokesman for Patriot Power."

What the hell was Patriot Power? Jacob received vituperative mail from all manner of groups, ranging from Kansas and Mississippi rednecks to little old ladies and church deacons. The public relations firm drafted apologies and explanations to the Anti-Obscenity League, the Advocates for American Tradition, and the Crusaders for Family Values. So who in this jihad, this holy war, were Patriot Power?

"What do you want, Mr. Jackson?"

"Me and my community demand that you remove that lewd and obscene statue from the headquarters of your fucking company by five P.M. on Christmas Day."

"You may direct your inquiries to my attorneys. This is a private number. If you call here again, I will immediately contact the police."

He was about to replace the receiver when something about the caller's demonic cackle arrested him.

"You still listening, dickhead? You whine to the fuzz, it won't do no good. If you don't remove that fucking statue, we're going to dynamite your whole fucking headquarters. You have insulted this whole fucking nation and all decent Americans. So get off your ass, Mister Toilet King, and get that fucking statue down." With another eerie howl the caller rang off.

Jacob slumped back heavily at the dining table. His first instinct was to call the police immediately, to put a tracer on the phone line. Or should he dismiss the threatener as another lunatic crank?

He took a deep breath and studied his Barnett Newman. He used the painting, a dark monochrome with one bisecting "zip" line, as a quick meditative fix. A few minutes' concentration on the monotone bed of color helped to vacuum his mind of all the junk and debris that clogged his brain. His zip painting suggested infinity, an eternal reality beyond the earthly phenomena of board meetings and stockholders and annual reports.

"Is it your stomach? Do you need your medicine? Shall I call Dr. Nathan?" Felice stood in the doorway, clutching the Barnes & Noble shopping bag of contributions for the bazaar: thalidomide teddy bears with stumpy paws, samplers, jars of homemade chutney, and mother-of-pearl trinket boxes. "Jacob, what's wrong? That phone call?"

He nodded grimly.

Felice put down the bag with a thump. "What now?"

"Some nuts called Patriot Power. A guy threatening to blow up headquarters."

"You look terrible. Maybe you should lie down."

He smiled wanly. "I'll be okay. I've been toughing it out all my life. I'll lick this thing. You'd better hurry. You'll be late for church."

"I'm not going. I'm staying here with you."

"Go. It's the bazaar." He knew how conscientiously she amassed the musty toys and crumpled paperbacks no one could possibly want.

"I'm staying with you." She had been looking forward to the bazaar and the carolers' committee, but, as last week's sermon stressed, charity began at home.

The Christmas/Chanukah season usually brought out the worst in the Karakoff marriage. He kept his seventeenth-century German silver menorah in his study and every night by himself lit the wicks in olive oil. Felice had her Limoges porcelain crèche. She tenderly arranged the manger and oxen and shepherds in the guest bedroom, where she had retreated to sleep last spring. She sent her own Madonna and Child Christmas cards to her friends. The mutual Karakoff cards, Jacob insisted, showed Santas or Japanese pagodas and only read "Season's Greetings." They had agreed not to disagree over the Christmas tree in the living room and the holly wreath on the front door. Both were, after all, pagan ornaments.

This year Felice and Jacob miraculously closed ranks in the face of outside danger. December spite and wrangling were forgotten. The gross absurdities of the Helena scandal had done more to cement their marriage than the counselors, the series of high-pedigreed Akitas or last-ditch trips to Bermuda. When Felice saw her browbeaten husband soldiering on, she recalled the twenty-five-year old bookkeeper she had married, so quietly determined among her own people of privilege.

"Every day the goddamned tabloids think up some new headline. We've canceled the photos of Dan's sculpture in the annual stockholder report. God forbid we fuel the fire with pictures of the offending object."

Felice slid away the plate of half-eaten sable. "You can't go on like this. You're going to give yourself another ulcer. I've made you an appointment with Dr. Nathan."

"What do I do? If I don't solve this half-assed screwup, the board won't renew my contract."

"What! You founded Belle John, you created the giant it is, you took it public, you still own thirty-nine percent of the stock."

"The adverse publicity is destroying us. It's a nightmare. Exxon and Mobil and Shearson Amex spend millions sponsoring cultural TV programs and blockbuster museum shows to promote their community image as patrons. We've spent our money and managed to do just the opposite."

"You've no choice. You've got to get rid of Dan's sculpture."

"And play into their hands?"

"Just have someone remove the thing in the night."

"What will I tell Dan and Giulietta?"

Felice had never warmed to Dan Helena. Was it his brazen machismo that annoyed her, or had it to do with the melting way Susannah glanced at him?

"Who cares about Dan Helena? And Giulietta will have to understand. Belle John is going down the, er, um, tubes"—she nearly said "toilet" and changed the expression in time—"because of a grotesque misinterpretation of a perfectly traditional statue. Get rid of the wretched thing and replace it with something noncontroversial, like a Henry Moore or a Calder."

"We gave Helena a contract."

"Compensate him. Swallow the loss."

"He insisted on a clause defining the sculpture as 'site-specific.' Which means it was designed for the plaza and can't go anywhere else."

"Pay him off."

"Helena's already rich. He doesn't care about money. He hardly spends a thing."

"Tough beans, then. Dan'll have to lump it. Get the nasty thing out of the plaza and the fuss will die down."

Jacob scratched his bald head. He had always tried to run a clean business, to behave fairly and do the right thing. He wanted to set an example to his management. He worked harder than all the rest, commuting out to Geraldine every morning at six, laboring to learn the names and faces of his employees, even eschewing first-class air travel on company funds. In the long run his rigorous standards had paid off. Until this.

"Let's sneak away for a few days together," suggested Felice.

"Juan Gomez invited us to join them on the *Esmeralda* in An-guilla. We could take up his invitation."

"We'd have to share a cabin. You wouldn't like that."

"I wouldn't mind. Not now." He would still sweat and snore, but she would endure it. In the eyes of God she was his wife, and her place was at his side in his troubles. And if Christian duty prompted her to let him invade her delicate flesh with his eight-inch erections, well, she would concentrate her thoughts on Ibsen. Anyone could put up with anything for a couple of weeks.

He glanced at her curiously. He had never expected they would share a bed again. "Let's go out for a walk," he said. "I could do with a breath of fresh air."

They set off along Madison Avenue. Although it was a Sunday and the store was closed, both of them subconsciously drifted in the same direction. The fluffy puppies scampered in the window in a sea of soft shavings and plastic dog toys. Soon it would be time to adopt Ezekiel IV, a new member of the dynasty of silken Akitas.

When Nick invited Delphine out, he kept the tone light and jocular. "You owe me a favor, remember?" He expected the erstwhile heiress to decline a real *date* with a mere commoner.

"Anything I can do." Noblesse oblige.

"Would you look in at a party with me on Friday?"

"Okay." She sounded indifferent, as if she had nothing better to do. She added earnestly and unexpectedly, "I still owe you a proper favor. Our plan failed, but you did your best."

He then spent an exorbitant amount of energy planning the evening. In Manhattan any halfway eligible heterosexual man could name his own price. As a handsome bachelor, with a Porsche, a view of Central Park, and the accent of Laurence Olivier, Nick had his pick of well-groomed singles.

An evening with Delphine carried more complicated reso-nances. Those snubs over the jellied eggs still rankled. He needed to show off to her his new toys and playmates. Choosing her a Christmas present became an obsession. The idea con-sumed every waking moment. He found it in the auction house, tucked away in the memorabilia sale. There were John Lennon's sunglasses, an old tuxedo of Marlene Dietrich's, and Joe Di-Maggio's umbrella. And there it was, the perfect gift for Delphine, staring him in the face: the top half of Che Guevara's army fatigues.

Why was he so driven to impress her? he asked himself as he wrapped in tissue and stuffed in a Bloomies bag what looked like a pajama top in a brown-and-green camouflage pattern. It smelled of dry-cleaning chemicals, which had not quite removed a greasy stain on the shoulder. How could he have blithely chucked away so much money on this rag of dubious provenance? (It was alleged to have been salvaged by a local peasant, fallen into the hands of a journalist, and eventually been acquired by the history department of a college in Ohio.)

Her face lit up as she unwrapped the tissue paper, and he knew he had scored a hit. She was sitting on his leather sofa, sipping her nightcap of diet Slice with Mandarin. She waved away the bottle of Taillevent Brut he had specially laid in for the occasion.

"Oh, Nick. This is beautiful." She hugged the stained fatigues to her chest and buried her face in the chemical-smelling folds. "It's hard to believe he really wore these in combat. I shall treasure them. I'll wear them to bed at night." She blushed at her own erotic allusions and took a quick sip of diet Slice.

Until Nick had presented the fatigues, the evening had been an unmitigated disaster. He had taken her to dinner at Petrossian. It turned out she did not like caviar or smoked fish. She had refused to order anything but a bowl of borscht, which make Nick regret his own choice as he waded through the baby monkfish with nori rolls in vanilla sauce.

Afterward they drove to the Broome Street party of a famous interior decorator, who smeared the walls of yuppie brahmins with a caking substance and implanted the surfaces with coins, junk earrings, movie ticket stubs, bottle caps, and nail files.

Nick steered Delphine through the crowd of his new friends. A member of the literary bratpack was holding forth to a rapt clique. Delphine hardly glanced his way. On the sofa an Olympic tobogganist was making out with a principal dancer from Martha Graham. Their bodies rocked lasciviously as she arched her neck toward the floor, sweeping up the contents of an ashtray with her hair. In the hammock a rock video artist who had just made the top ten on MTV was selling five grams of cocaine to a kid who had discovered a Spanish galleon off the coast of Curaçao.

"Whom would you like to meet?" Nick asked.

She shrugged, and the festoon of fine silver chains jingled on her arm.

Nick became embroiled in conversation with a jewelry designer, who took one look at Nick's green eyes and clung like a suction cup. Delphine escaped to the kitchen, where she hid out the rest of the evening with the bartender.

"There you are," said Nick, proffering his glass for a refill. "I've been looking for you everywhere."

Delphine introduced the bartender. "He's the only interesting person in this place. Let's get out of here, Nick. These people are all so boring. You want to go to Valhalla?"

He winced. It had taken him such fawning and many dinner checks picked up at 150 Wooster to get invited to this party. He half wished he had brought one of his other girlfriends, who flitted around him like adoring moths. An insidious voice whispered that without Delphine's approval, the whole evening had gone rancid.

Now they were back in his eagle-nest apartment. He stretched an arm along the sofa, letting his fingers brush the nape of her neck. He almost regretted that she was so pretty. He did not really need Delphine's lithe body or her princessy face, with the canopy of long lashes. He craved her acceptance, the blue ribbon that signaled his ascension from mediocrity.

She ignored the tickle of his fingers. "You've got no pictures on the wall," she noticed. "No photos, no posters, nothing. You work in the art business, yet you collect nothing. I don't get it."

"I haven't lived in this apartment long." How could he tell her that he was still haunted by the same paranoia that had kept his walls at Oxford bare? Nothing he could acquire was quite good enough. Supposing he framed some sketch or lithograph, what inferences might his guests draw? Would they "place" him by his taste or snicker behind his back that he was struggling to overcome his middle-class roots?

She stood up and yawned unself-consciously. "It's peculiar. Everyone I know collects something. My father. Jacob. Even Felice likes Victorian dollhouses. She goes all over the world buying miniature furniture and tiny cups and saucers and little curtains and things."

"And Susannah?"

"Poor Susannah." She looked reflective. "I used to be quite horrible to her. I was jealous of her glamour, and she was intimidated by my education. People think Susannah's so sure of herself, but underneath she's vulnerable and lonely."

"It's normal that you resented her. You were an only child. . . . "

"And my father drove a wedge between us. We were competing for him. Now he's dumped us, there's nothing left to squabble over. And we've flown the coop at the same time, together. It's created a real bond between us. We're Emil's casualties. Living with Papa is like living with the devil. People make their pacts with him."

Nick avoided that delicate subject. "And what do you collect?"

"I don't believe in acquiring stuff. It's all a bunch of bullshit. People think because they've put together paintings or stuffed tigers or even a crowd of famous friends, it'll somehow make them immortal. Ever since I was a child, my father used to take me to auctions. He wanted to teach me about buying art. I'd see the treasures go under the hammer, and I'd always think about the old man or woman who'd owned them, lying dead somewhere, while we watched their collection getting split up and sent away all over the world." She stared out thoughtfully at the nocturnal skyline.

"Hmm. You can't take it with you. Can I get you another diet Slice?"

It was easy for her, he thought, to dismiss that primitive instinct for accumulation. Delphine still had assets. Like her empty co-op, with a few crates and the one wing chair. She had recently put the co-op on the market to raise some quick cash, so she need not have to keep borrowing from Susannah. Real estate prices were soft, she told him, and there was no knowing when she would be liquid again.

When she mentioned collecting a crowd of friends, did she

mean Nick's chic party tonight, which had failed to impress her?

He had a hunch he might be able to get her onto his water bed. When he looked at her hungrily, her eyes glazed and her lips parted a fraction. But then tomorrow? Making her moan and thrash on the undulating billows of the mattress would in itself not earn him her respect.

She turned around abruptly from the panorama of the ultramarine night, where the buildings of Harlem, opaque as cardboard cutouts, twinkled at the distant north end of the park. "Nice view."

"I like it."

"Nice car, too."

He had driven her tonight in the tomato-colored Porsche, which he garaged downstairs at great expense (while he usually ended up taking taxis).

"Yes, it is, isn't it?"

She brashly yanked open the front wardrobe, where his cashmere coat from Armani brushed against the Dunhill tweed. On the overhead shelf he was storing his new snorkeling equipment. He had already booked a luxury singles deep-sea-diving cruise in the Galápagos Islands for February.

"Nice clothes, too. Dinners at Petrossian. How much money do you make, Nick?"

Her directness took him aback. No one asked such questions except Delphine. He blinked.

She persisted, "Twenty-five thousand dollars? Thirty?"

"Twenty-eight."

"I figured. So where does all the rest come from?"

It was the night of the jellied eggs all over again. She stung back just as he stupidly fancied he was gaining ground. How long had Papier's inscrutable daughter been brooding over his life-style behind the canopy of lashes?

"I've had a good year in the market. Waste-disposal equities. Garbage-dumping companies. Got a couple of hot tips."

She slid her own coat off its hanger. "Uhn-uhn. I don't believe it. You're getting paid by someone. I thought maybe at first you were dealing drugs or something, but now I'm pretty sure it's my father. That's why you're so scared of him."

He cursed his fatal compulsion for bringing her back to his aerie at Trump Parc, for wasting the caviar on her and showing off the Porsche. Emil had warned him often enough not to flaunt his luxuries.

"Don't be silly, Delphine."

She stuffed Che Guevara's fatigues back into their Bloomingdale's bag and plumped out the tissue paper. "Thank you very much for the evening, and the wonderful Christmas present. You needn't come downstairs. The doorman will get me a cab." She moved up close and leaned to kiss him three times, Swiss style, on alternate cheeks. "It's your business, Nick. But remember one thing. When my father's through with you, he'll throw you away like a dirty Kleenex." She nodded contemptuously at the gleaming bachelor apartment. "Don't get seduced by all this. It's an old trick. He buys everyone. You, me, Susannah. It's small change for him. Your Porsche, to him, is like buying a Big Mac with fries. Thanks again for dinner. Let's keep in touch."

The shock waves from the George Washington affair traveled far from the epicenter. In the annals of art history, the reshuffling read thus: Belle John stock plummets; shareholders put pressure on Jacob; Emil and Giulietta, bound by friendship and PAP Fund obligation, are drawn into alliance with Jacob; Dan, in disgust, distances himself from his dealer, Giulietta; Peter Dante, rival dealer, rushes in to scoop Giulietta's loss; Dante offers Helena the use of his gallery for a poetry reading to rally support for Dan's cause; Susannah volunteers to organize the event.

Poetry readings, after having bottomed out during the seventies and early eighties, were enjoying a fashionable renaissance. The intelligentsia inked the important dates in their engagement diaries. The Manhattan downtown poetry circuit was as intimate as the art world and linked to it tangentially. All the creative parameters were expanding. Artists practiced poetry; poets practiced art making. Both camps expressed themselves in performance. Caspar Peacock, who also wrote verse in his spare time, helped Susannah compile the list of guest speakers.

"You're so efficient," marveled Dan with newfound respect. "I could never have put all this together myself."

They sat in Emil's former study, freshly repainted in cheerful yellow and remodeled by Susannah as headquarters for their campaign. She had donated the hulking leather-and-mahogany furniture to charity, dispatched the paintings to auction, and exchanged the prized Giacometti for a two-million-dollar credit to her bank account. She decided to keep the shelves of glossy art books. They might come in useful for reference.

Susannah telephoned the caterers and ticked off the list of RSVPs. She had invited—with some guidance from Dan, Caspar, and Peter Dante—every intellectual heavyweight she could think of. "We have ninety-four acceptances," she told him. "And people will likely bring other people. We'll need to get in extra chairs."

"Not for a poetry reading," Dan explained. "The best people always sit on the floor at readings. Sixty-five chairs will be plenty."

She reread with trepidation the list of art historians, deconstructivist philosophers, famous critics, and professors. Will they really come to my reading? she wondered. What would Xavier think of her now, wherever he was, retired in Laguna Beach?

They did come. They pounded up the stairs to Peter Dante's gallery on Prince Street, a motley crew in leather, denims, chinos, tweed, Luke Elliot printed T-shirts, peasant skirts, hotpants, jogging suits, fishing boots, granny glasses, knitted hats, and nylon jackets invisibly lined with real fur. Some of them brought blankets or small prayer mats to sit on. Dan was right about the chairs.

Delphine, in a crushed velvet Versace bodysuit, hovered with the Wagnerian Hero by the yakitori chicken skewers. Dan and Susannah greeted the audience spilling in. She was seriously dressed for the occasion, in black brogues and an old calf-length skirt from 1982.

"Delighted to meet you, Ms. Bishop," mumbled a professor from NYU, teeth tightly clenched around his pipe. "We all admire your courage supporting artistic liberties. The torch of civilization is easily extinguished. We don't need any more Ayatollahs or Tiananmen Squares."

"Ah, yes. Salman is here with us in spirit," said Susannah. "Understandably he couldn't make it in person."

"Hey, Suze." Caspar Peacock bounded up. "I want you to meet Jacques. He says you remind him of Simone de Beauvoir."

Susannah gravely shook hands with the famous eighty-nine-year-old French philosopher, poised delicately as a heron on his burnished cane, his tiny feet planted in satin bedroom slippers. "I am so sorry," he enunciated in his bell voice, "that Jean-Paul has passed to a better world. He would have enjoyed himself tonight. I have not seen such a dedicated group since the Sorbonne rallies in sixty-eight."

"We're honored to have you," said Susannah. "What a beautiful cane."

"A small gift from Marcel D. He found it in Macy's bargain basement years ago. He always said it was too overwrought to be a 'readymade.' May I present you to my friend Henri Claud, the master of referential simulationism?"

She shook hands with another Gallic philosopher, who reeked of Gauloises and wore an eye patch.

Peter Dante clapped his hands for order. Obediently the crowd ranged themselves on the chairs provided and three deep on the floor alongside. Dan Helena hoisted himself onto the sturdy table at the back of the room, where the liquor bottles were arrayed, and sat swinging his long legs like an overgrown urchin.

"Welcome to our reading," boomed Peter Dante, "and to this opportunity to hear some of our most gifted young writers. First, however, I would like to introduce Ms. Bishop, whose efforts and tireless energy have made this entire event possible, and I know that Susannah would like to say a few words about the menace of artistic censorship, the brewing storm cloud that has brought us all here tonight."

The gallery vibrated with applause. Some of the more vigorous people thumped and stamped their boots, and a couple of enthusiasts whistled. Susannah half expected to hear rumbles of "Amen, brother!" In a haze of noise and body heat, swirling smoke and bright lights, she stepped up to the helm with Peter Dante.

Her blood pressure sagged. She felt quite overcome before such an eminent audience. The clapping petered out; they waited expectantly. She was reminded of the itinerant preachers of her youth, the self-designated prophets who set up spontaneously at a busy intersection or outside a movie house or department store and called upon the passersby to repent in the name of the Lord Jesus. Timidly she scanned the rows of faces, assembled from the corridors of academia, the press, legendary thinkers who had crawled here tonight like bats and beetles from their caves. Above the horizon of heads, Dan Helena sat on the makeshift bar, swinging his legs like a scarecrow in the wind. He grinned at her devilishly.

The floor solidified again beneath her sturdy brogues. Dan needed her now, as he had never needed her or anyone else before. Her insolent sculptor, who had gotten himself accidentally embroiled in a cause célèbre, could transform megatons of steel, but he could not organize caterers, assemble guest lists, solicit funds, compose thank-you letters, follow up phone calls, schedule itineraries, woo journalists. He required a mediator to interface with civilization. He would be lost without Susannah's skills.

The rank and file was on her side here. This group had come to celebrate her, not to jeer. She was grafted to them by a mighty common cause. She took a deep breath.

"Artists, writers, teachers, precious friends." She bowed her head demurely. These were to be her friends. No man is an island. She would never feel quite so alone again. "Thank you for coming forth tonight. As you all know, our most fundamental freedom of self-expression is under siege. And where is this exercise of fascism being perpetrated? Not in Red China, not in Iran, not in Johannesburg or Latin America, no, right here in the United States, but a few miles across the Hudson, in Geraldine, New Jersey." She hit a crescendo. Maybe it was a gift of hers, this sudden aptitude for preaching. She knew she was touching them now. "Many of you know Dan Helena personally, and you all are acquainted with his work. One year ago, the board of directors of Belle John, Inc., entered into a binding contract with Dan, commissioning him to design a 'site-specific' three-dimensional art work for ornamenting the plaza outside the company headquarters. As conscientious postmodernists you all are sensitive to the exigencies of the site-specific clause." Exigencies! The postmodernists twitched with appreciation. This woman was indeed a born speaker.

"Complaints from certain materialist-minded shareholders threaten Dan's sculpture with removal. I am confident there's not a soul amongst us would take such a desecration lightly. We are accordingly gathered to support Dan Helena and to sign our names to this petition, which I now take the liberty of circulating." In full view she handed the paper first to the aged Jacques, who unhesitatingly signed with a flourish worthy of John Hancock.

There followed a general seething and shuffling as the writers and artists searched their pockets for pens. Behind them, Dan gave her the thumbs-up of approval and beckoned for her to join him. She made her way, radiant, down the aisle. On either side well-wishers beamed at her, patted her elbow, and murmured their congratulations. "Excellent," Dan whispered hotly in her ear as she wriggled next to him. "Wherever did you learn to make speeches? They hung on every word."

She glowed inside. "Hush up. They're commencing."

Peter Dante briefly introduced the first poet of the program. A lanky young man in an overly large raincoat proffered a lamentation for the garbage barges, forced, like wandering Jews, to drift from port to port without permission to unload their debris.

Styrofoam egg cartons, TV Guide, *cigarette butts,*
Light Entrée Dinner trays, laddered Supp-Hose,
burnt light bulbs, emery boards, padded envelopes,
soggy tea bags, razor blades,
single socks, Baby Ruth wrappers, coat hangers,
buttons, clumps of hair, Skippy jars, crumpled giftwrap, packets of
soy sauce,
Trojans, playbills, Popsicle sticks . . .

Susannah tried to give due observance to the solemn litany. Outmoded were the LSD-inspired rambles of the sixties. The new generation was direct and provocative, showmen all. A few rows in front, another poet was catalyzed. He took out a small notebook and began scribbling wildly.

Dan wrapped an arm around her waist. She straightened her back proudly. If only Emil could see the army she had mustered. If he could hear her address her congregation with newfound religious fervor. What did he think to hear her name linked with Helena's? Such *glasnost* would have been unthinkable a few months ago. Now she could consort openly with whom she liked; and here she was, carving herself a footnote in cultural history.

The garbage elegy was winding to its conclusion.

Charmin rolls, shoeboxes, dried-up nail polish,
hotel keys, letters from local congressmen, soap slivers,
soda cans, Handi Wipes, wedges of pickle, bottle caps,
snipped price tags, Oreo packages,
Pampers, stray gloves,
business cards, small brown paper bags . . .

16

BETWEEN THE CRACKS

*L*ong after she stopped working at the Siamese Twin, Kitty still awoke with the stench of coconut in her nostrils. She thrashed across their best-quality orthopedic mattress (they had dumped out the lumpy, leaking one on the corner of Avenue C) and reached for the empty space in the bed beside her. Luke often stayed out all night in the newly rented studio on Mercer Street. He claimed to be working, or "pacing," as he put it, conceiving novel colors for a fresh batch of stripes. Yet when she telephoned the studio late, even at four A.M., there was no answer.

She screwed her eyes shut and struggled to sink back to sleep. The curse buzzed in her brain. Don't wish for anything too hard or you might get it. During the lean times, when she scrimped and saved in the peanut-butter jar and her shoulder blades ached perpetually from lugging stacks of plates, she had fantasized about their selling an occasional painting. Without warning, Luke's career had exploded in a cosmic bang. And now she would have given anything, almost anything, to put the clock back.

It had been fun at the beginning, buying a few little things for the apartment: a wok, an armchair, a cappuccino maker, a twelve-inch TV, and lamp shades to cover the naked bulbs. She ordered a hundred dollars' worth of groceries from Dean & DeLuca. Whenever she opened the cupboard doors, she thrilled at the sight of those sun-dried tomatoes, blueberry vinegar, and kumquats in cognac. She paid a professional plumber to come in and fix the dripping faucets and a plasterer to seal the window gaps Luke had never gotten around to.

But each time she glanced at her husband's sallow cheeks, she knew the small comforts had been bought at a cruel price. She would have willingly been poor again, just to bring back the topaz glint in his eyes, now permanently pink-rimmed (he pretended from the turpentine).

"Take a break," she begged. "Let's go away to Wyoming or Vermont and breathe clean air and forget all this."

"Wyoming? It's February."

"Or anywhere. You can leave instructions for Cher and Madonna. They do all the work anyhow. When we get back there'll be ten new paintings waiting."

"I can't leave SoHo. I need to be seen. That Brazilian restaurant wants the mural for the dining room ceiling, and I've got the biennial coming up." He pointed to the new microwave oven. "What do you think pays for all this?"

The pleasure of the money was dwindling. She loitered in the boutiques on Spring Street and West Broadway, listlessly trying on tunics and skirts made in olive sack and cocoa burlap. Sometimes she bought an earth-tone linen jacket or some stiletto ankle boots so delicate the heels broke off on the first wearing. She felt like an intruder in her own neighborhood, hauling the smart, shiny shopping bags from Agnes B. or the French Connection back into the derelict streets of Alphabet City.

Now when Dan or Caspar stopped by late at night for a look at Luke's latest stripes, Kitty could offer them vodka or bourbon. Before it had been just a glass of water.

Kitty asked Caspar Peacock what he would do if success were suddenly thrust upon him.

"Man, I'd buy a piece of real estate high up on a mountain in Hawaii, with a real observatory and my own huge telescope, and study the stars and moon and planets. I really get into all that stuff."

The Japanese flag paintings had not aroused excitement in the market, and Caspar was currently experimenting with "Milky Way" videos. He scattered a mix of Ajax, sea salt, and flour in spirals across a black tabletop and recorded hour-long tapes of simulated skies on the camcorder.

Caspar drained his vodka. "Will Luke be back soon?"

She shrugged helplessly. "No idea. He's painting the ceiling at the Ipanema Grill. He and the bimbos work nights."

Luke had accepted the commission to decorate the Brazilian club restaurant with turquoise and verdigris stripes. Giulietta persuaded him that he would benefit from the publicity to be derived from striping the hippest up-and-coming night spot in Chelsea. Cher and Madonna did all the heavy physical work, while Luke slumped beneath them, over his piña colada. With a glazed stare he watched the rhythm of their thighs and neat buttocks. *Art Insider* was already planning the cover for the April edition to show Luke and his two nymphs perched on stepladders as they rolled the bands of verdigris.

Caspar registered her stifled sigh. "Listen, I know it's been a rough season for you. I want to give you a present. My *Japanese Flag Number Seventeen*. It's a masterpiece. One day it'll buy you a vacation in Hawaii."

"Wow. Thanks." She tried to look suitably impressed. With great hoopla, they all gave one another their paintings at stirring moments. Kitty had already jammed several of the Visual Scientist's slashed underwear panels at the back of the closet. Oh well, maybe one day Caspar's ship would come in, too, and the flag would actually be worth a trip to the beach.

The next morning she woke up alone again. After she had meditated, defrosted the fridge, watered the window boxes, and hand-washed Luke's favorite graffiti socks (he would not trust the dry cleaner), she could think of nothing else to do, so she got out a hard-bristle brush and cleaned the cracks between the floorboards. Like us, she remembered, that's how we used to live, between the cracks. It was so safe and snug down there with the dust and plaster and asbestos shavings, while the giants thumped overhead and left us alone. Kitty would not dare engage someone to clean for her on Avenue C. The news would soon leak. Her barrio neighbors already eyed them suspiciously as they watched each new crate of furniture being delivered.

She signed up for a lecture series on deconstructive feminist cinema. "Jean Luc Godard: Woman as Image; Betrayal and Paralysis." Kitty hummed the title of her seminar to herself as she strolled down Avenue B. "The heroines of Godard's films," scribbled Kitty in her notebook, "betray their men out of a sense of despair and isolation. Advertising, packaging, media, billboards, and newspapers have overwhelmed real people and forced them into ambivalent relationships."

She stopped off at Valhalla for a drink with the Visual Scientist. It killed time. The Visual Scientist launched into a debate with the Wagnerian Hero over distinctions between "content" and "context."

"Hey, look who's here! It's Saint Kitty. How've you been? How's your celebrity husband?" The bartender slid a glass across the bar.

"Fine, great. Maybe a little bored," she admitted. "I don't have a whole lot to do with my unstructured time."

"Have you ever thought of returning to your old job?"

"My waitress job?" Her voice expressed horror. "Anyway, they closed down the Siamese Twin. It was bound to happen. One visit from the Department of Health."

"Sanitary violations?"

"Opiates. They were spiking the food. Anyhow, I'm busy signed up for a course. The cinema"—she lectured the paint-spotted regulars at Valhalla—"can only speak in neologisms." No one, all the length of the bar, knew what a "neologism" was. The bartender, taking responsibility for his flock, hurriedly offered her another Rolling Rock on the house.

Luke was lying on the orthopedic mattress when she got home. She could not see his body from the foot of the steps leading to the loft alcove, although she could hear Ella Fitzgerald on the new compact disk player. The high-ceilinged room smelled faintly of turpentine.

"Have you been painting?"

"Touching up a few black and egg-yolk yellow stripes. The new picture for the Milholland Collection." Although he painted in the Mercer Street studio now, he also worked on odd canvasses at home when the spirit moved him. The stretchers stacked against every wall. "Come on up here. I'm lonely."

She perked up at his rare expression of libido. Maybe he was snapping out of his torpor; maybe his former personality was breaking through the wall of drugs. It had been months since they had made love. It only depressed her each time she looked at her diaphragm in the drawer. One night, when Luke was staying out, in a pique of misery, she had thrown it away, into the trash can with the uneaten calamari salad she had bought him at Dean & DeLuca.

She yanked off her boots and mounted the flight of steps to the loft bed. Luke lay sprawled on his back. He reached for her foot as she approached the mattress and pulled her off balance until she collapsed on her knees and rolled beside him. He tugged at the buckle of her wide embroidered belt, reaching for her haunches beneath the gabardine skirt she had bought at Alaia. Wildly she panicked that their sex might have lost its power. Did she dare to put it to the test? But the moment she felt him astride her, she knew that however many Chers and Madonnas and nineteen-year-olds he had been poking and pounding, she wanted him anyhow, for he was hers by right.

Afterward he asked her, "What happened about the sprinkler man? Did he call back?"

"Yeah, he says it'll cost us three thousand to fix up a high-grade system, but it's important with your canvasses stored here and all the flammable art materials."

"When are they coming?"

"Next month. These guys get real booked up. Luke, can I ask you something?"

"Sure."

"Do you know what a neologism is?"

He took a drag of his Camel and aimed the cloud of smoke away from her face. "It's like using a new word in place of an established word. Why?"

"Nothing. Forget it." Oh, why did he have to be such a disaster of a husband when he was the only person in Alphabet City who knew what a neologism was?

When she had flirted with Luke at Unemployment, he had infected her with his excitement over paintings and books. His ascetic poverty and his egomania had seduced her. "Art isn't only what you turn out," he had instructed her as she scooped up the check at their coffee shop, "it's a way of life, a discipline to nonmaterial pleasures. Which eventually become more satisfying than the material ones."

Where had it gone, his conviction? Or had it never been more than a projection of her own aspirations? At least Dan Helena could still remember the old Luke.

"I never had any education," said Dan. "I haven't read all those art theory books, like Luke, and I don't know much about philosophy. But I understand one thing. People are shallow. You can't take so-called success too seriously."

"Luke hangs out now with young kids he meets at Mars and Nell's, who only use him to get dealers to look at their slides. He's stopped going to Valhalla. His old friends there bitch and snipe at him. I guess they're jealous. Only you and Caspar stayed loyal. Oh, Dan, look at him."

She nodded to where Luke, in a Hawaiian shirt with a dirty collar, swayed slowly from one foot to the other while he circled a rusty jungle gym. In one hand he gripped a paper plate with some strawberries and a glob of Brie. Red strawberry juice was smeared all around his mouth and chin.

They had all trekked out to Queens to P.S. 1, the mecca of the avant garde in the back streets of Long Island City. It was a private Sunday lunchtime party for the latest show, which consisted of smashed swings and seesaws and other playground detritus.

Dan put an arm around Kitty's shoulders. He felt protective, the way he looked after his dog. "What's he doing?"

"He does so many different drugs I've lost track. I made him get up this morning and come out here." The females wandered around them with their cavewoman hair and black dyky lace-up shoes; the males had ratty ponytails and multiple pierced earrings.

"I need to tell you something, Dan. Can we get away from the crowd?" They ducked into the wide stairwell. "Last week I found him heating a test tube over the gas burner in the kitchen."

"What!" Dan's even voice became sharp. "Test tube of what?"

"Two parts baking soda, one part cocaine. He was doing crack. He heats it, and he cools it, and heats it and cools it and so on till it turns into a hard, flaky chip."

"Jesus. Hey, watch these stairs. They're rotting away. We're going up to the roof."

The peeling, pockmarked plaster and the corroded pipes gave P.S. 1 its unmuseumlike character.

"The stupid asshole." Dan guided her up the final steep flight of steps. They emerged into the sunlight, like a ship's deck. "Doing crack—he must be crazy. He's got to stop. Or else it's detox."

"He says it's fantastic, better than snorting. He won't stop. He won't listen to me. Could you talk to Giulietta?"

The asphalt of the roof and the hooded exhaust pipes were caked in dust. The rising green towers of the Citicorp office buildings sparkled against the clear March sky. It was so quiet and peaceful up here.

"I'm sorry. I can't help. Giulietta and I have bust up over this fucking Belle John scandal. She said if I started any legal proceedings, she wouldn't go on being my dealer. So when my attorney served Belle John, that was that."

"How long have you been with Giulietta?"

He scowled. "Twenty years. When the big money got in the way, she knew which side her bread was buttered."

"Why did you serve them, Dan? Why did you have to do that?"

"I can't let them get away with it. It's a matter of principle." His face became grim. "Artists have been abused too long. My contract says the sculpture's site-specific. I'm not going to let them haul it away to some warehouse. Or even worse, Billy Berrymouse tried to buy it from Jacob for one of his biblical theme parks."

"George Washington in a biblical park?"

"He wanted the head and uniform rewelded to look like Moses."

"I can't believe you'd go ahead and sue them. They're a mammoth company. They'll bleed you to death."

"I'm a rich man. I've never spent much money before, 'cause I've never wanted to buy much. I can afford to take them on."

"They'll clean you out."

"Who cares? It's worth paying for. I'm doing this for artists everywhere."

He scuffed at the asphalt with his toe. A cloud of dust billowed around their knees. How did men find such intricate ways of destroying themselves? She did not want to see Dan go under, sucked into the vortex of his legal crusade. It was an odd match, yet they had become real friends.

She hooked her arm through his. "We'd better go downstairs. I ought to keep an eye on Luke."

"You're a brave woman. A lot of other people would have cleared out. You'll find some way of getting through to him, I'm sure you will."

Dan was right. The next day Kitty got the lab results. It was important to break the news carefully. She could not predict how Luke would react. He had become so volatile and temperamental. Earlier they had been too poor to consider the luxury of a child, and recently he was usually too stoned or tired or bad-tempered or overagitated or depressed to discuss anything.

When she telephoned him at the studio, Madonna answered the phone. "We're busy," she drawled in the squeaky, nasal voice that she used for unimportant people like Luke's wife. Madonna had gone to Sarah Lawrence and some fancy art school in Antibes, where she wind-surfed and smoked pot with the children of famous Abstract Expressionists.

"It's important," Kitty insisted.

"What do you want?" Luke picked up. He sounded far away. She heard the beat of Louis Armstrong in the background. "We're finishing *Haven't,* the aubergine stripes for the biennial."

"Can we have dinner together tonight? I need to talk. It's important."

Cher or Madonna was giggling near the phone. What was going on? "Okay. Okay," Luke agreed. "What time?"

"I'll come to Mercer Street at eight."

Nothing could deflate her buoyant mood. Anyhow, Luke always sounded crotchety during the day. She imagined how he would brighten when he heard her news. They would eat at one of the tiny East Village bistros, where half a dozen tables clustered against a brick wall below street level. His topaz eyes, long glazed like a sick dog's, would flicker again.

She smiled vaguely at everybody on the street. They all smiled back, even a surly gang with striped T-shirts and roaring ghetto blasters. Although the trees were still bare, the Village nestled in milky spring sunlight, and groups of children played with hockey sticks, squealing happily outside. A beggar was leaning against a crutch and exhibiting the suppurating sores on his leg beneath the rolled dirty trouser. Kitty gave him five dollars. She thought as she hurried away from his singsong chant of blessings, That pitiful creature was once a tiny baby, clean and pink and untainted by the evil out there, and no one could have guessed the vile direction his life would go.

She thought, I want my child to grow up far away from SoHo. Maybe Luke will finally agree to buy that house in Vermont I've been bugging him about; we could live there half the time and still stay in Manhattan.

Luke would want the child to paint, before it could walk or speak. He would teach it to use chalks and poster paints and Silly Putty. On St. Marks she bought a book entitled *Eight Thousand Names for Baby* (although they would doubtless end up with something eccentric like Willem or Jasper, or Serra or Stella for a girl) and a juice squeezer. From now on she was going to live on fresh oranges and spinach and whole grains.

There was time to go home for a couple of hours before she met Luke in SoHo. She did not want to put him in a bad mood by arriving too early at the studio. Besides, she had promised the drug dealer downstairs, the only other occupant of their squat, that she would feed his cats every day while he was away on one of his mysterious business trips to Miami. Better to get the chore over with.

In Tompkins Square Park the homeless were already setting up their fires for the night. The stench of fuel drifted with the breeze over the park railings. Someone had hung one of the park streetlights with a row of running shoes, dozens of pairs of Nikes and Reeboks, raided from a yuppie athletic store.

Would she bring her baby here to Tompkins Square? Or to the junk gardens, where the neighborhood mothers sat in a semicircle on sideways grocery crates? Or would she rock her carriage outside on the stoop with the Puerto Rican women on Avenue C, where they sipped sugary sodas and played loud Latin music on the radio?

At her back a crimson sunset licked the sky, a salute to a magnificent day. The light stroked the sad walls of the barrio, glistening on the fortress windows and the lampposts decorated with mosaics of broken plates. She loved these streets with their defiant murals of cartoon characters, flamenco dancers, and muscled athletes; scenes of fantasy animals, children, and flowers; or walls coated with mysterious silhouette fugitives. She loved the bright colors rising from the stripped lots, decorated like gardens with flags and chunks of mirrors and old TVs. The sunset intensified the wash of chipped paint on Jose and Ramon's Deli and the barber and *lavandería*. The store windows were smeary with old grease and draped with coils of fairy lights. The facades glowed, their moldings as frilly as wedding cakes, their blown-out windows stuffed with towels.

Luke said it was no longer fashionable to live here. The yuppies on Avenue A had colonized and gentrified the area, where they refurbished bistros and performed Shakespeare readings. Only Avenue C, farther east, was still a real barrio. Luke said those artists who could afford to took up pricey quarters in a SoHo loft, and those who roughed it were moving out to Queens. Kitty did not care. This was home.

On the corner of Avenue B, she heard the wail of a siren. A cop was diverting traffic, and a small crowd of children scurried in the direction of the noise. Any commotion on the streets of Alphabet City quickly drew an audience.

Someone yelled, "*¿Que pasa? ¿Que pasa?*"

"*Hay un incendio.*" There's a big fire. "*¡Se está quemando una casa!*"

"*¿Donde?*"

Another siren howled closer. Kitty was accustomed to police busts at all hours, when the cops raided the crack houses or the gangs assaulted the vulnerable windows of the late night delicatessens. By the time the cops arrived at their least favorite

beat, it was usually too late. All they found was a litter of frac-
tured glass.

No trouble tonight, she prayed. No delays. I only want to
feed the cats, change into some fresh clothes, and get out across
town to meet Luke.

She smelled the overpowering smoke before she turned into
her block. Two police cars were blocking access, and a caravan
of fire engines was lined up. The police held back the curious
crowd.

A cop bellowed into a bullhorn, "Everyone get back. There
is a danger from falling buildings and smoke. I repeat, this is
a very dangerous situation."

Luis, who owned the audio store and had survived half a
dozen major break-ins, leaned against a lamppost with a knowing expression. An excited cluster of women pointed and gabbled.

"I have to get through," Kitty pleaded breathlessly. "I live on
this street."

"I'm sorry, ma'am. No one allowed. It's too dangerous."

It was only when she crossed the avenue that she saw where
the gigantic hoses were directed and the smoke billowed. She
screamed.

"*¿Que pasa?*" The old woman who worked in the Funeraria
Santa Maria hobbled next to her. She always wore a wool beret
and earrings that clattered like a rosary.

"It's my house. My God, it's my house that's on fire. Oh, my
God!"

"You not to get scared. The firemen put it out."

"It's my house. Everything I own!"

"Shh! Someone, get her a can of soda. She'll be okay. Shh,
child. We all praying for you."

"I don't believe it. What do I do?" She clawed at the old
woman's arm.

"You come with me," suggested the woman. "We wait in my
office."

"No, no, I can't! Why is no one going inside? Why don't they
put up the ladders?"

"It's too hot," someone explained. "They can't get close. A
couple of walls have already caved in."

Smoke surged from the second-story windows where she and Luke had lived and built and scavenged furniture and planted window boxes. Six firemen on the street directed the nozzles of their hoses, which seemed impotent against the malevolent dark cloud.

"The paintings," whispered Kitty. "So many paintings."

Somebody had summoned one of the cops. "I'm sorry, ma'am." He tilted his head respectfully. "I understand you live there. We need to confirm there are no other occupants at this time."

"It's empty. There's no one there." Only a couple of stray cats, she thought wildly, and stacks of valuable stripe canvasses. And my pots and pans and bedspread and rug and the patched-up sofa I rescued from Orchard Street. Only my peanut-butter jar where I hoarded my tips.

The officer insisted again, "Ma'am, you are certain there is no one else living there?"

"The guy downstairs...he's away...thank God...and my husband, he's out this afternoon."

She turned in a frenzy to the manageress of the funeral home. "The phone! May I use your phone?"

Inside the funeral parlor the woman brought her some tea in a china cup. She was experienced at dealing with bereavement. She had soothed hundreds of relatives as they sobbed and heaved in her musty parlor, beneath the enamel Virgin Mary and plastic replicas of saints. Hunched on the velveteen cushions, over and over Kitty dialed the Mercer Street number on the old-fashioned rotary phone. It was constantly engaged. And did it matter, anyhow? What could Luke do, when even the fire brigade did not dare approach the collapsing structure?

The woman patted her hand. "You'll get a nice new apartment. This street's no good for you anyway. People look at you funny, they think you got too much money. Maybe someone even start that fire on purpose." She crossed herself.

"No! I can't believe that! We had all these paints and canvases and solvents. I guess it was pretty dangerous. We were planning to get a sprinkler system. We should have got it sooner. Oh, Jesus, why did this have to happen now?"

"You were lucky. *Gracias a Dios,* no one was hurt."

"Yeah. You're right. Thank God."

A mysterious calm descended on her. The woman was right. Maybe there was a kind of invisible providence. They had plenty of money now, unlike the rest of their poor neighbors. They could buy new furniture and a new sofa. It was only material things that were being incinerated in that gruesome furnace. She was safe, and Luke was waiting in Mercer Street, and deep down inside her a tiny seed was bursting into life.

"You don't like tea? You want some tequila?"

"Thanks. No. I have to go."

"You wait here and take it easy a minute."

"I have to find my husband."

Someone from the car service next door gave her a ride across town. Gratefully she slumped beside him on the front seat. His St. Christopher medallion swung between them like a hypnotic pendulum as he raced the lights. The driver turned to her kindly. "Where do you want me to drop you?"

"Right here. Thanks again." She tried to give him ten dollars.

He waved it away. "Keep it, señora. I'm sorry about what happen to your house."

She let herself into the building and unlocked the elevator, which opened directly on Luke's floor. How was she going to tell him? Would he care about the apartment or only about the stacks of canvasses all destroyed in a few seconds of curling flames?

Kitty opened the door to the studio. Cher was lying on the divan, fixing her mascara and eating from a carton of sesame noodles while she gossiped on the telephone.

"Where's Luke?"

"Hold on a second. Someone's at the door." Cher turned her head slowly in Kitty's direction and yawned. "Oh, it's you. Luke left."

"Where is he?"

"He'll be back soon." She yawned again as if even the effort of a few words with Kitty bored her. She plunged her plastic fork back into the carton and twirled a strand of noodles slowly around the prongs. She swallowed the noodles, sucking them through garnet-colored lips.

"Where did he go?"

Cher shrugged. "He said he was going home to your apartment for a nap. That was about three hours ago. He was a little—" She touched her forehead. "Well, you know. He was smoking that glass pipe. He'll be okay when he's had some sleep. Hey, what's wrong? Watch that painting. It's for the biennial. We've been working on it for days."

It was too late to save the stripes. Kitty stumbled and pitched forward, catching her heel in the center of the canvas that lay on its stretcher by the door. She could not stand straight and she could not breathe. The harder she gasped for air, the worse the suffocation compressed her. The baby, she thought as she fainted, skidding over a band of wet paint, what's going to happen to my baby?

17

THE WARRIORS' REST

Nick Jones shivered every time the expert's secretary buzzed him to step into the boss's office for a moment. Had security discovered the virgin videocassettes he substituted, or had someone noticed him sneak into Georgia's office for a glimpse of the auctioneer's book? The instruments of justice might strike at any time. He waited for his accusers to arrive like the Gestapo in the night. Even when safely locked in his luxury aerie, he half expected the ring of telephone or the wail of the intercom to sound his treason.

What was the very worst they could do to him if they caught him red-handed? He would be fired and disgraced; he would never find another job in the art business; they might pursue him for fiduciary breach and strip him of everything he owned. Or maybe not. The reputation of the august auction house was also at stake. Perhaps they would choose to hush up the scandal instead.

On the threshold of the expert's office he waited, at attention. What had he been summoned for this time?

"Ah, Nick." The expert looked up from the art he was examining. He seemed to be in a cheerful mood. "I'd like you to meet a couple of the trustees from the Lausanne Museum. Gentlemen, my assistant, Mr. Jones."

The duo nodded jerkily, like marionettes.

"I'm delighted to offer you gentlemen a look at the Picasso napkins before we ship them to the baron." The expert held out the objects.

"The Baron von Tislowicz! The pair of table napkins!" exclaimed one of the trustees.

"We nearly bid for them ourselves," said the other trustee. "Is it true that von Tislowicz is planning to give them as a wedding present to his fiancée?"

The other chimed in, "There were so many stories in the press. *People* magazine reported that she nearly became Miss Switzerland."

"*Vogue* said she nearly became Madame Papier."

The expert struggled to look discreet and knowledgeable at the same time. "I'm not in a position to comment on that," he mumbled. "All we know for certain is that Picasso made these sketches in the early seventies during a bouillabaisse lunch in St. Paul de Vence. He was always one for scribbling on tablecloths and napkins and so forth, and these happen to be masterpieces. Fortunately the waiter had the presence of mind to preserve them."

The expert knew perfectly well how the baron had filched his rival's flesh-and-blood ornament. Everyone in the contemporary department was aware by now that the powerful Emil Papier had been jilted by his fiancée. The beauty pageant semifinalist had left him without warning for von Tislowicz, who had an old family title, some inherited Rubenses, and a reputation for playboy escapades. The baron was eight years younger than Emil and probably, Nick judged, more fun. Papier was as tightly coiled inside as a Swiss watch. The baron, whose grandfather had been a close buddy of Archduke Franz Ferdinand, rumbled with Viennese enthusiasm for expansive eating and drinking and flirting.

The scandal titillated the contemporary department. After all, who knew better than they how Papier and the baron had been dueling for years over Dalis and Magrittes. Emil, with his PAP Fund, had ultimately beaten out his long-standing rival on the auction floor. For all the social and historical cachet of his Austro-Hungarian ancestry, von Tislowicz could not begin to muster the newly assembled resources of the mighty fund.

He was not the man to lay down his fencing saber. The baron happened to be single at the moment, and Helga, while no intellectual heavyweight, was a beautiful creature. Equipped with his innate finesse (he was related to Metternich on the maternal side), he set about introducing a new variant into the game. The art world watched with fascination as von Tislowicz neatly walked away with Papier's girl.

The two trustees leaned forward with anticipation.

"It's unusual," said the expert, "to find such a gem of draftsmanship on a paper napkin." He glanced to where Nick still lingered near the threshold. "Ah, yes, Nick." The expert cleared his throat. "Would you be so kind as to bring us some coffee? My secretary's away from her desk."

"Delighted to. Be right back." He hurried down the corridor toward the corporate kitchen, where the chef and the *plongeur* were busy in the kitchen, unmolding the guava soufflé for a high-level tapestries and armor luncheon taking place in the boardroom next door. A dozen plates of beef Wellington, cleared from the main course, waited to be stacked in the two giant dishwashers. When Nick relayed his orders, the *plongeur* obligingly broke off to fill the Georgian coffeepot and arrange some candied grapes on the silver-plated tray.

"Thanks," said Nick. He carried the tray carefully, balancing the stack of Worcester demitasses, the jug of cream, and the sugar bowl.

He paid attention not to let any drop of coffee slurp from the beak of the pot onto the linen tray cloth. The blonde from the estates department passed him in the corridor outside the oceanic offices. A group were returning from lunch. She gave him a wave and returned to giggling with her stewardess friends.

He had been dating her less often and spending more time with Delphine. Sometimes Delphine treated him like dirt; the princessy habits were so ingrained. Other days she exuded charm, melted his resistance, and wore his defenses down to putty. The alternating hot and cold behavior threw him off balance. Delphine was the only girl who had ever given him such a rocky ride. He shrank from the tiniest physical gesture that could be open to misinterpretation. He touched her waist lightly as a feather as he guided her into the Canal Bar or the Ipanema Grill and brushed her cheek decorously with his lips when he left at the end of an evening. Nothing else. He wanted her, at times even painfully. However much, it was not worth the price of risking rejection.

Delphine's temporary cash squeeze had not crimped her. She went on living in undiminished style, running up bills and borrowing from Susannah. Eventually she sold the pearl choker, which had provided her with the equivalent of the expert's annual salary.

Once or twice when she was being specially nice to him, Nick was tempted to confess to her the whole sordid deal with her father. He held back. The worst women to confide in were those who exercised fascination.

The trustees were still exclaiming over the baron's table napkins when Nick returned to the office. The expert motioned to an empty surface; Nick gently deposited the tray.

He listened to their oohs and ahs and little grunts as they examined the precious napkins. How high had von Tislowicz bargained in order to woo away Papier's fiancée? What exactly was it that each man had promised her, in his fervor to worst the opposition?

"No sugar for me, thank you." The trustee was riveted by the Picassoid loops and swirls.

Nick filled the four demitasses with coffee and held out the plate of candied grapes. Each trustee took a grape.

The nearer one reached out for his cup, then withdrew his hand. "A splash more cream, please, if it's not too much trouble."

Nick nodded obligingly and performed the honors.

The expert sipped thoughtfully. "We are fully aware, gentlemen, of your budgetary constraints. Almost every museum in the world—with the possible exception of the Getty—is hard-pressed to compete with the private market. We are, however, mere auctioneers. We do not set or inflate the prices. Yes, yes, I know the auction houses all took some flack over helping to finance those van Gogh irises. Since then I'm sure we've learned a lesson."

The art market was losing some sheen. No one was certain what was going on. Sandy Pike and several other important collectors were unloading. The doomsayers insisted that the bloom was off the rose and auction levels had peaked; the Picassos and van Goghs were artificially inflated by borrowed money; the very purchasers who had invested billions in the latest "in" contemporary works were propping up a South Sea bubble in the fear that the whole racket might collapse upon itself and leave them with a lot of worthless daubings.

Nick twirled the additional blobs of cream around in the demitasse.

The trustee answered the expert, "Despite a major recession in the entire Western economy, great paintings still hold their own."

The companion trustee added dryly, "*Great* paintings, we mean."

The expert nodded with understanding. The Klines and de Koonings should withstand some air pocket turbulence, but who could be sure about some of those minimalists and conceptualists and appropriationists?

The trustee leaned forward to pluck a grape. The other raised Picasso's napkin devoutly to the light, for a final look.

Nick stepped closer. "Your coffee, sir."

As Nick brought over the cup, his foot came down on a runaway grape that had escaped its bunch to roll across the carpet. His weight ground the crystallized coating with a crackle and squelched the juicy interior, sending him skidding. He regained his balance without actually dropping the fine bone china demitasse. It all happened so quickly that no one had time to react. The trustee let out a gasp, like a punctured tire, as a splatter of coffee lashed through his trouser leg against his thigh.

The very next moment seemed to freeze like a video frame,

as the guest held up the delicate tissue of Picasso's napkin, soaked through with the mocha stain. The expert's mouth fell open and hung there. He was beyond speech.

If the expert had been holding a gun, he would have pointed it between Nick's temples and fired at point-blank range. When he finally spoke, his voice vibrated with the fury of a man who would never forgive. "Get out," he hissed at the Englishman.

"It was an accident. I'm terribly sorry."

"And who do you think will be held responsible?" The expert quivered. The auction house insurance would cover artwork up to the point of delivery. But there was going to be hell to pay for this one. Now and then small objects were stolen or broken; that was the inevitable consequence of handling such volume of consignments. A napkin worth three-quarters of a million dollars . . . the claim would affect next year's premiums. To say nothing of the baron's wrath. They could kiss that valued client good-bye as of this afternoon. He would lose no time in taking his business to the rival auctioneers.

In a mounting rage, oblivious of the stunned trustees, the expert turned on Nick. To think how he had been so delighted with the Englishman's performance and even considered grooming him for promotion. "Get out of this office and never show your face here again. I'm calling security. They'll escort you while you clean out your desk."

"You mean I'm fired?" It was a foolish question, yet full of genuine astonishment. The road to catastrophe had taken such an unexpected twist.

"You bet your sweet ass you're fired. For having irreparably destroyed a masterpiece of twentieth-century art. And don't you dare set foot in this building again. You're finished."

Nick returned to his apartment in a dazed state of shock. He lugged a grocery bag full of his office paraphernalia: a dictionary, some pens and a ruler, a paperback *Who's Who*, a box of Kleenex, and a bottle of after-shave.

He mixed himself a strong gin and tonic and sat down heavily on the leather sofa. He had been fired for a stupid, clumsy accident. It was embarrassing and idiotic, but no one could imagine for an instant that he had acted on purpose. The expert was known to be hot-tempered. The other auction houses and the galleries would surely understand. He would find some other job soon, with Emil's patronage and gratitude behind him.

He swallowed some more gin and felt better. At least it was all over with, the spying and lying and sneaking around corners. Perhaps now he could get on with his life. Perhaps he could even enjoy a decent night's sleep.

On an impulse he reached for his cordless phone and extracted the antenna. He was sick and tired of having no friend in the world to talk to, no one he could really confide in. The emotion of reprieve made him light-headed. This once he was going to break his strictest self-imposed rule.

He dialed Delphine Papier's number.

"It wasn't your fault what the stupid klutz did." Jacob filled his guest's glass and wondered where Felice kept the midnight emergency supply of cashews. In the Moghul casket, maybe, with the Kashmiri daggers? "After all that, to get his ass fired for spilling a cup of coffee. What are we going to do about him?"

Jacob and Emil pondered their dilemma over the dregs of Corton-Charlemagne. Felice had excused herself and retired upstairs to bed.

Emil ground out his cigarette. "The British imbecile came whining to me yesterday about my getting him another job. I told him to get lost. He's no use to us any longer."

What did the boy imagine, that Emil would raise him like Lazarus from the dead and tuck him away in some swanky SoHo gallery? Emil needed him in the auction house and nowhere else. Emil had hung up the telephone on Nick in midsentence. Actions spoke louder than words.

He told Jacob, "Let him go back to London, and eke out a living again in some backwater. We gave him his chance."

"And he blew it. A short stretch in the fast lane."

The two men relapsed into that precious silence derived from the longevity of their friendship. It brought more comfort than words and reassurances.

Jacob gazed at his beloved magenta "zip" painting (companion to the Barnett Newman that hung in the dining room) and let his mind flush itself of spite and anxiety and petty vengeance. Tonight even the abstract oil hardly produced its cathartic effect.

"Screw the Englishman. We have enough info from the auctioneer's book to last us several seasons. Most important, we've got our new ammunition. Luke Elliot's stripes."

Emil beamed. It always cheered them to remember their cache of stripes.

"Giulietta thinks we may get close to a million apiece at the November sales."

Jacob whistled. "Astonishing what a tragic accident can do for promotion. Everyone loves a dead artist."

"It's rule number one in our business. When Jackson Pollock smashed his car against a tree, the price of his paintings multiplied by ten. And not only *his* paintings. All the Abstract Expressionists'. Before Pollock's untimely death, they sold almost nothing."

"We're going to make a killing," Jacob predicted. "We have the monopoly on Luke's work. We bought up all the early paintings except for the ones the wife salvaged from the studio, and everything else was stored in that tenement apartment." He made a gesture of conflagration. "Pouf! All burned to cinders."

"Which means the supply is finite. Our stripes will be our golden egg. We'll end up with a ten thousand percent rate of return. No one's ever done as well as that."

Jacob looked thoughtful "It far outperforms our Klines and Pollocks."

"Our limited partners will be orgasmic."

"Over the moon," Jacob agreed. "The PAP Fund will be the most successful private placement in the world. We'll show those jerks from the Shining Squid Corporation who calls the shots."

Emil thought of the man who had made him a laughingstock and undermined his masculinity. "We'll show Tizz, too."

"The Austrian putz. He's nothing. Forget him."

Emil prickled. He would never forgive the baron for having punctured his wedding plans like a needle in a balloon. He blamed the nation and all its Hapsburg history for his private disgrace. "The only people in the world who could claim Hitler was a German and Beethoven really an Austrian."

Jacob snorted. "To hell with Austrians."

Emil raised his glass. "To hell with von Tislowicz."

The loss of Helga wounded Emil beyond any reasonable proportion. She was the prize for all his decades of hard work and solitude, and his pleasure derived from watching the envy of other middle-aged men. Helga's departure kindled his phobias of age and death. She had guessed that his was a rotting ship. She had abandoned Emil for his rival von Tislowicz because, with her young woman's sixth sense, she concluded that the baron, not Emil, was ascendant. Emil's English governess had long ago explained to him how they sent the canaries into the Welsh mines ahead of the men, to test the air for toxicity. The death of the canaries presaged danger. Exquisite Helga survived where canaries perished. She had flown away.

"Cut the crap," said Jacob. "She was too young for you anyhow."

Emil grunted. It was all very well for his old friend to crow a little. His marriage to Felice (described by Jacob not so long ago as the "frigid shikse") had miraculously righted itself. For the first time in years they seemed to be functioning together as a genuine couple. It was remarkable what reconciliation an outside threat could effect. Nothing would cure the frigidity, Emil suspected. Just because Felice had moved back into the master bedroom upstairs, where she was probably curled up right now in her Lanz woolen nightgown, it probably meant she was earning an Oscar for convincing her husband that she was enjoying the ordeal. It was astonishing, Emil reflected, how far middle-aged men would go to fool themselves. Then he remembered that he too belonged to that club, and the smile died from his lips. "Just because you and Felice . . ."

"It's more than that. This Belle John grief has put a lot of stuff into perspective for me. You know, my wife may be stuck-up and snooty at times. She hasn't got the world's greatest sense of humor. And she's so Yankee cheap it's pathological. If I let her get away with it, we'd be living on a diet of hot dogs."

When he described Felice's failings, his voice took on a tone of real affection. Emil noticed, however, that he was steering well clear of the bed problem. Felice must really be earning her Academy Award for acting.

"My mother—may she rest in peace—was against the marriage from the beginning. She wanted me to marry a decent Jewish girl. She always predicted there'd be trouble with Felice, and she was right." Jacob pointed toward the molded ceiling. "I even thought once or twice she was putting a curse on us—from up there."

"Mothers," said Emil. He knew.

"I know my family life's not been all roses. I'd have liked some kids, maybe. I've never understood how you could have that beautiful daughter, and go on fighting with her for so long. Don't frown at me like that, I'm giving you the benefit of the truth, as I see it.

"Anyhow, when Helena went berserk over that stinking statue, then Felice showed her true colors. She was magnificent. What a fighter. I couldn't have gotten through these last months without her."

"You're a seasoned CEO, Jacob. You did what had to be done."

"It got pretty mean. The hate mail, the fights with the board, the extraordinary meetings of the shareholders—all those things I could deal with. Even when they tried to get me to sell my warrants and resign from the board. When Dan Helena went completely ape-shit, though, and rounded up the petition of intellectuals—can you imagine how it feels to be the culprit of a manifesto signed by half the major artists, writers, and thinkers in America?"

Jacob winced. It still hurt to remember. He had blinked in horror at that list of eminences who were rallying with Helena to decry the removal of the controversial statue from the plaza. Cultural decay in the country was endemic, read the petition. They accused Karakoff of personal collusion with the evil corporate oligarchy that trammeled the sacred rights of free expression. Jacob Karakoff, by removing George Washington from the battlefield of public controversy, was aligning himself with the forces of fascism. Dan's slightly confusing rhetoric was signed by the painters Jacob had patiently been collecting and the writers whose books he had devotedly waded through for years. How had he ever managed to incur such hatred? Maybe he would have been better off making a quiet, modest living, a bean-counting ant, as he had begun.

He had turned to his wife in despair. "What do I do now?"

"Get rid of that statue. Who cares about a petition? Don't let those intelligentsia intimidate you. It's only their fashionable cause of the moment. You have a Fortune five hundred company to run. A lot of people depend on you for their livings. And their plumbing."

He had ordered them to remove the statue at night. Swiftly and discreetly. He insisted on watching the whole proceeding from his office window. By the clammy beams of the plaza floodlights, under a sickly moon, they had dismembered George into four segments—legs, head, and torso—and hoisted the steel masses onto their trucks. The giant president was dead.

The four parts of the body now lay in a secret warehouse in Trenton, waiting to be reassembled one day in an alternative location, when the furor died down.

The morning after the midnight removal, Jacob's office was flooded with faxes and congratulations from all over the country. Several members of the board called personally to affirm their support. A group of the secretaries generously pooled their own money to send an order of four dozen white roses.

And amid all the well-wishing, Dan Helena's process server walked in. The sculptor was suing for breach of contract.

"He's wasting his money," commented Felice. "What kind of case does he have, anyhow?"

"The contract specifically states that the work shall be 'site-specific.'"

Felice put her wispy arms around him, so he could feel the psychic current of her strength flow to him. It permeated, like osmosis, through the skin. How had he never realized that his goyishe angel, with her fragile bones and undyed blond hair, was such a rock of support?

He told Emil, "When all this is over Felice and I are going to take a real vacation. Just the two of us. Every winter Juan Gomez invites us along on his yacht, but I'd rather do something private. Like newlyweds."

He smiled at the magenta field of his Newman zip painting.

Serenity roosted. Marriage was a compromise, but in the end it offered the only long-term happiness. "Hey, old buddy, you want to sleep over here tonight? You can have the guest room. The bed's made up." He was suddenly sorry for Emil, returning so late to the suite at the Carlyle. Emil had taken up residence there, since he could not set foot in the East End Avenue apartment.

He really doesn't want to go back alone, thought Jacob. "It's no trouble. I insist. We'll all have breakfast together tomorrow. Felice will be pleased, too."

So Emil borrowed a pair of Jacob's jumbo pajamas and tumbled groggily into the narrow bed. He might have been more comfortable at the Carlyle, but Jacob was right. He did not want to be alone tonight.

It helped somehow to know that Felice and Jacob were sleeping on the other side of the wall, only a few feet away. In the morning they would all get up and drink orange juice and eat bagels together. It had been so long since he had breakfasted with anyone but business associates.

Before he slept, he heard the noise unmistakably. The bedsprings were howling, and something was thumping hard against the wall.

He's showing off to me on purpose, thought Emil. Just as I would have indulged my own vanity with Helga. As for Felice, well, Joan Crawford and Bette Davis, move over. Mrs. Karakoff was earning her Oscar again tonight.

"I must find me a regular secretary," Susannah sighed, as she plowed through her stacks of correspondence. Delphine did her best to help organize their computer files, but the business of championing artistic freedom was becoming a full-time industry. They needed staff. Mornings were so busy. Iris brought her a pot of hot chocolate into the study. Susannah took a few bites of muffin between phone calls.

William Doyle, the auctioneers, called with the welcome news that yesterday they had successfully unloaded the stone three-headed Cerberus, purchased by a rich widow as a graveside ornament for her deceased spouse. Splendid. Another one down. Susannah had been shipping off crateloads of the anthropomorphic furniture and decorations. The Dalis and Magrittes had been removed from their sinister vigils on the paneled walls. A museum in Westphalia had bought the Gothic suit of armor.

She took a mouthful of muffin and answered the next phone call.

"Susannah, my dear," warbled Jacques. "I'm calling to congratulate you on your successful soiree." Susannah and the sage philosopher were becoming fast friends.

"You think it went well? We went through twelve pounds of Beluga." Last night she had invited a few score of her new congregation around to the palazzo.

"You've fallen in with a hungry crowd of have-nots." The intelligentsia rarely said no to free caviar.

"A grand heap of haves, too. Yesterday we raised fourteen thousand dollars for the Artistic Liberties Brigade."

Dan and Susannah had hatched the ALB right here in Emil's former study. They hoped the highfalutin label would serve as a brand name to attract a formidable coalition of artists, writers, minorities, staunch conservatives, limousine liberals, dyed-in-the-wool Democrats, new wave Republicans, anarchists, and First Amendment fanatics.

Following the poetry reading at Dante's, Susannah was barraged with requests to press on with the campaign. She chartered a riverboat and cruised the Artistic Liberties Brigade around the island. At fifteen hundred dollars a pop, the event mainly had engaged the wealthier bracket of supporters. But they flocked.

The petition meanwhile grew longer, as every name intellectual vied to keep company with his peers. Susannah's brigade sutured all manner of unlikely and disparate factions. They rallied around her beacon, legions of the influential as well as the oppressed. With practice, her rhetoric was becoming wondrously rousing, with its untutored directness, inspired by distant memories of street-corner evangelists and the lascivious minister. Somehow, she warned, during the runaway eighties, there had arisen a vocal and invidious chorus of backwater bigots from the eddies of the American cultural soup. They were obscuring the tragedies of poverty and prejudice with ridiculous decoys for attention: flag trampling and Bible burning, subliminal song lyrics, quibbles over local community standards of decency.

"We need every cent," she told Jacques. "The lawyer bills are astronomical."

"Thieves and vultures," he snorted. "But what choice does one have? When one goes to war against corporate America, one must hire mercenaries of the enemy's caliber."

"Cheltenham near declined to take our case. They claimed we might run into conflict with their other big corporate clients."

"A ploy to charge you double, I expect. Those law crooks will take on anything for money." Jacques's contempt for late capitalist society was unbounded. "They're all carpetbaggers."

Cheltenham, Arbuthnot & Crewe had formerly prospered during the Wall Street boom, before the senior partner Ariel Lamb had departed under a smudge of impropriety. Cheltenham now came up with a brilliant counterargument to Belle John. Karakoff's counsel argued that it was Belle John's decision *when,* if not *where,* to display the statue, and that the warehouse in Trenton represented a temporary storage place. Susannah's lawyers rebutted that, under such terms, Karakoff was obliged to warehouse the sculpture in perpetuity and thus prevented from selling it to Berrymouse's theme park.

Susannah said good-bye to Jacques and looked up. Delphine, with a fresh cup of coffee, was stomping bad-temperedly around the study. Susannah noticed dark shadows under the girl's eyes that should not have been there.

"What's wrong, sugar?"

Delphine scowled into her coffee mug. "Nothing. I didn't sleep too well. That's all."

"Is your thesis bugging you again?"

Delphine was disheartened about the validity of her work. She had dedicated years to collecting evidence of the evils wrought by American aggression. Yet since the Sandinistas' defeat and the collapse of the Eastern bloc, she questioned whether history had somehow caught her napping. Maybe she had gotten herself stuck in a historical quagmire. Maybe she should shelve her studies in U.S. imperialism and focus for now on the more pressing dangers of deforestation and toxic contamination.

"No, it's not my thesis. It's—it's something else." She picked up a rubber band from a tray of papers and twisted it around her index finger.

"You're not upset about your daddy again?"

"Stupid old bear. No, I try not to think about him."

Susannah rifled through a new file labeled "Vomit Show—Leningrad." The National Endowment for the Arts was threatening to cut the funding for the scheduled exhibit of a dozen of the Wagnerian Hero's paintings at the Hermitage museum. Perhaps the Artistic Liberties Brigade should stage a protest. An aborted post–cold war Soviet cultural exchange would provide a popular rallying point.

She looked up at Delphine. "It's none of my business, right?"

Delphine frowned. She looked for a moment like her father on the rare occasions he had misjudged the direction of the franc or yen. "I don't have secrets from you anymore, Suze. You know that. I—I just don't know what I think."

"What about?"

She catapulted the rubber band into the trash can. "Nick Jones says he's going back to London."

"Why?"

"Remember how he was fired for wrecking that Picasso napkin? He still hasn't got another job, and he can't afford to go on paying his rent and all his expenses."

"He's a pleasant young man, I agree. Well schooled, smooth as silk, and with some get up and go in him, too. I've noticed you giving him the eye once or twice. But why should you be caring?"

"I don't know. I only know I don't want him to go away. Disappear and never come back."

Susannah studied her curiously. "You like him that much?"

"I don't know what I think. All the time I've known him, he's never come near me. Nothing. Do you think he's gay?"

"You never can tell. But I don't think so, no."

"Then why isn't he interested? Does he find me unattractive?"

"What rot."

"Then why? Why?"

"Maybe he's—intimidated."

"I thought of that, too. It's all to do with my father."

"With the old warthog?"

"It's a long story."

"Don't frown like that, sugarpie. You'll be getting premature wrinkles and look like an old gator. Okay, tell me. I'm listening."

It took a while to recount the saga. Susannah put on the answering machine and ignored the flood of incoming calls while Delphine explained the diabolical pact between the Englishman and Emil. The story spilled out, piece by piece, just as Nick had confessed to Delphine in his hour of desperation.

Susannah drew in her breath sharply. "The nineteen-million-dollar Pollock! Emil snatched it out from under the Shining Squid Corporation?"

"More than that. All the other Klines and Rothkos and de Koonings and Warhols and Stellas."

"And nobody—*nobody*—ever suspected?"

"Never. There was a girl who worked there—he swears she's no beauty—who had a kind of crush on him. He stole her key."

Susannah digested the elaborate subterfuges. "What would happen if we blew the whistle?" she asked at last.

"We can't do that. Nick would get into even worse trouble. They might even send him to jail."

"I guess you're right."

"Besides, it would be very complicated. The auction house would move heaven and earth to cover up the scam. It could be the end of their business. Not only would they be legally liable for billions of dollars to many underbidders, but their entire reputation would be wiped out."

Susannah nodded. She marveled afresh at Emil's ingenuity. This manipulation of the Englishman was his most brilliant coup. No one had the standing to incriminate him, neither his puppet Nick Jones nor the art establishment, whose very underpinnings he threatened. Everyone would rather keep the lid on, except perhaps a few underbidders who would never be able to prove anything.

Susannah snatched at the tiniest germ of an idea. "Nick Jones, does he have his own copy somewhere of all that information he's been stealing, the order bids and the videos and suchlike?"

"More or less. He recycled the videos, but he has written records of them, plus the lists from the auctioneer's book of every bidder and every price."

"So he's well apprised of who all's chasing what all over the world."

"He knows exactly. But what's the use of all that secret knowledge without Emil to pay him for it?" Delphine collapsed back, exhausted with the strain of the telling, "Can you help?"

"What exactly do you want, girl?"

Delphine intently braided a thin skein of hair and mumbled, "I don't want Nick to go away."

When he was feeling glum, Emil often stopped off at his favorite bookstore, seven blocks down from the Carlyle. Here he could steal an hour's solace, browsing through the shelves.

He flipped through the latest philosophical treatise of Jacques Boucher, noticing it had been autographed on the flyleaf in a baroque flourish.

Emil's hand jerked to his chest. He thought his heart was going to fly out of its cavity. "Susannah! What are you doing here?"

"It's a public place."

He stared at her fixedly. She was wearing a short skirt, which showed off her racehorse legs to their best advantage. One-in-a-thousand legs that had belonged to him until recently. Her eyes crinkled with confidence under her wide-brimmed fedora.

"Susannah," he repeated dumbly. "It's good to see you."

"You're looking well, too. But I can't be stopping here long. I'm lunching with the editor of *Art Insider*."

"You? You know him?"

"Yessir. I'm fixing an interview to discuss the Belle John affair."

Emil winced. New York was abuzz with rumors about her and Helena. At first Emil closed his ears to the malicious reports, dismissing Susannah's "rabble-rousing" as mere rebellion geared to irritate him. Bit by bit doubts niggled at his ego. That sculptor was reputed to be attractive to women. Emil's testosterone sizzled at the inkling of competition.

"Come back to the hotel for a small aperitif with me," he proposed. "Or next door to Les Pleiades if you prefer."

"I've got better things to do than hang around and pass the time of day with you."

Even to Jacob he had not fully confided how he missed Susannah. She knew him so well, and how to organize his life. He missed the menus she specially ordered for him, the bowls of musty apples in the bedroom, and the flowers arranged just so. Jacob, however, had not been altogether fooled. "Maybe you should take her back," he suggested. "The two of you had a strange relationship, but all relationships are strange from outside. At least you knew where you were. Better the devil you know."

Did he really know her so well? This determined creature who swept between the bookshelves as if she owned them all, as she now owned the cursed apartment on East End Avenue, had acquired a new assurance.

"A quick drink and a short chat," he pleaded. "What's the harm?"

"You can contact me through my attorneys at Cheltenham."

"I don't want to talk to your fancy lawyers. There's no business left between us. You have a signed contract and you got everything you wanted: my apartment, my beach house, my pictures, my furniture, my books." He could not entirely strain the bitterness out of the word *books*. The glossy spines around him concretized his final loss.

"Let's not dispute it. Some things don't bear going into. Make it snappy, Emil. I don't have time to waste. I lost nineteen good years already."

He squirmed. There was nothing so alien to his nature as a public display, and here, of all places, in an intimate store where he was personally known... "Let's try again," he said softly. "Come back to me. Come to lunch, come to bed, come to Switzerland. Come back."

"Not for all the tea in China." Then, in a smaller voice, she added, "You cheated me."

The contract divided them like an explosive-mined frontier. They both knew he had intentionally never signed it, and that he, who held all the cards, had despicably duped her. And eventually she had managed to dupe him back. He stammered, "I—I was always afraid you would deceive me. That you'd run away with some younger man and steal my money and paintings."

"I'm well fixed now. I've got me a pile of money, and I don't need you to front the bills."

"Yes, you do need me! Not for my money, that's the least of it. You need me for my brain. I made you." He tugged scornfully at a handful of her hair. "Just as your sculptor once modeled you in clay, I modeled your whole mind and behavior and—and—"

"Buy yourself a box of paints and some charcoal next time you feel the creative urge coming on. Maybe you can make people. I know you can buy them. But they're still people, and they'll turn on you sooner or later."

He blocked her passage, challenging her helplessly. "Is it true about Helena, you and that raving lunatic? Do you really have a liaison with that charlatan? Don't you realize his career is washed up? It's a shame. All that talent wasted on account of stubbornness. If he hadn't kicked up such a fuss, Jacob could have discreetly removed the statue, and the whole incident would have blown over. Since they transport entire temples from Egypt and medieval cloisters from France, why all the fuss about one sculpture?"

"That's not the point. Dan's work is site-specific."

"Don't throw that Postmodern jargon at me." He moved a step closer. The more she enraged him, the more furiously he coveted her. "I know you've been lonely for a long time. You need a pet stallion. I don't care, as long as you conduct yourself discreetly. Come back to me and keep the mad sculptor as a hobby. Until you get bored with him."

She had to smile, and her anger went limp. She touched his crisp sleeve lightly. "I'm sorry. Sincerely sorry. I never did mean to leave you, but you're the one made me do it. It wouldn't work if I came back. You'd remind me and I'd remind you of a heap of resentments better forgotten."

He looked her up and down once more, from the legs to the

floppy fedora. "You were my creation, Susannah. I not only taught you to eat snails and asparagus. I not only introduced you to the art of the subconscious. I also formed your spirit. It seems even I can't take that away now."

As she stepped toward the door, she blew him a little kiss from her fingertips. "I declare, you may be a mean and evil old bastard, but you still are a real connoisseur."

18

FOR SERVICES RENDERED

*I*n her cubbyhole office Georgia collated the stacks of pink order bid slips for the auctioneer's book. Lot 12, Frank Stella, $250,000; lot 17, Hans Hofmann, $500,000; lot 37, Luke Elliot, $450,000. She sighed and picked up the telephone.

"Hallo, Georgia. Nick here."

"Nick! I've been worried about you."

"Nothing to worry about. I've been lying low for a bit. I've worked my way though *The Brothers Karamazov* and *Gravity's Rainbow*. And I saw the Delacroix exhibit a couple of times, and the futurist show . . . "

"Any news on the job front?"

"Um, well, various irons in the fire . . . "

"I don't know if it's of any interest to you: I did hear of an opening. If you'd like me to put in a good word for you—I'm afraid it's not in contemporary, and it's probably a notch down from your old job here. Still, it would be somewhere to hang your hat for a while."

"Kind of you to think of me."

"Don't be offended. It's not a very high-powered position. And it's in the other auction house."

"Jumping ship to work for the competition?"

"You know what it's like in our business. Everyone knows everyone. It's like that when there are only two real games in town. They're looking for a new cataloger in the objets de vertu department."

"Objets de vertu? Objets de vertu! Snuffboxes and eggcups and thimbles!"

"Please don't be insulted. It could be an interesting change for you. And if you stick it out a while, sooner or later you'll get back into contemporary. You know how people move around at the auction houses."

"Of course I'm not offended. I think it's extremely decent of you. Thank you very much indeed."

He bought himself an ill-smelling falafel and a can of soda and settled down to reread the classifieds for jobs. Unemployment meant empty hours to kill while everyone else was occupied and important. At the beginning he had soldiered along determinedly, padding out the vacuum with cheap distractions: walks, museums, library books, the zoo, the Staten Island ferry, the Roosevelt Island tram. Soon his resolution wavered. He could no longer concentrate on the novels of Dostoyevsky, and it took too much trouble to get dressed up in his pinstripes for hanging out in art galleries. In case he ran into acquaintances, it was important to look like a busy, self-employed consultant.

He scraped together interviews at galleries and museums. All the positions were lowly and paid less than a dog walker's salary. Anyhow, he did not get them. The rejection letters stacked up. The evenings were filled in with networking from his Rolodex. He gossiped, dropped names, whipped his résumé from his breast pocket at the opportune moment, and exhausted his rapidly dwindling savings on expensive bar tabs, which he picked up to prove he had no financial worries.

The money ebbed. All Emil's funds had been sucked into the maintenance of the extravagant life-style. The bills were steep, and there were many of them. Nick had saved nothing, after settling for rent, garage parking, the health club, the house in Quogue, exotic vacations, the upmarket video club, Armani, Brooks Brothers, Indochine, the Ipanema Grill, and the Quilted Giraffe.

He told his cleaning lady he was going away for a long trip to London; he would call her when he got back. He put up the Porsche for repossession. He bought himself bags of tokens and slunk down the subway steps past the beggars. Only on those days he felt crushed with despair did he break down and treat himself to a taxi. When his circle of yuppie friends stopped phoning, he let the relationships lie fallow. It was too much strain to implicate himself in a web of lies and excuses.

Delphine sympathetically insisted on picking up several hefty dinner checks—"Just until you're back on your feet." He hated her patronage. However tactfully she tried to help, it still reminded him of those original snubs. Poverty was temporarily bearable as long as he had his lofty apartment in which to sit it out, hermitlike, and stare at a fuzzy, wavy television, now stripped of cable service. What he could not endure was that Delphine should witness his disgrace. He did not want her to know he sat in his kitchen eating macaroni and cheese and scoured the sink and scrubbed the floor and ironed his own shirts and gave skimpy tips.

When they cut off his phone, he did nothing about it. He actually felt safer knowing that no one could call him. He used the public phones on the streets when he needed to, as for calling Georgia today.

Good old Georgia, coming up with this last-ditch interview. If by some miracle he got the job, at least, as she said, it would restore his foothold in the auction house world. Never mind if he would spend his days researching the provenance of Victorian pincushions and enameled oyster forks. Never mind if they paid him eighteen thousand dollars a year for the privilege. It would be better than reading *Finnegans Wake* by the Central Park boat pond or watching the orangutans' flirtations in their cage.

* * *

"Two hundred and twenty thousand dollars . . . two hundred and forty? Sixty on the phone. Eighty. Do I hear three hundred? Three hundred anywhere? Down it goes, then, at three hundred thousand dollars, fair warning at three hundred thousand dollars." Rap, rap. "Lot number thirty-six, the Diebenkorn, sold for three hundred thousand. Lot number thirty-seven is the Elliot."

The turntable spun. The stripes of pea green and dried blood swam into view. Mrs. Milholland III wriggled excitedly and sat up straighter on her metal folding chair. The entire room seemed to draw breath. Everybody was curious to see how high Luke Elliot's *Isn't* would soar as a result of the young artist's tragic accident last spring. Although she could take no direct credit for the young man's untimely death, Mrs. Milholland congratulated herself. She had purchased her first Elliots while the artist was still unknown. What a stroke of luck that Emil Papier had happened to be in Giulietta's gallery to tip her off to a future megastar.

Nervously she crossed and uncrossed her legs and hitched down her shocking pink miniskirt over her thighs. The catalog lay spread on her husband's lap beside her. She envied Joe Kominski, the seller who was putting *Isn't* on the market. Rumor had it (such stories, she comforted herself, were often apocryphal) that Kominski himself had bought it for a couple of thousand dollars right off the wall from one of those funky, counterculture dives on the Lower East Side.

Mrs. Milholland reached for her husband's wrinkled, freckled hand beside her.

"Take it easy, pussycat."

The chief auctioneer paused theatrically, to grab the attention of the room.

"Starting the bidding at one hundred thousand dollars."

Behind the Milhollands, the Baron von Tislowicz flared his Hapsburg nostrils. It pained him that Luke Elliot, the discovery of that vulgar PAP Fund, should become the flavor of the month. Of course, he reminded his friends, it would be an error to confuse luck with strategy. Emil Papier could not have foreseen his remarkable good fortune arriving in the form of the fire. Well, perhaps not good fortune for Luke Elliot, but think of all the people who had prospered as a result.

Helga, Baroness von Tislowicz, flashed her husband a sugary smile. She noticed that raffia hats and red eyeglass frames were fashionable this season. She yawned at the stripes on the platform and decided they were the ugliest thing she had ever seen. Not that she would admit to such an opinion. She knew when to keep her mouth shut.

"Three hundred and sixty... eighty... four hundred thousand from the gentleman near me... four hundred and twenty on the telephone."

Peter Dante, ever vigilant for the tiniest flicker of a paddle, surveyed the room. When his gaze fell on Giulietta's expansive black behind, he seethed. Why couldn't his own vomit painter have been the one to be immolated in fire? Why should it be Giulietta's artist who met such a newsworthy, profitable fate?

"I have seven hundred thousand on the aisle. Do I hear seven fifty? I have eight at the back. Eight hundred thousand. Make it eight fifty."

In the auxiliary gallery next door, Kitty and Caspar Peacock were following the drama on the video monitor. Kitty, pregnant to bursting point, had turned down one of the coveted seats in the main gallery. The auxiliary hall was better ventilated, and she did not want to feel faint. Besides, if she and Caspar sneaked out nimbly, they might be able to avoid the swarm of press.

Caspar and Dan Helena had counseled her against going tonight. Labor was due any time. She had been determined, however. She still owned the handful of paintings that she had rescued from the Mercer Street studio, preserved from the flames. Tonight's sale of *Isn't* would provide another benchmark of their value. The legacy of those stripes would provide her, and the unborn child, with the financial security of a lifetime. But she was here for sentimental reasons, too. This was her widow's valediction, a private tribute to Luke's living struggle, to the time they had spent together sleeping on a lumpy, leaking mattress and eating leftover frogs' legs in doggie bags from Kitty's restaurants.

The auctioneer's voice (broadcast into the auxiliary gallery) dropped to a stage whisper and rasped, "Nine hundred and fifty thousand on the telephone, give me one million, will somebody give me one million dollars?" The cameras zoomed up to his face. His rubbery, poker features wreathed in an explosive smile. "One million dollars. I have one million dollars!"

Kitty never discussed Luke, not even with Caspar or Dan, since his death. She knew, quite simply, that she would never love anyone as she had loved her dead husband. She would never want to. Unless you had experienced passion you had not lived, but love was a mixed bag, and hers had brought such misery and frustration in its wake. Once was enough. Luke had left her with a rich store of memories, the valuable stripes, and the child.

"One million two. Three. Four. Five. Six. Not yours, sir. The gentleman in the center. One million seven hundred thousand dollars."

She and Dan knew that Luke had been long headed on a one-way street to destruction. It was shocking how he had perished—yet had he survived, what then? Maybe he would have tried detox. Kitty doubted it. She had seen the crazed look in the topaz eyes. He was hell-bent on slow-motion self-annihilation.

If only he had not been so weak.

"One million nine hundred thousand dollars. Come on, let's make it two million. Nice round number, who's going to make it two for me? Say two. Say two. Thank you, sir. I have two million dollars."

Two mil. Phew. Caspar Peacock shook his head wonderingly. I mustn't be jealous, he reprimanded himself, of my dead friend's success. It was better to be alive and still painting. Caspar was optimistic. Where there was life there was hope. It was all a question of timing. He accepted now that he had been mistaken about the appeal of his Japanese flags. He had hawked the slides around SoHo. Everyone missed the point.

"Two million five. Six. Seven on the phone. Eight in the gallery. Nine. Three million dollars. Three one on the phone. Three two. Three three."

Painting, Caspar always argued, was a dinosaur. Even the

flags. From now on he would compose entirely on a keyboard, creating computer graphics unmarred by the fallible human touch. This was twenty-first-century art, unswerving and unwavering as the hand of God. It would not be long before all traditional media, oils and acrylics, tempera and watercolors, were quaintly relegated to the status of the steam engine and the airship.

"Three million six. Three seven."

Holy cow. Mrs. Milholland could hardly breathe for anticipation. This could be the most thrilling day of her life, as important as the inauguration ceremonies for the opening of the Milholland Wing of Twentieth-Century Art. She gripped her hands tightly in her shocking pink lap. *Go on, Luke,* a voice roared in her head, *you can do it.*

The auctioneer's own adrenaline skyrocketed as he announced each new bid to his mesmerized flock. "Three eight. Three nine." He searched the room imploringly. "Will no one give me four million dollars? No one?"

He looked lingeringly toward the row of stewardesses with their telephones, spinning it out, playing for time. He looked back at the audience, one arm raised in midair. His eyes bored into every spectator.

"Four million dollars."

The room burst into spontaneous applause. The release of tension was audible.

"Fair warning, then, at four million dollars." The gavel rapped. "Sold for four million dollars. The next lot is the de Kooning, number thirty-eight in your catalogs."

"I have a plan," said Susannah. "For helping Nick Jones."

It was three A.M., almost time for closing up at Valhalla, where she and Dan had stopped off for a nightcap. He ordered for them and put Jimmy Hendrix on the jukebox. The bartender was busy at the far end of the bar, rinsing glasses, as the regulars drifted off home into the deserted streets.

Dan checked out the latest display of panty hose spun over the bar like suspension bridges. "Why are you going to all this trouble to help him?"

"I'm doing it for Delphine. She wants that Englishman. She doesn't even know how much she wants him. I know."

"I still don't get it. The Brit's got himself a new job in the other auction house. He was fucking lucky to get employed again after the paper napkin disaster. Let him make his own money."

"Do you realize how much those people pay him? He can hardly settle his bar bills. I don't want Delphine getting mixed up with some penniless pauper." Susannah recalled the drab hallways, disinfectant smells, and rattling doors of the Palace West Hotel. She had lined her nest so as never to have to deal with poverty again. It had no romantic appeal. It was all very well to be Dan Helena, as she pointed out, living his bare-bones Dumbo existence with that dog. He was an art star, and his asceticism was his trademark. She and Delphine were women who were not equipped to sleep on a futon mat in an ill-heated loft.

He squeezed her thigh, hard. "This is a major caper you're getting mixed up with. The English kid has been stealing information worth millions, maybe billions, of dollars."

"Who cares? The art market stinks. It represents everything evil we've been fighting against. You hate these people, Dan Helena. They ruined you. Giulietta and the Karakoffs and Juan Gomez and Billy Berrymouse, what do you care if they cheat on one another?"

He considered the argument. She had something. From that angle there was a kind of moral grandeur in accelerating the decay of a corrupt and degenerate system; a certain Dadaist-style victory in crusading to topple the whole bourgeois machine. Why should he care whether the Shining Squid Corporation outbid the Milhollands or Billy Berrymouse? Why did any of those ruthless, gluttonous fat cats deserve to own a Picasso more than anyone else?

She pressed on urgently with her strategy. "We're meeting tomorrow, you and I, with the man from Shining Squid, to discuss your new commission." The Japanese corporation, eager to patronize the most talked about sculptor of the year, was hiring Helena to design a monument for its headquarters in Osaka. "Maybe the Japs will give Nick Jones a job. Leastways I can inquire."

"Okay." He took Susannah's hand (the bartender was still occupied clinking glasses around in soapy water) and slid it between his warm thighs. "Ask them," he agreed. "But don't fuck up my deal."

He leaned back against the bar and closed his eyes. He had never cared about any of the other women. He had used them, and let them use him, in a celebration of libido. He had no idea what had become of any of those velvet creatures who creamed for him like pools of runny paint. When they had had their fill of the pagan sex he dished up to them, they had drifted off, and he had never pursued. Susannah was different. Sure, he talked gruff and never let on that he gave a damn. Once in a while, though, the realization startled him. What would he do if she went her own way? She organized his Belle John campaign, she appeased him, she excited him, and sometimes, when the bartender was not looking and the lights were dim, she would even swiftly go down on him under the bar. A fine combination.

The next afternoon he gripped her arm tightly as he wheeled her along the corridor of the Carlyle.

"We're going to be late for your meeting," she protested. "The folks from Shining Squid said they'd be in the bar at five-thirty."

"Don't argue with me, woman." His authority was adamant. He pushed her abruptly through the gold-and-white door marked with a female silhouette.

She stiffened. "Not here . . . we can't."

The old woman who passed out the fresh hand towels looked up indolently from her knitting. She had a quiet routine. Nothing unexpected ever happened, except for an earring dropped down the sink or a spilled powder compact. When she saw Dan Helena's towering frame, her stare traveled in frozen horror from his size eleven boots up to his leather safari jacket. She opened her mouth to yell.

Before she could bring out a whimper, Dan whipped a hundred-dollar bill from his pocket and placed it delicately amid the dimes and quarters that clustered in the old woman's saucer for tips, next to a small jug of anemones.

The woman had been born in a Sicilian village, where the

townspeople swore the local saint came down from heaven to perform miracles for those who prayed in earnest. She mouthed her own small prayer of gratitude to Santa Benedicta dei Fiori as she stretched out her swollen fingers for the folded bill. This was New York, where people were crazy, but her saint had never deserted her. She squinted at the elegant red-haired woman with a kind of awe, even though she realized that they were about to commit the sin of fornication.

Her gnarled finger pointed toward the closest of the four stalls. Dan ushered Susannah through the door.

"Someone else may come in!" Susannah hung her Fendi purse on the door hook.

"Shh! Come closer."

She felt him lift the hem of her skirt and peel the panty hose from her hips. She did not step out of her high heels, which rocked dangerously on the pink-and-white marble floor. The wallpaper was salmon, with silver gray flowers, like wrapping paper for a wedding present. It was a solid white door, thank the Lord (she suspected he would have done it anyhow, if it had been slatted). The old woman could see their four feet underneath. Here, between the narrow pink-and-silver walls, in the most proper hotel in Manhattan...in the hotel where she had first set eyes on Emil Papier...was nothing sacred, nowhere? Then he was thrusting inside her, clutching her ass with both hands, until she could no longer control herself from moving back and forward against him. She clenched her hands to stop herself, letting escape a stifled moan.

At the point of no return, her breath came faster and she cared about nothing but the gathering climax. He withdrew and, sitting, made her stride him, so it was her turn to ride him. As he felt her thighs begin to grip, he ordered, rasping in her ear, "Do it for me. Give it to me. Now." And she did.

Afterward, squeezed like sardines in the stall, they wriggled to adjust zippers and nylon. She took a comb from her purse and ran it through her hair.

"I'll do that." Taking it, he combed the red waves for her, separating the tangles with exquisite gentleness. She leaned her head into the caress of the comb. Dan could at one moment batter her into welcome submission and touch her at the next with the delicacy of the finest sable brush.

He showed her his watch. "It's five twenty-eight. See? We're on time."

The old woman's knitting needles clicked furiously. She did not look up. But when Dan threw a couple more quarters into the saucer, her face crinkled into a ribald grin.

The man from Shining Squid and his interpreter entered the Bemelmans Bar at five-thirty-one. He bowed gracefully, first to Dan and then to Susannah. "Good evening, Mr. Helena. You permit? I have invited my interpreter to join us. That way I do not make single mistake."

The man from Shining Squid spoke fluent English, and particularly as far as numbers were involved. Otherwise the corporation could never have dispatched him to the bidding wars, where millions turned instantly on a word or a gesture. He liked to bring his interpreter along, however, for support.

The Japanese both chose Jack Daniel's. Dan Helena drank orange juice, and Susannah ordered a martini.

The man from Shining Squid launched his opening volley. The interpreter translated solemnly. "The Shining Squid Corporation is proud to commission a forty-foot steel sculpture of the honorable President Washington, in identical proportion to the thirty-foot statue executed for Belle John, Inc., of Geraldine, New Jersey. We regret the misunderstandings arisen between the Japanese and American people, because our small country has bought so many American companies and so much American real estate. We admire your Hollywood movies and your Rockefeller Center and your system of democracy. Our corporation wishes to set an example, by adorning our headquarters in Osaka with a forty-foot sculpture of your honorable president."

"Forty feet," exclaimed Dan. "You want a bigger one than Belle John?"

Both Japanese nodded vigorously. Up-down-up-down. "The Shining Squid Corporation is the leading manufacturer of silicon chips and transistors in the Osaka area. We are able to afford a bigger statue than the Americans."

"My fee for such a large-scale work is nine-hundred-thousand dollars. The proceeds will be paid directly to the Artistic Liberties Brigade to fund my lawsuit. I guess you know that the Belle John piece has provoked a controversial backlash."

The Japanese glanced at one another surreptitiously. On the one hand, they were anxious to avoid taking sides in the internecine American wrangle. On the other, if this sculptor won his case, the value of Shining Squid's forty-foot George would be vastly increased on the books. In a country where the tiniest plot of real estate had become prohibitively expensive, and earth the size of a foot sole could be worth so much, why not a forty-foot mammoth of steel?

"It is the choice of Mr. Helena where he will spend his money."

Dan proceeded cautiously, too. "My contract must state clearly that the work is 'site-specific.' Do you know what that means?"

The man from Shining Squid jerked his head and rattled off a torrent. The translator conveyed, "A postmodern work of art should relate to its environment, and set up an intellectual dialogue with the site of its installation."

Dan looked impressed at the translator's command of English. Nevertheless he hammered home, "Which means it can't be moved or relocated."

"The statue of the great Buddha at Nakamura has guarded the temple for eight hundred years. The statue of the honorable President George Washington shall remain in place for two thousand years."

That would have tempted any artist.

"We have brought these photographs for your inspection. We would like you to come soon as our guest to examine the site of our headquarters." The translator turned to the man from Shining Squid, who sharply attacked the combination lock on his briefcase and produced two 24- by 13-inch glossy Cibachrome prints of the ingress to the Shining Squid corporate offices.

Susannah peeped at them over Dan's shoulder. The pagoda building, with layers of overlapping roofs, was set in a landscaped park amid spotted deer and paper-white plum blossoms.

The Japanese explained, "Our country is in transition. We

are proud of our imperial past, yet we are also a modern nation. Our art is greatly influenced by the West. The Shining Squid Corporation continues to acquire for investment and recreational purposes the finest twentieth-century American paintings."

"We know," Susannah interrupted brightly. "And I have a proposal for you on that subject." It was her first remark.

Both Japanese turned their faces in surprise. They belonged to the old-fashioned Oriental school firmly rooted in the creed that women should be silent, decorative objects. "You, madam?" The interpreter could not disguise his distaste.

She went on, unfazed. "As everyone knows, the PAP Fund has been collaring all the best work that comes up at auction."

"They have a lot of money. And we also have money."

"I know you do. What you need now is know-how."

"Ah, know-how." The word was on everyone's lips in Tokyo these days. The Japanese business world was obsessed by the differences in American and local management practices. Oriental companies leaped to sponsor their up-and-coming brass to acquire MBAs from Harvard and Wharton.

But how to apply that education to acquisitions in the international art market? "You confuse us," replied the man from Shining Squid. Annoy us, too, the translator's tone suggested. Who was this intrusive Western woman who dared to interfere with serious masculine business?

"Every season," Susannah reminded them pointedly, "the other bidders use up their funds, bumping each other higher and higher like a Ferris wheel at a county fair, and end up overpaying for the works. When something really superb comes up, they're near broke, and the PAP Fund moves in double quick for the kill."

"We have noticed this phenomenon."

"What an advantage you would have if you could be wise to how high your opponents were prepared to go, and you knew who all exactly they were."

"An advantage, yes. But it is impossible."

"It is not impossible. I know a person here in New York who is a specialist in that very area."

The man from Shining Squid and the interpreter stared at

her, their eyes bubbling like carp. They took time out for a voluble flurry of Japanese exchange.

The interpreter finally said, "We wish to know whether this person is expensive."

"He's worth it. His information is the best."

"And he's available to work for the Shining Squid Corporation?"

"He's a free-lance. A hired gun."

"Excuse me, what is a hired gun?"

"A mercenary. He works for the most generous employer."

The Japanese consulted again. "How can you guarantee his information will be accurate?"

"It will be. He's well placed, he's bold, with a heap of initiative and a flood of fine sources."

"And he will continue to provide consistently over the long term?"

"As long as folks buy and sell works of art." Susannah had confidence in Nick's ingenuity. He had gumption, and he could steal cleaner than a weasel. The information he had already stolen from the auctioneer's book would last out three or four seasons at least. Meanwhile he had plenty of opportunity to reenact his thefts and espionage across the street at his new employers'. Nick Jones would use his charms to unlock the necessary combinations. "If you hire him as a consultant, you will pay him a retainer of one million dollars a year. Why, gentlemen, that's a speck of nothing for a flourishing corporation like yours. A drop in the ocean. You spend millions on paintings."

"We would like to meet this person."

"That can be arranged."

The Japanese nodded. They could squeeze the retainer out of the sixty million they had earmarked for November's acquisitions. The Shining Squid Corporation would soon be completing the construction of its art gallery adjacent to headquarters, and they were determined to cram their museum with the finest. Management was expecting an influx of tourists from all over Japan, far exceeding the numbers attracted by the Berrymouse Noah's Ark theme park in Nagasaki. Western visitors would be arriving in droves, too, to ogle at their treasures.

Although the man from Shining Squid was reluctant to do business with a woman, in this one incidence he capitulated.

He bowed stiffly. "We would like a six-thirty breakfast meeting with the hired gun."

Felice and Jacob sent out Luke Elliot "Season's Greetings" calendars. To avoid the December holiday season, which had so long brought out the worst in their marriage, they agreed they needed to spend a few intimate days away together, far from the fracas. It must be a compromise, a Moslem or a Buddhist country. So when the Egyptians invited Belle John, Inc., to tender for the plumbing project, Jacob decided to combine work with pleasure.

"It's a sizable contract," he explained to his wife. "They want low-water-consumption flush toilets in eighty-five thousand homes, to say nothing of sinks and shower units."

In the cradle of civilization, where gods once walked and five-thousand-year-old bodies of pharaohs lay embalmed in the museum, thirty million peasants inhabited the banks of the Nile. They lived with their children and chickens and buffalo, in one-room mud huts almost as primitive as those of their ancestors of 3000 B.C. The locals left their outdoor fires to huddle around the single television in wonder. In the mud villages Jacob, with his three-gallon-flush toilets, was a new pharaoic god, providing the bewildered inhabitants with miracles of plumbing that approached sheer magic.

The Karakoffs were staying in the Nile Hilton, where Jacob treated dignitaries from the Ministries of Sanitation and Urban Development to lunch in the Isis Coffee Shop. Deal makers gathered in the bright, airy restaurant to order an "American hamburger." Government officials mingled here with the remnants of Cairo society. Mature men pampered their mistresses with "American fried-chicken drumsticks"; it was the "in" place for adulterous affairs. During the day Jacob held court over "American blueberry pancakes," negotiating porcelain and U-bend pipe supplies and sewage and drainage systems.

When Jacob had a lunch appointment with a big cheese from the Department of Hygiene, Felice announced that she had

some private errands of her own to run. Jacob smiled. She was
doubtless planning a shopping excursion to buy him some little
Christmas something, although she had already given him a
charming Paul Klee watercolor and a new exercise bicycle before
they left New York.

"Be careful," he begged. "It's dangerous in the back streets
of the souk. Do you need more money?"

"I have plenty. I'll get the cabdriver to come with me. He can
translate."

Jacob and the senior engineering manager of hygiene finished up their cups of pungent Turkish coffee, and the senior
engineer took off for his siesta. Everything came to a standstill
in the excoriating afternoon heat. Jacob sat a while in the shade
by the pool, flipping through his business notes, and wondered
what had become of his wife. Maybe she had stopped off for
sightseeing in one of the mosques. Or gone to the museum. He
decided to make his own excursion.

Beyond the perimeter of the sweltering city streets and as-
phyxiating exhaust fumes, they waited, the pyramids of Cheops,
Cheophren, and Mycerinus. The busloads of tourists and post-
card hawkers milled in the car park like ants. Jacob left his taxi
and set out alone through the sand, which puffed in clouds
around him.

He stopped between the paws of the Great Sphinx. She
greeted him as she had greeted Alexander and Caesar and Napoleon in their times. The millennia had eroded the stone, but
her paws were still firm and her rump arched proudly. Great
Sphinx, thought Jacob, I'm glad we decided to make this trip.
When I look at your pyramids, your statues, and your temples,
my own troubles slip away. You put our skirmishes into proportion, Sphinx. The shareholders, the board of directors, the
patriotic protesters, and the intellectuals with their petitions are
like shadows compared with you. So what if I can provide cut-
ting-edge plumbing technology to hundreds of mud-caked villages; so what if the Shining Squid Corporation of Osaka is
determined to erect that forty-foot Helena sculpture among the
plum blossoms; so what if a few curators and postmodern critics
have labeled me the Attila of cultural imperialism? The limbs

and torso of George Washington lie helpless in the Trenton warehouse, while you, Sphinx, watch your horizons of sand.

He bought a papyrus scroll as a souvenir for his secretary and located his snoozing taxi driver in the car park. They drove back to the hotel, where Felice was waiting with a smug, secretive expression.

Felice made an effort that evening with her appearance, shrouding herself in a heavy cotton caftan she had bought in the hotel boutique and an amulet necklace that the seller had promised was guaranteed to stave off the evil advances of men. Jacob did not know if the touch of glamour was intended for him or for Jesus. He had to keep remembering that it was almost December 25; the gaudy Christmas tree in the lobby looked out of place amid the palms, and the Hilton management pumped the strains of "Silent Night" through the dining room, over and over again. Jacob ran his hand across her hips as they stepped into the dining room and groped for the bony gentile pelvis beneath the stiff folds of the cotton.

"Did you have a nice day?" Felice asked.

Jacob glanced through the window at the wide, torpid goddess Nile, so dark and flat and strangely female, as no other river he had ever seen. The lights of the traffic bobbed along the nearby bridge that spanned her. The maître d' hovered anxiously over their table, bowing and smiling in his scarlet fez.

"Uh-huh." He did not tell her about his private interchanges with the Sphinx. The desert cat had left him becalmed; his philosophical musings were too intimate to share.

"I have a surprise for you."

What on earth has she found, he wondered, in the dirty, crowded souk where they bargain for trained snakes and plastic junk and sequinned slippers?

"I had an appointment this afternoon with the director of Mohammed's Orphanage for the Lambs of Allah."

"Are you meshuga or what?"

"Don't get excited. It's bad for your blood pressure. I would have told you earlier, except I wanted it to be a surprise. Oh, Jacob, if only you could have seen the children. They're so cute and well behaved."

He took a deep breath. Come back, Sphinx, come back to me quickly, before I lose the tranquillity I found in the desert. "What were you doing in an orphanage?"

"His name is Ibrahim, and he's six years old. He's lovely, you'll melt when you see him. He has enormous, liquid brown eyes and thick, curly black hair. He only speaks a couple of words of English, but he's obviously intelligent and I'm sure he'll learn fast."

"Learn English? Why?"

"I want him, Jacob dearest. You'll want him, too, I'm sure, when you see him. And he's cheap, too. Only a couple of thousand dollars. Do you realize how much it would cost us if we arranged to adopt an American child? Fifty, sixty thousand at least."

"It's not the money, for God's sake. You can hardly buy a blue-chip lithograph for that these days."

"I know, I know. Think of the good we can do. We can give Ibrahim a real future, educate him, send him to Harvard or Princeton, groom him for an executive post at Belle John ... "

"You are talking about an Arab street orphan."

"The adoption papers can be arranged right away. There's only one condition. They insist that he's allowed to go on practicing Islam."

"You want to take this kid to New York to practice Islam?"

"He'll have to leave school on Fridays. We'll get a prayer mat and there's a mosque up on Third Avenue. He can go there, can't he? It'll be fine, I'll take care of all the details. Say yes, please say yes."

Jacob heaved and pushed away his unfinished pyre of French fries. Outside, the great brown Nile schlepped relentlessly toward its delta in the faraway sea.

S'iz bashert. "Yes, Felice. Whatever you want, honey."

Amen kayn yehi ratzon. God's will be done.

19

TOGETHER

The servants left Emil a slab of roast goose under the breast-shaped dish cover, in addition to the usual heap of dried beef. Although he had not ordered it, someone had mixed up a pitcher of *Glühwein,* with nutmeg and cloves, probably in the expectation of increasing the Christmas tips.

He left the goose untouched. Behind the faint curtain of snow he could sketchily discern the frosty light of Montreux below and the smudge of the castle of Chillon. There would be activity in the casino, he reflected. Tourists would be sipping hot chocolate in the cafes, ice-skating, or playing vingt-et-un. As he gnawed at his mouthful of dried beef, Emil was struck by the wild idea of ordering his car and driving down to Montreux, for the sake of human chatter and light. No. That was absurd. He rarely ventured out of his fortress, and least of all on Christmas night, when the vagabonds and dregs of society would be stalking.

The villa was silent. The snow muffled the wind and the creaking of the pines. The servants had all departed for their Yule logs and families; only the substitute nightwatchman prowled downstairs, smoking his pipe and muttering to the Alsatians. Emil was alone, a prisoner of self-imposed confinement, with no company but the crags of the Dents du Midi across the lake.

He tried telephoning the Karakoffs, who were still in Cairo. There was no reply from the hotel room.

He succeeded in getting through briefly to Giulietta. She was celebrating the day with her multiple generations in Scarsdale. She answered with her mouth full. Giulietta always put on another kilo at Christmas. Emil heard a jabber of child and adult noise in the background. She was obviously busy. Emil wished her a merry one and hung up. It was more depressing to hear other people's happy sounds than to sit in silence with the snow.

The snow was thickening now, veiling the outlines of the mountains. The lamps flickered. Not tonight, panicked Emil, don't let there be a power failure. It was bad enough to wait in silence as the snow stole away the landscape. It would be terrible to be trapped in blackness.

In case, however, he lit the candlesticks in the Raoul Epinard candle holders on the sideboard. Delphine had given him those candlesticks, shaped in the form of iguanas' mouths. Where was his daughter tonight? Living it up with her anarchists and revolutionaries? How sharper than a serpent's tooth is an ungrateful child.

He reached impulsively to dial the number at East End Avenue. He had no idea whether Susannah was actually there. She might be anywhere with that crazed sculptor, fomenting trouble, drawing attention to herself, and piling ridicule on him. No. However lonely he felt, he would not compound the gloom by talking to Susannah. At least the market in Tokyo would open in a few hours. Trading would be thin the day after Christmas, but it would take his mind off brooding.

Emil clasped a hand to his left side, where he felt that dreaded tightening. Not here, not tonight. Even his father had not been caught alone and morose, deep in the snowy night. The electricity shuddered again. Perhaps he should one day forgive his daughter. She was the last of the Papiers, after all.

Emil picked up the jug of *Glühwein* and carried it downstairs, groping for the treads. How petrifying to slip in his own house and be discovered later by the watchman, in a crumpled, broken heap, the general manager of the largest art fund on earth.

He called out to the watchman as he reached the landing. "I'm visiting the basement apartment."

"Very good, monsieur. *Joyeux Noël.*"

Iris was spending Christmas Day with her sister, Pansy, in New Jersey. Susannah roasted the eighteen-pound turkey herself. Delphine helped with the oyster stuffing. The creamed onions disintegrated, and something went mysteriously wrong deep down in the innards of the bird—maybe they should not have tampered with the oyster recipe—but everyone attacked the dinner gallantly and managed to praise the asparagus.

Afterward Dan stoked up the fire in the living room until it blazed like a sinking warship, and Nick passed around cups of coffee, taking extra care not to drip on Susannah's recently acquired Chinese silk rug.

Kitty arranged herself with the baby on her lap in a sea of Susannah's new fluffy cushions.

"Will you be comfortable there?" Everyone was paying special attention to Kitty and her three-week-old, making a great fuss of them.

"We're fine." Kitty adjusted the baby's sleeping sack and kissed her forehead. "Aren't we, Stella?"

Her infant daughter was named after the artist Frank Stella, as surely Luke would have wished.

Nick sat down next to Delphine. This was the best Christmas Day he had ever had. How delightful to be here in the palazzo with Susannah's menagerie rather than in Wiltshire listening with his dull family to Queen Elizabeth's dull broadcast speech.

Susannah finished lighting the last of the candles. "Let's open the presents. Start with that big blue box. It's for Kitty and Stella."

Kitty slid away the gold ribbon and ripped off the blue paper. "Finger paints! Stella's going to love them. She's inherited Luke's talent."

"Maybe three weeks is a little young, but soon she'll be painting up a storm—we'll fix her a show: the youngest artist in SoHo. Is this for me?" Dan held up a box that rattled. "Wow! A bear-hunting knife. What a blade." He ran his thumb appreciatively close to the razor edge.

Delphine coughed and looked away discreetly. Although everyone knew how she disapproved of animal slaughter, Christmas was no time for ideological warfare. She took a box from under the tree. "Ozone-friendly eau de cologne. Thank you very much."

Susannah was stripping the paper from a large flat square. She held up a Cibachrome print of Caspar Peacock dressed up as Napoleon.

"That's from me and Stella," Kitty explained. "Caspar designs the entire thing on a computer keyboard and prints it out like a photo. Since you're redecorating, I thought you needed something fresh for your bedroom." Kitty read aloud from another label. "'To Stella. Love, Delphine.'" From out of its swaddling of tissue paper a stuffed plush whale was brought to light.

"I got it at the Save the Wildlife annual dinner," Delphine told her.

Susannah gave Dan a sweater that turned out to be several sizes too small for him. "Never mind, it'll fit Judd. He needs a winter sweater when we go scavenging on cold mornings."

Delphine provided a rubber whale dog toy for Judd.

Kitty gave Dan a cassette course guaranteed to teach fluent Japanese in nineteen days. "Maybe it'll be useful for your trip." Dan was scheduled to leave for Osaka shortly, on his first scouting visit to the site of the Shining Squid headquarters.

The pile of presents was diminishing. Kitty gave Susannah Roland Barthes's *The Pleasure of the Text* as a tribute to her hostess's new intellectual stature. There was a box of organic fudge from Delphine to everyone, a chunk of which nearly broke Dan's front teeth.

"Would anyone like some more dessert?" asked Susannah.

There were cries and rumbles of protest from all around.

"I'm stuffed."

"I couldn't eat another mouthful."

"I'm going on a diet tomorrow."

"What are you trying to do to us?"

"Stella and I have to get home," Kitty said. "Thank you all very much for the wonderful presents."

"And thank you for yours."

Kitty held up her baby's cheek against her own. She was gradually getting used to handling her. "Aren't we lucky, Stella, to have such terrific friends?"

Susannah fetched Kitty's coat.

It had been such a happy day that she had hardly even missed Luke. She remembered the Christmases they had spent together eating turkey TV dinners and trying to seal the crack in the windowpane where the blast of frigid air whipped through. Valhalla was closed on Christmas Day, so there had been nothing to do but go to bed early with the radio, a pack of Camels, and a couple of candles wedged in old 7-Up bottles and make love on the lumpy mattress.

As she gave the cabdriver the address of her new condo on Avenue A, she thought, Of course it'll never be the same with anyone else. But life goes on. Was there an invisible purpose behind the chaos? Luke had always coveted a hero's end. Maybe he would have preferred it this way, having collectors all over the globe scrambling and jockeying to own the famous stripes.

The cab pulled out. The main thing, she thought, is that I have Stella. Life goes on.

Upstairs, Nick was looking for Delphine. He poked his head into the laundry room, canvassed the dining room and the kitchen. He finally found her in the conservatory, feeding Gauguin crumbs of the organic fudge and scowling furiously.

Delphine was the only one who had not had fun. She envied the others' contentment. Susannah and Dan had found their strange peace together, writing manifestos and leading the avant garde into battle. As for Kitty, she had the child to dote on, and besides, as everyone whispered behind her back, she was better off without that crackhead loft rat to drag her down. Nick certainly had nothing to complain of, with his restored income, a new Porsche fully paid up, and the leggy stewardesses from both auction houses fawning over him. Delphine, his "friend" and confidante, knew exactly the origins of Nick's phantom funds. She had even feigned congratulations when he had exultantly relayed to her his arrangement with the Japanese. Inside she boiled. What were his revived fortunes to her?

Delphine gritted her teeth when she thought of Nick Jones. It depressed her to sit next to him on the sofa, watching him passing around coffee and unwrapping boxes and telling jokes that made everyone laugh. For Nick was surely using her again, just like Rudi and the others. She had been naive enough to believe they could become real friends over time. Fat chance. She was no more than Papier's Daughter again.

When they saw each other, Nick was a paragon of good behavior. He was always on time, always insisted that Delphine choose the movie or night club, inquired after her ecological activities, praised her jewelry or clothes, brought her little presents, exotic zinnias and camellias, and tiny objets de vertu from work.

Every token of esteem made her madder. She had no use for perfume vials or Victorian pillboxes. She thought of that blonde from the estates department whom he was still seeing. Delphine ran into them together one evening at the Ipanema Grill. Nick had his arm around the girl at the table. He introduced her awkwardly to Delphine, who nodded coldly and did not linger.... Whenever she visited him at Trump Parc, she sneaked into the bedroom to search for clues. Once she found a pair of earrings on the windowsill. In an uncontrollable rage, she threw them out the window while Nick was busy on the phone to Osaka. Once she spotted a couple of cigarette butts—stained with *lipstick*—in a saucer by the bed. The evidence made her so livid that her stomach hurt. Worst of all was the evening she discovered the package of opened condoms in the medicine cabinet in the bathroom. It was no use throwing them out the window. He would only buy more. She came out of the bathroom looking flushed, told him she was coming down with a bug, and left without even finishing her takeout sushi.

Some women complained how they were used by men for their bodies. It was a lot worse not to be used.

Perhaps Nick was impotent. Or a latent homosexual, even if

he did have sex with the blonde from the estates department, just to prove his manhood. Maybe he snored; maybe he was emotionally stunted. It was his business anyhow whom he saw or slept with. Maybe he felt brotherly toward Delphine. Or maybe he didn't find her attractive. Dammit.

"Oh, it's you," Delphine grunted sourly. She pulverized a lump of organic fudge between her fingers and held it up to Gauguin's perch.

"I've been looking for you. Let's get out of here. Susannah and Dan want to be alone."

"There's nowhere to go. Everywhere's closed on Christmas night. Anyway, I'm tired. I think I'll go to bed early."

"What's wrong? You look miserable."

"Nobody liked my organic fudge."

"Come on. What is the matter?" He crumbled a hunk of the rocky fudge and fed it to the parrot.

"Not again!" squawked Gauguin. "My dick's going to fall off."

"When's Susannah going to do something about this foul bird? What's bothering you, Delphine? Is it about your father?"

She winced. That's what I mean to him. Papier's Daughter. Even now, after Papa and I have been estranged for a year, when Nick looks at me he's thinking about how useful we've all been to him and how useful we can go on being.

"Papa was always gloomy at Christmas," she replied indifferently. "We never went out. He has a theory it's the time of year the most terrorists strike."

What about that ugly girl from the order bid department at his former job? Did he still string her along, too?

"We've done it three times," Gauguin interrupted. "Let's eat now."

"Will you and your father ever be reconciled?"

Was that all he cared about? She looked at him sharply from under the canopy of lashes. "Maybe. Maybe not. It's better this way for now. I need some space to make my own life. I never again want to go back to being Papier's Daughter."

"You're absolutely right." He sat down on the wicker bench below the parrot's perch. "Come here. I want to talk to you."

"What about?"

"Sit down."

"Be quick. I'm tired and I've got a headache."

"You owe me something."

"What! I do?"

"When I arranged for you to meet Emil after the auction, you promised me that one day you'd return the favor."

"Oh, that." Why did he have to bring that up now? What did he want, anyway, after all this time? Money? Introductions? Leverage? "Can't we discuss it some other time, Nick? For God's sake, it's Christmas."

"I want to ask you now."

"All right, all right." She was so weary she could almost burst into tears. She had an inkling of how it must feel to be her father. People always wanted things from you.

"You agree, then? I can have what I want?"

"Yeah, yeah, I agree. Whatever I can do." She leaned her neck back against the prickly wicker. Why didn't he get it over with?

"I want to marry you."

She stared, as if he were speaking a foreign language. For a moment the words made no sense. Had she heard him right? She looked up sharply. "You want what?"

"I want to marry you."

"Why me? I'm disinherited. I don't exactly starve, but I'm no heiress, either."

"I want to marry you. I want you. You, not Papier's Daughter."

Overhead, Gauguin insisted, "Fuck my brains out. Now, baby, now."

Nick lifted a strand of silky brown hair and put his lips close to Delphine's ear. He whispered, "I think that's a fine idea. What are we waiting for? Let's get your coat and go home."

Susannah moved slowly around the living room, scooping up wads of crumpled gift wrap, gold cord, and rosettes. Iris would be back in the morning to straighten out the ravages of the holiday. Meanwhile Susannah shuddered at the wreckage of boxes and tissue paper littering *her* living room. All hers. She was becoming house-proud, as she relished the pleasure of ownership.

Outside the window a tendril of smoke sketched the thin, cold air across the East River. The traffic murmur at last was still. Even the twenty-four-hour city stole a few hours' sleep on this rare night of the year. Only a solitary plane, taking off from JFK beyond the bridge, ferociously blinked its red wing lights in the cloudless dark.

Dan stood slowly from the sofa where he had been examining his new knife and stabbed at the embers with the poker. "This was a fine day," he said. "You did a really nice job." He threw in a handful of fir cones and some reindeer paper. The flame sizzled and darted up again.

"Coming from you, that's a big compliment. I've never known you to be any more concerned with festivities than a bear in the woods. Still, it probably does you no harm to eat a decent home-cooked meal once in a while." She fished out a loop of tinsel from under her new chintz armchair.

"People change." He stretched his arms toward the coffered ceiling as if the spacious living room were too cramped for his massive frame. "Now I know what people mean when they say they feel tired all the way in their bones."

"You need a rest. Belle John has worn you out after all these months of wrangling. That and the trash food you live on. It's no wonder you feel weary at times."

"You're right. I'm just tired. And Japan seems a long way to go next week."

"You'll sleep on the plane. You've the gift of sleeping anywhere. And by the time you get back home, I'll have licked this spat with the NEA over the vomit exchange to Leningrad."

"Let that Wagnerian Hero fight his own battles. You have your hands full already with mine."

She laughed at his sharp reaction. "Sweet Jesus, I do believe the lofty Dan Helena is jealous."

"Are you nuts? Jealous of those third-rate vomit smearings?"

"Indeed you are. Why, it irks the pants off you." He, who knew he could make her flutter like the tiniest twitch on a kite string.

"Dan, we can't use the Artistic Liberties Brigade as your exclusive machine. When I accepted the chairpersonship, we understood my mission was to stamp out censorship and bigotry everywhere."

"You're right. I guess I am being self-centered."

Joining him in front of the fire, she wrapped her arms around his middle and clung for a moment, as if he were a gigantic, weatherbeaten sequoia. "All artists are self-centered, one way or another. I'm used to them."

He plunged his fingers into the well of her swirling hair. "I've had it," he announced emphatically. "Let's get the hell out of here."

"Where to?" Wherever did one go at eleven P.M. on Christmas night? Valhalla and all the other dives would be shut tight.

"Out altogether. I can't take it with this sewer of a city any longer. These drug-infested streets, where the grass is brown and the trees are shriveled and the rats parade. New York is washed up. Everyone's leaving who can."

She gazed up at him in shocked astonishment. "You thrive on the danger and loneliness. I thought the urban sterility inspired you."

"It used to. That was fine during the minimalist years. Gravel pits and rolls of barbed wire and corrugated metal—that stuff's had its day. It's not exciting here anymore. There no hum in the air. The greed generation has truly fucked us over and left this town a bomb crater. I'm dried up. I want to breathe clean air again and watch the horizon."

"Take your truck and go scavenging. When Manhattan gets to be too oppressive you just need to pick up and leave for a spell, and when you come back it's all fine again."

He shook his head slowly. "This time I'm getting out for good. I'm going home."

"You mean ... ?"

"Yep. I'm going back to the Rockies. I want to wake up in the mountains and smell the pines. I've enough money left, even after what's been shot on the lawyers. We'll build a comfortable wood cabin, heat it with solar energy, set up a studio for me next door."

"We?"

He ignored the tiny question. "We'll live simply, like mining people. Get a couple more dogs, grow our own potatoes and raspberries." Swept up in his vision, he became uncharacteristically eloquent. "We'll have to get a phone, I guess, and a fax and a satellite dish. Though we won't read newspapers and all that media shit."

"We? We?"

His face took on a solemn expression, almost comical in its intensity. He swept his arm around the walls, where the Magrittes and Dalis had been replaced by Fragonard drawings. "You don't need all this."

"Are you asking me to go out to Montana or Idaho or wherever and live with you?"

He wrinkled his nose like an embarrassed schoolboy. "Yeah. I guess I am."

The confirmation took her breath away. "Sweet Jesus Christ crucified! And you so in love with your privacy, too." She remembered the many times when she would have eagerly thrown up the palazzo and all her toys to run away with him to Dumbo. If only he had asked her then.

He scuffed at the Chinese rug. "Like I was saying, people change. Maybe I'm getting ready for a small dose of company now. Not too much—but you'd respect my solitude, I'm sure." He frowned fiercely, as if he were surrendering machismo drop by drop. He opened his broad palms in supplication. Hands that welded and tamed and trammeled the steel. "Let's try it. See what happens."

There were men who put chains around you, bound and gagged you and brutalized your will into submission, locked you in gilded cages like Emil Papier, enmeshed you in nets and traps of all kinds, brainwashed you and blustered, like Zachary and his brethren. She wanted to keep Dan on her side, away from all that. She never wanted to see her outlaw change or spoil.

She answered hesitantly. "You helped me get free. Now leave it be."

"I never asked for anything before, except when you wanted it, too." He took pride in his self-sufficiency and in demanding no favors.

She nodded. She needed to find an explanation that would

not wound him. She wished she could tell him that if she had been nineteen or twenty-five or thirty-five, even, she would have jumped at his offer. Anytime then.

She swiveled around the room, taking in the drawings and vases and polished tabletops, china and mirrors and celadon glass, and she wanted to blurt out, "I'm not inventory any longer, a listed item in the insurance catalog." But she feared he might misinterpret.

She took his giant hand with its rough skin like uncured leather and long dark hairs. "Thank you. It's a grand offer and well meant. But it's not feasible. I can't go with you."

"Why not?" Now his surprise.

"I've a heap of business to be getting on with here," she protested gently. "There's your statue to be restored, and all the other exploited artists to be defended, too. And besides, I like New York."

"This dump?"

"I like it here," she repeated stubbornly. "I don't care if folk are moving out in droves to Maine and Colorado and West-chester. Maybe it'll be a better place when some of them go. I like it, and I aim to stay."

She pressed her face to the windowpane. The glass felt cool against her forehead. With a muffled moan like a hoot owl, a barge announced its lonely passage. She sensed Dan's body behind her, although he made no sound.

"You've gotta do what's right for you," he said finally.

She turned to him almost gaily. "All the same, if you do leave, I'll be fixing to come and visit often, if that's okay by you."

"It's okay by me."

She flung open the window. They stood together, inhaling the frosty blast. The chain of green lights winked along the girders of the bridge. Most of the windows on Roosevelt Island were dark now. Only a few faint stars managed to emit feeble pinpricks of light. Susannah took a deep, invigorating breath. In a few days she would be delivering her new speech at the New York Jurists First Amendment luncheon, stirring their blood with her preacher's rage. *Truth stumbles in the public place, and honesty can find no entrance.*

She shivered happily. She had worked hard. Even greater

challenges lay ahead in her mission. She had her own flock and apostles to minister to now. The leafless branches, the cloudless sky and points of light, and the river below her, the dark, thrilling world beckoned at her feet, seductive, rife with possibilities.

Emil steadied the jug of *Glühwein* and fitted his key in the lock of the private basement apartment. Not even the watchman ever unlocked that door. The maid was allowed in to clean once a week. They left the food on a tray outside the door. It was often sent back untouched.

As he turned the handle, Emil could hear the crooning of Ella Fitzgerald or Sophie Tucker, or whatever he was playing now. Even though the basement apartment was insulated like a sound studio, sometimes Emil imagined he could hear the vibrations of Luke's music two floors above.

"What do you want?" The emaciated figure looked up irritably from the floor, where he sprawled.

Luke Elliot was half-naked, dressed only in the top of his pajamas, and he had not shaved for days. Emil stepped forward cautiously. Perhaps it had not been such a good idea to come down here. Luke smelled, too, as if he had not bathed, and his hair hung in matted clumps.

"I came to visit you. It's Christmas night."

Luke rolled over on his side. He lay in a pool of comic strips: *Doonesbury, Garfield, Andy Capp,* and the *Wizard of Id.* He read nothing else, except occasionally to flip through *National Geographic* on the days when his brain was half-lucid.

"I didn't invite you."

Emil sat down by the fireplace. "I brought down this *Glühwein.* I thought we could have a drink together. If you can cope."

Luke trembled wildly. Supposing he were to have one of his paranoia crises, Emil thought. Would the watchman get here in time if I rang the alarm button for help?

"Why don't you leave me alone? You keep me prisoner like an animal. Isn't that enough?"

"You agreed. We made our deal."

"Deal!" Luke dribbled. "What kind of a deal do you call it? I'm cooped up in here with no one to talk to, ever. I can't go out, I can't see anyone." He began to sob in raucous, rattling gasps.

"Don't cry," Emil cajoled. He was used to Luke's tempests of self-pity. "You can swim in the pool, you can paint, you can read. I'll send you a woman if you want that."

Luke glanced contemptuously toward his naked groin. "Forget it. I can't do it anymore anyway."

Emil soothed him. "You're one of the highest-priced living painters anywhere. Three million, four million . . . and for every item I sell, I give you ten percent. You're a rich man, Luke Elliot."

"And what am I to do with it? I can't leave here."

"What would you do outside anyhow? You're an addict." When he saw an ugly glint in Luke's puffy eye, Emil continued hastily, "I'll see that your daughter gets her share when she's older. That was our deal, too. What's this?" He picked up a rectangle that lay face downward. A few carpet strands clung to the paper that Emil detached from the floor. "You've been working again."

"I can't do stripes any longer. My hands shake. I can't hold a brush or a roller. I can only use my fingers."

"Ah, well, it keeps you busy." Emil held up the infantile smearing of yellow and blue thumbprints.

"When will you sell it?" Luke demanded petulantly.

"You know I can't sell it. You're dead. You hear me? Dead. Nobody wants to know about your living genius. If they ever discovered that you were still alive, and I was hiding you here, the bottom of the market would fall right out. You don't want that, and neither do I. Be reasonable, Luke. I've guaranteed you immortality. Your stripes sell for the same prices as Monets and Renoirs. One day they'll be hanging in museums next to Rembrandts. That's what you wanted."

Emil reached for the plastic tumbler on the table. He only allowed him plastic; it was too messy when Luke broke glass and cut himself on the jagged edges. "Have some *Glühwein.* Merry Christmas."

Slowly Luke raised himself and hobbled toward his captor. He looked at him for a moment giddily. Then, raising a feeble arm, he suddenly struck the *Glühwein* out of Emil's hand. It splashed like a wave of blood across the carpet.

"Get out of here. Leave me alone. I hate you. Go away."

"Very well. Calm down. I'm leaving."

When Emil had closed the steel door firmly behind him, Luke slithered in slow motion back to the floor. He lay there for a moment, recouping his energy. With great effort he began to crawl, deliberately, on all fours, to the corner where it was waiting for him, his precious pipe.

It took another bout of concentration to light the flame. There. It was burning now.

He inhaled deeply. The voice of Billie Holiday became sweet and distant, like a lullaby of the sea. Emil was a creep, but he was right. He, Luke Elliot, had won. He had gained admission to the most exclusive club of all. He had conquered death. He would be crowned with the ultimate wreath: immortality. The body would decay. It did not matter. His stripes would still hang on walls next to the masters, long after the worms were eating Emil and Giulietta and Peter Dante and all the rest of them. Luke Elliot's stripes would bear witness to the indomitable power of the human spirit.

Next to Rembrandt. Next to Titian. Up there with Michelangelo.